GOOD GUYS

ALSO BY SHARON BALA

The Boat People (2018)

GOOD GUYS

A NOVEL

SHARON BALA

McClelland & Stewart

Original trade paperback edition published 2026

Library and Archives Canada Cataloguing in Publication

Title: Good guys : a novel / Sharon Bala.
Names: Bala, Sharon, author
Identifiers: Canadiana (print) 2025028507X | Canadiana (ebook) 20250285088 | ISBN 9780771005237 (softcover) | ISBN 9780771099083 (EPUB)
Subjects: LCGFT: Thrillers (Fiction) | LCGFT: Novels.
Classification: LCC PS8603.A463 G66 2026 | DDC C813/.6—dc23

Cover design by Andrew Roberts
Cover art: (airbrush texture) Sytnik, (shiny texture) Soho A studio, (burnt texture) nikkytok / Adobe Stock; (concrete texture) Dvorko Sergey / Shutterstock
Typeset in FS Brabo by Daniella Zanchetta
Printed in Canada

McClelland & Stewart
A division of Penguin Random House Canada
320 Front Street West, Suite 1400
Toronto, Ontario, M5V 3B6, Canada
penguinrandomhouse.ca

1 2 3 4 5 30 29 28 27 26

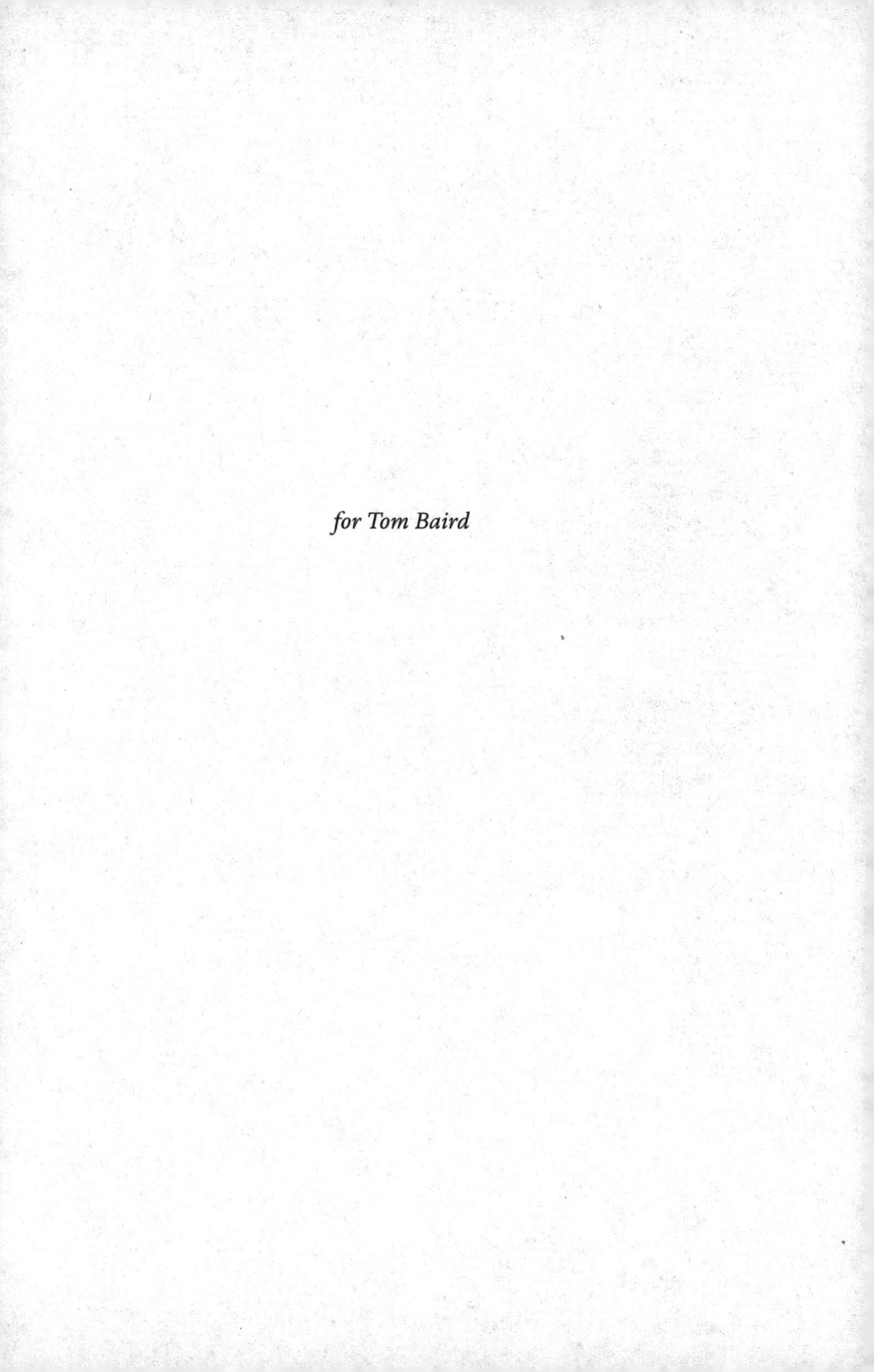

for Tom Baird

Wealth is like an orchard.
You have to share the fruit, not the trees.

—CARLOS SLIM

Charity creates a multitude of sins.

—OSCAR WILDE

Foreigners

Lucca

In the village of Pueblo Bonito, the first bus of the day arrived after dawn, screeching to a halt at the plaza opposite the church. The driver pulled up the handbrake, and a dozen passengers filed off, bleary-eyed and silent, rucksacks and jute bags slung over shoulders. Under their sarapes and striped pullovers, they wore identical mud-brown uniforms. Stitched over the breast pocket was a crest embroidered with the name Children of the World.

Exiting the village on foot, they took the turnoff toward Los Altos, the mountains looming larger with each step. A couple of the men carried on a spirited conversation about football while up ahead a woman twisted her braid into a bun as she walked, a hairpin clamped between her lips. The road was heavily potholed and bracketed by deep concrete gullies. The greenery was thick on both sides, ferns and pines with scrawny trunks and bushy leaves that formed a canopy overhead. This leg of the commute took thirty minutes, and as they neared their destination, the road narrowed and turned to dirt, pebbles and red-brown dust kicking up with each step.

The children's home where they worked was set on ten acres enclosed by a high fence. Inside sat a trio of concrete buildings. The pediatric clinic was nearest the entrance, a blue rectangle with a white *H* emblazoned on the door. Thirty feet away was the dormitory, children in the east wing, foreign volunteers in the west, with the cafeteria where everyone took their meals in the middle. A cheerful mural decorated the walls of the school, which was set on its own plot with a playground, swings, and space for ball games.

At the gates, the group paused to exchange news with the overnight staff. The guard reported that he'd caught a raiding party in the kitchen.

Diablillos, he said, affectionately calling the boys little devils as everyone chuckled. I dragged them back by their ears.

But there was tragic news too, said the night nurse, lighting a hand-rolled cigarette she had pulled from the pocket of her scrubs. A two-year-old with dysentery had died, too malnourished for the antibiotics he'd been given to take effect. The mother was inconsolable, and when one of the gringas from overseas had tried to put an arm around her, she'd let loose a torrent of obscenities. The clinic staff had kept their distance while the mother raged, spewing saliva and invective, stalking the space and emphatically gesturing at the bug-eyed volunteer, whose total ignorance of Spanish was, for once, a blessing.

The nurse said she'd never heard such inventive blasphemy in her life. She took a long drag of her cigarette and added: It's not right to call it cursing. Truly, it was poetry.

For a moment, all were silent, thinking of their own losses—the infants born too soon, the cousin crushed in a mine collapse, the mother struck down by a motorcycle, the friend drowned because she couldn't swim. Then they traded places, day staff streaming in, overnight crew exiting. The night nurse passed her cigarette to her daytime counterpart. The woman with the plaited bun stood on her toes to kiss the guard who would retrace her steps, returning home to their children.

From deeper inside the compound, Lucca da Silva watched the shift change with a dull yearning. He missed the days when he'd been in the thick of a team, one of the gang and not its leader.

He and his second-in-command were loading the rusty jeep, readying it for a scouting trip into the mountains. Thiago was breaking the news that yet another nurse—their most experienced one—had quit. Lucca didn't need to be told the clinic was dangerously understaffed and losing people because they couldn't guarantee shifts. He was the one who made the schedule and balanced the shrinking budget.

A few hours here, a couple there, no one can make a living like this, Thiago said.

I'll speak to Head Office, Lucca said.

The water heater is still broken, Thiago added. Some volunteers are complaining.

Did they lose their way to a five-star resort and end up here by mistake? Lucca asked, exasperated.

Hot water is a human right, not a luxury, Thiago said. Didn't you know?

When Lucca asked for an update on the school they were building in the nearby village, Thiago reported the cost of materials had risen. They would soon run out of concrete if Lucca didn't loosen the purse strings. The bricks would be next. And then they'd have to halt construction altogether.

Lucca signed. Half of his job was going cap in hand to Head Office. Skyrocketing inflation had devalued the peso, causing a run on the banks that led to a paper shortage, which in turn prompted people to trade in U.S. dollars, further depreciating the local currency. Volunteers paid for their trips in dollars, and now he'd have to convince his bosses to part with more of those.

A slight woman with a gait like a ram marched over, head and shoulders jutting out, forehead leading the way.

I can't explain division to those hooligans, she told Lucca.

Beatriz was a gifted educator. Or maybe she had a gift for silencing a classroom. Either way, no one else could teach the students as effectively.

Give me something else, Beatriz wheedled. I'll plunge the toilets for the rest of the week. I'll clean the pig pens. Anything.

Whether you're scrubbing bathrooms or drilling the multiplication table, it's the same paycheque, Lucca said.

How many empty beds do we have in the dormitories? Thiago asked her.

They should all be empty, she said. You should be taking the children back to their families, not bringing more in.

She stared at Thiago as she spoke, but Lucca understood the complaint was directed at him. When neither he nor Thiago replied, she grumbled: It's not right. Children need families. Proper homes. Otherwise they become broken, not right in the head.

What good are relations if they can't feed you? Thiago said, and Lucca thought of the mother now grieving at the clinic. Ten minutes ago, he'd phoned into Pueblo Bonito for a priest.

A couple of volunteers—young women chatting in languid English—strolled by in shorts and sleeveless shirts. Beatriz dropped her voice, conspiratorial.

One of the new girls was crying in the bathroom yesterday, she said.

The gringos always cry, Thiago said, sliding into the driver's seat. Day one, they're excited. Day three, they cry. By the end, they are excited again, because it's almost over. The criers are not the ones to worry about.

Beatriz sucked in a sharp breath, and Thiago nodded. The ones who are too eager, the ones with roving hands, that's who you need to watch. You'll learn.

A group of labourers heading for the fields with their scythes and rakes parted for the dawdling volunteers. In the sea of worn and threadbare uniforms, foreigners were always conspicuous in their peacock colours and swathes of reddening bare skin, the ball caps they wore instead of more practical wide-brimmed hats, the sunglasses that rendered them aloof. Lucca watched them go, eager to exit this conversation.

Thiago leaned out the open window and said: You should speak with the doctor.

Yes, Lucca said and made his goodbyes. He was a few paces away when he heard Beatriz ask Thiago: Is it true you get a bonus for every child under five you bring in?

Lucca cringed. This was an idea Head Office had floated a few months earlier. He'd swiftly shot it down and never mentioned it to anyone, yet somehow the story had spread as rumour.

Don't be foolish, Thiago said. There's no such thing.

Good man, Lucca thought.

During Lucca's job interview, Head Office had lauded Thiago. He could restart a car without jumper cables, sweet-talk his way out of tight situations, had a knack for predicting the weather, got the best rates on currency conversion, *and* he was an excellent parallel parker. He's a genie, they promised. Your wish is Thiago's command.

Of course there was nothing magical about Thiago. He was organized and reliable, the kind of man who kept a Swiss Army knife in his pocket and three weather apps on his phone. The rest was local expertise. Everyone knew whose palm to grease to fast-track visa applications and which money changers were crooked. Thiago had been with the project from the start, outlasting all of Lucca's predecessors, the revolving door of country directors. If Lucca's bosses spoke Spanish, they'd have put Thiago in charge.

Children of the World was one of hundreds of foreign NGOs operating in the small Central American country of Santa Rosa. They had founded the orphanage a decade earlier and later added the school and clinic. But most of the compound was dedicated to farming. At first, there'd been great expectations about the farm's profitability. But in reality, they barely produced enough to feed themselves.

Lucca toured the long rows of crops, exchanging pleasantries with the day labourers and volunteers. He was spinning out time, delaying the inevitable confrontation with the doctor who must be seething about the nurse's resignation because he'd been predicting this outcome for months. What was Lucca to do? Head Office kept shrinking payroll, pressuring him to do more with less.

He paused, hands laced behind his head, and leaned back to take in the green-sloped mountains, thin bands of clouds bisecting their blue tops. The air smelled light and clean with bright notes of chlorophyll. At this higher altitude, there was no hint of the pollution that hung about at sea level.

Steeling himself, Lucca shoved his hands in his pockets, hunched his shoulders, and headed to the clinic. The facility was a rudimentary operation with cots and privacy screens on wheels. A cart of medical supplies. IV poles. A room in the back that had been built for an X-ray machine that never materialized, and another on the side that they called the doctor's office, which housed a cramped desk and a locked drug cabinet.

It was barely seven, and already a dozen patients waited as volunteers checked vitals. The clinic was only equipped for primary care and the doctor was a pediatrician, but it was free so people of all ages brought their ailments, major and minor. Foreign donors thought only children—and occasionally their mothers—were in need, but in Santa Rosa the staff didn't discriminate. Beatriz might not like the way they did things here, Lucca thought, but what would happen to all these patients if the compound didn't exist?

Dr. Juan Flores Ramirez had a stethoscope pressed to an old woman's back. Next to her, an emaciated baby, swaddled like a burrito, was being fed through a tube.

Juan pulled the stethoscope from his ears and slung it around his neck. Lucca could tell from the deep furrow in his forehead that he didn't like whatever he'd heard. Some physicians took formal histories, ticking boxes on a questionnaire. Juan casually asked patients about their lives. Where did they live? Who else was in the home? What do your sons do for work? How long ago was that accident? Lucca crouched to join the conversation. The story the woman told was a common one. The child's father was paralyzed, injured on the job. His mother was doing her best, but there were two older children and food was scarce. The grandmother, Lucca guessed, was giving the baby her portion.

When Juan examined her fingers, Lucca saw the blueish tinge around the nail beds. The doctor knelt to check her feet. Swollen, like her hands, Lucca noted, and when the doctor squeezed, one, then the other, he saw the telltale dimples.

The woman was focused on her grandson, fretting over his condition. The doctor explained that the concoction they were feeding him was full of vitamins and nutrients.

The boy would plump up, be well enough to return home in a few weeks, but then what? Sometimes it seemed to Lucca that all they did was postpone the inevitable. In two, three months, maybe a year, Death would return to cash in the IOU. For now, he sent the grandmother to the cafeteria with the promise of a meal.

Is there room in the nursery? the doctor asked after she'd left.

Don't let Beatriz hear you, Lucca joked, then was chastened by Juan's scowl. I'll advertise for a new nurse, he lied. Today.

Lucca was fond of Juan. In different circumstances, they would have been good friends. Instead, he was forced to be the man's adversary, the one who frustrated his efforts.

From the doctor's office came a keening wail. A couple of volunteers jumped out of their skin. One of them whispered, Is that—?

The priest is on his way, Lucca said, in English for their benefit.

Juan peddled his feet, rolling his stool to the next patient—a middle-aged man complaining of poor vision—and Lucca followed.

The tricky thing will be convincing the grandmother to leave the child, Juan said in English.

She doesn't trust us? Lucca asked.

Not us, Juan replied in Spanish. He rubbed his thumbnail under his lower lip.

Across the room, one of the volunteers, a Canadian physiotherapist, was wrapping a measuring tape around a child's arm. This group was brand new. Two nurses and three physiotherapists, they outnumbered the local staff. Juan reported that they were full of enthusiasm and energy, keen on saving lives.

The tall one asked me where we keep the EKG, he said in Spanish, and even the patient guffawed.

In the back room with the CT scanner, Lucca said, but this, too, failed to elicit so much as a smirk from the doctor.

Beatriz appeared at the door with the priest, a stout Black man Lucca didn't recognize. A missionary, he guessed, waving Beatriz over.

Are there free cots in the nursery? he asked.

No, she said, crossing her arms and scowling.

The mother who had lost her child in the night began banging something in the office. The legs of a chair? Her head against the wall? Lucca saw Beatriz glance toward the baby being fed through a tube and swallow hard. She had sons of her own, the youngest only a toddler.

Excuse me, one of the volunteers called. Dr. Ramirez?

One moment, he said in English.

What lies do they tell these foreigners to convince them to come to Santa Rosa? Beatriz asked.

You'll save a hundred lives. You'll be a national hero, the doctor said.

In Gringolandia, you're no one. But in Santa Rosa, you'll be superman. They'll put a statue of you in the capital, Beatriz added.

Lucca snorted. You'll have the best videos on social media; all your friends will be jealous.

His contribution was met with silence.

If I worked in a full-service hospital, I would not spend my vacation here, the doctor said finally.

Lucca wondered if this was a warning. At a larger facility, Juan would have access to real equipment and other specialists.

You use your senses to diagnose, Lucca said. These ones from abroad, without gadgets and gizmos, they're helpless.

What good is a diagnosis if it doesn't come with a cure? Juan muttered in English, rolling away to the volunteer who was crouched beside a fourteen-year-old girl.

What's wrong with her? the volunteer asked.

Nothing. Her treatment is complete, he said, sitting the patient up. Close your eyes and count to three, he instructed the teenager, before swiftly pulling the tube, hand over hand, out of her nose.

The door of the office opened, and the grieving mother emerged, cradling a limp bundle close to her chest. The priest, at her side, intoned a prayer. Lucca, Beatriz, and the doctor paused to cross themselves.

We can make room in the nursery, Beatriz told Lucca. Two can share a crib.

Hail Mary

Claire

At Children of the World's headquarters in Toronto, Claire Talbot sat at the weekly all-hands meeting, see-sawing a pen between two fingers. It was a Tuesday in mid-September, humidity still thickening the air, summer refusing to relinquish its clammy grip. They were an hour into the meeting, and everyone was wilting as Anya Mueller presented the quarterly financials.

Anya was director of operations and stood with the posture of a dancer, straight-backed and proud. A non-profit lifer in her early sixties, she had a sharp wit and a voice like a handful of gravel. They'd weathered bad years before, but this one was a catastrophe, Anya said. It's an *unprecedented* disaster.

Claire was distracted, self-conscious in the presence of the charity's founder, Crispin St. Onge, whose face had papered the walls of her childhood bedroom. She still owned a complete collection of his albums, his music the soundtrack of her youth. At her job interview, it had taken Claire a moment to reconcile this Crispin—early fifties, ever-so-slightly bow-legged, mismatched socks—with the leather-jacket-clad rocker of her youth who had gritty vocals and whipped his shampoo-commercial hair in circles on the stage. Now, Crispin sat across from her, head in hands, as Anya took them through the balance sheet and income statements. The figures were in red. Donations. Corporate sponsorships. Volunteer income. All of it way down. It was a bloodbath.

Anya pressed her palms on the table and leaned forward. So. Does anyone have any ideas? She looked around the silent group, her steely gaze pausing at each of them in turn. We need a Hail Mary, Anya said, lingering on Claire. Anything at all.

Anya's eyes were grey and ponderous, deep-set into her face. Claire experienced them like a set of oncoming headlights.

Claire was the most recent hire, having joined in the spring. After her two decades in the corporate world, the non-profit's constricted budget had come as a shock.

Fine. Anya shut her laptop and took a seat. She waved a vague pen in Claire's direction and said: Let's have the comms update. Claire's got an internet thing to show us.

Around the table, eight eager gazes turned on Claire, willing her to save, or at least distract, them.

It's a new website, actually, Claire said, syncing her laptop with the projector.

The old one was a relic, and Claire was proud of her facelift, but she was nervous, too, because it was the first big project she was presenting to Crispin. The redesign had been her idea, one she'd executed solo, teaching herself web design, and troubleshooting on her own. The result was a polished new interface with easy-to-find information and eye-catching images. Good riddance to busy backgrounds and broken links.

Everyone ready? she asked.

Crispin drumrolled the table, and Claire grinned as the memory of huddling beside a dumpster in minus-twenty weather to get his autograph flashed through her mind. Bolstered, she typed in the URL and said, Voila!

Wow, the events manager said, when the homepage appeared, all clean lines and white space. What NGO is that?

Claire laughed. Sure, there was a mousetrap in the corner, baited with a dusty smear of Cheez Whiz, but their online avatar was now dynamic and inviting. She demonstrated the site's features, the ease of navigation, emphasizing how everything subtly led visitors back to the donate button.

It's certainly aspirational, Anya said, turning a Lucite bracelet on her wrist.

Claire knew better than to take Anya's wariness personally. Anyway, it was Crispin's opinion that mattered.

This is where we're headed, she said, donning the armour of total confidence she'd always worn in pitch meetings at her old job. Then—what the hell?—she threw in a cliché for good measure: The website is the first step in the right direction.

It's our vision board, the office joker guffawed, before becoming contrite as he saw Claire's face. It's fantastic, really, he said. It just seems . . .

It's very slick, Crispin said slowly. Claire, you've done a brilliant job. But is it authentically us?

Claire was stung. She'd expected enthusiasm, for Crispin to have one of his excited outbursts where he paced as he spoke and got everyone riled up.

It's giving boutique with five white sweaters and no price tags, the office joker said. But we're more like . . . bargain basement deals-deals-deals.

This *is* us, she said. Sure, we have a bootstrap ethos, but that just means the operation is lean. Our brand promise is a robust ROI. But overseas, we're on the vanguard. It's who we've always been, and now everyone will know it.

As she spoke, she watched Crispin's expression—at first open and thoughtful—fall. Too late, she realized the foolhardiness of her words. What the hell was she doing telling the founder his business?

She was grateful when Anya said: It's an improvement. That's the important thing. Show us more.

Here's the drop-down menu for our overseas projects, Claire said, demonstrating. Each country gets its own page.

What happened to the DRC and Sierra Leone? Crispin asked. Where's Ghana?

Officially, Children of the World had operations in fifteen countries. They had moved into regions with bullish expectations, but things hadn't always gone according to plan. The failures in Africa had been an unwelcome revelation, and Crispin's explanation—we had to make some tough decisions for the overall health of the organization—had inexplicably left her feeling shamed.

But what did Claire know about running a non-profit? Her job was to protect the brand. So, she'd quietly deleted the evidence, not just on their site but across the rest of the web, suppressing search results that led to the old projects. When she stumbled on a blog post by a disgruntled former employee in Senegal, she'd buried that too.

Noticing the missing regions, Crispin got uncharacteristically touchy. Every project, every country, they're all important, he said.

Of course, Claire agreed. It's just that some of them haven't been operational for years, and I'm not sure—

You're not sure? he thundered. They've been *temporarily* deprioritized. We haven't abandoned our responsibilities.

Claire shrank back. Her colleagues fell silent, staring fixedly at their hands, at the walls, at a spot on the table.

Leave it, he snapped. Don't change anything.

But . . . Claire was confused. Did he want her to scrap the whole project? The old website was incompatible with smartphones and glitchy on some browsers. It took three clicks just to get to the donation page. She glanced at Anya for support.

There's no need to get into the weeds, Anya said. She turned a page in her notebook. If there's nothing else on comms, let's have the volunteer update.

After the meeting, Crispin and Anya stalked out, heading in different directions, and the boardroom erupted into speculation. Was this why they hadn't hired anyone to cover the HR officer's mat leave or replaced the country director in Senegal? The finance director whispered that Crispin had stopped drawing a salary in the summer, that cash injections from his personal account were the only thing keeping them afloat. If something didn't pan out soon, the layoffs would begin. Starting with me, Claire thought as she slipped away.

Back at her desk, she flicked between emails, unable to focus, shoulders crunched to her ears. Children of the World was headquartered on the top floor of a nineteenth-century red brick building that had once been a meat-packing plant. They had long ago outgrown the space. Ten people crammed tight, hemmed in by novelty cheques, emergency kits, files, event gear, two decades worth of detritus. Through the grimy window on her left, Claire could see the coin laundry across the street and the pay-day-loan place beside it. She stared at the company's logo until the dollar sign blurred. She *couldn't* lose this job.

Before coming to Children of the World, Claire had been at a huge public relations firm, representing weapons manufacturers and blood diamond miners. *Reputation management.* Justifying oil spills and corruption scandals and, increasingly in recent years, men who'd been caught with their hands down other people's pants. The worst part wasn't that she'd been good at her job. The worst part was how much she'd relished her competence, taken the public rehabilitation of the most loathsome clients as a personal challenge. She was revolted now, when she thought back on that work and the person who had done it, the tactics she'd deployed that her colleagues had lauded as ingenious.

Even her current salary—a fraction of what she'd been earning—was a balm, a necessary corrective to years of ill-gotten gains. And she didn't mind her shiny new halo either, the moral superiority she felt visiting her old office or meeting former colleagues for drinks. She was committed to non-profit, but if she failed at this, her first shot, who would hire her? She'd have to go back.

Everyone returned to their open-plan desks, and soon she was surrounded by the usual drone of her colleagues, the steady thump of a stapler, the aged copier laboriously ejecting pages.

Crispin's and Anya's workstations formed a pod, L-shaped desks touching with a shared recycling bin between them. They usually sat back to back but were huddled together now, voices low, his placating, hers fretful.

We have to make a decision, Claire heard Anya say.

We just need a little patience, Crispin said.

At the rate we're going—

Crispin dropped his voice when he replied. Claire's jaw ached, a familiar gathering pain that would soon spread across the back of her skull. Restlessly, she tapped her fingers against her keyboard without typing any letters, and watched Crispin spin away to his desk while Anya glowered at his back.

All around her, Claire's colleagues were introducing themselves on cold calls, leaving voice mails that would go unanswered. She heard the desperation in their voices. White-collar begging, that's what working in non-profit was all about.

She was acutely aware of being the only team member whose work was dissociated from money. While the others processed volunteer fees, applied for grants, and wooed sponsors, she watched TikTok. All that effort she'd put into the new website, her one tangible contribution, was futile. She snuck a glance at Crispin. He pressed a palm to his forehead and seemed to be holding in a long breath.

In the nineties, Crispin had been the front man of the alt-rock band Resurrection. They'd been huge for a time, with world tours and guest spots on *Saturday Night Live*. At its peak in the mid-aughts, Children of the World had been hip, the brand luxe and fearless, with a keen masculine energy. Concerts had been their marquee fundraiser, Crispin convincing all his buddies in the music industry to play for free, ticket sales powering most of their revenue. But two decades on, the charity's star had diminished. The donor base was made up of Resurrection fans, people like Claire who had grown up with the music. Young adults with disposable income when the organization was founded, they were creeping into middle age now, their donations and engagement drying up as they got caught on the treadmill of careers and caregiving, all generosity redirected inward, around the nucleus of family. Sure, kids are starving in the DRC, but have you *seen* the cost of hockey camp?

At the job interview, Crispin had asked about Claire's clients. Corporate sponsorship is a key aspect of our fundraising, he said, and she felt a prick of doubt. Was this why Children of the World wanted her—for the clients she was eager to shed? Instead of getting derailed, she squashed her reservations down and pivoted the conversation to an untapped donor pool. Gen Z and young millennials, she'd declared, are more socially conscious than any previous generation. She'd talked a big game about using social media and online influencers to gain relevance and new income streams. Six months on, she'd done nothing of the sort and felt like a fraud on the verge of exposure.

She could stomach a firing so long as Crispin wasn't involved. She'd rather it was Anya, brisk and no nonsense, bringing the axe down fast, a clean and ruthless stroke. The unbearable thing would be telling her ex-husband, who'd lord the failure over her.

Hail Mary. Out of habit, she switched tabs to check their Instagram feed. Her latest post about Santa Rosa was generating buzz. The tiny country was home to one of Children of the World's more stable and established ventures, with a child rescue arm that Claire thought was underleveraged. Scouts regularly scoured the nearby mountain villages, searching for children in need. Poverty was high, and even a routine illness could prove deadly in the absence of antibiotics and basic medical attention. When a scout alerted the centre, the rescue team mobilized—a convoy of jeeps, canoes, an ambulance, even pack animals, whatever was needed to bring the child to safety. It was a jewel of a program, ready-made for publicity. If Claire had her way, she'd hire a documentarian—an up-and-coming talent with something to prove—and commission a short film. A tear-jerker with a rousing soundtrack that followed the rescue team for a day. Something arty but accessible that they could aggressively pitch to all the festivals, with a view to an Oscar nod or a Palme d'Or.

The country director was a man named Lucca who seemed intent on ignoring her. All she wanted was a video of one of the rescue operations, a couple of photos after the fact, but Lucca was taciturn, so she'd turned to the volunteers, cultivating relationships with them through social media. An undergraduate from Montreal had obliged, sending photos from a medical rescue that had taken place the previous day.

Before the meeting, Claire had uploaded a photo of the child, sucking on a bottle, in the volunteer's arms. The composition was suboptimal. Claire would have tightened the frame, focused on the volunteer's rapt expression and shown less of the child's torso, which was a little too scrawny. Or waited for a moment of eye contact. As it was, the child's gaze was narrowed and turned away from the volunteer.

Claire was diligent about reading the comments. She tried to engage with each one and recognized most of the regulars. The wordless message with the holding back tears emoji and the hashtag #realheroes was so unobtrusive, she almost missed it. Seeing the handle, she jolted—could it really be?—and clicked on the account. Yes, it was.

Dallas Hayden, thirty-three, alumnus of the long-running teen drama *Musical High*, lead actress in three critically acclaimed and commercially successful films, the newest superhero in the *Sentinels* franchise—this same Dallas Hayden had just commented on Claire's Instagram post.

Claire pushed back her chair and stared at the ceiling. Surely, she was dreaming. Dallas was a triple threat: a legitimately gifted actor with a pretty face who was universally well liked.

Notoriously private about her love life, she was savvy on social media and charmed followers with a pretend cooking show where she hammed it up from her kitchen. Recently she'd had a celebrity chef teach her how to poach an egg.

Her standalone superhero movie, *Freya*, had been the summer's blockbuster, and rumour had it her role in the upcoming ensemble was central. Dallas's star, steadily rising, had catapulted into the stratosphere.

Claire replied, *Takes one to know one #realheroes*. Immediately, the heart beside her comment turned red.

Guys, she called, a swooping thrill in her chest. Then louder, more urgent: Guys. Guys. You won't believe this.

As her colleagues crowded around, she exchanged quips with Dallas in the comments before smoothly migrating into her DMs.

Oh my god, oh my god, the finance director said.

Pinch me, the volunteer coordinator said.

The office joker began droning a Hail Mary.

Claire was all adrenalin and instinct. I'm messaging with Dallas Hayden, a terrier-like voice in the back of her mind yelped in all caps. DALLAS HAYDEN.

Anya crossed her arms. You're sure it's not a fan account?

Blue checkmark, Crispin said. It's her. What now?

Watch, Claire said and typed: *We'd love to have you join one of the rescue teams. As our guest of course.*

Say the word, she said, turning to Crispin and hovering a pinky over the return key.

Do it, Crispin said.

Wait, Anya said sharply. We can't—

Afford not to, Crispin said. We'd be fools to let this opportunity go.

Anya exhaled loudly. Fine.

Claire hit send and got an instantaneous reply: *OMG I'd love that.*

It would be our pleasure, Claire responded. *When would you like to go?*

ASAP! Dallas replied, adding there was a break in her schedule next month. *I'll have my assistant email you*, Dallas promised. *Let's make this happen.*

Amid high-fives and cheers, Claire turned to Anya, triumphant. You wanted a miracle.

Ask and ye shall receive, the office joker quipped.

Anya was mulish. We'll have to get Lucca on board, she warned.

But Crispin was jubilant. It would be Lucca's honour to host Dallas Hayden, he declared.

He'll get that, right? Claire asked. Surely even someone as recalcitrant as Lucca would play ball under these circumstances.

Don't count on it, Anya said, as she and Claire returned to the boardroom and dialled Santa Rosa. Then she added, Let me do the talking.

True to her word, Dallas flew to Santa Rosa a few weeks later. Claire tracked the flight's progress obsessively, waiting for an update from Lucca, a single line on Slack to confirm he'd met her at the airport.

If there was a problem, we'd know by now, Anya said.

Dallas would be used to an A-lister's welcome. How would she react to a truculent host?

Doesn't Lucca understand? Claire asked, hovering at Anya's desk. She's not just some random influencer; she's a star with a dedicated fan base. Millions of young people all over the world *want* to emulate her. Those are the eyeballs we could get. If Lucca plays his cards right, this could change everything.

Anya put her glasses on and bent toward her screen, engrossed in a spreadsheet. I told you what he's like.

Something wrong? Crispin asked, glancing over.

Claire checked herself. Affecting a breezy voice, she said, Nope.

In the end, it was Dallas herself who announced her arrival through a series of Reels and TikToks, which Claire scrutinized on her phone, alert for disappointment. But Dallas was upbeat, delighted by every fruit tree and milk cow, the orphans who crowded her, even the spartan accommodations. Lucca at least had given her a private room, so she didn't have to bunk with the hoi polloi, though doubtless she'd have made lemonade of that too.

Claire showed Anya one of Dallas's videos. She was crouched with the chickens, joking about the smell, not afraid to stick her hands right in the straw and collect the eggs.

Doesn't get more local and free range than this, Dallas joked. The project aims to be self-sustaining, and you can help. Then she rattled off the website's URL and the number to text with a donation. It was as if she'd swallowed all of Claire's marketing materials on the plane.

I didn't ask her to do that, Claire said. That's all Dallas.

She knows how to direct a scene, Anya said. I'll hand it to Lucca, though. It was good of him to play along.

It was the development manager who explained. The eggs would have been gathered at dawn, hours before Dallas landed. Otherwise, they were liable to rot. But this video is gold, he assured Claire. Donors will love it.

The rescue was scheduled for the following morning. Claire was the first one in the office, her stomach a riot of nerves. She had no clear idea of how things would proceed and what role Dallas would be given. Claire's worst nightmare: Lucca, on a flimsy pretext, leaving Dallas behind.

Bright and early again, Crispin said, arriving thirty minutes later.

Claire shrugged. It's a big day.

During weeks when her ex had the kids, Claire worked overtime to avoid being alone in her depressing basement apartment, but she wasn't about to admit that to Crispin.

I've been meaning to talk to you, Crispin said, glancing around the deserted space. And listen, I know I should have said this sooner.

Claire became nervous, certain she was about to be called out for a faux pas or mistake.

I'm sorry about how I behaved at the all-hands.

Oh. No, that's fine, she said, relieved and embarrassed.

I shouldn't have lost my temper, he said. It was profoundly unfair of me.

Really, Crispin. It's long forgotten.

You know I don't care about *optics*, he said, making air quotes, then spinning an index finger to indicate the office. But with the projects overseas, we have to project a certain robustness.

Sure. Of course, Claire said, chiding herself. Appearances were everything. She of all people should have known that.

Donors are fickle, he said. A new CEO comes in and decides to overhaul priorities. Just like that, the funding we rely on vanishes. It's the children who pay the price. It's been our toughest struggle.

Was Crispin taking her into his confidence? She was reminded of the first time they'd met. It was minus twenty that night and only a few diehards stuck around after the concert. His bandmates had hurried into the tour bus; Crispin had posed for photos and cheerfully signed autographs.

This was right before their third album went platinum, when the band was still playing small venues and felt like Claire's secret, their screeds against capitalism and proxy wars written for her alone. Resurrection were known for their punk ethos as much as their social conscience. They had hits called "Sweatshop Couture" and "Hutu Commandments." Crispin wasn't just another rock star. His lyrics had opened her eyes to injustice and atrocities, made her pay attention to the news.

I have all your albums, Claire had gushed as he scribbled in marker on her CD cover. The new one is the best.

You don't find it too dark, too much of a downer? he asked, with a mischievous wink.

Oh no, Claire said earnestly. It's honest.

Crispin tapped the marker against her CD case, smile fading. Some people say we should leave the activism to the professionals and stick to being entertainers.

Claire was caught off guard by this disclosure, the way he held her gaze and seemed genuinely curious about a fifteen-year-old's opinion.

Can't you be both? You've taught me so much about stuff that like *actually* matters. I wouldn't have known about Rwanda.

Behind her, the line shuffled impatiently, but Claire had the pleasure of Crispin's full attention, his intelligent eyes alight, focused squarely on her. Emboldened, she told him about the presentation she'd given in social studies on the genocide, which had reduced some girls to tears, how afterward she'd taken up a collection among her classmates for UNICEF.

Sounds like you have a future in international aid, Crispin said, returning her CD with both hands like he was holding a platter. You have no idea what that means to me. Thank you, Claire.

Claire had never heard those words paired together before—*international aid*. Later, she would repeat them aloud to herself, testing her tongue on the consonants and vowels, enjoying the heft and gravitas of their sounds, thrilling at the fact that he'd spoken her name (that he even remembered it!), that her actions, which had felt so insignificant at the time (a meagre fifty-dollar donation), had touched him.

Nearly thirty years later, in the office where they worked, Crispin's voice was breaking as he told her about Ghana, how he'd gone there to wind down the operation himself. He paused, crestfallen, then shook himself and said, But we forge on.

Crispin was unlike anyone Claire had ever worked for. He wasn't afraid to be vulnerable, owned up to failure but didn't let it crush him.

It was nearly eight a.m. in Toronto. Six in Santa Rosa. Claire refreshed her browser for the umpteenth time and was rewarded with a video. Posted two minutes earlier.

It's begun, she said, increasing the volume on her computer as Crispin leaned in.

Santa Rosa was awash in early morning light and the shrill din of birdsong, so many and of such variety that their calls and whistles pitched together sounded like a dissonant and beautiful choir.

Today's the day we save a child, Dallas said, out of sight, panning her phone across the scene. There was a peach-coloured single-storey building, long and squat with a corrugated sloped roof. Steps leading up to the front door and ferns all around. The trees were bright green and capacious.

Claire had expected a bevy of vehicles and a team of staff, or at least a couple of medics. Instead, there was only a jeep with an overturned rowboat strapped to its roof rack. A man—was that Lucca?—circled, checking the tires and adjusting the wing mirrors, before slamming shut the trunk.

Dallas flipped the camera view to face her, then held the phone overhead and tilted as she added: We're headed into the mountains. Into Los Altos. But first we have to cross the Río Bueno.

Her voice was husky, with a depth that suggested gravitas. Claire was impressed by how quickly she'd grasped the geography after arriving.

There was the muffled sound of the driver's door closing, and Lucca's shoulder appeared in a corner of the screen. The engine revved, and then they were moving. Was there really no one else accompanying them?

Infant mortality in Santa Rosa is over fifty per cent, Dallas said, as they drove, quoting the copy Claire had written for the new website. These children, the ones in the mountains, they don't have enough food. The water is contaminated. Every day, dozens and dozens of babies die. At Children of the World's facility, they have food and medicine, even a clinic. But the mothers in the mountains haven't got a way to bring their kids there. So, Children of the World goes to them. Every day matters, Dallas added, a concerned crease in her brow. Every hour. Every second.

Elation pulsed through Claire. Dallas Hayden was the shiny new thing that would attract donors, make corporations pick up the phone and call Children of the World. They could reopen the shuttered projects in Africa, expand the existing ones, move into other countries. Save more lives. And Claire had done this. *She* had made this happen.

We've got a long day ahead, Dallas said, the camera jostling with the jeep. She appeared fresh and lively, unfazed by the early hour, as she added, Stay tuned.

Claire and Crispin rewatched the video several times, euphoria increasing with each viewing. Jittery from too much coffee and nerves, too little sleep, Claire was overheated, her armpits uncomfortably damp.

On his phone, Crispin was logged into the fundraising software and reported the updates in real time. It was only a trickle, but already the money was coming in. It would ramp up, he predicted. Turn into a deluge before the end of Dallas's visit. Crispin raised both his palms, and Claire slapped them. We did it, she said.

You did it, he corrected.

She glanced at Anya's desk with its towers of files and wilting ivy, the cardigan slung over the back of her chair, the tableau poignant and grubby. In an hour, Anya would be here, scowling at her screen, pointedly ignoring Dallas's updates.

The project in Santa Rosa was Anya's brainchild, and Claire suspected she was territorial and jealous. She'd come up against Anya's type before, the kind of woman who had clawed her way to the top and, rather than reach a hand down to help a sister up, regarded her as a threat and trod on her fingers instead. Claire decided to be magnanimous.

It's Santa Rosa that caught Dallas's interest, not me, she said.

Claire remained riveted all day as Dallas documented the complicated journey into the mountains in real time, millions of fans lapping up videos of the actress in sporty leggings, ponytail trailing out the back of a baseball cap, lithely leaping from the jeep, gamely taking the oars of a rowboat, winding around a mountain on the back of a donkey. And all the while, Children of the World's follower count rose. The phones rang non-stop. The donations team couldn't keep pace, and soon even Claire was logging in the new sign-ups.

The day had a carnival feel, another injection of excitement every time new content arrived, and everyone gathered around Claire's monitor to watch. Only Anya absented herself, barricaded in the boardroom for a marathon call with India.

What do you know about the child we're rescuing? Dallas asked in one of the videos.

Lucca was driving, a toothpick sticking out the side of his mouth.

Very sick, he said. The mother is saying she has pain and cries.

The jeep was passing through a town. Goat crossing, Dallas announced, flipping the camera to show the animals who were holding up traffic. She zoomed out to take in more of the scenery. Men in straw hats carried firewood on their backs, the branches cut and tied together in an ingenious kind of backpack. In the opposite lane, an open-backed truck waited its turn. Passengers in colourful dresses stood on the bed.

It was midafternoon when they finally arrived. The place where they found the baby was a clearing bounded by greenery, trees and ferns. Clothes were inexplicably laid across every bush. A woman in a yellow dress stood in the doorway of a shack, if you could call it that, formed of uneven planks. Lucca conferred with her while Dallas swept the area with her camera. The roof was flat and made of tin sheets weighed down with rocks.

Santa Rosa is one of the poorest countries in Central America, Dallas narrated off-camera. I know it's depressing, but we cannot look away. We owe it to these people to bear witness.

Another woman crowded into the doorway, and Dallas paused to zoom in on them. Both were aged and ageless, faces gaunt, limbs browned and thin. Then the camera tilted down to show a boy in shorts and a *Toy Story* T-shirt standing in front of Dallas.

Hola, Dallas said to him. Como esta?

The boy didn't speak but began to reach out until a harsh word from one of the women—his grandmother?—made him whip his hands behind him and step back. At the entrance, Lucca beckoned, and the camera followed. Inside, the hut was a single open room, the only light a dim glow from the pane-less windows. Cooking pots, plastic tubs, clothes, and the rest of the family's meagre possessions were piled up against the walls. Everything was chaotic and disordered.

This is where they live, Dallas narrated in a whisper while the others spoke in Spanish, their voices a babble in the background. Dirt floor, she added, swivelling the camera down and lifting a foot to show the imprint left by her shoe. The little boy was close by; his filthy bare feet fleetingly appeared in the frame.

The sick baby lay in a hammock, whimpering and gulping. Is this her? Dallas asked.

The child's face was round, and her dark eyes were set close together. She had a listless vacant expression. She was naked, save for a cloth nappy, and her feet—extremely pigeon-toed—briefly caught Claire's attention. Dallas must have knelt or crouched because the camera angle dropped to the baby's eye level. Her hand appeared, stroking the child's hair off her forehead. The Spanish voices were clearer now.

She's burning up, Dallas said.

The sight of the child, the pathetic gasping cries, the crack in Dallas's voice when she said: We have to get her back. We have to save her. Anguish and pity welled up in Claire, visceral memories of her babies at their sickest, their plaintive, mewling wails. She put a hand to her mouth.

The intern, crouching beside Claire's desk to watch, said, That's so . . . so . . .

I know, Claire said, and rubbed her thumbs against the corners of her eyes. It's heartbreaking. She noticed the intern frowning. What? she asked.

Well, I mean, doesn't it seem a little exploitative? I dunno. It just makes me uncomfortable.

We *need* to feel uncomfortable. That's what makes this footage so powerful.

But they're vulnerable, the intern said. And Dallas didn't even ask permission to film, let alone broadcast their private lives to strangers.

Claire recalled the time her youngest caught croup, the terrible goose-honking cough, his struggle to breathe, and how helpless she'd felt. She said: Their baby is starving and sick. Believe me, this video isn't their priority. It isn't even on their radar.

Yeah, maybe, the intern said, but she could tell from their frown that they were unconvinced, and she watched them leave the office, unsettled.

But the others were congratulatory. Now the child would be saved, they agreed. And you couldn't buy this kind of promotion. Dallas's empathy was astonishing, how generous of her to be so candid. No one who saw these videos would be unaffected.

Still, Claire wasn't satisfied. She couldn't drum up any media interest. What part of *a Sentinel rescues a baby IRL* don't they understand? she asked, frustrated after hanging up with another polite but uninterested entertainment reporter. She'd spent so much of her career conducting evasive manoeuvres with news desks and investigative heavy hitters that she wondered if the problem was a lack of contacts in lifestyle.

Anya scoffed. Celebrities were always jetting off to muck around with the poor overseas. Didn't Claire know that? It was hardly breaking news. *Charitainment*, she added, with sarcastic emphasis, may as well be mandatory in Hollywood. I'm surprised Dallas isn't already affiliated with another NGO.

But Crispin was sanguine. Press coverage or not, the donations are coming in. Ghana, Sierra Leone, the DRC, he said, catching Claire's eye with a grin. Told you those closures were temporary.

Small at home and mighty abroad, she said, parroting his motto. We should thank Lucca. He's been a good sport.

Oh, you thought that was Lucca? Anya jutted her chin at the screen, where the video was paused on the driver, and laughed. That's not Lucca. He wouldn't have wasted his day on this.

Fait Accompli

Lucca

Lucca circled the building site where construction on the new school had ground to a halt the previous month. The scaffolding was gone, exposing the partially erected walls. Already there was graffiti. He took photos of the spray-painted genitals, the last brick laid in an unfinished row, then stepped across the threshold and aimed his phone at the blue sky through the nonexistent roof. It was futile to think he might shame Head Office into sending more money, but he'd email the photos anyway.

This was the problem with relying on foreigners for infrastructure. They had more ambition than forethought, put up schools or clinics but didn't pay for staff. Then the buildings sat abandoned, a beacon for vandals, looters, and eventually stray dogs.

Early in his career, Lucca had installed merry-go-round water pumps in villages all over Mozambique and Zambia. A multimillion-dollar initiative, backed by some of the world's wealthiest philanthropists, it was utterly impractical. The merry-go-rounds were more labour intensive than traditional pumps. Within a year, a quarter were broken.

Lucca drove the jeep back to the compound, snaking along the muddy river and the green-carpeted foothills encircling the valley. He honked in solidarity as he passed a convoy of tractors in the oncoming lane, people riding on top and clinging to the backs. They were headed to a protest in the capital, agricultural workers flocking from all over to take part. Santa Rosa was in the middle of a years-long megadrought, the aquifers and irrigation tanks drying to dust even as private industry kept drilling into the water table to slurp up the little that remained, leaving small farmers and locals without a drop. Ladrones de agua, they were called. Water thieves. His staff had asked for time off to join the water defenders' protest. If it was up to him, Lucca would have given them his blessing and sent the children along just for the experience. But one of their biggest sponsors—the one whose name was chiselled into the gates of the compound—was a mining operation and the worst offender, so that was that.

The sun was high in the sky, another cloudless day without hope of rain. He felt the oppression of dark thoughts and ill will and recognized it as a sign he'd lingered in Santa Rosa too long. Usually by the time he began to consider the endemic and systemic problems of a place, it was time to leave.

Lucca had been a humanitarian worker since his early twenties. For most of his career he'd worked in six-month stints, parachuting into conflict zones and providing just-in-time aid. New places. New people. Improvising on the fly. Challenge. Catastrophe. These were the things he thrived on. The past, the future, both became irrelevant in the white-hot thrill of a dangerous present.

He'd held out longer than most, despite the creaky knees and back spasms, but it was impossible to ignore how quickly he was aging even as the aid workers around him remained eternally young.

When Anya got in touch, said Children of the World needed someone experienced and resourceful to lead the operation in Santa Rosa, it seemed a reasonable compromise. But two years into the job, Lucca was antsy.

When he returned to the compound, it was somnolent, palm trees throwing long shadows. It was siesta, the shutters closed, children asleep under spinning fans, the staff lazily throwing down cards or napping in chairs. Only the day labourers were at work, the pungent smell of manure rising from the fields.

On the steps of the main building, three volunteers snapped selfies with one of the children. They wore impractical oversized costume jewellery and took turns posing with Moisés, cooing over his Coke-bottle glasses. The child was nine, one of a handful of true orphans at the compound. It was Thiago who had christened the boy after finding the infant at the gate, wrapped in a Mickey Mouse blanket. No note. No identification. Just a baby so hungry he hadn't the energy to cry. And though Thiago hadn't started the rumour about the basket, he didn't dissuade it either.

Lucca knew better than to play favourites, but Moisés had latched onto him early, and despite himself, he was charmed. They even looked a little alike with their dimpled chins and curly black hair. Moisés was a great mimic and had taken to parroting Lucca's gestures, the way he rested a fist on his lowered forehead when he was thinking hard. Now he sat glumly in a stranger's lap as her friends squealed *queso*, his magnified gaze slanted sideways, and fixed on Lucca.

Some children became attached to the volunteers, only to grieve when they inevitably left. Others checked out entirely, refusing to warm to anyone, and were alarmingly anti-social. Moisés swung back and forth, latching on to some strangers and taking against others. He was affectionate with the local staff, though he'd begun acting up with some of the other children, a development that worried Lucca.

Oh, you're so cute, the volunteer with heavy eyeshadow said, tickling Moisés as he squirmed and batted her away. How would you like to come home with me?

It was the same meaningless nonsense all the gringos prattled. The children in their matching uniforms, the idea that they were all alone in the world, inspired fervent pathos and empty promises.

Ladies, Lucca said, adopting the friendly Midwest accent he'd perfected because its bland, casual arrogance provided cover when he wanted to get his way. I need to borrow Moisés for a while.

Vamos, he said, and Moisés held Lucca's trouser as they legged it inside. In Lucca's office, Moisés listed the countries of Southeast Asia.

Myanmar, Thailand, Laos, Cambodia, he said, pressing his fingers in the air as if touching points on a map, one he had seen in a classroom and fixed in his mind. Vietnam, Philippines, Malaysia.

Brunei, Lucca said, logging on to email.

Have you been there? Moisés asked.

Not yet.

Me neither, Moisés said. Singapore. Indonesia.

There was a message from his eldest brother, another from his mother. These Lucca trashed unread.

Don't forget East Timor, he said.

Is there a West Timor? Moisés asked.

Yes, but it's part of Indonesia.

Why?

That's complicated. Do you really want to know? Lucca turned away from the computer, ready with the answer. Moisés was voracious for geography. On the right day, he could be a patient listener.

Moisés raised his index finger. I didn't tell you! The movie star is here.

Lucca had forgotten about their unwanted visitor. Did you meet her?

It's not really her, Moisés said, and Lucca chuckled, ruffling the top of his head.

The week before, he had gotten his hands on a bootleg copy of *Freya* dubbed into Spanish, and they'd given the children an impromptu movie night in the cafeteria. For days afterward, Moisés stripped the sheet from his bed, tied it around his neck, and ran in circles, looking back to see how it flapped in the wind. Until Beatriz lost patience and gave him a smack.

There were three emails from the publicist demanding to know how Dallas was faring. Was she settling in? Had he arranged for a photographer? Was everything okay? The emails had arrived in thirty-minute intervals, each one more agitated than the last. Lucca deleted them. He had a contentious meeting coming up at the clinic (he still hadn't hired a new nurse), and there was a customs headache—a donation stuck at the border, old shoes and school supplies—that would require a diplomatically worded email to an acquaintance in government. Because of course this box of diverted landfill had been flagged for search and slapped with import duties. The actress was the last thing on his mind.

Has she come to take one of us? Moisés asked.

Who told you that?

This was the rumour circulating among the children, Moisés informed him.

Foreign adoption seemed a rite of passage in Hollywood. To Lucca it was silly, but then he thought children were always an act of ego, regardless of genetics.

Would you like that? Lucca asked.

I want to stay with you.

And when I leave?

Then I'll go with you, Moisés said. And his tone was so earnest Lucca swallowed back the instinctive laugh.

It might be dangerous where I go, he said. Bombs and bad guys. Wouldn't you rather live in a superhero's mansion and fly around the world with her?

Moisés's expression lit up. To Brunei?

You'll have to show her where it is, Lucca said.

His landline rang. Unlisted number. Lucca answered without thinking, then cursed himself when he heard Paolo's voice.

We've brought Papai home, Paolo said in Portuguese.

It was always like this with his brother, who launched in without preamble, as if every exchange was a continuation of the long-running dialogue they'd been conducting since the day Lucca was born. Sometimes he suspected the conversation carried on in his absence, with Paolo taking both parts.

The doctors had exhausted their options, Paolo was saying now. Pain relief was all they could offer.

Moisés began toeing a partially deflated football. The black and white pentagons spun across the linoleum floor. The ball rolled Lucca's way, and he faked right, kicked left. Moisés dove right. The child's sight was weak, almost nonexistent in one eye and very bad in the other. The glasses he wore weren't nearly strong enough. Lucca was willing to bet that what Moisés needed could be found in California, a cutting-edge therapy, an intrepid surgeon wielding lasers. Pocket change for a movie star.

Through the phone, his father growled: Lucca, are you listening? For a petrifying split second, Lucca was yanked back to the terror of his childhood.

This is important, his brother added, sounding like himself again.

All their siblings were returning to Rio, Paolo said. Even Carla was coming.

Carla goes with the others, Lucca said, slipping into Portuguese.

Is your heart a stone? The man is dying.

Moisés was knocking the football between his insteps, whispering to himself as if announcing his plays. The sight of the child, lost in the security of his imagination, gave Lucca an unpleasant pang of recognition.

He switched to English, neutral ground, a conciliation. Paolo, you're a good man. The ass doesn't deserve your sponge cake.

Hanging up, Lucca turned to Moisés. Did you meet her?

Moisés didn't look up as he shook his head no. She's gone with Thiago into the mountains.

Too shy, Lucca guessed. He checked the time and stood.

Freya might be a big deal out there, he said. But in here, you're the important one. Come on.

When Head Office had first called him about this business with the actress, they presented the plan as a fait accompli.

We'll need to arrange transport from the airport, Anya said.

By *we*, she meant *you*. There was no *we* in Santa Rosa. There was only Lucca in his small office with the noisy ceiling fan and scuffed walls, the smell of frying tortillas and the cacophony of the kitchen coming from next door.

There's a chauffeur service, Anya said. Thiago has the name. We'll want something comfortable. Not the usual.

But keep it authentic, Claire added. I'll email the flight details once the tickets are booked.

She was efficient, the publicist. Lucca pictured her as an eager girl Friday type, dumpy with spectacles and a pinched face. She was asking about volunteer orientation—could they do something special for Dallas, perhaps a welcome ceremony with the staff and all the children? Could he hire a photographer?

Lucca made noncommittal noises as he filled out the schedule. Anya, he had met. She was tall and long-necked, with a grey bob she pushed her glasses up into and cheeks that sagged like saddlebags. This movie star business had to be the publicist's idea. She was keen, he'd say that for her. She had a lot of suggestions, prefaced with phrases like *Wouldn't it be nice* and *What do you think*. His strategy was evasion, answer every third or fourth email with a bland *Sounds great*, and delete the rest.

Social media will be key, and we really want to capitalize on Dallas's time there, Claire said. So ideally the rescue would happen on her second day.

They acted as if medical rescue was an item on a menu, something they could pre-order via mobile app.

Lucca, are you still there? Anya asked.

We do one, maybe two missions a month, Lucca said. This isn't an on-demand service.

I thought they were routine, the publicist said.

Her voice went up a notch when she got anxious. It was a quality Lucca had noticed on previous calls. Perversely, he found it a turn-on.

It depends on what Thiago finds when he goes into the villages, Lucca said. There are no guarantees.

This is a major opportunity, Claire said.

One we can't afford to squander, Anya added.

The publicist had outplayed him. Still, he resisted.

I've enough to be getting on with without having to babysit an actress, he said. It was an expression he'd picked up at Eton, and he employed it, inflected with a British intonation, whenever he wanted to adopt a high-handed stance.

Lucca. Anya's voice contained a warning, though it sounded hollow from fifteen hundred miles away.

Lucca was tempted to defy them, give Thiago a week off. But then he'd have an actress to entertain. Sending her on a rescue would at least get her out of his hair for a day.

Dallas won't be any trouble, Claire promised. She's completely down to earth.

Lucca had worked with celebrities. He knew their type. Once, he'd been trapped in a bunker with a punk band while two warring factions traded fire outside. The musicians—three guys in their mid-twenties who'd rose to sudden, unexpected fame—were catatonic with terror for three blissful hours, then spent the next five airing old grievances and arguing bitterly, each of them appealing to Lucca to take his side.

Another time he'd loaned his flak jacket to an actress and given her a crash course on how to crouch and run zigzags when a sharpshooter appeared on a roof. She'd been hysterical, bawling *I'm going to die, I'm going to die*, while he'd patiently lied and assured her, *No, you won't*. He'd gone into humanitarian work to save lives, not be a war-zone tour guide.

Claire said goodbye, and he and Anya turned to other business. Lucca explained about the clinic's personnel issues.

You've had a steady influx of volunteers since March, Anya said.

Volunteers whose Spanish was so poor they required the doctor to double as an interpreter, he wanted to say. Volunteers whose presence gave Head Office an excuse not to hire full-time staff. Mutiny was brewing, but try explaining that to Anya.

There are qualified nurses here, he said. Eight hundred dollars a month to replace one full-time position. That's all I'm asking.

I'll bring it to Crispin, Anya said, giving him her usual brush-off.

She asked for an update on the other volunteers. Two days earlier, a family had arrived to work on the farm. A retired couple and their five teenaged grandchildren. The old man had gotten ill on tap water. One of the girls suffered heatstroke. The others were up before dawn to milk cows and feed the pigs, but without skills or training, they only got in the way.

Why does Crispin insist on this charade? he asked Anya.

For a moment, there was silence, and he wondered if she might give a genuine answer, but then Anya sighed. This is our fundraising model, Lucca.

The couple had organized the excursion as a gift for their grandchildren. They were good sports about the spartan dorm rooms and communal cold showers, polite to the staff, and friendly with the children. They were kind people who meant well. Still, Lucca couldn't help adding up the numbers. Seven economy flights plus volunteer fees and visas. Nearly forty grand.

How many teachers, nurses, and labourers could Lucca have hired if they'd cut a cheque instead? But people didn't shell out like that unless there was something in it for them. He had resented the family then. How smug they looked returning to the dorms every afternoon for siesta, so self-satisfied by the illusion of their largesse. He'd despised himself, too, for taking this job despite his qualms.

I see the numbers, Anya said, as if reading his mind. You're doing good work. Don't overthink it. Stick to the plan.

The actress wasn't part of the plan, he said.

Lucca, we're drowning here. Can you please, just this once, throw me a buoy?

The lunch service was winding down, and the cafeteria was quiet. Most of the volunteers had left for their post-siesta shifts. Of the children, only the older ones remained, hunched over schoolwork or volubly gossiping and joshing. Standing at the entrance with Moisés, Lucca was scanning the room when Beatriz sidled up.

What do you think? she asked, wiping her hands on her apron and jutting her chin toward a table where a young woman sat alone, tearing a tortilla to sop up refried beans. She wore leggings, a nondescript T-shirt, and a trucker cap, the bill pulled down low. He was surprised to find her so quiet and self-contained.

Nearby, the volunteers who had accosted Moisés earlier were whispering together. Breaking away from the group, one approached Dallas cautiously. A moment later, the girls had surrounded her, all of them grinning for selfies.

Lucca was curious to know how the medical rescue had gone and what theatrically circuitous route Thiago had taken, but he wasn't about to broach the subject with Beatriz.

She seemed to read his mind and said, They brought a baby in.

Head Office insisted, Lucca said. You know the gringos; they make plans without asking us.

Beatriz talked over him, She's six months and has an ear infection.

Lucca shook his head in frustration. This was the problem with the theatrics. A child who could have been treated at home was now occupying a crib.

The baby is no trouble. The actress does everything for her, Beatriz said, making it clear where she laid the blame. Anyway, Maria will be cured and go back to her mother soon, she added, touching the crucifix at her throat. Won't she?

Yes, Lucca said.

Beatriz fiddled with her braid, coiling it behind her head. Did you hear about the protests? They're continuing next week.

Saint Beatriz, Lucca said, eager to change the subject. Thank you for taking care of the actress. Then he gave her a break and promised to clean up.

Lucca was used to being surrounded by other foreigners—journalists and aid workers, like-minded people with whom to share beers. This was what he craved after hours: blowing off steam with intelligent conversation or light banter, a harmless flirtation or a no-strings dalliance. But the staff at Santa Rosa were locals tethered to families and domestic responsibility. Most had grown up in the area and had networks of extended families nearby. They were generous with Lucca, invited him into their homes for christenings and parties, insisted he not be alone at Easter and Christmas. Occasionally, he accepted these invitations but only out of obligation. Inevitably, someone would attempt to play matchmaker. They pitied his bachelorhood, the very thing he prized.

Lucca was comfortable with solitude. It was the monotony he couldn't abide. Years ago, he'd been riding a jeep in Baghdad when a grenade was lobbed inside. Everyone had flung themselves out, while the vehicle, unmanned, drove on ahead, bursting into a fireball in the middle of the dirt road. The hours right after, coasting on the wake of near annihilation, were the most buoyant he'd ever known. Without the drone of fighter planes and thrumming adrenalin, daily life felt flattened.

He was rinsing dishes, sleeves folded up, Moisés toeing the deflated soccer ball, when the actress entered the kitchen.

Is the internet down? she asked.

It happens, Lucca said. We have power cuts too. Might come back in five minutes or tomorrow. He expected her to pout, to get the restless fidget of the addict, but she said okay and put her phone away.

This is Moisés, he said. He's our number one top scorer. Nuestro mejor goleador.

Moisés blushed and tucked his chin further into his chest.

Hola, Moisés. Soy Dallas, she said.

It didn't take her long to draw him out, and soon they were kicking the ball back and forth while the boy practised his English, Lucca translating for them.

Moisés wanted to know if Dallas could drive. Did she own a car? How many cars? Could she fly? How big was her house? What did she think of his country? Did she like it here?

Outsiders were usually uncomfortable with Santa Rosan curiosity, mistaking friendliness for prying, but Dallas didn't appear bothered. Lucca was amused, wondering when her patience would wear thin.

No, she didn't have children. Well, yes, she did hope to have some one day. No, she wasn't married. No boyfriend. Not at the moment.

What about the Aphid? Moisés asked. Dallas laughed. Freya was dating the Aphid, but she, Dallas Hayden, was not. Yes, she had a brother. No sisters. Her parents lived in Idaho. They were from America, like her.

No, Moisés said, shaking his head at the sound of *America*. You're from the United States *of* America. That's only one country out of thirty-six in the Americas. It's not even the biggest.

Oh! Dallas said, taken aback. I don't think that's right.

Moisés nodded, returning to his ball. No, I'm right. Ask anyone.

Lucca almost guffawed. It tickled him to think of how appalled Anya would be to witness this scene: Dallas in the kitchen—with its faded walls and greasy surfaces—receiving a geography lesson from a nine-year-old. Anya would not think Moisés was funny and clever. She would call him impertinent.

Dallas was still looking stumped when Moisés said he liked her bracelet and Lucca translated.

I have it? Moisés asked in English.

Dallas acted without hesitation, pulling the leather band off her wrist and slipping it onto his, wrapping it around twice.

It suits you, she said. Muy guapo.

The bell rang and Lucca sent Moisés to class: Go before the teacher comes.

He expected Dallas to leave, too, but she picked up a dish towel and began drying plates.

Cute kid, Dallas said. She was the sort who didn't find silence companionable.

He doesn't always warm to people, Lucca said, and explained that Moisés was a foundling, left by the front gate in a basket. He's a big fan of the Sentinels, Lucca added and described Moisés with the bedsheet, pretending to fly. All the while, he was watching, out the corner of his eye, as Dallas stacked dishes. Her face was unadorned. She wore no jewellery at all, only an analog watch.

He wants me to adopt him, Lucca said.

Will you?

I have nothing to offer. This isn't a place for a child like that.

He's seven? she asked.

Nine. He's small for his age, but he's bright and has good reflexes.

Maybe he'll be a soccer—football—player one day, she said.

Lucca shook his head and explained about Moisés's poor eyesight. We don't have the means to send him to specialists, he said.

That's so sad, Dallas said.

Lucca shrugged. We do our best, but what Moisés really needs is a proper home, a real mother. A good school. To join a fútbol—soccer—club.

Do you have kids? she asked, and Lucca flinched.

Oh, now I sound like Moisés. That's so personal.

It never appealed to me, he said. Though now I'm responsible for seventy of them. But it's not right. Children should be raised in families, not by strangers.

Your work must be so meaningful, she said.

Other aid workers told themselves stories about changing the world, but Lucca didn't flatter himself. He was good at his job, thrived on the parts that terrified most people. He was resourceful and took risks, liked immersing himself in other cultures so fully the person he really was vanished. Everyone needed a vocation, and this one suited him.

But he kept these thoughts to himself—they weren't *on brand*—and made a vague reply. He wanted to bring the conversation back to Moisés. If he could improve the child's lot, his time in Santa Rosa would have been worthwhile.

Don't you ever get overwhelmed? she asked. By just . . . the poverty. She dropped her voice. And the malnutrition and . . . and . . . She fluttered her hand vaguely. All the rest of it.

Lucca recognized her crisis of conscience, a common volunteer affliction. The news wasn't enough. Books weren't enough. People only reckoned with inequality, the vast chasm of their own privilege, when forced to confront it first-hand. But it was only a pinch of unease, quickly forgotten when they returned home. Hardly worth mentioning in the brochure.

The baby, Dallas said. The place where we found her, it was so—she put her hands over her eyes in a *No, I can't watch* gesture—hopeless. How can people live like that?

People live in all kinds of ways, he said mildly.

Privately, he was annoyed by her horror of the ordinary. Worse, her assumption that he would agree. It made him want to put her in her place. *Listen, Princess . . .*

You're lucky to have found this work, she said, as if she herself had never had any choice in the matter. God, she said. Acting. How facile. She circled her bare wrist absently.

Lucca wiped his hands and picked up Moisés's forgotten football, holding it out to her. Sometimes the best thing you can do is improve the life of one child.

Those people, she said. There must be others like them.

It took him a moment to understand she was referring to the family of the baby she brought in.

Millions, he said.

Everything was filthy, she said and shivered. There was a little boy there too.

She dropped her voice lower and relayed how he'd urinated by a tree, then returned to playing. Without washing his hands, she whispered. I don't think the baby had even had a proper bath until we got her here. No wonder she's sick.

Foreigners liked to think the poor were slovenly by choice, that it was a moral failing. Exasperated, he reminded himself of Moisés and kept his voice level as he explained how climate change and private industry had left hundreds of thousands in Santa Rosa without clean water.

And water is privatized, he added. Only those who can afford it can get it.

But that's awful, she said, crossing her arms and holding her biceps, shoulders up toward her ears. Why isn't someone doing anything about it?

He almost laughed at her ignorance. Not every problem has a solution, he said, still offering her the ball.

Salvation

Anya

Dallas. Dallas. Dallas. Was it to be a whole week of this? Anya wondered, arriving at the office the Monday after the baby rescue to find everyone fixated on the actress's latest online antics and ignoring their work. Children of the World was on the verge of bankruptcy. Surely, she'd made that clear. They were six months—a year tops—away from dissolving operations. Not that you'd ever know that from Crispin's self-satisfied chuckle as he made the rounds, pausing at desks to chat about people's weekends, like a benevolent monarch bestowing his blessings. Crispin was hell-bent on making everyone like him. It wouldn't do him any favours when it came time for the layoffs.

Alone in the kitchen, Anya scooped coffee grounds into a basket. All this brouhaha on the internet—exposure, Claire would call it—was well and good, but in the real world they were desperate for cash, and so far, what had come in was a pittance.

She'd spent the weekend running scenarios. Cutting two staffers at Head Office and shuttering operations in Nepal and Indonesia would buy them four or five months. Axing Santa Rosa—their most expensive venture (Anya preferred the word *robust*)—would give them a year. But no way was she doing that; she'd quit first.

The project was *hers*, one she'd masterminded and built from the ground up, its genesis a conversation on the beach with her son that she'd fleshed out on paper as their flight lifted off, Santa Rosa's jewelled coastline appearing underneath them. It was the reason she was here.

Children of the World had always flown under Anya's radar, too inconsequential for her attention. But what she'd planned, this one project that would benefit from her decades of experience, required someone like Crispin. A millionaire with a floundering vanity project, yes, but one who wasn't too proud to let her take the wheel. Within a year, she'd hauled the organization back from the brink and into modest prosperity, and in exchange he'd given her carte blanche to move into a new region and bring her vision to life.

If Crispin was a different type of founder, he'd have insisted on pulling up stakes long ago, but he knew what Santa Rosa meant to her. This was Crispin's problem: he didn't have the stomach for disappointing others. It fell to Anya to make dispassionate decisions and be the heavy.

Leaning her forehead against the cupboard door, she tried to imagine closing Santa Rosa, valiantly giving the other locations, all those other children, a fighting chance. The prospect made her ill. She couldn't admit failure. Not again.

From the workstations, there was a cheer so loud Anya startled. She knew they wrote her off as a curmudgeon, but she had good reason to be cautious. Before this job, Anya had headed up fundraising at CONCERN, one of the country's largest foreign aid NGOs. For two years, she'd courted the head of an investment firm, a reclusive billionaire whom she'd met by chance at the ballet and had, with great tact and subtlety, signed up as a major donor. Her colleagues were skeptics. He'd never given away a cent; why start now? Anya, imprudent in those days, dismissed the naysayers as jealous.

The Pink Fund was the donor's idea, a cache dedicated to improving the lives of girls in sub-Saharan Africa. They launched it with great fanfare, Anya and her new friend beaming on either side of the oversized cheque. Lights, cameras, microphones, all the media there for a rare gawk at one of the world's richest men. At the podium, Anya praised the donor's leadership, explaining the seven million was seed money, that he was going to match every cent donated by the public and had promised to leave his entire fortune to the fund in his will.

Within a month, Anya was promoted to vice-president. Within two, the billionaire was charged with running a Ponzi scheme. His sentence—predictably short—had ended long ago, but to this day, when Anya googled his name, the footage of the two of them with that worthless cheque came up. A dozen years on, her cheeks still burned at the memory as Crispin sauntered in.

New video just dropped, he said and pressed his phone on her.

Dallas was in the nursery, the rescued child bouncing on her knee. Someone else was behind the camera this time. Little Maria Garcia was six months old and had an ear infection. Easily treated by a round of amoxycillin, Dallas explained, gesturing to a syringe on the table at her side.

The baby was almost unrecognizable, bathed and dressed in a pale yellow onesie, the type that buttoned on a bias and was easier to manoeuvre and therefore more expensive than the kind that fastened under the crotch. She wore a crocheted cap, knit in white with teddy bear ears, and the incongruity of the toque and her bare legs was charming, though Anya winced when she saw her high arches, the way her toes and heels pointed inward. Club foot, rare in the West, was far more prevalent in poor countries and especially pernicious in Santa Rosa.

We got her just in time, Dallas said, tickling the child under the chin to elicit a gurgling laugh. This angel would have lost her hearing if we'd been even an hour later.

Through the years, Anya had seen variations of this philanthropic song and dance in videos and stills, in commercials that featured her employers or competitors. She'd grown disdainful of the cliché; could no one else see through it? But this time, the show was taking place in Santa Rosa, at a project she had founded, and when the baby laid a sleepy head on Dallas's shoulder while the actress planted a kiss on her crown, pride swelled in Anya's chest.

They wouldn't be there if not for you, Crispin said, shaking the phone. Nothing in Santa Rosa would.

And then she was anxious again, burdened by the weight of responsibility. She'd put up no resistance when Crispin decided to fly Dallas down with dollars they couldn't afford, and when the cheapskate tried to send her cattle class, it was Anya who had insisted on upgrading to business because she'd be damned if the actress's first impression of her project was marred by a cramped flight.

But will it pan out? she asked, rubbing her fingertips together in a money-money gesture before reaching for the creamer.

Crispin shook his head. Anya, you of all people know the power of celebrity.

Anya jolted, mid-pour, sloshing half-and-half all over the counter.

Woah, Crispin said, grabbing and steadying the carton.

After his arrest and trial, the Ponzi-scheming billionaire had achieved a dubious fame. Meanwhile, Anya, who had for many years been a favourite of headhunters, her resumé a checklist of blue-chip charities, became an industry pariah overnight. How quickly celebrity could turn into infamy, two sides of the same coin.

Crispin, unaware of her shame, was cheerfully wiping down the counter. No need to cry over spilled milk, eh? he quipped.

Yes, well, donations have barely ticked up, Anya said, returning to the steady ground of the present. What we need is cash. A lot more cash.

Something's bound to turn up, Crispin said. After the rescue—

Let's not speculate, Anya said. How were your meetings with Cannabliss and TrustEx?

Not bad, Crispin said. Cannabliss asked about the clinic in Kenya. They want photos for their employee newsletter. And an update.

Claire, forcing her way into the cramped space, piped in: Oh, it's going really well. I'll send you some copy.

You told TrustEx the clinic was theirs, Anya reminded Crispin. The CEO and his wife went there with a photographer. They posed with staff and patients. It's splashed all over *their* website, she added. But of course he was thumbing away at his phone, a grin stretching his face.

Anya made a strangled noise of frustration. They were forced to play fast and loose with sponsorships sometimes. Every millionaire wanted to stamp their name on a new building, but once the ribbon was cut, mundane expenses, like payroll and hydro bills, were left to the charity, stretching operational budgets thin, necessitating more fundraising to attract more major donors who demanded more buildings. But hey! The robber barons got to jack off their egos. That was the most important thing, right?

What are the odds— Crispin started to ask.

We can't risk it, Anya began, but before she could say more, Crispin announced that Dallas's manager had sent him an email. He wanted to speak with them. Right away.

In the boardroom, Anya listened to Crispin's pie-in-the-sky predictions while scowling at the fluorescent lighting flickering overhead. Claire, as usual, was enthusiastically agreeing with his every frivolous word. The table wobbled, and Anya had to crouch to readjust the old phone book propping up the short leg.

If we're gonna be famous, how about springing for some new furniture? she grumbled.

The phone rang. To Anya's surprise, Crispin didn't vault up. Instead, he closed his eyes and squeezed his hands, as if steeling his nerves. Here we go, he muttered before pressing the green button.

The manager's voice floating out of the speaker was surprisingly tinny. Dallas was having a transformative experience in Santa Rosa, Hugh Coren said. She felt a connection to the land and the people. She was humbled by their resilience and in awe of everything. I asked her, Dallas, are you sure you're coming home?

Anya had to admit Claire was right: Dallas had to be low maintenance if she was having a good time despite Lucca's neglect. Or perhaps her charm offensive had won him over. More likely they'd slept together.

Crispin raised the corner of his mouth at Anya, showing his dimple, and she rubbed the tips of her fingers together again.

Hugh began talking about the child Dallas had rescued, how the relationship blossoming between them was an inspiration. Dallas is keen to take a more active role with your organization. Perhaps as a spokesperson.

A goodwill ambassador, Crispin said. We'd be honoured.

Anya glanced at Claire, who was leaning toward the speaker expectantly, hands clasped. Her extravagant promises about internet strangers—*influencers*—transforming their donor base, maybe it wasn't all bluster. Anya had come up in the days of direct mail and infomercials and was bewildered by the bizarre and unnavigable landscape of social media.

Just so we're clear, she said, we distribute contraception. Antiretrovirals. Is Dallas comfortable championing—

All of it, Hugh confirmed. She's keen to visit your other locations too.

The joy in his voice stirred Anya's own, and she quickly tamped it down.

You can't imagine what this will mean for the mission, Crispin said, raising his eyebrows at Anya in an *I told you so* expression.

She scribbled the word *catch?* in her notebook and pushed it toward him. But before either of them could speak, Hugh added that just as an aside, he also repped Hercules and the Aphid. They, too, were curious about joining a rescue team. And now Anya felt a swoop in her chest. She imagined a global fundraising campaign, Dallas and her fellow Sentinels the stars of a major ad push, the donations flooding in. She'd finally get Santa Rosa on track.

Claire crossed out *catch?* and scrawled the words *celebrity ambassador program* in Anya's notebook, underlining the phrase twice. Crispin grinned and shook his head, and even Anya shrugged her shoulders to her ears. Claire cupped her face in both hands. Is this actually happening? their expressions asked. Can it be real?

Everyone was giddy. Wow, they kept saying to each other, to the manager. Wow. Hugh was clearly enjoying himself, said making this call was the highlight of his week.

Anya felt chastened. Witnessing suffering first-hand could inspire private revolutions. Who knew that better than her? She was only surprised Dallas wasn't on the line to share the good news herself.

The rescue mission flipped a switch, Hugh said. That's how Dallas describes it. If you could hear the way she speaks about the little girl.

The videos are wonderful, Anya said. She's obviously smitten.

Oh, yes, the baby adores her, he agreed. The truth is this has become personal for Dallas. Which brings me to the big news.

Here it comes, Anya thought. The windfall that would be their salvation.

Dallas is ready to adopt her, the manager announced.

Anya frowned, confused. What on earth had given— But, already, Crispin was saying yes of course, Dallas could have whatever she wanted. Anya put her hand out, pressed twice on an imaginary set of brakes.

I think there's been some confusion, she said. I'm not sure—

Dallas understands the girl has a difficult road ahead, Hugh said. Surgery, rehabilitation. Dallas is prepared to do everything in her power.

Anya had forgotten about the child's feet. Untreated, it would cripple her for life. She leaned closer to the speaker and raised her voice a notch. To my knowledge, the baby *has* a mother.

From the corner of her eye, she could see Claire frantically waving traffic controller arms, signalling stop, stop.

Of course, as a token of her commitment, Dallas would make a donation, Hugh continued.

Crispin raised his palms in a placating gesture. He said, That's extremely generous—

Let us speak to our director in Santa Rosa, Anya said, shaking her head at Crispin, tapping an index finger on the table twice. I'd like a better handle on the situation.

We'd have to take some time to confirm the exact figure, Hugh said. But five hundred, six fifty . . .

Claire mouthed her name, eyes bugged out in remonstrance, but Anya was overwhelmed by this roller coaster of a phone call and how quickly information was coming at her. She resented Dallas for sending her middleman instead of having the guts to come on the line and make this brazen request herself.

We don't facilitate adoptions, Anya said.

Even seven figures isn't out of the question, he finished. As I said, Dallas is keen.

Crispin got Anya's attention and sternly pulled an imaginary zipper across his lips.

Dallas's generosity is incredible, he said. If we sound overwhelmed, it's only because we're astounded. Give us a day or two to get our heads around what's been discussed and then we'll be in a position to respond.

Thank you, Claire said, leaning forward toward the speaker, hands on the table for maximum leverage. Please tell Dallas. We're so grateful.

Anya waited for the dial tone to play before letting loose. Who the hell does she think she is? She swans in on a poverty porn tour, spends five minutes in the country, gets her feelings in a tizzy, and thinks Oh! oh! whatever shall I do? I know! I'll take home a baby. Keychains are for plebeians. *I'm* Dallas Hayden. I need an *elite* souvenir.

Crispin watched her, face like thunder. Are you done?

Anya suffered a split second of humiliation before remembering herself, that she was his elder and infinitely wiser.

Crispin tapped a pen against the table as if preparing the nib, ready to sign the adoption papers himself. On any other day, this would be an amazing opportunity, he said. Today, it's a life saver, and I won't have you or anyone jeopardizing this organization—*my* organization's—one chance.

There was a mother in that video, Anya said quietly. There's a father, too, for all we know.

What means can they have if their child is in our care? Crispin argued, his voice gentle. Anya, you know the life she'll have there. Pain, deformity, infection. She might never walk. He turned to Claire then, appealing: But in California, with Dallas, she'll get treatment. By the time she gets to kindergarten, it'll be like it never happened.

I noticed she was pigeon-toed, Claire said. I didn't realize it was serious.

He said: There's a reason you never see club foot here. They catch it on ultrasound and treat it at birth. That's if it even happens.

No one knows why, Anya added, for Claire's benefit. My guess is malnutrition.

Crispin jammed the pen so hard into the table, the point stuck. It's a damn waste. She could be an athlete or a dancer. A Nobel Prize winner. These kids could be anything if not for an accident of birth.

Anya shook her head. Of course, she agreed with him. Of course, she was enraged by the scale of the injustice and what was too often their sheer helplessness.

There are two orthopedic surgeons in Santa Rosa, Crispin said. Two. For nine million people. And one in every thousand babies is born with club foot.

Anya winced, recalling the heated exchange they'd had with Lucca in the summer, when he'd pummelled them with these figures. She wasn't surprised that Crispin had them memorized. He took failure to heart, as if he was personally to blame for how the children suffered.

Anya drummed her fingers on the table. If Dallas is such a long-time fan, why haven't we heard from her before? For that matter, why adopt now?

Claire held her phone up, a still photo on the screen of the baby cherubic in sleep, thumb in mouth. She said: I'm sorry, but I don't understand why this is even a discussion. How can we deprive her?

Anya could see why Dallas was besotted. But being a single parent . . . She thought of Zach, nearly forty and still living with her. Probably sleeping in. Dallas was either selfless or a lunatic.

We have what . . . seventy children under our roof in Santa Rosa? Crispin said. And how many in India? Cambodia? All over the world? That's hundreds of kids who'll be on the street if we don't find a solution.

A million-dollar solution, Claire said quietly.

If a donation comes in, Anya said. It hadn't escaped her notice that Dallas's manager had dangled that carrot whenever she'd tried to interject.

Anya put her fingers to her temples. All those years ago, even after the bombastic public announcements, the oversized cheque boasting its seven figures, the Ponzi-scheming billionaire hadn't ponied up. Weeks before the police broke down his door, he'd already stopped answering Anya's calls.

Why are you assuming the family won't agree? Claire asked.

Would you? Anya asked.

If it was a choice between lifelong disability and treatment? If I couldn't give my child what she needed and there was someone who could? I'm not saying it would be easy. But it would be wrong to trap her in poverty if there was another option.

You'd give up Charlotte? Anya pressed. You'd give up Theo?

Claire's nostrils flared, and she sat forward. What about Zach?

Anya knew how it looked, a woman her age still saddled with a forty-year-old son living at home. Everyone wrote Zach off as a mooch and her an as enabler, but what they didn't understand was how much she cherished his companionship. She pictured Zach at six, whimpering with a stomach bug. Zach at thirty-three, his forehead bouncing against a train window. Zach at twenty-seven, handing her a shell on the beach in Santa Rosa, saying, *Start your own charity*. She couldn't imagine being deprived of a single prosaic moment, the fond pity that overcame her as she imagined her grown son.

Not for anything, she said. I'd never let him go.

She saw the crumple in Claire's expression, how Anya's certainty had wounded her. Then a terrible memory: calling the police. Because this was the only way to admit someone to a psychiatric ward against their will.

What Anya mourned was not the person Zach was but the life she hadn't given him. All his potential that she'd squandered.

Because she'd been a single mother with a demanding career, too preoccupied to heed the red flags. Who would Zach be today if he'd had a more courageous mother, one who'd acknowledged his problems sooner?

She shook her head at Claire and said, But sometimes parents make selfish choices.

Claire slumped back and said, We do.

A better mother would put her child's needs first, Anya said.

Yes, Claire agreed. A better mother.

It's not just this one kid, Crispin said, pointing out that this would change the trajectory of the whole family's lives. One day the baby would return to lift them all out of poverty, he predicted.

Dallas could do it now, Anya said. She could make the million-dollar cheque out to them, if that's who she really cared about.

Even I'm not naive enough to expect that, Crispin said.

There's a new Reel, Claire said, showing them her phone.

This video had been shot at the clinic. Dallas panned the camera around the space, taking in the patients and staff, the volunteers doing blood pressure readings, making notes on charts. She spouted off stats about the number of patients they saw every year, how everything was accomplished on a shoestring.

Text the number 7368 to donate, she said. Every dollar counts, but monthly donations go the furthest.

Check out the comments, Claire said. The engagement is off the charts, and it's only Monday. Dallas's trip is going to change everything for Santa Rosa.

The hum of a headache was gathering at Anya's temples. She resented the proprietary way Claire spoke of Santa Rosa, as if it was hers, as if she'd been the one to find and resuscitate Crispin's flailing charity, build it up from nothing, toil heart and soul for twelve years, only to watch, helpless, as it hung in the balance.

Twenty minutes ago, we were worrying about Kenya, Crispin said. Soon we'll have Hollywood fundraisers. We won't know what to do with the money.

His enthusiasm could be infectious, but today Anya was immune. Dallas could rescue them all—the child's family, the project in Santa Rosa, Children of the World—without this rigmarole, but the rich demanded fanfare. Her expression must have betrayed her contempt because Crispin caught her eye, frowned, and said: You have an issue with Dallas. Fine. Step away. Claire can take the lead.

I don't have an issue—

He shook his head. Anya, you said it yourself. Without a serious cash injection, we're finished. We don't have a choice.

He meant *she* didn't have a choice. Her contributions didn't matter; ultimately, this was *his* organization.

She has a mother. It's not our call, Anya said.

My point exactly, Crispin said. We'll bring it to the mother. She'll do the right thing.

Golden Opportunity

Lucca

When Anya demanded they speak—*Now. Right away. It's imperative.*—Lucca braced for a long-distance tongue lashing: He wasn't being hospitable enough to their special guest. He was squandering a golden opportunity. And furthermore, his paperwork was months behind.

Whatever it was, it must be serious for Crispin to be involved. Lucca had not spoken to the NGO's founder in months.

Lucca, Crispin said. Thanks for making the time.

We know how busy you are, Anya added, and he couldn't tell if her tone was goading.

There was a stress ball on Lucca's desk, a relic left behind by his predecessor. He squeezed it.

We appreciate how you've taken the reins in Santa Rosa, Crispin said. We don't say that enough.

The numbers speak for themselves, Anya continued. Child rescues are up, dorms are at capacity, the volunteer surveys are glowing.

Lucca relaxed his grip on the rubber ball, confused by the surprise performance evaluation.

And hosting our special guest on short notice, Crispin said. It can't be easy, the additional work when you're out there on your own.

Anya said they'd just spoken with Dallas's manager. She's having a life-changing visit.

And ready for this? Crispin said. She's making a donation!

When he named the figure, Lucca pushed the chair away from his desk and whistled. Crispin told him to make a list. Whatever was needed. They could afford it all now.

This is a game changer, Crispin declared as he and Anya began daydreaming about butcher shops, artisan cooperatives, and pies in the sky. While Anya imagined a utopia of women weaving baskets and braiding bracelets, marketing their tchotchkes online to suburbanites overseas, Lucca knew half a dozen underemployed seamstresses who would kill for a commission to sew the children's uniforms, if only they weren't being donated by a foreign company.

I'd like to invest in the local economy, Lucca said at last, finding diplomatic phrasing. Give this donation back to the community, but not as charity. Then he named the vendors he wanted to hire, neglecting to mention that some of them happened to be cousins or brothers or nieces of the staff. Only gringos could network. Try that here, and Head Office called it nepotism.

The prospect of the donation had made even Anya receptive to hiring locally, and soon the three of them were brainstorming ways to share the wealth. Lucca offered to draft a proposal. He was imagining how far those U.S. dollars would stretch. Finally, he could stop worrying about insurrection.

I knew Dallas's visit would mean big things, Crispin said.

Anya said this was all down to the rescue and asked what Lucca knew of the family: Was it a two-parent household? How many children? How stable was the father's employment?

Lucca was bemused. Anya was incurious about individuals, only ever pressed him for statistics and numbers. It was the publicist who harangued him for details.

Dallas has bonded with the child, Anya said.

Maria Garcia, Lucca said.

Dallas is going to adopt her! Crispin made the announcement as if declaring a prize.

Maria? Lucca repeated, thinking of the childhood game of telephone—the message must have gotten garbled in translation.

This is the best thing that could happen for the girl, Crispin said, then hesitated before he added: In the States, she'll have access to specialists. Anything she needs.

Lucca wondered what Crispin was talking about and why he sounded almost ashamed, but he didn't want to reveal that he hadn't laid eyes on the baby.

Maria has a family, Lucca said. But there's another child. Then he told them about Moisés, feeling no compunction about the embellishment of the basket. It was too bad Claire wasn't on the line to appreciate the technicolour of the tale.

Dallas likes Moisés, Lucca said. They've—

Crispin said it would be best if Lucca met the family to put the offer on the table, do it face to face. Of course, he used the royal we. *We* should meet with the family. *We* should let them choose. All that bombast about wish lists. Lucca should have known. There was no such thing as a gift; there were only strings donors could yank to make recipients do their bidding.

It's impossible, Lucca said, pointing out the bureaucratic hassle. If she'd been born at home, Maria might not have a birth certificate. She definitely didn't have a passport. Odds were the parents were illiterate.

Crispin cut him off. You don't have to worry about the details. Dallas's people will handle everything.

What happened to giving the Garcias a choice? he said. I thought *we* were going to meet with the family and let them decide.

Of course, Crispin said. We'll take our lead from you.

Lucca squinted, vision narrowing to a dent in the filing cabinet. Anya usually took charge on these calls, leaving Crispin to play hype man. But today, Crispin was doing most of the talking. Not browbeating like Anya did—Crispin was savvier, using persuasion to build faux consensus—but strong-arming all the same.

What do *you* think, Anya? Lucca asked, trying to recall if she had children. Should the parents be forced to do this?

They will want what's best for the baby, Anya said.

It was clear from her tone what she thought *the best* meant and that Lucca was expected to lead the Garcias to this conclusion if they didn't arrive there on their own. He flung the stress ball in disgust.

Dallas is offering to reverse the child's fortunes, Crispin said. Think of what that will mean for her future, for her family's future.

Her family! Lucca almost spat the words back. There would be a web of relations, all of whom would have an opinion on whether this was a loss or a gain. Crispin and Anya, remote at Head Office, had no clue.

Anya cleared her throat and said: When you speak to them, it would be prudent to go alone. Don't take Dallas or the child.

Bureaucracy is slow and inefficient here, he warned. Even if all are in favour, it might take months. Years.

Lucca knew his arguments were futile. They would send him on this hateful errand, like it or not. He dug his nails into his cushioned armrests, the action briefly satisfying until his hands cramped.

It's better than a storybook, Crispin said. Dallas is a real-life fairy godmother.

Make them see that, Anya said, sounding grim. You have to make the family understand.

That evening, Lucca went to visit Maria who, because she was only nominally sick, had been moved to the nursery. Some of the children around her were asleep, but most were awake, babbling to themselves or staring into space. A three-year-old in diapers banged his head against the bars of a padded crib. Many of the children had the same flat bland affect, a result of genetics or malnutrition or both.

Dallas was in a folding chair by the window, Maria cradled in the crook of her elbow, hands on the bottle, eyes locked on each other.

Oh, you're so delicious, Dallas cooed at her. I could eat you up.

The cafeteria closes soon, he said. Don't miss your chance.

He saw the proprietary way she held Maria to her chest, the kiss she gave her before laying her in the crib. To Dallas, the child was already hers.

I won't be long, she promised, tickling the baby under the chin to hear her giggle before hurrying away.

Maria lay on her back blinking at Lucca as he looked down at her. Usually, the children who arrived through medical rescue were severely malnourished and needed feeding tubes. But Maria, though small for her age, wasn't scrawny.

Thiago was proud of his country and did not relish putting people's vulnerability on display. Lucca understood why he'd chosen a robust child for Dallas's rescue. If only they'd taken the medication to the family and returned empty-handed.

He unwrapped the swaddle carefully, unsure of what he'd find. When he saw Maria's feet—how the heels pointed down while the toes revolved inward—Lucca immediately understood Crispin's hesitation, his vague word choice.

For years, they'd run a weekly club foot clinic that people from the surrounding areas had relied on. To compensate for its doctor shortages, Santa Rosa had a system of clinical officers, licensed medics who trained and apprenticed alongside physicians and specialized in areas like obstetrics and oncology. Children of the World had hired an orthopedic officer to set up shop on Wednesdays. The treatment was straightforward: a series of manual manipulations, weekly casts, and eventually a brace. Watching a child walk out of the clinic for the last time was one of the most satisfying things the staff got to witness, and finding afflicted infants had been a routine part of the medical rescues. But Head Office claimed the program was too expensive, and a few months ago, they'd forced Lucca to shut it down.

He sighed. Both Maria's feet were affected. She was doubly unlucky.

Juan arrived for his evening rounds and declared himself satisfied with his patient's progress. Maria can go home any time, he said.

And her feet, Lucca said, treading carefully. Isn't there anything we can do?

We? Juan said. Yes, of course. *We* can reopen the Wednesday clinic.

Lucca had seen the orthopedic officer at work, holding a misshapen foot, the deft series of movements that appeared like a sleight of hand. The intervention was so basic.

He gathered his nerve and asked: If I can find a brace, couldn't you treat her? Just this one child.

You think because a specialist makes it look easy, the method is simple, something any imbecile can learn from YouTube?

Lucca flinched. You're right, Juan. I'm sorry.

Juan tapped the side of the clipboard with the flat of his hand. And what about a new nurse, he said. You spoke with the bosses today?

Lucca's jaw tightened. He'd told no one of the meeting, yet they all knew his business. He considered sharing the news of the donation but held back. Inflating the clinic's hopes always backfired.

Every day we are receiving more and more patients, Juan said. We need at least two nurses overnight and three during the day. This part-time situation isn't enough.

They say there is no money.

No money. Who understands this better than us, the doctor said. Ask the actress if she has any money.

Lucca nodded at the child, still alert, eyes wide open and watching them from the crib. The actress wants to take Maria to California.

The doctor scoffed. For treatment she could easily have here?

Yes. And to live there, as her daughter.

The angry flush that had been creeping up Juan's neck reached his cheeks. Los pinches gringos, he said viciously. Their arrogance is astounding.

Vindicated, Lucca had an urge to vent, to tell Juan all about the call with out-of-touch Head Office. But he quickly stopped himself. Juan was his direct report, not a peer.

I'm to speak to the parents tomorrow, Lucca said. They'll understand what her condition means for her future, but I'll have to tell them there is nothing we can do. In the U.S. of course . . .

Lucca wanted to ask him: if you were in my position, what would you do? But they had never been confidants. Still, he hoped Juan would offer a third option, a way to get Maria treatment that didn't involve emigration.

I don't envy you, Lucca, the doctor said, his features softening. As to what is best for the child, that I cannot say. It is for her family to decide.

All Good Things

Claire

When the notification appeared on her phone, Claire blinked at it dumbfounded. It was a text from Dallas, a selfie of her and the baby, faces squashed together. Claire had communicated with an assistant to set up the trip, never with the actress herself. She glanced around, wondering if the message was a prank. But her colleagues were diligently at work. Even the office joker was on the phone, and from his patient, earnest tone, she could tell he was speaking to an elderly donor.

She checked the photo, the phone number. It was legit. Dallas Hayden was reaching out to her directly.

Too cute, Claire typed back.

I love her, Dallas wrote. *Did Hugh talk to you?*

It had been four days since their conversation with Dallas's manager. Later, Crispin and Anya had emerged from the boardroom, their expressions—hers grim, his elated—revealing no hint of how the call with Lucca had gone. Claire, still stinging from being sidelined, was too proud to ask.

Now, she paused, vexed. Claire was the one who'd brought Dallas in and, let's face it, upgraded Children of the World to the grown-up table. All the serious aid organizations had celebrity ambassadors, and now Children of the World had a chance at one too. But that counted for nothing, it seemed, and Anya and Crispin still hadn't seen fit to give her an update. She had a brief, irrational urge to stride over to their desks and wave her phone.

Instead, she typed back *Yes! Very exciting!* and added a fingers-crossed emoji. A heart materialized next to her reply. Claire stared at the screen, waiting for more.

What did it mean that Dallas seemed to be fishing for intel? Anya must have argued with Lucca and sabotaged everything. Or maybe the baby's family was undecided. All week, Claire had been pondering Anya's challenge: Would she give up her own kids if it guaranteed them not just a better life, but the *best* possible life? Under what duress would she hand over Theo or Charlotte? She thought of the mothers who threw their babies out of burning buildings to strangers down below, willing even to break a precious limb if it meant saving their lives. The ones who sent their kids across borders, hidden in vans or squeezed onto lifeboats. For unlucky parents, these choices were heartbreakingly cut and dry.

Her ex-husband's voice came to her unbidden, his tone mocking: *The easiest choices are the ones you make for other people.* Simon liked to invoke heritage in these types of conversations, likening emigration to murder, a severing of cultural and familial ties that would forever haunt, radiating phantom pains. Bollywood levels of melodrama for a guy who was born and raised in Canada. Claire banished Simon and his scorn from her mind.

At a loss, she scrolled through her social media, searching for clues. Dallas had been churning out TikToks and Instagram Reels, keeping her fans abuzz. Unlike the footage shot by volunteers, these videos were edited with a professional influencer's savvy.

In one, she played a clapping game with a little girl. It was morning and children in uniform moved through the frame, chattering in Spanish, occasionally harangued by a teacher. Dallas and the girl sang a rhyme. Claire caught a couple of words: *marinero*, *mar*. *Sailor*, *sea.* Both of them were giggling, as if in on a joke. The rhyme ended, and Dallas and the child turned to the camera, waved, and called adios.

Other videos focused on the clinic. One of the most popular TikToks was of a malnourished child being fed through a tube, with a concerned Dallas, stethoscope on, listening to his heart. The little boy was emaciated, his head huge atop a frail body, an image that gave Claire a twinge of discomfort. She tried not to interrogate this feeling, distracting herself with the comments, which were awash in high-fives and clapping emojis, people asking how they could help. Claire chimed in: *Sign up as a monthly donor. #realhero.* She got an endorphin rush every time she did this.

Claire found a video of the baby and scrutinized her feet. The parents would of course agree to the adoption. How could they not when the alternative consigned their daughter to a lifelong disability? She watched the rescue again and tried to imagine a wheelchair in the shack.

The workday was winding down when another message arrived. A grey wall of text sent from the airport in Santa Rosa, where Dallas was waiting to board her flight home. Anxiety spiked Claire's pulse. Dallas wasn't scheduled to leave until the following day. Had Lucca's rudeness driven her off early? But scanning the message, she read only positivity.

Thank you so much, Dallas wrote in closing. *Your invitation was life changing. All good things —Dx*

Claire lingered on the sign off, charmed by its quaintness. *All good things.* She liked the ring of that. And the casual first initial. The modest lowercase *x*. Dallas Hayden was texting from her private phone number. Dallas Hayden was sending an electronic kiss. To her. What is my life? she wondered, jubilant.

The office joker rolled his chair backward into her workstation. What's that grin for, Talbot? He whistled low when she showed him the message. Next thing you know, she'll be flying you to Cali on her private jet, he said. Crispin better watch out or she'll poach you. Smooch. Smooch.

Get outta here, she said and pushed his shoulder. He peddled away with his feet, and Claire thumbed back a reply: *It's been entirely our pleasure. We're all looking forward to working with you longer term. Safe travels.*

She debated awhile, adding and deleting a lowercase *x*, before finally leaving it in. Of course they weren't really friends. But they were friendly, and with any luck, soon they'd be practically colleagues. She scrutinized Dallas's message again, searching for the subtext, dying to know: Was the adoption going ahead? Is that what Dallas meant by *life changing*?

Crispin had been cloistered in meetings for most of the day and was finally emerging from the boardroom. She showed him the texts, and he waggled his eyebrows but didn't answer her unasked question. Instead, he said: I'd like you to put some thought into the celebrity ambassador program. Think big. And don't limit yourself to actors. Obama. Beyoncé. We could have anyone.

Anya, flipping through files in the cabinet nearby, snorted. Sure, sure, count those chickens.

Something must have gone wrong in Santa Rosa, Claire decided, plunged back into agony. Lucca, with a heavy assist from Anya, had ruined everything, and this was Crispin's subtle way of telling her to reach into her hat and produce another bunny.

On social media, the excitement and engagement were rising every day; but offline, the phones had gone silent, and donations had flatlined. Yes, they'd signed up seventy-five monthlies, a respectable number, but seventy-five new supporters wouldn't save their skin.

She'd always have a place at the agency. Her former boss had made that clear.

Is it a question of compensation? he'd asked in his typical straight-talking way, when she'd given her notice. Her last bonus had been a couple thousand shy of what she'd expected, and he thought she was making a power play. Because if it's about money, or a promotion, I'm open to negotiation, he said.

I've been working here since I was twenty-three, Claire said. Almost twenty years.

You have seemed a little disenchanted recently, he agreed grudgingly.

It's time to turn the page, she said.

At the agency, her work was high-octane. They likened themselves to firefighters, dousing the flames that threatened their clients' brands. Burnout was common, but Claire had been proud of her stamina and the cool-headed neutrality that allowed her to improvise game plans rather than crack under pressure. Claire's a savant, her colleagues joked. She's playing ten-dimensional chess.

Meanwhile, at home, Simon's complaints about her long hours (which Claire had always written off as his unwillingness to do his share of parenting and housework) had morphed into moralizing.

He lambasted her clients, called her complicit in their villainy, and denounced her salary as blood money.

Green oil, he railed one night, with exaggerated air quotes, about a client's offshore drilling. There's no such thing as environmentally friendly fossil fuels. They're poisoning the planet, and you're helping.

Jesus, Simon. Can you take it down a notch?

It was late, and Claire had just returned after a fourteen-hour day. She'd barely kicked off her heels and was rubbing her swollen feet. She was exhausted and dehydrated and wanted very badly to kiss her sleeping children and ideally pass out on the floor next to one of them.

This is the planet we're talking about, Simon said, trailing her as she hobbled to the kitchen for a drink. The one we're supposed to be leaving to our kids.

You forgot to clutch your pearls, she said, miming holding a string of baubles at her throat and mouthing the words *Think of the children*.

Well, one of us has to think of them, he said.

This was rich, coming from the father who never packed lunches or dealt with calls from principals. Oh, *I'm* the bad parent? she said and demanded he recite the names of their daughter's friends, after which they plunged headlong into their favourite fight sequence, lashing out at each other with well-practised choreographed moves.

What happened to international development? he asked, referencing her degree. What happened to doing good in the world? What happened to the girl I fell in love with?

She grew up, Claire snarled. Why didn't you?

Well, I'll always do the right thing for my children, he said. *My children*. As if they weren't hers. As if she'd forfeited her right to call herself their mother.

It wasn't the argument that ended the marriage, but maybe this particular fight, which continued for weeks, inflamed by the successful rollout of the client's green oil campaign, was the final straw.

One day, a couple of months into her separation, Claire attended a new client meeting. A consumer products conglomerate was facing down the residents of a small town over a scandal that was about to break. Claire and her colleagues sat on one side of the boardroom table, with the clients on the other, as the company's president outlined the issue. A rare and deadly cancer was afflicting kids in the area around one of their paper mills. It had been going on for a couple of years, a medical mystery with no clear answers. So far, the public fallout had been contained to the tiny local paper.

But Claire already knew this story. The town they were talking about was the one she'd grown up in, alongside the parents of the sick children. For months, her former classmates had been agitating on Facebook, saying surely the cause was an environmental toxin and what else could be poisoning the water or air but the town's sole industry? Four children were dead, a dozen more still sick, their bodies riddled with aggressive tumours.

Claire felt a sickening dread as she listened to the brief, noting who the client had brought to this council of war: the president, two executives, their lawyers, and the board chair. All dressed in uniform black suits, a murder of crows. So it was true: they *were* responsible.

The room took on an unreal, underwater quality. Her colleagues scribbled notes, asked questions, and nodded with sympathetic gravity, but Claire couldn't play along. The most recent child to die was five, the same age as her daughter.

After the client left, they discussed strategy. This is capital-B bad, one of Claire's fellow directors groaned. I mean kids with cancer? *Come on.*

And they expect us to make it disappear? said another colleague. We're comms experts, not magicians.

Claire's a magician, someone said. While we were all sweating it, bluffing for the client, you were in your mind palace mapping out a multipronged strategy, right?

It was an off-the-cuff compliment, voiced by her rival, of all people.

A *killer* strategy, someone joked.

Too far, the others tutted.

What about these moms, Claire's rival said, flipping through his notes. This Darlene woman seems to be the ringleader. Step one: we bury her.

Oh yeah, because that's who people love to hate, the mom of a dying kid, Claire snapped, heartrate spiking at the mention of her high-school best friend.

Her outburst startled the room. Everyone stared at her agog. In a calmer tone, she said, An authority figure is a better target.

The doctor, her boss agreed. Smart thinking, Claire. Question his credibility; turn him into a charlatan.

Soon they were foraging for complaints on Rate My MD, outlining a smear campaign while Claire felt sick to her stomach because the target was now on her former pediatrician's back, the one who'd seen her through all her childhood illnesses. By month's end, she had resigned and joined Children of the World.

A ping from Claire's computer demanded her attention.

The *Herald* wants to interview you for a big weekend feature, she told Crispin.

Finally, her media outreach was gaining traction. An in-depth long read in a national newspaper, just the kind of publicity Crispin thirsted after, and Claire hadn't even pitched it. But then she read on and frowned.

Something wrong? Crispin asked. He was buttoning his coat.

They've assigned Emmanuelle Clemmons, she said. Do you know her?

Don't think so. Should I?

Claire was friendly with most reporters. The *Herald* editor whose email she was reading, for example, was an old acquaintance. He was the solicitous type who always asked after her kids when they crossed paths off-hours. But the journalist he'd chosen had a chip on her shoulder.

Emmanuelle Clemmons reported out stories with a thoroughness that was rare. Even in media circles, she had a reputation as a troublemaker. Claire had warned more than one junior colleague to watch themselves around her. That Emmanuelle had been given the assignment at all was unexpected. She'd had a regular column at the *Herald* but lost it. Or maybe she'd quit. She'd started a protest or some kind of job action—Claire couldn't recall the gossip—but either way the split wasn't amicable.

She wrote that exposé on the factory accidents, Claire said. I'm just surprised she'd agree to a fluff piece.

Crispin popped his collar. Who says we're fluff?

—

Later that evening, while Charlotte splashed in the bath, Claire sat on the closed toilet seat, elbows on knees, phone cradled between thumbs. There had been no new texts from Dallas, and Claire was reduced to rewatching footage of her time in Santa Rosa: Dallas singing songs from *Mary Poppins* and preparing a syringe of medicine.

Mama, Charlotte said.

Just a second, Chicken.

Claire depressed the buttons on her earbuds. Dallas was telling the camera, Here's my little trick. She squirted the white goop into the baby's mouth while affecting a series of dramatic fake swallows. The child, expression puckered in mutiny a second earlier, began imitating her, hypnotized by the performance.

All done, Dallas said, rubbing the baby's back. See? Not so bad.

How did Dallas know to do this? Claire wondered.

Earlier, there had been a fight in the park when Claire had tried to persuade her hangry daughter to eat a yogurt cup. Not the one with the fruit in the bottom, Charlotte had complained. Mama knew fruity yogurt was her enemy. She'd toed the sand furiously, then kicked it at her brother who raged and came at her with his fists. Prising them apart, Claire had taken a foot to the shin. Already she could feel the bruise blooming. And here was Dallas convincing a child she barely knew to take her medicine.

Dallas's certainty with the syringe—perhaps this was the trick: complete confidence. How she'd made a game of it until she earned the girl's trust, the child's eyes following her. The swiftness of her method and the comedic distraction. She was a natural.

Why not bring the medicine to the family? a couple of Negative Nellies asked in the comments. *Are the dramatics necessary?* But these were fringe complaints, swiftly drowned out by the positive-vibes pile on.

Mama, Charlotte called again. Mama. Are you listening? She turned on the faucet, and water rumbled out full blast.

I'm listening, Claire said and nudged up the volume on her phone. Dallas had dropped a final TikTok right before her plane took off from Santa Rosa, a compilation of stills from her week set to an upbeat Taylor Swift song. The photos sped by, and Claire had to rewatch a few times to get the full effect.

She had a better idea of the compound in Santa Rosa now and even recognized some of the staff by name. The only absentee was Lucca, who never showed up on Dallas's camera. A grumpy Polkaroo.

Mama! Charlotte slammed a hand into the bathwater, creating a white cap that sloshed onto the floor, bringing Claire's attention back to her bathroom. Eyes on me please, her daughter demanded, repeating a phrase she must have picked up from her teacher.

Claire yanked out her earbuds. She was a terrible mother.

Sorry, Chicken. What were you saying?

Charlotte splashed her toes up and down. You know my dadu?

Claire, shamed, knelt on the floor, shampoo bottle in hand. She wondered why Charlotte was bringing up Simon's father. I know him, yes, she said.

It's my dadu's birthday, Charlotte announced. I'm gonna go to the party, right?

Claire's former in-laws did nothing by halves. This seventieth birthday would be a five-star production. Live music and a dance floor under one of those outdoor canopies. Caterers. Guests in silk saris and three-piece suits. Children in their finery tumbling across the manicured lawn. Bottles of Veuve Clicquot by the crate.

Of course you're going, Claire said, massaging Charlotte's scalp, bubbles foaming between her fingers. But it's not until April, so we have lots of time to think of a present.

The only child of older parents, Claire had grown up lonely in stifling quietude and was delighted by her ex-husband's large and spirited family, the easy way they folded her in. But after the separation, she never heard from any of them again.

Charlotte said she'd been promised a new party outfit and would meet all her aunties and uncles and cousins in India.

From India, Claire corrected, lifting her out of the tub.

In India, Charlotte said. I'm gonna ride an elephant. But not Theo. He's still a baby.

When's all this happening? Claire asked, wrapping the towel round tight, enclosing Charlotte in a hug.

When we go for my dadu's party.

Claire held on a couple of seconds longer, staring at the lowering water level, her vision blurring with rage.

Later, she stood on the back steps and tried to keep her voice low as she said into the phone, You tricked our child into doing your dirty work.

I was going to tell you, Simon said.

They'll need vaccines and passports. You don't get to make these big decisions on your own. Claire heard her voice rising. She took three steps up into the bald patch of yard and asked more quietly, When's this trip anyway?

April. It's a long way off, he said. And the flights aren't cheap. To make it worthwhile, we really need six weeks.

A month and a half! she exclaimed.

Simon made a pitch for heritage. The kids had extended family to meet and a homeland to see. It was Sara's idea, he said, punting the blame to his eldest sister. The siblings were going to hire cars and drivers, travel the country with their families.

Claire could imagine how he'd sold this to Charlotte and Theo—an epic road trip, an unending sleepover with their cousins during which they'd be spoiled rotten by their grandparents.

It was a gift for his parents, Simon said. They weren't getting any younger and might never go home again.

Did he expect her to buy this last-chance golden-years nonsense? Over Easter, Simon's parents had climbed Machu Picchu. They still worked full-time, heading up their respective departments at a busy uptown hospital.

Still, Claire tried to be judicious. If the kids were a little older, she said.

I know you hate to be away from them, Simon said, and her grip on the phone tightened.

Theo will cry the second you land in Delhi and he realizes I'm not there, she predicted. Charlotte will last four days max. What she didn't say: You might be the fun one, but I'm indispensable.

The kids want this, he insisted.

Six weeks. Simon wanted to take the kids from her, and not just for a while. This was a test run for primary custody, for total alienation. And he would use his parents' Visa Black Cards—how else was he, an elementary school teacher, funding this excursion?—and her lack of resources against her.

That's not how this works, Simon, she said. Call your lawyer and get him to explain the custody agreement to you, if you don't understand.

Hago lo necesario

Lucca

TWO DAYS EARLIER

Lucca asked Thiago to drive. The sun rose, burning the morning dew, and a veil of mist lifted off the fields. The road curved along the mountainside. In the left lane, their wheels hugged the cliff edge. Below, the Río Bueno snaked through the valley, its waters gradually blueing in tandem with the sky. The jeep was heavy, weighed down by a packed trunk. Water bottles by the gallon. Live chickens in a cage. A box of shoes. Sacks of rice and lentils.

Lucca was perseverating on the call with Toronto, Crispin's insistence that this was in the child's best interests and Anya's command: *Make the family understand*. The week before, he'd summoned Thiago to his office and given him an assignment: *Find a child for the clinic. Just for a night or two. Doesn't have to be an emergency.* How he wished he could rewind and erase both conversations.

How are you finding it, having the actress with us? Lucca asked.

You have worked with celebrities, Thiago said.

Too many, Lucca said.

Thiago replied with a huff, lifting and lowering his shoulders in a wordless reply Lucca deciphered as *I appreciate your joke, but don't mistake my amusement for collaboration; we are not allies.*

Lucca tried to explain the reason for the visit to the Garcias, but of course Thiago already knew. A heated debate had taken place during last night's shift change, Thiago revealed. Beatriz, no surprise, had been vehement in her opposition. And her husband, Enrique the nightwatchman, agreed it was a shame any time a child lost a family. But nurse Josefina argued that these situations must be taken case by case, and ultimately wouldn't Maria benefit?

Enrique objected to Dallas's marital status. Children needed mothers and fathers, not a flighty divorcee. Beatriz didn't like that Dallas wasn't Catholic. Maria's life on earth was of little consequence. To deprive her of heaven would be a sin.

How did this stupid gringa expect to raise Maria when she doesn't even speak Spanish? added Yolanda, who oversaw the dormitory.

Neither does Maria, Josefina pointed out.

Luis, the farm manager, disagreed. Maria understood Spanish. She just couldn't speak it yet.

Beatriz said this was her point exactly. Maria would lose her mother tongue and cease to be Santa Rosan. She would be forever estranged from her country and even herself.

She will raise that poor child in her image, Yolanda had said. Just what the world needs: another fucking gringa.

Yolanda is protective of the children, Thiago said ruefully. You know how she gets.

Lucca waved away the apology, admitting he'd been wrestling with the same conflicts all night. Why had they excluded him from the conversation?

They'd never say these things in front of you, Thiago said. You're the boss.

And an outsider, Lucca thought. Never mind about being Brazilian, to the locals he may as well be a gringo. A gringo who hadn't let them take the day off to protest. Of course there were other discussions happening behind his back. How naive he'd been to only just realize it.

Thiago kept his eyes on the road as he negotiated a tricky uphill, reversing to give a truck in the oncoming lane room to manoeuvre. From the back, the hens clucked and rustled their feathers in alarm.

There must be many private conversations. Why tell me about this one?

Because this is different, Thiago said. He had a habit of chewing a toothpick as he drove, keeping it clamped between his teeth and sticking out the side of his mouth.

And what's your opinion? Lucca asked.

Immaterial, Thiago said. I do the necessary.

Hago lo necesario. Thiago's motto.

Lo necesario being whatever Lucca chose. Elbow on the armrest, he squeezed the skin on his forehead between thumb and forefinger. These were dilemmas he never had to adjudicate in Beirut or Kinshasa.

In the cup holder, his phone lit up. His brother Paolo again, asking Lucca to reconsider visiting Papai. There was still time. Lucca swiped away the message. *Time.* What a joke. His father would hang on forever while his siblings stayed in Rio, their lives elsewhere on pause, as the old man held them in his grip, a tyrant to the end.

I'll tell you this, Thiago said, speaking around the toothpick. Jorge Garcia has a woman in the city and two small girls. Whenever he is working, he stays with them.

Lucca smothered a groan. Was there a father alive who wasn't a scoundrel?

They pulled up in front of a rudimentary home formed of uneven planks with a corrugated tin roof. Rain barrels lined one wall. The property was pleasantly shaded. Lucca tried to find the deprivation Dallas had seen, but what he noticed instead was a bicycle leaning against a banana tree, laundry strung like bunting, onion tops poking out of an industrious patch of land.

A woman and a small boy who'd been stacking firewood paused to watch as the jeep approached. They ran over before Thiago raised the parking gear.

Where is she? Inez asked, as the boy jumped up and down trying to see through the windows. Thiago explained that Maria was still at the clinic and needed more medicines. Then he busied himself unloading the trunk, while Lucca showed Inez photographs and videos of her daughter.

You didn't bring her? Inez asked again. She touched the screen with tender fingers, her chin trembling.

Lucca considered lying, saying that Maria was too sick to travel, but in his periphery a lanky man appeared. Addressing both parents, Lucca said: Maria improves. The doctor is happy.

Jorge remained in shadow, leaning against the doorway.

How do you get on? Lucca asked Inez, taking his time with pleasantries, dropping into the plastic chair she offered, accepting a fizzy green drink even as she remained empty-handed, drawing the story out gradually. The older sons worked on a coffee plantation. Inez's sister had gone to the United States—Lucca understood this was a case of paying an agent and slipping in undocumented—and from time to time, she sent something home. Jorge's back was not good, and that made it hard for him to work. They were fortunate the boys had jobs and that her sister could help.

As they spoke, Inez's eyes never left Lucca's phone, nestled in the cradle of her hands. She watched and rewatched the videos, returning most often to the one of Maria asleep on her stomach, her diapered bottom high in the air, rising and falling with every breath.

It is eight of you here and the baby? Lucca asked, turning to address this question to Jorge, who hadn't moved, his eyes like obsidian. Jorge hadn't been present during the rescue. In the city, no doubt, *working*. Lucca wondered, Would he have allowed it, or would he have kicked up a fuss? A man like Jorge would bristle at charity, resenting the idea that anyone could offer his family something he could not.

My mother stays with us, Inez said. She's collecting water.

Maria's feet, Lucca began and paused, searching for the right words. Her little feet are twisted, he said in the end, adding the suffix -ito as a softener. *Piecitos chuecos.*

Yes, Inez said. My brother was born like this. There is nothing to be done.

There is a cure, Lucca said, and described the process, emphasizing its humane and non-invasive aspects. Your daughter need not suffer.

Inez shook her head. We cannot pay, she said.

Jorge grunted, speaking for the first time: You people always come with your hands out.

Lucca asked if Inez remembered the woman who had been here with Thiago, then explained who Dallas was. She wants to help, Lucca said.

Jorge spat on the ground. And what does she want in return?

Lucca's jaw clenched. He knew Jorge's type, patriarchs for whom children were trophies, proof of virility. Crowing about their offspring's accomplishments in public, privately dismissing them as a nuisance, leaving their care to others. What sort of man would send an old woman to lug water?

Inez asked what Maria was eating, and Lucca was grateful to Thiago who said she was doing well on formula. Then, holding out the box of shoes to Inez, Thiago added, It is made with vitamins and nutrients to help her grow strong.

I have no milk anymore, Inez said, lifting an unconscious hand to her chest.

There is no substitute for mother's milk, Jorge said. Now we must buy this special *formula*.

The actress wants to take care of Maria, Lucca said. Gently he took his phone from Inez and showed her another video, this one of Dallas with the baby. Where she lives, there are special doctors, Lucca said.

She will pay for everything, Thiago added.

Come away from there, Jorge shouted at his son. The boy had been racing around the jeep and had climbed onto the rear bumper, palms and face pressed against the windshield.

He does no harm, Thiago said and went to open all the doors so the child could satisfy himself that his sister wasn't in the glove compartment or under a seat.

When will you bring Maria home? Inez asked. She'd returned to the video of the sleeping baby.

The actress wants Maria to go with her, Lucca said.

She went, Inez said, gesturing to Thiago.

Yes, they are in our clinic now. But she is offering to take Maria to California. To see the doctors I told you about. And they have better schools there too.

At the mention of school, Inez's demeanour changed, posture straightening. Education was the rope ladder to opportunity, upward mobility, for anyone who could afford to climb.

Maria could go to school in the U.S.? Inez asked.

The best school, Lucca said.

She might be an engineer or a doctor, anything at all, Thiago added, surprising Lucca.

What does a baby want with school? Jorge scoffed. He'd begun circling the property, strutting like a rooster.

While she's still a baby is the best time for doctors to cure her feet, Lucca said. In a year, she will walk like other children.

Don't waste time, Thiago added. These early months are important. In the U.S., they begin treatment from the day the baby is born.

Lucca had asked Thiago to drive because he knew the route. He hadn't expected him to join the conversation. But did I know he would? Lucca wondered. *Hago lo necesario*.

Jorge kicked the jeep with one slippered foot. Because she is rich, she thinks she can take better care of Maria than us.

Can't she? Lucca wanted to ask. He disliked this man's entitlement. This man who postured as if he could support two families on an occasional labourer's salary. This man whose sons toiled while he leaned in doorways. It would be Inez who looked after the children, who was burdened by their needs while Jorge dicked around in the city. And it was Inez now who was asking was it true, was this woman from the U.S. really going to pay for Maria's doctors and school? Her food, the uniform, all of it?

Yes, Lucca said. All she wants is your permission.

In Gringolandia, they have nothing better to do with their money than spend it on strangers, Thiago said without smiling.

Foolish woman, Jorge said. You would give my daughter to a stranger?

I am not giving Maria to anyone, Inez said. She is *our* baby.

Jorge pointed at Thiago. If I had been here when you came, I would have . . . He took a stride toward Thiago, and Lucca stepped between them. Jorge poked his finger right in Lucca's chest. You bring Maria back to us. Bring her back today.

Just think, Thiago said. Without treatment, Maria will be crippled.

Gently, Lucca touched Jorge's wrist and lowered his arm. He said: The actress, her name is Dallas Hayden. I have seen her with Maria, how well she cares for her. She will give your daughter everything.

And see how she laps it up, Jorge said to no one. My wife lives in a dream land.

Inez shook her head. She is my daughter. I am not giving her to anyone. But she must walk. And she must go to school.

She will, Lucca said.

The little boy had sidled up to his mother and taken Lucca's phone. They were out of cellular range, but he'd found his way to the music app and was dancing to a bossa nova track. It made Lucca think of Moisés, all the ways he, too, would benefit from Dallas's donation.

I've heard enough— Jorge began to say.

Lucca gestured to the chickens and other items Thiago had unloaded. He said they were gifts from Dallas. There was more where they came from.

No doubt, there would be a financial clause in the adoption agreement. Whatever pittance Dallas tossed their way would be life-altering for the Garcias. They had six sons and would in time have more children. These kinds of people always did. They couldn't help themselves. His own family elbowed their way into his thoughts: the image of his umpteen siblings gathered around the sick bed. Irritated, Lucca shoved them aside.

My daughter is not for sale, Jorge said.

You would stand in the way of Maria getting an opportunity? Lucca asked, knowing full well a man like Jorge would not want his daughter to have anything he didn't.

Maria must have every chance, Inez said.

Dallas Hayden is very fond of Maria, Lucca said. She will give her the best of everything.

And then she will bring Maria back?

No doubt Dallas would. Celebrities liked their adopted children to *connect with their heritage*. How they might do this without language or customs Lucca didn't know. But what was the good of heritage anyway, this invented notion of nationality, an ephemeral value when set against U.S. dollars and all the privilege they could buy. With Dallas, Maria would be pampered and spoiled. And then she'd be able to send money back, if she wanted, lift the whole family out of poverty, maybe extend a hand to her half-sisters in the capital too. She might be weak-hearted like Paolo, who even now was probably texting Lucca entreaties.

Maria will come back, but it might take some time, Lucca said.

Don't trust a word, Jorge said to Inez.

You are giving Maria a gift, Lucca told her. Jorge could fall off a cliff for all he cared. Inez was a decent woman. She would be sad for a while, but then she'd be pragmatic. Lives out here didn't leave much room for sentimentality.

It is difficult, Thiago said. But we all must make sacrifices for our children.

The return journey seemed to take twice as long. They got stuck behind a line of trucks ferrying fruit and logs down the mountain and had to reverse uphill when they met oncoming traffic on a narrow pass. Thiago played the radio. Lucca read the hysterical messages from his brother. The paterfamilias was suffering middle-of-the-night seizures. His right side was paralyzed, his speech garbled. By the time they returned, Lucca was thoroughly demoralized.

At the compound, Dallas fidgeted with a multicoloured carrying cloth, Maria nestled inside. She'd tied the sling inexpertly and kept adjusting the slipping straps. Nearby, Moisés dangled off the monkey bars.

Dallas approached the jeep. Did they—?

Lucca nodded as he jumped down. Then warned: But it was only one conversation. Nothing is confirmed.

Dallas clapped and did a half hop. Maria, awkwardly torqued in the sling, wailed.

Can you? Dallas asked, and together they worked to untie the wrap. Lucca gingerly held Maria under the armpits, slightly away from his body, as Dallas shook out the blanket. Maria was squirming and bawling, her cries rising in pitch. Was she hungry? Tired? Bewildered without her mother? Lucca recalled the tender way

Inez had stroked his phone. It didn't matter about the shoes or the chickens, that Inez's mother wouldn't have to collect water for weeks. He, a stranger, was holding her only daughter.

I had it a minute ago, Dallas grumbled.

Here, he said, returning the baby. He stood at her back and deftly tied the carrier, a task any twelve-year-old Santa Rosan could perform blindfolded.

Thank you, Lucca, Dallas said. I was convinced they'd say no.

Nothing is finalized, he said, raising his voice over the baby's screams. You can't expect the Garcias to make the decision in a moment. He snapped his fingers. Like that. Maria is their daughter.

Secure in the wrap, the baby's wails were even more pathetic. Dallas wrapped her arms around Maria protectively. I'm only trying to help, she said in a wounded voice.

The Messiah

Emmanuelle

When Emmanuelle Clemmons got the call from Art Whylie, her former boss at the *Herald*, she understood his offer was motivated by guilt.

I need someone to write a feature on Crispin St. Onge for the Saturday edition, Art said.

The drummer from that band? Emmanuelle asked. What's he done?

Lead singer. Resurrection, Art said, then explained that Crispin ran an NGO and had recruited Dallas Hayden as a volunteer. You really haven't heard? Art said. Are you living under a rock?

Pop culture isn't exactly my beat, she said.

Emmanuelle had no interest in aging rock stars and their hackneyed reinventions. Her last major project had been an investigation into a series of accidents at an industrial bakery where a worker had died. Over several months of reporting, she'd discovered that the company cut corners on safety, hired refugees under the table, and sent them to work, untrained, in dangerous conditions. The death made headlines, but Emmanuelle had discovered a pattern of serious accidents as well, several that had gone unreported.

The series ran in the *Globe and Mail* to acclaim. There was talk the paper might put it up for an industry award. But apart from a fine, the company hadn't faced any consequences, and nothing had changed for their workers. Since the bakery series, she had been writing more pitches than stories.

You always were my best columnist, Art said.

I thought I was a pain in the ass, Emmanuelle replied.

That too, Art said. You want the assignment or not?

Emmanuelle read the publicist's email with one eyebrow cocked. *We're all great admirers of your journalism, and we're thrilled you're penning a profile*, Claire Talbot wrote.

Penning a profile. Who spoke like that?

Crispin St. Onge was giving a talk at a private club in the Financial District, Claire went on to say. She'd finagled Emmanuelle a ticket. *Crispin thought you might find it helpful to attend, just as background.*

Before the lecture, Emmanuelle did her homework. Until the call with Art, she'd never heard of Children of the World. For an unknown organization, they seemed to have reach—projects in fifteen countries, if their marketing materials were to be believed. Their website boasted all the usual tropes. White saviour surrounded by grinning Asian kids. Check. White saviour cradling awkward-looking Black boy. Check. Skeletal child with a feeding tube. Check. Flies on face. The full bingo card.

In her youth, Emmanuelle had been a churchgoing do-gooder, serving in the soup kitchen and arranging donations at bazaars.

As a young teen, she'd even given up her Friday nights to what they called an inner-city ministry: a group of suburbanites traipsing downtown to save the souls of fallen women.

Emmanuelle despised these memories, the blithe assurance she'd worn in those days. *Have you considered letting Jesus Christ into your heart? His love is unconditional.* What did she, a middle-class virgin, know of homelessness and pimps, of anything at all? She'd been so bloated with arrogance, so secure in the righteousness of all her actions, the delusion that she knew what was best for complete strangers. Everything changed the year she was sixteen and an artery in her father's brain ruptured while he was writing a sermon. The Lord in His mercy will always provide, Reverend Clemmons used to say. But when he left his homemaker wife and eight children without a pension or savings, it was the church that provided. On the receiving end of charity, Emmanuelle had experienced such benevolence differently.

Over the years, her distrust of philanthropy had become more entrenched. She'd watched as the internet made the exercise even more artificial, noting the way glamorous causes monopolized attention and resources, leaving others orphaned. The recent online fad of forcing gifts on strangers and broadcasting the interaction without permission—so-called random acts of kindness—was so preposterous she'd mistaken it for a prank. And crowdfunding. Surely *that* was the Wild West. No oversight. No regulation. Just influencers flexing for the gram with their quirky online challenges that raised unprecedented dollars. Then what? she wondered, reading a blog post Dallas Hayden had supposedly *penned* during her junket in Santa Rosa—*the children have taught me so much about bravery and resilience.* What did a rinky-dink charity do after they won the lottery?

—

The Devonshire was a red-brick Victorian institution on a narrow lane off King Street. Membership by invitation, fees unlisted, gentlemen only for two centuries until finally, in the eighties, a court order forced the locks and women began trickling in.

The club's crest was carved into the front door, and when it was opened for another patron, Emmanuelle held her breath and breezed through behind him. In the lobby, she was intercepted by an officious butler.

Miss, yours is the west entrance, he said.

Oh, no, she said. I'm not here for *that* kind of work. Then she flashed the embossed invitation for the event and asked to be shown to the John A. MacDonald room. There was a flicker of hesitation in the man's eyes. She'd read the dress code and wore a suit under her long wool coat, and six-inch heels that made her tower over him. Nothing was ever good enough for these people.

I'm a journalist, she said, gesturing to the board advertising Crispin's talk. I'm writing a piece on tonight's guest speaker? She turned her voice up into a question, so he wouldn't write her off as angry.

You're early, he said, stepping back and making a flourish with his arm.

First pick of the worms, she said and click-clacked off in her heels, making sure to come down a little harder than usual with each step.

The John A. room was the usual sort of thing. Dark walnut panelling. Heavy curtains. Thick carpet that muffled sound. A fire blazed and above the mantle, decorated with autumnal gourds, a decapitated moose gazed over the room with the dead-eyed benevolence of a deity. Armchairs were circled around tables. The projector screen on the tripod stand was the only blight. A clipboard was propped on the lectern. The first page listed the attendees; Emmanuelle snapped a photo before choosing a corner by the fireplace where she could discreetly watch the room. Her table was small with only one other chair across from it.

Waiting for everyone to arrive, she glanced over the attendance list. The familiar names jumped out at her. The founder of an ethical fashion label that ran sweatshops in Bangladesh. A hedge fund executive who, rumour had it, had a penchant for teen girls. A telecom magnate whose son was taking him to court over a racehorse. Plus, a handful of politicians. Other surnames she recognized from hospital wings and art galleries. All the usual suspects searching for a new laundromat for their filthy reputations.

The suits arrived all at once, shaking meaty hands and clapping one another on the back. None of them were encumbered by coats, and Emmanuelle became uncomfortably aware of hers, folded over the back of her seat. Of course she hadn't thought it strange to walk in here with outerwear on.

A text from her partner, Ben—*Have you seen this?* and a link to a tweet. Some joker had drawn a caricature of Crispin in white robes with a red sash, microphone in one hand, the other holding a dinner plate behind his head. *Q: What's the difference between Crispin St. Onge and Christ? A: Jesus doesn't think he's a washed-up rock star. #realhero*

It was one of those anonymous accounts that poked fun at local news and noteworthies. Emmanuelle snorted and checked the time stamp. It had been posted an hour earlier.

A woman strode over. Emmanuelle? I'm Claire Talbot.

Claire was of average height and weight and had one of those forgettable faces: long beaky nose and straight brown hair brushed off a wide forehead. Her tortoiseshell cat-eye glasses, an accessory that could be removed and swapped, were tellingly the most memorable thing about her. Emmanuelle distrusted this kind of aggressive ordinariness. It seemed painstakingly cultivated, a way to hide in plain sight.

Claire wore a turtleneck under a charcoal-grey skirt suit and silver studs in her ears. Emmanuelle had wound her braids into a low bun and painted on a red lip to offset the plainness of her black suit, but shaking Claire's cool hand, she felt outlandish and wished she hadn't chosen her largest gold hoops. Naturally, the butler had taken Claire's coat.

The lecture was about to begin, and there was no time to meet Crispin. That was just fine with Emmanuelle, who was unsettled by the reminder that she was, like the bulky projector at the front, conspicuously out of place.

After a stilted introduction by a wheezy old man, Crispin rose to applause, lifting the lectern and moving it aside. A consummate entertainer, he spoke without notes or microphone, projecting his voice so even Emmanuelle in the back corner could hear. His humour was self-deprecating. His whole manner conveying the message *we're all just friends here*.

What does a washed-up musician know about global conflict and international aid? he asked. I don't have an MBA or a degree in international relations. I'm just an aging rocker who thinks he's the chosen one.

And then he took out his phone and read the tweet she'd just seen. Emmanuelle wasn't surprised Crispin was thin-skinned—his sort often was—but revealing this weakness was another thing.

The publicist's expression was a mask. If Emmanuelle was Crispin's handler, she'd be appalled. The account only had a few thousand followers. Why cop to having seen it?

But Crispin clearly knew his audience because they bristled. A number of people put their own phones away. The crowd seemed to sit a little straighter, at attention, ready to fight. And then Crispin laughed it off.

Well, maybe I am the messiah, he said. And if that's the case, I've come to preach the good news.

Crispin's speech was bullish, even as he spoke of poverty and malnutrition, reducing them to pablum the audience eagerly slurped up. Emmanuelle took note of the body language around her, the looseness of their limbs. Crispin was talking about Haiti, a subject Emmanuelle knew something about because an old J-school friend was an international correspondent who had reported there after the earthquake. Children of the World, too, had flown in during the crisis, and today they were a fixture. Crispin had a lot to say about how wretched the country was, how the land was fractured and aid agencies had come together to repair the earth. No mention of the centuries of foreign rule and stolen resources, the decades of so-called restitution paid to France after a hard-won independence, the U.S. occupation and the brutality of those years, the cholera spread by aid workers after the earthquake. As Crispin explained it, the only foreign intervention in the country was benevolent: education and health care.

Crispin described the stench of open sewers, the women conducting business on the side of the road. Haiti is not for the faint of heart, he said. Then he rubbed his belly, adding, And believe me, you'll need a strong stomach too. A few chuckles at this quip and even Claire had the decency to cringe. Emmanuelle's cheeks burned at the hubris on display.

There's a lot of cynicism these days, Crispin said, especially online. But here's the problem with the keyboard warriors. That nihilist attitude, it leads to apathy. Do I want to dwell in negativity? No. And let me show you why.

A graph appeared onscreen, a falling line, and Crispin announced: The fact is that since 2000, we've made huge progress on HIV and malaria. Mortality in kids under five, that number is down by 2.65 million per year. That's more than seven thousand children saved every day. Here's one of them.

Crispin projected a photograph of a boy in a classroom with his hand raised. Emmanuelle winced. Now hers wasn't the only dark face in the room.

This is Akello, Crispin said. He's alive because of volunteers in Uganda.

The volunteers in Uganda turned out to be a white girl shoving a bottle at a naked, malnourished toddler, all thin limbs and distended belly. The child kept a wary distance from the crouching stranger, his head stuck out to suck on the bottle while the rest of his body hinged away. Emmanuelle tensed.

Akello was found on the streets of Kampala, lost and alone, likely abandoned by his family, Crispin said. He had worms and was severely malnourished, but worse: he tested positive for HIV.

Emmanuelle sucked in a breath so sharp Claire turned her head. To disclose a child's diagnosis to total strangers was so appallingly unethical.

I know, Claire mouthed. Isn't it awful?

That was a few years ago, Crispin said. Today, Akello is ten and thriving, thanks to life-saving antiretrovirals.

A new photo. A different set of white girls, sunglasses in their hair, forcing friendship bracelets onto the wrists of a group of children.

Africa has so many challenges, Crispin said. But generous donors and volunteers, medications, mosquito nets, these are all giving kids a fighting chance.

He brought the graph back onscreen and said: This is a phenomenal success story, but we are at a dangerous moment. This is when we risk getting complacent. Why should you give? Well, there's the tax receipt.

These millionaires don't need tax receipts, Emmanuelle thought. They had more efficient ways to stiff the public purse.

But seriously, Crispin went on, do it for children like Akello. Do it because it's the right thing to do. Give because this level of extreme poverty is a crime.

Nearby, the sweatshop mogul and the hedge fund pedophile were sharing a loveseat. One had his arm slung over the upholstered back. Elsewhere in the room were people who profited off weapons sales. And here was Crispin bringing up a photo of an emaciated woman with a child wrapped against her chest.

Why am I here? Emmanuelle wondered. The *Herald* wasn't paying her damn near enough.

It doesn't have to be this way, Crispin said. This mother, her child, *they* are why you should give. Not just generously. Give till it hurts. Give an amount that has a tangible impact on your life. For some of our donors that's fifty, maybe a hundred dollars a month. But I know all of you can do a lot better. Do you really need that second and third home? Do you really need the yacht, the plane?

Was Crispin actually asking these guys to hawk their Muskoka mansions and write him a cheque with the proceeds? The room had gone silent in an uncomfortable way. Claire's back was ramrod straight. The publicist had known this was coming, Emmanuelle thought. Crispin wasn't going off script. Perhaps now he'd misjudged his audience.

And I *know* your lovely wives don't need those procedures, Crispin said, and that cracked the ice a little.

Ballsy, Emmanuelle thought. Maybe Crispin was worth interviewing after all. Twice this evening he'd surprised her.

The Global South doesn't need charity, Crispin said. We owe them wealth redistribution. Is it right to send your children to private school when this woman can't feed her baby?

Emmanuelle tipped her head to the side, bemused. All around, people were fidgeting; a couple of phones had emerged from pockets.

And listen, if none of those reasons convince you, look at the numbers, he said, pointing to the graph. When this line gets to zero, when child mortality under five gets to zero, then I promise to retire. If nothing else, do it to make this trumped-up Jesus shut up.

He stretched his arms out horizontally like Christ on the cross. Emmanuelle couldn't stop the laugh that burst out. The whole room roared as Crispin twisted his palms up and encouraged them with a *bring it on* gesture. He was grinning the whole time.

During the Q & A, Crispin spoke of the charity's inception. All these Richie Riches with their foundations had the same hackneyed origin story. *I was walking along the beach in Africa. I was humbled by the people, their resilience.*

Crispin's epiphany came to him in Cambodia, where he'd gone to find himself after the breakup of the band. While his agent urged him to launch a solo career, a burned-out Crispin searched for a worthier second act.

Living with the locals, witnessing their simplicity (Emmanuelle almost groaned at the word choice), how carefully every possession was used and reused, had reminded Crispin of his own frugal upbringing, made him ashamed of his profligacy and indolence. The cash hoarded in his investment accounts.

Peak first-world problem, Emmanuelle thought. And instead of putting money into people's hands, he'd set up this elaborate middleman scheme. Peak first-world solution.

Everything got quiet in Cambodia, Crispin said. I was thinking a lot about the next phase of my life. Who I wanted to be. What legacy I was leaving. I went to escape. But after a while, the idea to found Children of the World was so compelling I wanted to run toward it more than I wanted to run away.

I. I. I. I. I.

The crowd at the Devonshire, buzzed on Chardonnay, and relieved at this pivot away from their real estate and plastic surgeons, lapped up the myth about the begging children who inspired Crispin to return the following year with a team and build a school.

A reedy man with large glasses raised his hand. Maybe those children had to work. How does your organization address root causes?

Crispin didn't pause for a moment before replying, If we build it, they will come.

A few agreeable murmurs from the crowd, but the man adjusted his glasses and said: As an educator, I can tell you there are many reasons for absenteeism in Canada. It must only be more complicated in Cambodia.

I've never been one to adopt a defeatist attitude, Crispin said. Nothing is actually as difficult as we think. We just need a willingness to make a difference.

The man's rebuttal was cut off by the moderator who called on someone else.

Emmanuelle was relieved to discover a fellow skeptic. How had he gotten past the gatekeepers? she wondered. As Crispin took questions—all the usual fawning things—Emmanuelle studied the attendees. This was it, she thought. Here was an investigation worth conducting: who was scratching whose back?

Once home, she drafted three different versions of an email, then called Art Whylie instead.

There's more to this piece, she said. The guest list at this thing, if I followed the money—

Emmanuelle. Whenever Art spoke her name, it always carried a ring of warning.

There's a story here, about the way philanthropy operates and who really gains.

This is the lifestyle section, he said. There's no need to make it political.

Everything is political, Art.

I assigned you a feel-good piece, he said. Don't get ahead of yourself.

Don't get ahead of yourself. Emmanuelle had graduated at the top of her class. She was diligent, worked twice as hard as anyone else, but none of that mattered. Twelve years into her career and she was freelancing. Her white classmates were rewarded for following their noses and asking tough questions. When stories became personal, they were praised for having a heart.

But when Emmanuelle went to report on one tenants' rights protest and got arrested after joining the peaceful sit-in, she'd lost her column. You can't be the story *and* the reporter, Art had lectured her in a closed-door meeting the next day. As journalists, we have to be neutral, Emm.

He might have left it at that, but it wasn't her first misstep and the higher-ups saw a convenient excuse to turf her. Deep down, Art knew it was bullshit, which is why from time to time he tossed her a consolation prize. Like this feature.

I don't disagree with you, Art said now, his gruff voice softening on the phone. There may well be a larger story here. But the contract is for a profile of Crispin St. Onge and his organization. Interview him. Write the story. Collect your paycheque. Why do you have to make everything difficult?

What happened to getting three sources? she asked.

Art said fine. Talk to the staff. Talk to volunteers. Talk to the man himself. There are your sources.

Persimmon Pink

Anya

The donor relations team had commandeered the boardroom, so Anya used an empty suite on the second floor for her call with Dakar, dragging a folding chair to one of the tall windows where an anemic sun was struggling to break through the clouds. The previous tenant had been a tech start-up and their signage, loud and hopeful, still adorned the walls. A decade earlier, there hadn't been a vacancy in the building. Even last year, there had been a cerebral palsy charity on three and an online activist magazine on four. Both had since left.

Today, Anya was grateful for Crispin's extreme frugality. In the week since their call with Dallas's manager, nothing more had been said about the donation. Meanwhile, the actress had flown home, was probably on set, shooting a new film, her memories of Santa Rosa fading. The adoption would take months to finalize and then Dallas would be ensconced in the fog of new parenthood. By the time she remembered her promise to Children of the World, they'd be past tense.

Anya had to break the news to Senegal that the country director search was on hold. But before she could clear her throat, Fatou launched in with a gripe. The electricity bill was past due.

I didn't realize there was an invoice, Anya said. Is it on the shared drive?

Overseas offices were supposed to log their payables into the finance database, but without a country director to keep her in check, Fatou had reverted to her own primitive methods, springing these code-red requests on Anya.

I know it's a hassle, Anya said for the hundredth time. But the auditors want paper trails.

Fatou got prickly when criticized, so Anya had to couch everything in questions and apologies. Fatou had already gone over her head once and complained to Crispin, accusing Anya of throwing her weight around. As if that was a thing Anya could do from afar. And then Crispin had taken whatever Fatou had said personally and been crabby for days. Crispin wanted everyone to love him and pouted when he discovered someone didn't.

They are threatening to cut the power, Fatou said.

Email me the invoice and I'll wire the funds, Anya said, keeping her own tone level. These minor quibbles weren't in her job description, but since the departure of the country director in the summer, the five local staff had become her responsibility.

This wouldn't happen if we had money in the account, Fatou said and began pushing for a float. Anya was wary of leaving too much discretionary wiggle room. The office in Senegal administered African operations. Without a country director at the helm, there was no telling what the staff might do.

We're responsible for projects in three different countries, Fatou said. We have couriers and taxes and travel and rent to pay. I can't keep asking you for every single thing.

Let me bring it to Crispin, Anya said. I don't disagree with you, but it's not my call to make.

Then Fatou said there was another problem. Anya squeezed a knuckle into the pressure point in her palm. All she had were problems. Sure, toss another on the pile, Fatou.

She listened, stunned, while Fatou relayed the absurd story. Crispin had recently bagged a couple hundred thousand from an agricultural company. Cash in hand, no strings attached. An actual win. The sponsor had even thrown in some rice seeds, shipping the bags direct to Dakar. But now Fatou was saying the farmers had rejected the gift and were threatening to protest.

They do realize these seeds are free? Anya said.

Nothing is free, Fatou said, sounding heated. These seeds are unnatural; they're made to self-destruct.

Anya squeezed her eyes shut and inhaled. AgriSeed was a leader in the field. They poured millions into R & D to perfect their products. Eight per cent of children in Senegal were malnourished, and these ungrateful people were turning their noses up at a gift anyone else would happily accept.

It's not voodoo, she explained slowly. It's science. They're designed to be high yield.

You're shoving these suicide seeds down our throats! Fatou burst out.

I'm what?!

That's what the farmers are saying, Fatou said quickly. We have our own seeds that are better for our pests and climate. We can buy them here very cheaply. My cousin—

Anya stopped listening. There was always a cousin. She had to tell Fatou there was no money, might never be more money, they all had to keep economizing. But she couldn't remain on this call a moment longer.

When she tuned back in it was to find, with some alarm, that Fatou was asking about the country director position, making a pitch for her cousin—was it a different cousin?—talking up his degrees, his rise through the ranks at another NGO. This seed misunderstanding wouldn't have happened if they had a director who was one of them and understood Senegal.

Sure, Anya thought. Local knowledge was a bonus, but having the chops to do the job was the most important thing. Country directors required a certain professional polish to represent the organization. They had to be meticulous about policies and procedures, and then there were the educational requirements. Fact was there weren't any aid workers in Senegal, anywhere in the developing world really, at the management level. But she couldn't say this to Fatou, who always misconstrued hard truths as a personal affront.

Tell him to apply, she hedged. We'll be ramping up the search in the new year. She ended the call by promising to pay for the electricity and more seeds with money they didn't have, saving the bad news for another day.

Then she lay across two folding chairs and stared at the ceiling. Sometimes she wished she could say to hell with the other projects and focus her attention on Santa Rosa. Funnel all her efforts into resuscitation. The original vision had been a self-sustaining operation, one that wasn't at the mercy of donors and their whims. She'd planned to expand their land holdings and sell the excess. A butcher shop. A greengrocer. An artisans' cooperative, their wares on sale to local and international buyers. The children would gain real-world skills, not just in farming and textile making but in accounting, marketing, and how to run a business. The whole enterprise would be revenue positive, a model for others.

But she'd been forced to make compromise after compromise. Because their donor base was small. Because they had no money. And now here they were, once again, hopes pinned on a capricious actor.

There was a buzz in her pocket, but it was only a text from Crispin: *where r u?* She'd been trying to get a hold of Lucca since Dallas's unexpected departure the previous Thursday. But after their truncated conversation about the adoption—Lucca spitting out yes, yes, he'd met with the family and they had agreed, then hanging up hastily, as if the building was on fire—he'd been screening her calls.

Had Dallas mentioned anything about the donation? Or returning to Santa Rosa as a spokesperson? Anya would accept any crumb. Lucca's evasion made her suspect he'd chased the actress off. Trust him to squander the opportunity.

Anya had been shocked by the family's swift agreement. She'd expected them to need more persuading, had half hoped they'd reject the proposal outright and put an end to the whole thing. Lucca had mentioned another child—as if anyone wanted a nine-year-old boy when there was a baby girl in the picture. Still, a more agreeable country director, or a savvier salesman, like Crispin, for example, might have convinced Dallas to adopt someone else.

She'd had great expectations about Lucca's hire. He was a veteran aid worker whose progress she'd casually followed. When she heard through the grapevine that Lucca was feeling his age and might be ready to settle down, she'd gotten his number through a mutual and called a few contacts just to make sure the

CV checked out. That was how recruiting at the higher level was done. Not this *my cousin knows a guy* stunt Fatou was trying to pull.

Anya had made a mistake with Lucca, she understood that now. But Crispin was so stingy it was impossible to hire anyone stellar.

In the office there was unexpected jubilation, everyone on their feet, calling over each other. The events manager and volunteer coordinator chanted: We're rich! We're rich!

What's going on? Anya had to shout to make herself heard.

Dallas's donation came in, Crispin said, grinning.

Guess how much, Claire called from her desk.

Five hundred? Anya said, thinking they were saved. *Saved.*

Two million! Claire yelped. TWO. MILLION. DOLLARS.

Anya covered her face and took slow, deep breaths, exhaling the warm air into her palms. Thank god, she whispered. Thank god. The relief, swift and absolute, threatened to knock her knees out from under her. She reached for the wall to keep steady.

You need to have more faith in people, Crispin said, putting an arm around her and squeezing her shoulder.

Anya barely heard him. Eleven years of uphill effort and she was finally, finally going to see her project through.

Lunch is on me, Crispin declared. Cancel your afternoon plans. We're celebrating.

There was a shout from a few feet away. Claire yelled: Come and see this. You won't believe it!

Dallas had uploaded another one of her videos. *An announcement*, she'd captioned it. Claire maximized the window on her screen, yanked the headphone cord out of the computer, and turned up the volume.

In California, against the backdrop of her sleek white kitchen, the actress beamed. And Anya did a double take because—

Is that the kid she rescued? the intern asked.

The dimpled dark-haired child blinked at the camera. Meet my new daughter, Dallas said, kissing the baby on the cheek as she squirmed and turned her head away. We're so in love.

Holy shit, the development manager said.

Fantastic! Crispin said.

Did you know? Claire demanded, sounding almost angry, the question directed first at Anya, then at Crispin.

California lawyers act fast, Crispin said.

Evidently, Anya said.

Lucca had spoken to the family exactly a week ago. When had this happened? Anya crouched at Claire's desk. Play it again, will you?

Crispin held court in the centre of the open plan, filling everyone in on how Dallas was going to be their new spokesperson. Meanwhile, Anya rewatched the video, Claire's headphones on. The child was in California. No sign of her parents. How was this possible?

And it's all thanks to Claire, Crispin finished as Anya slipped out of the office and into the stairwell.

Her fingers were trembling so hard she could barely hold the phone. She was furious with Lucca. How could he let them find out this way? His voice on the recorded message only increased her ire.

I would have appreciated a heads-up, she said, speaking into the void of his mailbox. Call me as soon as you get this. I mean it, Lucca. Not an email. Not a text. Phone. Me.

Back in the office, the joker was saying: That vision board manifest destiny stuff really works, huh? Then shaking his head in disbelief, added seriously, Nicely done, Talbot.

Anya pulled Crispin aside as everyone was putting on their coats. I have a bad feeling about this, she muttered. How do we know it's legitimate?

Crispin told her to relax. The baby wouldn't have been able to cross the border without—

Thousands do it every day.

They don't just let anyone take a child on a flight, Crispin argued.

Anya was unconvinced. People like Dallas Hayden were bound to a different, slimmer rule book. Crispin said this was his point exactly. Everything was smoother, faster in her world. Then he told her about the time their drummer lost his passport in Barcelona. Our manager called the embassy, pulled some strings, I dunno, Crispin said. He did the rest of the tour without a passport. We didn't miss a beat.

Breaking away from her, he rejoined the group and said, This is all you, Claire.

The others were mock-threatening to carry Claire out sports-fan style as she laughed.

Persimmon Pink, Crispin said, taking the baby's new name for a spin. I kinda like it.

At the noodle place, Anya took her usual spot to the right of Crispin who was doing what he did best: hyping everyone up. Dallas's donation is more than a gift, he said. It's proof of her faith in us. We've been entrusted with these dollars—

Two million of them, *baby*. Two. Million. Bones, the joker said, eliciting a round of cheers.

It won't amount to much if we don't treat it like an investment, if we don't use it to earn more, Crispin said. More major gifts. More corporate sponsors. More celebrity ambassadors. More schools and clinics and children's homes. More lives saved. We *owe* it to those kids.

Anya told herself to believe him. What choice did she have? She couldn't call Dallas's manager and insist on seeing proof. This was Santa Rosa's only chance for survival, and she wasn't going to risk that. Anyway, the child's parents had agreed. It was what everyone wanted. Anya forced her qualms aside and tried to be carried along by the team's optimism.

You'll need to go to Santa Rosa, Crispin said. See for yourself what needs doing before we invest.

How long since you've been there? Claire asked, and Anya found herself reminiscing about one of her earliest trips when they'd broken ground on the dormitory, the compound's first building.

In Santa Rosa, she told Claire, she had aspired to build a different kind of venture, without any of the design flaws that had hamstrung all the other efforts she'd seen, and laboured on herself, during her decades in non-profit. Her specialty had always been coaxing donations from individual philanthropists, the one per cent who set up private foundations with the sole purpose of distributing their wealth.

They make their fortunes by stiffing employees, then funnel the excess into vanity projects that supposedly help the very people they exploit, Crispin said.

Stamping their names on hospital wings and law schools, like dogs marking a fence, Anya grumbled, and her sarcasm was rewarded when Claire spat up a mouthful of water.

It was the absurdity of the system that irked Anya, too, all the well-intentioned bureaucracy that tied their hands in red tape. But in Santa Rosa, things could be different.

We knew we'd need a few big donations to get the ball rolling, but the end goal has always been independence, she said. The problem with foreign aid is foreign aid. No one is saying *How can we give people a hand up and, once they're on their feet, let them take charge?* But in Santa Rosa, we'll prove it can be done.

She'd been addressing herself to Claire but soon realized she had a captive audience, the whole table silent and riveted. Crispin caught her eye and raised his water glass and they clinked in mid-air.

Anya was reminded of the night she'd pitched him the idea. It was a year into her tenure, when they were at the start of a financial upswing she'd single-handedly orchestrated, and Crispin was in a good mood. They'd been the last ones in the office when she'd suggested a drink. At the dive bar, she'd ordered two pints of lager and been surprised to discover Crispin was a lightweight.

You're changing my charity, he'd said, glass only half drained.

Do you mind?

He took a swig and grinned. Not at all.

Have you ever been to Santa Rosa? she asked.

What Anya liked about Crispin was how open he was to ideas. If you pitched it with enough gusto, he was happy to go along.

Let's do it, he said when she finished explaining.

It's a major commitment, she warned. We'll need a dedicated country director. Significant infrastructure. You should think about it.

Nope. He'd tapped his nose and pointed at her. You, Anya Mueller, can do anything. You'll make it happen.

Now, she pictured herself—Santa Rosa in the rear-view—taking her show on the road, teaching other NGOs how to wean their own projects off charity. She'd start with CONCERN.

Entertainment Tonight, Claire announced, glancing up from her phone. They wanted Crispin on that evening. A live double-ender.

Their orders arrived, fragrant bowls of noodles, steam rising in clouds. The finance director broke apart her wooden chopsticks and slashed them together like a chef sharpening knives. I'm surprised she announced the adoption like that, she said. Dallas usually keeps her private life quiet.

Claire pointed out that Dallas was always going to let the news go public. If it wasn't on social, she'd have found another way to let it slip. A quiet word to a trusted outlet—*People* mag or the like—and Dallas would be spotted pushing a carriage.

She'd starred in an art-house black comedy that had won an audience award at the Venice Film Festival in September. There was buzz about a potential Oscar nomination. Her publicity team would be working overtime on her bid.

What do you mean her bid? Anya asked.

Claire poked her udon and shrugged. It was well-known, wasn't it? The way these nominations happened. It was all behind-the-scenes lobbying and front-of-camera wholesomeness. Not that Dallas hasn't done enough, Claire added. She's basically America's sweetheart.

But adopting an orphan won't hurt her chances either, the intern said.

When younger colleagues spoke with this knowing cynicism, Anya felt her age. She had a pang of doubt. Had Dallas only done this to advance her career, the child a prop in a drama she was staging to win fans and prizes?

She checked her phone. No word from Lucca. Around the table there was a celebration. Anya knew behind her back they called her Eeyore. She told herself to relax, recalling the rescue video, the birth family's grinding poverty. A disabled child would have been the least of their problems and one they couldn't have solved.

Claire was smirking to herself, thumbing frantically on her phone. Check it out, she said, leaning across the table, and Anya saw the video on her screen. The baby on her back, kicking her feet in the air, and Dallas bending over her prone form, tickling her toes and cooing.

Is that online? Crispin asked.

Dallas just sent it to me, Claire said. On text.

Let me see, Anya said.

She watched the baby giggle, eyes wide open, pink tongue sticking out.

You did this, Anya, Crispin said quietly. You changed her life. And now we have the means to change thousands more.

Who's the sweetest baby? Dallas asked. Who's the nicest, cutest baby?

Dallas's voice was pitched high in that faintly ridiculous way women got when they engaged with small children. She fluttered her lips like a horse, unconscious or uncaring of how silly she sounded. It brought Anya right back to early motherhood, that complex stew of emotions, but strongest of all pure, unadulterated love.

Here was affection that could not be faked. Anya knew what it was to hold a child in her arms and never want to let him go. Secondary motives notwithstanding, this baby couldn't do better than having Dallas Hayden for a mother.

Ábrelo

Lucca

THE WEEK BEFORE

Lucca phoned Anya, eager to be finished with this hateful task. He squeezed the stress ball. His foot tapped an impatient rhythm under the desk.

I spoke to the Garcias.

You met them? In person? Anya sounded astonished. There was a shuffling on the line that indicated she was on the move. I'm putting you on speaker, she said. Crispin is here too.

Lucca recounted the morning's events and the parents' reservations, trying to temper their expectations.

But they agreed? Anya asked, her voice loosening as if from a noose.

The Garcias understand this will benefit Maria. But when it comes time to sign the papers, they could change their minds.

That can't have been an easy conversation, Crispin said. Thank you, Lucca. Thank you.

From Crispin, too, that tone of amazement. As if he'd done them an unexpected favour instead of grudgingly carried out orders. He leapt up, infuriated, and began to pace.

Dallas must bring Maria for visits, Lucca said. Annually, at least.

Of course, Crispin said. Anything. Really, Lucca. We're so grateful. You have no idea what this will mean.

Nothing is guaranteed.

Dallas's team will see to the rest, Anya said.

My involvement in this business is over. I have real work to do.

And soon you'll have the resources to do it, Crispin assured.

I'm advertising for two full-time nurses, Lucca said.

Anya cut in: Let's hold off until—

Today, Lucca said. If the doctor resigns, the clinic closes.

I didn't realize the situation was so dire, Crispin said. Whatever you think is best.

And when Dallas's donation arrives, we can restart construction on the school, Anya said in a placating tone.

She's scared I'll quit, Lucca realized and felt the power of the upper hand. He said: A local crew. No volunteers.

When Crispin began talking about next steps, Lucca hung up, determined to never speak of Maria Garcia again. Brokering adoptions wasn't his responsibility.

He went straight to the clinic. It was past one in the afternoon, and the queue stretched out the door and around the corner. People sat on the ground, children slumped against chests and shoulders, adults dozing with hats over their faces. A nurse, one of the casual hires whose name Lucca didn't know, was triaging cases, a volunteer at her heels. This one at least had decent Spanish.

Nearby, a group of high-spirited boys was playing football. The two teams chased the ball and Moisés chased them, calling for passes that never came his way. The world was unjust. Usually Lucca didn't let it get to him, but today, seeing Moisés ignored by the only children he'd ever call friends, knowing that

Dallas had chosen another child over him, was more than he could bear.

Inside, every cot was occupied. It took Lucca a moment to spot Juan in the far corner, resetting a dislocated shoulder. Striding up to him, Lucca said: The nurse outside. Is she good?

Very, Juan said. He was kneeling next to the bare-chested patient, holding the man's arm at a ninety-degree angle, one hand around the wrist and the other under the elbow.

Hire her. Full-time. And a second one.

Juan raised his brows but remained focused, coaching the man to relax as he gently moved the arm. The patient gritted his teeth and took shallow breaths through his nose. Sit a little straighter, Juan said gently. It's almost done.

Lucca was full of restless, righteous indignation. What else do you need? An X-ray machine? EKG?

Truly? Juan asked.

Make a list, Lucca said.

Finished, Juan told the patient, adding, Feel better? And the man gave a wry twist of the head.

Juan stood and finally turned to Lucca, who nodded and said, Things are going to change.

It was the first time he'd taken a hard line with Head Office, and he felt good, full of confidence. On a whim, he said: Why can't Moisés see? What's wrong with his eyes?

Until now, there hadn't been any point in asking.

I have a theory. But an ophthalmologist would have to confirm it. Juan shrugged as he said this as if to ask *What was the point?*

Please make an appointment, Lucca said.

Head Office has approved? Juan looked skeptical.

They'll pay, Lucca said. For the treatment too.

He'd asked a mother to give up her child, a hideous burden Head Office had foisted on him, one they themselves would never have carried out. He'd bring Moisés to the specialist himself. The boy deserved his share.

Two mornings later, Thiago came into his office, toothpick in mouth. The blinds were closed. The fan rustled the papers on the desk. Lucca had his sleeves folded up, the top few buttons on his shirt undone. Not even ten thirty, and already his forehead and chest perspired.

A situation with a group of boys in Beatriz's classroom was occupying his mind. There were always issues in the compound, and he disliked these interpersonal ones most of all. As a child, Lucca had been prone to ferocious tantrums, lashing out at the slightest provocation, any time he felt blame or disrespect. Rage had won him no friends. As a teenager, he'd learned to control himself. Now his strategy was a charm offensive, but this wasn't something he could teach the children here, many of whom could barely look each other in the eyes. So, he was glad to see Thiago, grateful for a distraction.

Until Thiago said: The actress is leaving today. They're asking what will happen to Maria.

They. The day before, Lucca had overheard Luis argue: The parents should be permitted to see their baby before they are forced to give her up. Then Yolanda had chimed in, and Lucca had turned the corner so he wouldn't hear her opinion. Even through the closed door, he could sense their volatility and chose to avoid the histrionics.

This damned actress. She'd been nothing but a nuisance, just as he'd predicted. Lucca turned from the computer and replied: That is not for me to say. We'll keep the child here until we are told otherwise.

Anya should have been the one answering these questions. She or Crispin who had dreamed up this scheme. He thought he'd made himself clear. But the emails were unrelenting, reply-alls landing in his inbox at all hours of the day, most of them from Anya, a back-and-forth between her and Dallas's manager. Just seeing their names made him antsy, and he'd deleted the messages unopened. The adoption—if it did happen—would take who knew how long to manage. And what were they supposed to do with the girl in the meantime? Now there were four babies in the nursery sharing cribs.

The actress says she's taking Maria with her, Thiago said, speaking around the toothpick.

This was news to Lucca. Since his visit to the Garcias, he'd been avoiding Dallas and suspected she was keeping her distance too.

Where did you hear this? he asked.

She has told Yolanda, Beatriz, Luis, everyone. Even the children know.

Lucca turned up his palms. There, you see. Arrangements have been made.

But have the Garcias signed some forms? Thiago asked.

Lucca opened the top drawer and scooped the keys. He'd planned to spend the day catching up on paperwork, but if the staff were going to be mincing around, wringing their hands, he was better off absent. He'd go to the capital and check on the shipment of donations that was stuck in customs limbo, maybe even spend the night there.

They must have, he said, standing. He should have known Dallas would get what she wanted. The wealthy always did.

Thiago spoke quickly: It's impossible. They cannot have given permission. It's happening too quickly. The Garcias must be allowed to see Maria again, at least.

Sidestepping him, Lucca reached for the door. Keep an eye on things while I'm gone, he said.

But if she tries to take Maria—

Leave it, Lucca said. It is not for us to decide what happens to the child.

The hallway was deserted, and outside he found an unnatural stillness. Children had paused in their games as staff conferred in anxious clumps. When Lucca followed their gazes, he saw Dallas at the entrance to the compound, a forty-litre bag strapped to her back, and a black Range Rover idling on the opposite side of the gates. The guard stood in the doorway of his hut, and even from a distance Lucca could tell the situation was heated, Dallas gesturing emphatically at the waiting car and the guard shaking his head and leaning backward.

Thiago hurried over and Lucca followed reluctantly, sick with apprehension, hyperaware of the volunteers who had emerged to watch the drama. He thought he saw one of them raise a phone.

They arrived at the guard's hut to hear Dallas demanding, You need to open the gate. Seeing Lucca, she said, Tell him.

The Range Rover honked twice. Lucca felt the eyes of the compound on him. The children holding skipping ropes and footballs, the patients who had edged out of line. The staff were muttering, a low grumble. Lucca spotted Moisés, peeling away from a cluster of boys, pushing the bridge of his glasses up with his index finger.

The dread that had been building now sounded an alarm. RUN, it screamed. RUN. He willed his legs to still, his mind to silence. Lucca thought of his brash conversation with the doctor, the two nurses they were about to hire. What would happen if he denied Dallas? He recalled his own words from a moment ago: *It's not for us to decide.* No matter what move he made, it would be the wrong one.

I have a flight to catch, Dallas said. She had a protective arm flung across the bundle on her front. Only the top of Maria's head was visible, a thatch of dark hair. Dallas had tied the bottom of the carrier in such a way that her feet were hidden. *Piecitos chuecos*, he'd said when speaking to Inez. Her little twisted feet.

For a moment, every possibility existed. He could deny the actress, and the compound would suffer the consequences. He could let her go and . . . No. This was *not* his responsibility. If Crispin and Anya were here, what would they do?

I need to go, Dallas said, stamping her foot. You can't keep me.

The baby, who must have been asleep, woke with a piercing cry. Dallas scowled at Lucca, as if he was to blame, then bounced up and down, patting Maria's back.

The muttering from the staff grew louder.

Ella no quiere ir, Luis called.

Ella quiere a su madre, Beatriz shouted, and soon their colleagues chimed in, repeating the phrases: *She doesn't want to go. She wants her mother.* A gust of hot wind rustled the foliage, carrying their voices. Some of the children took up the refrain: Ella no quiere ir. Ella no quiere ir.

Sweat beaded Lucca's neck, trickled down his back, the sun blistering in the unshaded patch where he stood. Maria's wails were frantic and breathless, and Dallas appeared on the verge of tears herself, whispering shh, shh.

At night the two sides of the fence were secured by a chain and padlock. During the day there was only a single bolt, retracted by a switch in the guard's hut that, when flicked, automatically opened the gates. The guard had slipped away. Thiago blocked the switch, standing with his feet apart, hands on hips.

Lucca caught his eye and nodded once. Thiago shook his head no, and the two men stared each other down. Thiago widened his eyes and made a guttural sound from deep in his throat—a wordless entreaty. *Please don't make me do this.*

Ábrelo, Lucca said. *Open it.*

Angels

Claire

Claire threw a coat over her pyjamas and dashed to the mom-and-pop at the corner to watch a bleary-eyed teenager take a utility knife to the shrink-wrapped stack of *People* magazines sitting on a pallet. When he handed her a copy, there were Dallas and Persimmon on the cover.

Dallas's Baby Bliss, the headline screamed alongside a photo of Dallas touching foreheads with Persimmon, both in matching pink. In smaller font: *The star opens up about her new daughter*. Claire nearly cooed.

Inside, the interview was even better. *What were the chances our paths would cross?* Dallas mused, adding: *It was meant to be. I truly believe Persimmon found me.* She described the baby as flirty and giggly. One hundred per cent personality. *But you can see in her eyes, she's an old soul.* The article ended on a quote: *She's made me a mother. She's given my life meaning.*

Best of all were the references to Children of the World and the yellow pull-out box where the editors had reprinted their fact sheet.

You in there or something? the teenager asked, curious now and straining to read over Claire's shoulder.

That's the charity I work for, she said. We made this happen.

She watched his face, waiting for recognition to dawn. Instead, he yawned and said, That's cool.

While he rang up her bill, she texted Dallas (*People! Amazing! You two were made for each other!*) and got a reply right away (prayer hands thank you emoji, blowing kiss emoji). It was four a.m. in California, but before Claire could ask why on earth she was awake, Dallas sent a still of Persimmon asleep on her chest, the milk bottle blurry in the background, and a single word: *trapped!*

Cutest hostage situation, Claire replied, impressed that Dallas hadn't outsourced the early morning feedings to a nanny.

At the office, arriving with spare copies of *People*, Claire was mobbed by her colleagues who exclaimed over the photos and declared the profile a triumph.

For the past month and a half, their phones had been ringing non-stop. Philanthropists and corporations, the same big spenders who used to screen Children of the World's calls, were now vying for their attention. They'd even been gifted a new office and were scheduled to move in a couple of months. Claire had, in a single stroke, reversed their fortunes.

Gold, the events manager declared, flapping the magazine. Gold!

Only Anya remained stubbornly at her desk, spectacles on, leaning toward the screen. Claire tried not to take it personally. Anya had come up in a time when the glass ceiling was lower. She probably couldn't help resenting a younger woman's success.

Later though, in the midday lull when the office was deserted, Claire caught her, phone in lap, screen angled under the desk, watching an Instagram Reel. Persimmon, her chubby legs in casts, squirmed on her tummy, diligently struggling to flip over, her face screwed up with the effort, a couple of false starts and then the triumphant moment when she landed on her back. If the sound wasn't muted, Anya would have heard the baby grunting with the effort and Dallas's cheers in the background.

Amazing, right? Claire sidled up and Anya dropped the device as if it was a hot coal. Claire almost burst out laughing. Instead, she bent to pick up the phone and said, Hours of physio went into that.

Is all that necessary? Anya asked. Wouldn't she have figured it out on her own?

You can't take a chance with these things, Claire said, appalled. Dallas is playing catch up as it is. She has weekly X-rays and appointments with the orthopedic surgeon. RT. PT. Nutritionists. The schedule's full on.

You two are still in touch? Anya asked.

That one's a little old. Here's the latest, Claire said, showing her a video that wasn't public.

At first, Claire had been cautious about texting Dallas, only replying, never initiating. But brief back-and-forths had evolved into longer conversations. These exchanges were different from the buttoned-up missives Claire sent about promotional plans and advertising campaigns, which, in any case, were always answered by Dallas's assistant. Over email, Claire was all business, wrote in full sentences with faultless punctuation. But in the messaging app, she and Dallas were casual and jokey, even confessional.

Persimmon screams and screams and I have no idea what she needs, Dallas had admitted, telling Claire how she'd tried everything (hungry? gassy? tired?) to no avail until finally she, too, had broken down in tears. This text block was punctuated by a photo of Persimmon, wet face splotched red, snot tracking from her nose, head tilted in a quizzical expression.

It made her finally stop crying, Dallas wrote. *Turns out that's all she wanted. To break me.*

Ouch, Claire thought. She vividly recalled those early days in the strange land of motherhood, where everything about the language and terrain was alien. How utterly alone and overwhelmed she'd been, how simultaneously responsible and helpless. It made her protective of Dallas.

Charlotte was 10% sleepy and 90% fury, Claire had replied. *It's a miracle I had another*. She didn't add that it was only because Simon had worn her down with his badgering. He'd wanted to try for a boy, of course. *It gets easier. I promise*, she wrote instead.

It better! (tongue out emoji)

In these vulnerable moments, Dallas revealed her humanity, giving Claire a peek behind the curated image she cultivated for the public. Dallas Hayden was no longer a remote, flawless actor. They were two single moms, supporting each other.

In the video Claire showed Anya, Persimmon lay on her stomach and lifted her upper body on two elbows.

This is major progress. Her muscle tone has improved a lot, Claire said.

She's gained weight. She looks healthy, Anya said, and the tight lines around her mouth eased as she took Claire's phone and replayed the video, eyes softening.

It was a rare moment, Anya with her defences down, and Claire guessed she was recalling her own son's babyhood. Anya wasn't the enemy, Claire thought. She was a struggling human. Another single mom.

Persimmon weighed next to nothing. She couldn't sit up, and her feet . . . Anya, you gave her a real shot at life.

This was your doing, Anya said, pushing Claire's phone back to her. You saw an opportunity and pounced.

What *was* this woman's damage? Claire's instinct was to lash out, but she stopped herself, deciding to be the bigger person.

Santa Rosa was *your* vision, Claire insisted. We wouldn't have found Persimmon if it wasn't for the compound, and that was *your* brainchild.

On the wall was a map of their territories, push-pins marking the overseas projects, strings connecting each one back to the red star stuck over Toronto. Claire turned and gestured to it as she spoke: Think of all the lives we touch. Not just the kids we feed and house and teach and vaccinate . . . I'm talking about the knock-on effects for those children's families and their futures and the jobs and families they'll raise one day.

Crispin had been pulling Claire into meetings with country directors. When Nikhil in Delhi outlined the expansions he wanted to make to their orphanage, or when his counterpart in Jakarta spoke of turning mobile clinics into permanent hospitals, she felt a thrill, knowing she'd made all this possible.

Claire indicated the green pins recently returned to Ghana and Sierra Leone, and the yellow pins demarcating ground they were planning to break in the new year, her voice rousing as she went on.

The work we're doing, sure it's underpaid and often thankless, she said. But it's important. Our actions have real-world *consequences*. Just imagine this map in twenty years. How many more Persimmons we'll save. And maybe you'll retire and maybe I'll move on, and others will take up the mantle, but this—she pointed again to the map—will never end.

Claire ran out of breath and stopped, aware of their colleagues trickling back and the unexpected audience.

Anya was watching her, leaning back in her chair, elbows on the armrests, fingers steepled together, a smirk on her face. You've learned a few things from Crispin, she said. But do us all a favour. Don't ape his overconfidence.

Crispin was going to lunch with prospective donors from a pharmaceutical firm and asked Claire to join.

Claire had been taking her own meetings. The day before she'd met with competing advertising agencies, all vying for the chance to pitch a *Sentinels*-themed campaign. Pro bono of course, they were quick to add. But this was the first time Crispin had invited her to a tête-à-tête with a prospective donor.

Anya thought you'd be an asset, Crispin said.

Really?

You're a fundraiser now, he said. Don't sell yourself short.

At lunch, Claire watched Crispin in action, admiring his poise, the seamless pivot he'd made from raspy-voiced stoner to serious philanthropist. He talked about mosquito nets and the economic cost of infant mortality. He had facts and figures at his fingertips but didn't lean on them to make a point, instead sharing stories about individuals.

She could see the suits were charmed, these big shots who'd begun the lunch by claiming they didn't have much time but were now lingering to hear more. They admired him, she realized, maybe for the same reason she always had: Crispin was doing something they weren't. Anyone could push paper, make a profit, sing a song. Crispin was bettering the world. She felt a flush of pride because she was too. A year ago, she'd been doing damage control for an oil company that was forcing a pipeline through Indigenous land, watching her client pressure the Mounties to haul grannies off the protest line. She couldn't even *think* of the conglomerate poisoning her hometown. Now she was on the side of the angels.

Claire's the bad guy's Cyrano, her ex had once joked at a party. Well, look at Claire now: an honest-to-god humanitarian, noble and self-sacrificing, one of the good guys.

By the time dessert arrived, Claire was eager for the pitch, curious to hear how Crispin would usher the conversation toward the ask. Anya had sent them off with a wish list and a slide deck, but the computer remained in its bag under the table.

You've captured eyeballs, said one of the suits—the head of marketing. We really admire that. Frankly, we're jealous.

Dallas's trip hadn't just enticed new volunteers; it had spawned imitators too. There were more TikToks than ever—young people in classrooms, surrounded by children, perched atop tractors, wielding pickaxes on building sites. They were taken in Guatemala, India, Cambodia, and Senegal. It was all free advertising, attracting more volunteers and donations in a virtuous cycle.

My kids are riveted, said Suit #2—the VP of corporate social responsibility. A few months ago, you couldn't pay these teenagers to put down their phones and touch grass. Now they're begging me to let them volunteer overseas.

That's all Claire's doing, Crispin said. We'd love for Orion Pharma to be part of our story.

My daughter had me watch one of those TikToks, Suit #2 said. And it gave me an idea.

Next to her, Crispin leaned imperceptibly forward, and Claire felt herself doing the same. Then she listened with dismay as

Suit #2 floated the idea of an overseas team builder. The clinic in the DRC desperately needed antibiotics, and the orphanage in Nepal was running low on measles vaccines. But here was the pharma company's head of philanthropy talking about his staff. It would be great to take the senior leadership somewhere, he said. Give them a once-in-a-lifetime experience.

Claire envisioned a group of white-haired men lugging bricks in sub-Saharan Africa. Peeling off their shirts to reveal soft middle-aged stomachs, grumbling with diarrhea, necks burnt in the equatorial sun. She waited for Crispin to swivel the conversation. Instead, he said: A corporate retreat. That's an idea.

We'd need a proper conference centre for something like that, she said afterward, reminding him of the no-frills cots the volunteers slept on, the rice-and-lentils meals.

That's a brilliant solution, Crispin said. We'll start a for-profit arm. A social enterprise with revenue donated back to Children of the World.

What's a social enterprise? Claire silently wondered. She'd always worked with profit-driven companies and big budgets. The charitable sector was a completely different beast, with its own arcana of rules and restrictions. Sometimes she still felt out of her depth.

One fact she was cottoning on to: unbridled optimism was Crispin's Achilles heel. Claire had begun to appreciate Anya's pessimism—even her snarky *do us all a favour*—as a necessary corrective.

But back at the office, Anya was uncharacteristically receptive, musing that because so few charities offered this sort of thing, they'd be able to charge luxury rates.

A social enterprise could be a stable, long-term source of funds, she said and mimed cracking a pencil in half. We break the feast-famine cycle.

Four-star facilities. Private rooms and quality meals, Crispin said. I'll convince Orion Pharma to sponsor it. Give them naming rights.

Anya suggested Santa Rosa as a location, adding that the country had the benefit of political stability, regular flights, and proximity to day trips. Typical, Claire thought. Ever since Dallas put the country on the map, Anya had become single-minded about her pet project. Out loud, Claire pointed out that India had all those points in its favour too. Plus, a country director who answered his phone.

Crispin clicked his fingers together. Who was that guy . . . the one who just won *Top Chef*? Isn't he from Delhi? We could recruit him for the kitchen.

Santa Rosa— Anya began.

Lucca will oppose it on principle, Claire cut in.

I don't think he will, Anya said. We've been having some fruitful conversations. He understands the value of investment.

This could be our new operations model, Crispin said. Think about it. We're constantly at the mercy of donors and their whims. Even now, we need drugs and vaccines, but what's Orion focused on?

Their staff, Claire said and added with air quotes, Team building.

Who do you think pays for all this? Anya snapped, gesturing at the rundown space.

Claire was taken aback by Anya's outburst, which had drawn the attention of their colleagues. For a couple of horrible moments, there was an awkward silence, only the laborious wheeze of the copier filling the air.

Anyway, Crispin said finally, clearing his throat. Here's a way for everyone to get what they want and the children too. Win-win-win.

Claire was aware of her co-workers staring, trading significant glances, a flurry of typing that suggested private messages were zinging around. Embarrassed, she turned to her computer, using Instagram as a pacifier.

Since Dallas's volunteer stint, the charity's socials were perpetually lively with a level of interaction that suggested followers were living vicariously. They requested updates about the kids and staff, people asking for Beatriz, Josefina, and little Moisés by name. They called the doctor a *snack*. Sometimes the curiosity and speculation, the silly emojis about the doctor, bordered on the uncomfortable. But Claire tried to keep things in perspective. These were well-wishers, harmless in the end. She watched the latest volunteer TikTok. Uploaded a few minutes earlier from Santa Rosa, it depicted a young woman crouched in the chicken coop, ferreting for eggs.

Anya, who had arrived at her side, scoffed. Bet Lucca loves that, she said, holding out a print job Claire had forgotten, still warm from the machine, a wordless apology.

Serves him right for going AWOL, Claire grumbled.

Lucca might have conceded to regular calls with Anya, but he'd gone to ground as far as Claire was concerned.

Have you given any thought to my suggestion? Crispin asked Anya. It's been a while since either of us had eyes on the project, and now we have the means.

Claire enjoyed a moment of amusement, imagining Anya parachuting into Santa Rosa unannounced and catching Lucca off guard. But Anya was fluffing her scarf awkwardly. Was it Claire's imagination, or was she uncomfortable?

That's a good idea, Claire said. Especially if we're going to build a conference centre.

Anya tapped the base of her phone against her jaw. Let's fly him up here instead. First thing in the new year, after we move.

Earlier that week, the whole team had trooped out to the west end on the streetcar to tour the new office. They'd been gobsmacked by its size and opulence. Floor-to-ceiling windows and blonde wood floors in a three-thousand-square-foot suite with a tech-enabled conference room, working elevators, even a concierge.

How big is this place-place-place? the office joker had asked, faking an echo. We'll never find each other in here.

If only we could lose you, the volunteer coordinator teased, pretending to shove him into the coat closet.

I told you Dallas's visit would mean big things, Crispin had said to Anya before rapping his knuckle on the door of a glass-walled office and announcing he'd ordered her a name plate.

They were slated to take possession in February and now Crispin was agreeing with Anya, saying that it was an opportune moment to bring Lucca in. There had been a time when this was routine, he told Claire. Country directors arriving at Head Office, taking up residence for a month or two to file field reports and make the rounds with Crispin, guilt-trip millionaires into turning out their pockets.

Anya floated the idea of hosting an open house. An afterwork cocktail party, she said. It would give us a chance to ingratiate new donors, woo potentials, and warm the space. We could introduce Lucca there.

Would he be up for something like that? Claire asked, imagining Lucca spending the whole evening hiding in a toilet stall.

Anya and Crispin exchanged grins. Lucca can turn on the charm when he wants, Anya said.

—

Her ex said he'd drop off Charlotte's swim gear.

On my way, Simon texted.

Meet us around back, Claire replied.

She did not want him to see her basement apartment. Simon's parents had helped him buy Claire out of her share of the house. During their weeks with him, the kids returned to their old bedrooms, had their trampoline and wading pool, the door jamb that recorded their heights. At her place, they shared a narrow den with a curtain pulled across in lieu of a door.

Leaning against the kitchen counter, she returned to her text exchange with Dallas. Dallas said they'd gone to a birthday party recently, an elaborate production with face painting, costumes, and a unicorn theme. Claire knew the details because she'd creeped them online. There were lots of kids, Dallas said. Some were babies, already babbling and recognizing their parents, though they were younger than Persimmon.

Claire was struck afresh by the depth of Dallas's sacrifice, the size of her heart. She recalled the hovel where Dallas had found the girl and shuddered.

Everyone thinks I'm crazy, Dallas confessed. *Because Persimmon has high needs, you know.*

Rude!

Right?

They're saying this to you? To your face?

I'm the flighty one, that's my rep. Short attn span.

Untrue, Claire replied, wondering, Was it true?

But Persimmon's so smart. They don't know her. She's already doing better. Like her motor skills and stuff. She's starting to know her name.

Amazing! Claire replied. *Great job, mom.*

Persimmon's been written off all her life but we'll show them. Gtg. Physio's here.

Claire had once stage-managed a comeback tour for a D-list comedian who'd disgraced himself in blackface. Now she was a professional altruist effecting real, tangible change, *and* making friends with an A-lister.

Outside, the children had their faces pressed to the chain-link fence, Charlotte touching noses with the white terrier next door, Theo reaching for his fur. The dog's tail was high and loose, wagging broadly like a windshield wiper.

Don't worry, I've been watching them, her neighbour Regina said.

You really didn't have to.

Claire had heard the podcasts and read all the articles. Stranger danger, the Satanic panic, that ridiculous Wayfair conspiracy theory, none of it was real, but try explaining that to Regina, who had no children and all the time in the world to spy and make snide comments about the height of the fence, how easily it could be scaled, and did you get that Amber alert—

Daddy, Daddy! The kids ran, flinging themselves against Simon's legs. Hugs received, they immediately returned to the dog.

Claire smirked. If the situation was reversed, they'd have been grasping her limbs, begging *Stay, Mommy, please*.

Simon had cycled over—of course he had—and his bike leaned against the fence. He knelt to rummage in the pannier and said: Sorry. Breakfast program meeting ran late.

There was no reason to volunteer the information, but Simon never did a good deed without expecting a pat on the head. He taught in a low-income neighbourhood and had begun the program when he'd noticed how many of his students never brought lunch.

How's Graham? she asked.

Graham was the blackface comedian. As part of his public rehabilitation, Claire had arranged for him to gig a fundraiser. Simon had turned his nose up when she'd floated the idea, but that hadn't stopped the principal from cashing Graham's cheque.

All that was a precursor for you, I guess, Simon said.

I mean a one-off for a local school, it's great and all. I'm happy I could get you that seed money, but what we're doing at Children of the World is on another level. We're global change-makers.

Have you given more thought to April? Simon asked, handing over the bathing suit. Naturally he'd forgotten the swim cap. Even though Charlotte was prone to ear infections. Even though Claire had reminded him.

Theo's only a toddler. He's too young—

I understand your concerns, he interrupted. But the kids won't.

That's because you keep riling them up.

Claire had the custody agreement on her side, but what use was the law against the desires of two small children? India was all they could talk about. Among their friends and teachers, the trip was a given. Claire was the only obstacle standing between them and the holiday of their lives. She felt the injustice of her position. Charlotte and Theo would go off for six weeks and every misery would be blamed on her absence, not the father who'd spirited them away.

You're right, he said. I should have run the trip by you first.

This was unexpected. It put Claire on her guard. I'm not going to be the one to tell them India is off.

He glanced toward the shabby low-rise with the three concrete steps leading to the flimsy back door, the window wells that grew mould after storms and said, If you're worried about the expense—

Yeah, well, humanitarian aid isn't exactly lucrative.

This had been another sore spot in their marriage, that Simon could simultaneously malign her salary while benefitting from its perks. When she'd first taken the job at Children of the World, he'd accused her of strategizing to deny him spousal support, and she'd laughed in his face. It had been a rare, fleeting moment when she'd had the moral upper hand. And she didn't mind reminding him of it from time to time. He might be teaching refugee kids to read and write and assimilate, but she was saving lives for a fraction of his pay.

I'll cover all the costs, he assured her, adding there were elderly relations who were anxious to meet Charlotte and Theo before it was too late, and you couldn't put a price on those memories.

He gazed away as he spoke, toward where the kids were now playing in Regina's yard, a game that involved chasing the hapless dog as he ran, crooked tail down, and Claire felt a pang. Here was yet another advantage he had over her. She had no family to offer the kids; even her parents were gone.

If the roles were reversed and you were the one who could give them this trip, wouldn't you want them to have it? he asked. Don't begrudge them this opportunity.

Anya was in her ear then, her voice blazing, with a strange déjà vu: *You'd give up Charlotte? You'd give up Theo?*

I just don't want them to miss out, he continued. We promised the kids wouldn't suffer because of our divorce. We said we'd be better than that.

Claire, on the verge of capitulation a moment earlier, flared up. Better than that? Simon was such a condescending prick.

Stop pressuring me, she hissed. I told you I'd think about it.

You're right, he said immediately. I'm sorry.

You always do this, go on and on and try to get in my head. This isn't life or death. No one's *suffering* because they didn't go on holiday.

Let's leave it—

You know what? I *am* being the better mother. I'm the only one who's thinking about how they're going to cope for six weeks.

When Simon was remorseful, he got the wide-eyed look of a gormless infant. Aflame with rage, she stared him down, ready to charge.

Woah, Simon whispered, putting his hands out and stepping back.

His startled expression brought her back to herself, panting hard, wondering what on earth she'd just said. Mortified, she scuffed her shoe on the dead grass.

You forgot the swim cap, she said.

Afterward, she went through the rigmarole of dinner, bath, and bedtime with the kids, feeling despondent. Sure, she had their loyalty now, while the emotional umbilical cord was strong. But how long could that last?

This was Simon's endgame. He would take the kids, not by force or a legal battle but with insidious stratagems. Eventually, it would be the children agitating for more time with him.

A terrible possibility: the birthday party was a ruse. The family was gathering for a wedding, and Simon would return from India married, an arrangement brokered by his parents. His new bride would move into the house, take over Claire's side of the bed. Everyone would assume she was the children's mother.

But no. This was ludicrous. Simon—who never did anything his parents wanted, the only child to reject med school—in an arranged marriage? She was being irrational.

After the kids were down, Claire went online and saw that Dallas had a new Instagram post: a photo of her and Persimmon on a hike, the pair of them paused on an elevation, overlooking the mansions and greenery of Beverly Hills. Dallas had her daughter strapped into a carrier and was holding up the baby's hands in triumph. They must have done this after physiotherapy. The night before, Dallas had been on late night TV, promoting her new movie. Filming on *Sentinels II* was slated to begin after the holidays, and she was learning the script. How did Dallas have time and energy for motherhood?

The next still was of a sleeping Persimmon, her cheeks cherubic. The caption was peppered with hashtags: #obsessed #blessed #mamalife. Here was Dallas on her own, just her and Persimmon, a duo. Claire felt uplifted. Families came in all sizes. She, too, could be enough for her kids.

The Gospel According to Crispin

Emmanuelle

The publicist's directions led Emmanuelle to a part of the city that was several blocks shy of trendy, with more abandoned warehouses than trees. Cigarette butts confettied the cracked pavement. At a five-storey red brick, she double-checked the address. Inside, the building appeared desolate, metal grates pulled across the fronts of deserted retail stalls, Out of Order scrawled on a piece of paper taped to the elevator. Taking the stairs, Emmanuelle stopped at each floor but found only empty suites. Was Children of the World the only occupant? Was this a front for something more nefarious?

At the top floor, there was only a laminated sign to indicate she was in the right spot. Emmanuelle had that uncanny premonition again. Like none of this was real, and Children of the World was just a couple of people squatting in an abandoned building and pretending to run a charity.

Then Claire came around the corner, and Emmanuelle shook off the daydream. Claire looked different out of the Devonshire, more like one of the moms she saw at the playground where she took her nieces. Without her glasses, her eyes appeared larger and more expressive. There was a jammy smudge on her scarf.

Keep your coat on. There's a problem with the thermostat, she said, adding: Crispin will just be a minute. Come meet the team.

When Claire led her down the hallway, Emmanuelle saw a motley collection of furniture and a lot of duct tape. It put her in mind of her old student newspaper. There, too, the space had been cramped and furnished with castoffs.

She couldn't square the charity's headquarters—which resembled the clubhouse of a grassroots protest movement—with their slick website. *Was* there a money trail to follow? Yet they boasted over a dozen international projects. There must be funds backing that up.

Claire introduced her colleagues, and Emmanuelle allowed herself to be charmed by the boisterous, friendly group who appeared to be enjoying themselves, despite the toques and fingerless gloves.

They said they were moving in the new year to a better location. Rent and utilities included, a generous gift-in-kind.

It was the only way Crispin was gonna agree to the move, someone said, and then the others chimed in about how it had been a team effort to convince him to spring for new furniture.

This is going in her article, Claire said. Crispin St. Onge is a cheapskate.

Well, he is, one of her co-workers replied, and everyone laughed.

Can I quote you on that? Emmanuelle removed an imaginary pencil from behind her ear.

I prefer the word *economical*, Crispin said, striding in and greeting her warmly.

Emmanuelle made a mental note to check into their new landlord. Giving away prime commercial real estate for a tax writeoff and good karma? In this economy? Doubtful.

This reminds me of a place where I used to work, she said, as they entered a meeting room. The memory of that student newspaper—she'd been the editor-in-chief two years running—put her in a sentimental mood. The dynamic there had been similar. Even though she'd been in charge, there was no tyranny of hierarchy, only a shared sense of mission, everyone pitching in. Had she misjudged Crispin?

She placed her phone on the table, but to the right where the recorder app would be less conspicuous, and asked about his childhood because that's what Art would have wanted. The picture Crispin painted was one of extreme frugality, if not deprivation. Father who kept the refrigerators running at a dairy plant. Mother who reused tinfoil and hung laundry on the line in winter. The family home was a drafty old place his grandfather had built, with squirrels in the walls instead of insulation, and a pot-bellied stove that had to be fed overnight, Crispin and his brothers taking it in turns to pad down in pyjamas and toss in log after log.

Emmanuelle was surprised to learn his was a churchgoing household—thirty per cent to the collections plate, and Sundays tithed to the Lord, all of them lingering after the service to volunteer—and how much his religious upbringing tracked with her own.

Crispin said his mother had chaired the fundraising committee for the overseas ministry. Every year trips were arranged, week-long stints where volunteers flew to Ethiopia or the Philippines to build churches or feed the hungry.

Emmanuelle was reminded of her father's dream of sending missionaries abroad. The Great Commission, he'd called it, the duty entrusted on them to make disciples of all nations. A moment from the deep past resurfaced, of the Reverend's voice, rich as a saxophone, saying: Christ has a plan for all of us. You, Emmanuelle, are his hands on this earth.

I don't understand the prosperity gospel, do you? Crispin asked, conspiratorial, then added that at Bethany Pentecostal they'd preached the values of poverty.

Easier for a camel to pass through the eye of a needle than for a rich man to enter the Kingdom of Heaven, Emmanuelle quoted, still half lost in the memory of her father.

Therefore blessed are the poor, Crispin quipped, and they grinned at each other, Emmanuelle, despite herself, charmed. Rare to find a former church kid in this city. Not the rural evangelical kind, anyway.

You're a believer, he said, and immediately she regretted letting her guard down.

No. Not for a very long time, she said.

It was unnerving to discover their childhoods had progressed down parallel tracks, that they'd both jumped off the train, and yet ended up in very different places.

Does how you were raised influence your philanthropy? she asked.

Well, I think it's clear I come by my fundraising chops honestly, Crispin joked, adding that he'd learned it all from his mother.

Then he told her about their most successful event: a karaoke night that had been his idea. Afterward, tallying up the earnings, wrapping stacks of hundreds in rubber bands, they'd shared a giddy, illicit glee.

We'd never *seen* so much money, he said. Of course every cent was earmarked for overseas.

Crispin said the families his church sponsored sometimes visited. These were highly anticipated trips, the missionaries' names spoken with near reverence.

We didn't have TV or magazines, Crispin said with a laugh. Missionaries were the only celebrities I understood.

That's interesting, given your careers, she said. Did you ever consider becoming a missionary?

My parents hoped I would, he said and laughed again, but this time the sound was hollow and his face stiffened, the smile on his mouth not reaching his eyes.

You would have been good at it, she said, bringing up an interview she'd conducted, the previous day, with a former volunteer.

As a teen, the young man had spent two weeks in Ghana. Five grand plus airfare had bought him an immersive adventure building a school outside Accra. He'd made exaggerated air quotes around the phrase *"building a school"* and spoke of his ambivalence, how unprepared he'd been for the poverty, which had made him feel simultaneously gallant and guilty, and how, though he'd accomplished very little, the experience had won him a scholarship, volunteering overseas being a shorthand for pluck and valour, rather than gullibility. But Emmanuelle didn't mention any of that to Crispin.

You recruited at his high school, she said instead.

Crispin beamed, the expression genuine now. School assemblies are a great way to spread the word.

The gospel according to Crispin, Emmanuelle thought.

It sounds like you're persuasive, she said, recounting the scene her interviewee had described: girls in tears, crowds signing up then and there.

It's the first exposure many of these young people have to the wider world, Crispin said, making a *what can I say* shrug of his shoulders, as if he was a neutral party and knowledge was the higher power spurring teenagers to action, not him.

Emmanuelle had a flashback of her father, wrapping up a sermon and urging the unsaved to give their lives to Christ. If the Spirit moves you, he called, come forward and be saved. Accept Jesus as your Lord and Saviour.

And from all over the congregation, men and women stood, picking their way out of the pews and into the aisles, streaming to the pulpit. Everyone on their knees, heads bowed, and her father's voice booming out, the particular, measured cadence of his baritone: Is the Holy Spirit calling? Come and be saved.

In one of her last memories of him, she'd sidled up while a congregant was praising his sermon. Her father leaned back, beaming, and put an arm around Emmanuelle, pulling her into the glow of his orbit. She could still recall the texture of his tweed jacket, a hand-me-down softened by wear, and the woodsy scent of his cologne.

For years after his death, these memories were tainted. How could someone so concerned with the afterlife have taken no precautions to protect his own family after his death? His impassioned oratory, those vaunted Sunday mornings, struck her as manipulative then, not acts of salvation but an exercise of power. Over time, her resentment had dulled. If the Reverend had been guilty of anything, it was of ignoring his mortality. It became possible again to dwell in that halcyon recollection, in the soft and woodsy crook of his arm. These ancient memories of her father were rarities these days, and it was a struggle to yank herself back into the present.

That sort of proselytizing zeal can be tremendously powerful, she said. Do you feel a responsibility to wield it with care?

Crispin furrowed his brow. I'm not sure I understand.

Surely, this guileless act was a sham, she thought, irritated.

Well, returning to missionaries for a moment. They're God's messengers, arriving from more prosperous countries, bringing money and the means of eternal salvation. They have incredible influence, which they haven't earned and don't deserve. They might not know anything about the land, its history, the people, their culture, their spirituality . . . That kind of moral certainty, the wealth disparity, the ignorance, it can result in abuse.

She was getting worked up and breathless, betraying her pique, but she couldn't help herself.

You equate persuasion with power, he said.

Because it is! she exclaimed. I watched you at the Devonshire. You had the room in the palm of your hand. You do realize you're something of a Svengali, right?

Crispin's posture snapped upright. Emmanuelle trembled, hot with adrenalin and righteous indignation. She was pleased to see the self-satisfied smirk wiped off his face, replaced first by shock and then unwelcome recognition.

A *Svengali*? he said, distaste spitting off his tongue, and for a tense moment, she was afraid he'd end the interview and kick her out. But Crispin rallied. Chuckling, he said: You give me too much credit. Well, in any case, I don't think persuasion is nefarious. You can't force anyone to do something they fundamentally don't want to do. It's about inviting people to broaden their horizons.

He was a master at deflecting threats to his ego. Emmanuelle changed course.

I was surprised by what you said at the Devonshire, about giving an amount that hurt, she said. That's not a pitch you hear often.

Honestly—and I say this from personal experience—wealth is an albatross. The only way to be happy is to give it away.

This was her father's favourite sermon, about Poverty and its bedfellow Godliness. Neither of which paid the mortgage. Guilt as the engine of philanthropy, Emmanuelle thought. *There* was an op-ed she could write with her eyes closed.

Crispin had veered back to the charity's origin story. Enlightenment in Cambodia. She wondered how much of it was fiction. Had he really lived in a village without running water? Used a squat toilet? At the Devonshire, she'd dismissed it as myth, but here in his derelict office, she had a change of heart. Crispin at twenty-something, yeah, okay, she could see him cross-legged on a low table with a local family, eating with his hands, swarmed by mosquitos.

I felt called to this work and that was my guiding motivation, even before I knew what exactly I was going to do. Resurrection. The concerts. None of it holds a candle to the lives we're changing, Crispin said. He probably didn't realize these were word-for-word the same lines she'd heard at the Devonshire. And that broke Emmanuelle out of her trance. This guy was a snake-oil salesman with a script.

What does it take to make positive change? she asked.

A willingness to do the work, Crispin said. Your intentions must be correct. An open mind and an open heart.

That's it? she wondered silently. No consent or cooperation with the locals. No understanding of land or language. Just chutzpah and empty slogans.

Crispin was absently drumming the table. He was the type who needed to be in perpetual motion.

Emmanuelle said, The other day, you mentioned there was a lot you didn't know when you first embarked on this journey.

The scale of the issues, he said, and his hands stilled. Unless you witness them first-hand, it's impossible to fathom.

When pressed for an example, he told her about Children of the World's first foray into Indonesia. This was soon after the tsunami, before they had a permanent presence in the country. They recruited a dozen volunteers, including a couple of emergency physicians and nurses, took medications, vitamins, whatever the volunteers could scrounge up. They formed a mobile unit, bringing medical care to remote villages. Crispin never wanted to be the kind of founder who led from afar, and this visit was instructive.

We were treating fifty, sixty kids a day, Crispin said. Most had scabies, worms, fungal infections. But there was also typhus, malaria, dengue, things we never expected.

The medics on the team, had they worked in the tropics? Emmanuelle asked.

Our volunteers were amazing. But they came from suburban hospitals. There was some culture shock.

I can imagine, Emmanuelle said. What she couldn't fathom was the gall. To waltz into a foreign country and play Asclepius without a shred of experience.

Don't get me wrong, Crispin said. They did their best. They read books, the internet, but there's not much that can prepare you for what you'll see when you get there.

You don't know what you don't know, she said.

And in a setting like that, without technology and diagnostics and so on, he continued. It was frustrating, how much we wanted to accomplish and how little was possible.

Emmanuelle watched his body language, how he leaned back slightly, shoulders and limbs at ease. She was glad Claire wasn't babysitting the interview.

Have you ever considered tackling inequality at home? she asked, pointing out all the communities that lived under perpetual boil-water advisories, over a hundred at last count.

It's unacceptable, Crispin said. To my mind, those issues are the government's responsibility.

Because . . .

Because for one thing, as a country we have the GDP, but only government policy can equally distribute wealth. I'm talking progressive taxation. I'm talking guaranteed income.

Yes, she said, once again surprised to find herself in agreement; how easy it was to like him when he spoke sensibly.

But then there's geography and bigotry and long histories of exploitation, Crispin said. These are complicated systemic issues, and beyond the scope of a charity.

As if Gordian knots didn't exist abroad, as if complexity was the prerogative of rich nations.

She cleared her throat to cover her exasperation and said: You could lobby. You're a persuasive speaker.

We're a non-political organization. In my experience, we do better by being non-partisan.

Interesting take, she thought, from a man who got rich performing political anthems. She was irked by his arrogance—how childishly certain he was that everything he touched would turn to gold.

At the Devonshire, you spoke passionately about equity and wealth redistribution.

Crispin leaned back, crossing his feet at the ankles and stretching his legs out so she had to scoot her own away. He said: It's not about charity. That's not what we're doing here. We're interested in social justice. Kids should be in school, not sweatshops.

Emmanuelle pounced: Let's talk about Nutty Butty Chocolate. They've been caught exploiting child labour, in Cameroon specifically, where they're also a long-time supporter of your work. She caught the startled widening of his eyes and jabbed again: How can kids attend the school you built, with Nutty's money, if they're working on a Nutty Butty cocoa farm?

You can't expect change just like that, he sputtered.

Emmanuelle smothered a smirk, pleased to have unsettled him.

Crispin sat straighter, gathered himself, and said, Our sponsors are committed to revolutionizing their business models.

And you believe they will? Even when it's not financially advantageous?

I see our role as being the better angels. We hold them accountable to their moral obligations.

Like a corporate superego?

A wha— Oh, you mean Freud. Haha. Fundamentally, I believe all our donors, whether they are private individuals, major multinationals, or mom-and-pop operations, they all want to make a positive impact. And we're privileged they've chosen to invest their philanthropic budgets with us.

There it was: the careful sound bite. Interesting that it should arrive just as they got on the subject of corporate sponsors.

Several of the companies you do business with have found themselves in hot water, she said, reeling off a list, taking pleasure as Crispin's face fell a little lower with every name. Do you worry they're using Children of the World—and the halo of charity—as cover?

But Crispin now had his armour on and was sticking to his key messages. As I said, our donors want to do good in the world, and we're grateful they've chosen to do that work with us.

He snuck a glance at his phone, and Emmanuelle decided to end on a high note.

Last question, she said. There's been a lot of new interest since Dallas Hayden's association. Thinking of the future, what excites you the most?

His posture relaxed and his eyes reanimated. Tech. Definitely tech. The ideas these young guys are coming up with . . . He held his head and flicked his hands away in a mind-blown gesture.

An app for malnutrition? she asked.

Anything's possible, he said. I'll keep you posted.

Missionary

Crispin

Jim Whalen was Crispin's number one fan.

I saw you at the Tranzac, Jim said. Ninety-two, ninety-three.

Wow, Crispin said. The early years.

Crispin and his bandmates sharing a couple of mattresses in a bachelor apartment, subsisting on ramen and dented cans of Chef Boyardee, playing every dive that would have them. He could still smell the cigarettes, feel the smoke sting his eyes, how raw and red they were in the mornings. That leather jacket he'd found at a Sally Ann and worn against the bitterest wind chill, through the sweatiest, most athletic performances. He'd loved that thing with its cracked and softened leather and treated it like a second skin, until he'd forgotten it on a bench in Chicago.

I know you were hoping to speak with my father-in-law, Jim said. But I couldn't resist taking his place.

Jim Whalen was the head of charitable giving at Robertsons, a grocery chain run by the country's fifth-wealthiest family. Crispin was doing double duty, hoping to sign up a new sponsor and secure a cheque from the family's private foundation, where Jim, as the new son-in-law, had a seat on the board.

Before he'd left the office, Anya had shown Crispin a list of the other non-profits the company supported. At a glance, he knew their types. Flashy brand names with inflated overhead and extravagant salaries that housed overseas staff in gated communities, with domestics and chauffeurs, so they could cosplay as maharajahs.

And this one, Anya had said, pointing out a small ALS charity.

Must be a personal connection, Crispin said.

Float the idea of donations at the cash, Anya said. And let's try to tap into their employee list. Send a request through HR with a sign-up for monthlies. Payroll deductions with corporate matching ideally. Robertsons will be motivated, she added, an oblique reference to the price-fixing scandal the chain was currently embroiled in.

Just whisper the words *class action*, the office joker said in a spooky drawl. Scare them into submission.

Recalling his interview with Emmanuelle Clemmons, Crispin felt a twinge of unease. This meeting is about *our* work, he said.

Right you are boss, the joker said. No need to put the fear of God into 'em. The media has that angle covered. Bad cop, bon cop this thing.

Anya chortled, and Crispin bristled. They were *not* running a laundromat for dirty corporations. He said, When Robertsons comes on board, it'll be because they're inspired by our mission and values.

What's your professional opinion, spin doc? the joker asked Claire.

It's a comms nightmare, and Robertsons is making a hash of it, she said. They need to change the conversation, not double down on petulant messaging.

No kidding, the joker said, turning severe. We aren't idiots. We *know* Big Grocery is a cartel.

Change the conversation how? Crispin asked Claire.

They can't fight this in the press. The headlines are too loud. But one on one, you can neutralize consumer opinion. I'd astroturf. Maybe engineer some TikTok content—a single mom who loves her job as a cashier, someone offbeat and quirky, a bunch of stuff like that. Hope one of them goes viral for a minute. And then pay a bunch of influencers to shill Robertsons private-label products. Pair the brand with anything and everything that isn't about price gouging.

Impressed, Crispin asked, Would it work?

Claire, whose expression had been alight with intelligence a moment earlier, suddenly appeared flustered and unhappy. Hugging her arms to herself, her voice was deflated when she replied: You can ride anything out. Eventually, the news cycle moves on.

Get them to pay penance, Anya told Crispin. Three Our Fathers and a big old cheque.

They'll want their name on a building, Claire said with unexpected sarcasm.

The corporate retreat facility in Santa Rosa, Anya said. They can put their name on that.

Image rehab's expensive, the office joker quipped.

Hardy-har, Crispin said, irritated. Okay, yes, in the past we made some compromises. Needs must. But that was then. The tides are changing.

There are risks to partnering with a company that has a sullied reputation, Claire said, voice savvy again. Farmer's has clean hands and a high-end brand, she added, referencing an upscale organic chain.

Too niche, Anya said. Robertsons are coast to coast.

We're not desperate, Claire had replied.

Crispin had been on the verge of agreeing when Anya had snapped: We're always desperate. This is non-profit. Get used to the scarcity mindset.

Crispin and Jim were meeting at the foundation's headquarters. Everything about the place exuded wealth, from its location in the historic Artemis Tower with its tin ceilings to the ten-foot Christmas tree in the lobby, decorated in gold.

Entering the elevator, Jim said: It was open-mic night, back at the Tranzac. My band played after yours. We weren't any good.

I remember you guys, Crispin lied. You were—

The drummer. Yeah! Wow. You really remember us?

Sure, you were great.

We were listening backstage and almost lost our nerve. The rest of us were just fooling ourselves. Resurrection. You were the real deal.

Not true, Crispin said. You guys had a special sound. The kind of thing you could sink your teeth into.

Jim's eyes grew huge. He was lost in the nostalgia of that time, staring at his own reflection in the false mirror Crispin held up. Making people happy was simple. All you had to do was listen carefully and tell them what they wanted to hear. And once they had the satisfaction of your attention, it was easy to make them do your bidding, even believe your desires were their own.

You think my band could have—

Absolutely. Half of it is dumb luck. If an agent had been there that night . . .

Well, Jim said. Roads not taken, eh?

Jim wore silver cufflinks and an entry-level Cartier. The tops of his ears ended in points giving him an elven appearance. Crispin stored these tidbits to chuckle over with Anya later. Since the reversal of their fortunes, the camaraderie between them had returned.

Congratulations, by the way, Jim said. Dallas Hayden. It's a hell of a thing.

That's all down to our publicist, Crispin said. She's a dynamo.

She must be. I can't go anywhere without hearing about Children of the World.

We've got a feature coming in the *Herald*, Crispin said and was immediately sorry to have reminded himself of the interview.

They'd been having a friendly conversation until the reporter went on a cranky tangent about power. If he was perfectly honest, he disliked this younger generation, whom he found puritanical and humourless. And here was Emmanuelle, faithful to her type, with her farcical notions about philanthropy being fascist or racist or whatever-ist.

He was still feeling injured—worse, unsettled by the sense he'd let her down—as the elevator doors opened on the top floor. Following Jim out, Crispin paused beside a painting of the reigning patriarch, Tilden Robertson, large as life and immortalized in oil, stern and crag-faced in three-quarter profile. How joyless these tycoons were. Once, he'd penned lyrics lampooning their greed. Now, he was knocking on their doors with his cap out. What would that long-haired rocker at the Tranzac have made of his older, pinstriped incarnation? For a discomfiting moment,

Crispin's own lyrics threatened to judge him: *Cutting moral corners. A contortionist's tricks.*

He had tried. Lord knew. He'd poured his soul into the music, the lyrics a rallying cry for a better world. But for all their success, Resurrection was only ever entertainment. Through Children of the World, he was effecting true change.

His strategy with power brokers was to finely calibrate their emotions: prick their social conscience without lavishing blame. In that sweet spot, they were liable to be generous. At the Devonshire, he'd waited until the crowd seemed receptive before taking his chance. *Give till it hurts.* Immediately they'd shut down. He'd taken a quick survey of the room, adding up the hundreds of millions in potential donations, and pivoted to a fail-safe: turning himself into the butt of the joke. *Make this trumped-up Jesus shut up.* They had roared at that, back on side. And Crispin had felt the old thrill in his veins, like he was onstage again, returning for the second encore, the reverb of an amphitheatre's ovation thrumming up his sneakers.

These captains of industry, they were just like fans, easy to win over once you stroked their egos and found the soft spots. Christ had been a fisher of men, friend to the poor. Crispin fancied himself a different sort of missionary, casting his net among the rich, gently converting them with the gospel of equity.

From behind his desk, Jim listened, elbows tented, chin on fists, as Crispin gave his spiel, outlining what Robertsons, the company and the family, had to gain from an association with his charity.

Your mission aligns with our values, Jim said. To me, it's a perfect fit.

Fantastic, Crispin said.

And if it was my call, I'd write a cheque this instant. But I gotta pitch it to the higher-ups.

The higher-ups being his in-laws. Had Jim dragged Crispin here just to get face time, a belated backstage pass? He recalled the list Anya had shown him, all those larger non-profits that were nothing like his own.

I'll level with you, Jim said, smoothing his tie and sitting back. This isn't really my father-in-law's kind of thing. It's part of the reason I wanted to take this meeting.

And why they were hidden away at the foundation rather than convening at company headquarters where Tilden worked, Crispin guessed. Did Tilden even know he was here?

I see, Crispin said, privately seething. He was tempted to announce that on second thought, it wasn't in his interests to partner with a morally bankrupt corporation. It was just the kind of tantrum Emmanuelle would relish.

You've read the news, Jim said. We're being pummelled. And Tilden, he thinks coming out guns blazing is the best response.

But you'd rather change the conversation, Crispin said, shrewder instincts kicking in. Jimbo here needed to impress his wife's daddy. Better yet, upstage him.

The C-suite's going to ask me, Why not CONCERN or another non-profit with broader reach? What makes Children of the World special?

The unique selling point. Jim might be an MBA, but Crispin, the high-school dropout, could wield the capitalist argot too. When his conscience rebelled, Crispin's wiser self reminded him that he was playing the game for the child in rural Cambodia. He'd win this one for *her*.

Let me ask you this, Crispin said. Can any of your charitable partners guarantee ninety cents of every dollar directly fund the mission? We run Children of the World like a start-up. Being lean and nimble allows us to invest far more overseas than we spend on ourselves.

That's a compelling case, Jim said, and Crispin heard the silent *but*.

Convincing colleagues can be a challenge, especially when they're entrenched in their ways, Crispin said.

An array of the day's newspapers was spread across the desk, every headline a variation on an unflattering theme. Jim glanced at them and said, The old ways can be a hindrance.

Crispin considered leaning into Robertsons' troubles, stoking Jim's anxieties. But no. He wasn't here for that. Instead, he brought up Robertsons' new chairman—a tech mogul in his early thirties, who'd sold a blockbuster app to Silicon Valley—and watched Jim's gears turn. Calculating how he might go over his father-in-law's head.

There are synergies between our organizations, Crispin said. We're partnering up to tackle global hunger. Robertsons could be a part of our solution.

But Jim's attention had wandered out the window where steel towers loomed, sun glinting off glass, and men in coveralls conducted their high-wire acts with buckets and squeegees. The clock was closing in on the hour, and Crispin felt the urgency of time. He caught Jim's eyes and held them.

If you could meet these kids as I have, Jim, you'd understand. In Santa Rosa, one in five babies dies before childhood, and what chance do the remaining four have? What are we losing—the next great invention, a solution to climate change . . . the cure for ALS?

Jim blinked, startled, and leaned imperceptibly forward.

Jim, you could save the child who grows up to do that, Crispin said. Think of the human capital that's being squandered every day, every hour, every minute to malnutrition, a problem that is easy to solve. That *Robertsons* can solve.

You really think a partnership will help with this? Jim asked, tapping a folded-up newspaper on his desk, his father-in-law's frowning face in black and white on the front page.

Crispin felt a triumphant frisson, an echo of the thunderous onstage elation. Let Jim play hard to get. The only question left was how much Robertsons would pony up.

Let me take you through the slide deck, Crispin said. I think we can work together to make customers think differently about your brand.

Band-Aids

Emmanuelle

Art Whylie had taken a sander to Emmanuelle's profile, filing down every word or phrase he deemed *too barbed*.

You're muzzling my work, she complained, flipping through the draft that was bleeding in red strikeouts.

It's pronounced *editing*, Art replied, leaning back and folding his arms over his ample belly.

They were in his grey-carpeted office at the *Herald*, the door behind her open to the drone of the newsroom and Emmanuelle's former colleagues clacking at their keyboards and whispering to each other. Probably about her.

You cut the volunteer's quotes, she said. That school he went to Ghana to build never even opened.

You don't know that for sure, Art said.

Then why aren't they bragging about it on their website?

They were interrupted by an employee collecting for the weekly 50/50 draw. As Art scrounged for change, Emmanuelle squinted at the new hire. Intern? Cub reporter? Her replacement? She'd been out of work for months, and things were tense at home. An accidental purchase of organic apples the day before (Emmanuelle's fault) had triggered Ben's anxiety, sending him into a budgeting frenzy that led to a tailspin about the future—they'd never afford a house let alone kids and would die childless and abandoned, not even in the discomfort of a nursing home, which was far too expensive, but here in this crappy rental—and ended with him begging her to quit journalism and get *literally any job that pays*.

To distract herself, she examined Art's office, which was decked out in CONCERN paraphernalia. The *Herald*'s vice-president was on the board of the local chapter, and the newspaper ran an annual employee campaign. A month of time-wasting distraction in the form of raffles and games.

Got it, Art said, counting out quarters and exchanging them for a ticket.

Emmanuelle didn't miss this part of her old job: the employer's fingers in her pocket, skimming her meagre salary to pad the coffers of the VP's pet charity.

When they were alone again, Emmanuelle gestured to the donation jar on Art's desk and said, If the paper believes in the cause so much, why don't they make giving a line item in the budget?

You're the Scrooge who doesn't add two bucks to your grocery bill at the till, aren't you? Art said.

Why should Robertsons get the credit for my donation? Emmanuelle asked. We wouldn't even need food banks if they didn't price gouge.

Art barked a laugh. Touché.

Does that mean you'll let me keep the picket fence?

LinkedIn sleuthing had led Emmanuelle to a former employee who'd filled her in on this particular folly. Children of the World had sent a team to Indonesia to erect a wooden fence, something the locals neither wanted nor needed. The village had living fences: plants as barriers, trees that bloomed fragrant red and pink flowers that were poisonous to vermin and attracted birds, bees, and butterflies that were industrious pollinators. Children of the World insisted on white pickets.

All because Crispin wanted to leave his mark with something quintessentially quote-unquote Canadian, Emmanuelle said. When was the last time you even saw a picket fence? In my neighbourhood, it's all chain-link.

Art tapped the arm of his spectacles against his teeth, watching her. She felt emboldened to continue. Unbridled optimism, that's Crispin's problem, she said. But all his piddly relief projects are band-aids. What difference can they make in the face of a total systems failure?

What's the story? You and Crispin go way back or something?

R & B is more my jam, she joked.

Art pointed his glasses at the red-penned pages in her hand and said, The tone seems personal.

He's a type, she said. Children of the World is a type. Absolute certainty underpinned by great globs of ignorance. And a dash of good intention, whatever that's worth.

Lifestyle section. Weekend edition, Art said. I warned you about having an agenda.

She flapped the pages over his desk. Whose agenda is this? I did notice the *Herald* and Children of the World share a board director.

Art pressed his teeth together and shook his head. Dog with a bone. I mean that as a compliment.

She leaned forward, elbows on knees. Then let me keep digging. This one's for lifestyle. Fine. But there's an investigative piece here too. Something a hell of a lot more interesting. Okay, I couldn't get confirmation on Ghana. Yet. But in Sierra Leone, they built a clinic they never opened and broke ground on an orphanage they didn't finish.

How on earth—

I talked to a doctor in Freetown, she said. Their volunteer model works fine for places like Santa Rosa and India, but it falls apart in less stable regions. And once they can't sell trips, they pull up stakes and leave. No explanation. No apology. They abandoned Sierra Leone just as the Ebola epidemic was beginning, when health care was most desperately needed.

You've really got a source on the ground? Art said.

Multiple sources. And photos.

Art's bifocals were now perched on the end of his nose. I'm listening.

Emmanuelle thrilled. She was sure there was a long read here, maybe even a multipart series.

I've seen their donor reports, she said. They're double- and triple-selling naming rights to schools, clinics, orphanages, inflating the numbers.

You think, or you're sure?

She exhaled. The numbers are murky, purposefully so.

So that's a no. What else?

There's something else in Jakarta, she said, then repeated the ugly story her source had shared about certain volunteers who were frequent fliers, too intent on the children, and a country director who looked the other way.

Empty gossip or skeleton in a shallow grave? he asked.

I'm working to corroborate, she said. I have a lead. But the country director was fired so obviously—

It's old news, Art finished.

Obviously, it's true, she corrected. I suspect—

Suspicion is not fact. And reporting it as such is libel.

Give me time, and I'll get the facts, she said. But she could see that just saying the word *libel* had alarmed him.

Emmanuelle, you're a cynic.

Compliment? Thank you.

He doffed an imaginary cap at her and continued, This business with the volunteers and the kids, what are the odds most, some . . . maybe all? foreign NGOs have a similar story in their vaults?

I'd take that bet, she said, recalling Crispin's self-satisfied air, the casual arrogance he mistook for virtue. But Crispin—

If every charity does this, if Children of the World is only a type, and a minor player at that, why single them out? Are they significantly worse than all the others? What's the hook?

Isn't it damning enough that even this small-time charity can wreak so much havoc . . . She trailed off. Art was already turning toward his monitor.

Send me your invoice, he said, waving a dismissive hand toward the exit. It's a good piece, Emmanuelle. Under all the sarcasm.

It's pronounced *journalism*, she muttered under her breath but only when she was safely in the elevator, having slunk through the newsroom, coat wrapped around her, collar popped up like a shield.

For a couple of months, Emmanuelle kept reporting out leads and pitching stories, spurred by indignation and injured pride. Late in January, she got a bite. *The Bullhorn* was a podcast with a small audience, but the host was eager to have her on. At first, it was just to talk about the abandoned construction projects; but when the episode generated chatter in a niche corner of the internet, he extended another invitation to discuss corporate philanthropy more generally.

You follow the money and see how deep the rot goes, she said. Multinationals swoop into a foreign country and extract natural resources at low cost. They union bust. Exploit child labour. Manipulate every loophole and get exemptions on paying domestic taxes. Trade misinvoicing and transfer misplacing practices, unregulated tax havens—

The host leaned back in his chair and held up his hands. Woah. Woah. Woah. What *is* all that?

She pointed the eraser end of a pencil at him, enjoying herself, and replied, Complex accounting trickery.

But even as she was speaking these words, she was hearing her own ire and sarcasm, and another, more critical voice in her head (which sounded suspiciously like Art) warned that she was tarnishing her credibility as a journalist just by being on this podcast and confirming everything her detractors called her. Angry. Biased. Unprofessional.

They're cooking the books, the host bellowed.

And Emmanuelle startled, recalling Art's warning about libel. No. No, she cried.

The host looked astonished by her vehemence, and she said more calmly: A lot of what I'm describing is legal. Unethical of course, but perfectly legal.

The game is rigged, she continued. Governments in the developing world are cheated out of what's rightfully theirs. And when their coffers are drained, of course they can't afford schools and so on. Enter the white saviour.

The host was white but so thoroughly invested in being an ally she knew he wouldn't flinch.

Sounds like plutocracy, he said.

It's a threat to a nation's democracy when the people calling the shots and deciding how to solve a country's biggest problems are outsiders with deep pockets and no stake in the outcome, she said.

The host, who'd been about to speak, shut his mouth abruptly. He twisted an imaginary light bulb over his head, then said: Wow. Listeners, take a moment to process what Emmanuelle's saying because it's deep. Philanthropy can threaten a country's very sovereignty.

I know it sounds extreme, Emmanuelle said, thinking of her time at the *Herald* and how she had to cushion every subversive idea in ten feet of bubble wrap. But the wealthy get fixated on things that aren't important to locals. Take Children of the World. They distributed mosquito nets when women asked for contraception. They partnered with a tech company that had spare laptops, so they shipped them to a village in Cameroon that doesn't have electricity. They flew volunteers to Kinshasa to build houses for thirty grand a pop instead of hiring locals who would have done the work for a thousand.

And this is just one minor charity, the host said. We aren't even talking about what the bigger guys are getting up to.

Interventions should be dictated by local needs, not foreign whims, Emmanuelle said. Of course what locals want more than anything is their due. But overhauling the system is difficult. Promising infrastructure you never build is easy.

BOOM! the host roared. Mic drop.

—

On the bus home, Emmanuelle was writing a stranger in Jakarta, someone whose employment at Children of the World had overlapped with the former country director, when Ben called.

He's selling the house, he announced before she could say hello.

He's not selling the house, Emmanuelle replied.

Emmanuelle and Ben had been renting a bungalow in Scarborough for over a decade. They had rent control in a marginally gentrifying neighbourhood, which was both a blessing and a curse.

We'll be priced out of the city, he moaned.

Ben spiralled, and Emmanuelle's guilt went along for the ride. Every January, their landlord floated the idea of selling, a perverse new year's resolution he always forgot by spring. Even Ben was generally Zen about it, but Emmanuelle hadn't made a paycheque since that feature on Crispin two months earlier and Ben was certain that this time the landlord meant business.

We're gonna be on the street, he said.

That won't happen. But if it makes you feel better, I'll scope out some rentals, she replied. It was important to remain calm when Ben got in this state.

It would make me feel better if you scoped out some jobs. Instead of doing whatever it is you've been doing.

Ouch, she whispered. But he didn't apologize.

Emmanuelle pressed her forehead against the seat in front of her as the bus jostled along. She fretted this crusade (Ben's word, not hers; Art's word, too, probably) was a colossal waste of time, a wild goose chase she'd undertaken as a distraction from her floundering career.

Where's it all going? he asked gently. All the research you're doing, what's the end goal?

Maybe it's a book, she joked, thinking of the files crowding her desk, stuffed with interview notes and academic articles, background reading on foreign policy and international aid.

In J-school, Emmanuelle's favourite professor had predicted she'd write a book one day, declaring her one-track mind and obsessive nature well suited to long-form. It was an old and secret ambition, one she hadn't nurtured long.

Emm, Ben said finally. Just give me a date. Please. Can you do that? Set a timer, and I'll shut up about it.

March first, she said quietly. And then I'll get a job as an Amazon drone or an Uber driver.

We don't have a car, he said.

I'll steal a car and drive for Uber. Or I'll steal cars for a living. That's definitely more lucrative.

They chuckled together in unspoken apology, and for a moment it felt like everything might be okay, but then she was off the phone and back on the chilly bus with her dark thoughts and the man at the back screaming obscenities in staccato.

She sent the email to Jakarta, without hope of a reply. Why would anyone confide in her, a perfect stranger who didn't even have a byline in an outlet of record? Emmanuelle felt like a fraud, taking advantage of her sources' generosity and time, their faith in her. She kept hearing Art in her head insisting none of this was newsworthy or timely. Worse, that it was driven by personal vendetta.

Idly checking on Children of the World's website, she was surprised to find there was news. They were throwing a party at their new office and hyping a special guest: the country director from their star project in Santa Rosa.

Emmanuelle pursed her lips. She had a fizz of premonition, thinking of the email she'd just sent. A long shot, but *what if* it was the same guy? Moving predators around like chess pieces, hiding them in plain sight—it was the oldest trick in the book. No, she thought, that was unlikely. Still, there might be some other angle. She'd sniffed out Crispin's trail of destruction in Africa and Asia. She'd bet there was one in Central America too.

She flicked over to Dallas Hayden's Instagram account, something she'd been avoiding because the adoption made her sad: that parents would be in a position where surrendering a beloved child was the best option. Dallas's most recent post was celebratory: one of the movies she'd starred in had been nominated for a slew of Oscars. Emmanuelle had to scroll and scroll before she finally found a still of the baby, buried under layers of newer photos and Reels. Was it suspicious, or was Emmanuelle desperate and grasping? She frowned out the window at the grey sleety sidewalks and tapped the phone on her knee. The first of March was four weeks away.

New Money

Lucca

The phone rang just as Lucca was slipping a passport into his backpack. When he flew north, he liked to travel in the guise of a U.S. citizen. Seeing his brother's name, Lucca sank into his chair and took a breath before answering.

Paolo's voice was scratched vinyl. Papai has passed, he said. Ten minutes ago.

Lucca focused on a corner of his desk where he'd constructed a tidy pyramid: novel, rolled-up compression socks, wallet. Ten minutes ago, he'd been finalizing staff assignments, typing names next to shifts and feeling the particular satisfaction of achieving a perfectly balanced schedule, and finally having a full staff complement to make this possible. Ten minutes ago, the electrician had dropped in with his bill, rubbing a sheepish hand along the back of his neck as Lucca praised his work and paid in cash. Ten minutes ago, he'd been savouring the upcoming break from the straitjacket of management, six weeks of inhabiting an easygoing version of himself and the high probability of finding a casual dalliance with a convenient end date. Ten minutes ago, he had *not* been thinking of his father.

The service is tomorrow, Paolo said. Mamãe wants us together.

It came as a surprise that he could no longer recall his father's face. Not really, not the precise details of eye shape and jawline. It was his overall form Lucca remembered. The bear looming, throwing his shadow. The deep bass of his voice. The roar of expletives.

I'm flying to Toronto tonight, Lucca said in Portuguese. For work.

Make a detour, Paolo said in English, that Etonian accent, another morsel of shared history.

In the background Lucca heard the hubbub—sobbing and distressed voices. The funeral would be a seven-day spectacle. Lucca couldn't work himself up to it, the effort of playing along or hiding his contempt.

Ten a.m. at the cathedral, Paolo said, still in English. Open casket.

Cancer consumed its victims. But when Lucca pictured the coffin, it was the grizzly in hearty middle age that he imagined. Nestled in velvet, hands folded over his chest, the heavy square rings that covered his knuckles, poised to strike.

Paolo, this is a sad day for you, Lucca said in Portuguese. I am sorry.

No, Lucca, his brother said. I'm the one who is sorry. If you change your mind, your family is here.

After the call, Lucca paced his office, grief ricocheting, threatening to break loose. His hands trembled, and he squeezed them together. Ambient sounds—a crow cawing, the ticking clock, volunteers talking as they passed his door—merged into a droning hum. His vision tunnelled, focusing on the duffle bag against the wall, the backpack slouched on top, one corner of his passport poking out of the front pocket. He had an instinct to grab his things and run.

But the car that was taking him to the airport wasn't due for another couple of hours. He had to give Thiago final instructions. There were finances to log and calls to make. The room shrank. Claustrophobic, he bolted.

It was midday, and the corridors were blessedly deserted. Turning into the children's wing, he heard the murmur of adult voices. Eager for distraction, he headed their way. Approaching one of the boys' rooms, he saw Luis and Yolanda. Her back to the door, Yolanda was speaking in rapid and emphatic Spanish, her voice suppressed but punctuated from time to time by an audible word or phrase. Vaguely, Lucca registered she was upset.

. . . nothing we can do, Yolanda said.

Luis shook his head in frustrated agreement. His reply was a low rumble.

That is the worst of . . . Yolanda said before her words dipped out of earshot.

Luis glanced up and startled, halting mid-sentence as Lucca's stomach sank.

I'm interrupting, he said, frozen in the doorway.

This wasn't the first private conference he'd stumbled upon or overheard through a closed door. The staff were freezing him out. Even the raises he'd announced at the start of the year hadn't helped.

We are speaking of personal matters, Luis said, and Lucca was injured by the lie.

Yolanda moved to one of the bunks and worked with a rote efficiency, snapping sheets, jerking cases off pillows, and flinging bundles into a wheeled laundry basket. Yolanda ruled the dormitory with more tenderness than discipline; even the older boys called her mami. Lucca watched her, feeling shut out from her affection for the first time. His hurt grew spikes.

Overhead the ceiling fans turned lazily, circulating the smell of bleach from a nearby bucket and the heady, earthy aroma of animal skin that Luis had carried in from the farm.

It's much cooler in here with the fans working, Lucca said, then added to Luis, Your brother-in-law has done a good job with the electrical repairs.

He's grateful for the business, Luis said, head bowed to hide his expression, revealing only a crown of thinning hair.

I'm grateful to *him*, Lucca said, suppressing his aggravation. What was worse: Luis's obsequiousness or Yolanda's passive aggression?

Moisés says he's seeing an eye specialist in the capital, Yolanda said, her tone suspicious.

In March, Lucca said. Juan arranged it.

There was a deflated soccer ball under the bed she was changing, and Lucca realized this must be Moisés's bunk. There was something poignant about the sight of the abandoned toy, collapsed on the floor.

Someone has to go with him, Yolanda said, rolling her basket to the next set of bunks. He's scared.

Lucca was taken aback. Moisés had been excited when Lucca had shared the good news. He was about to say as much, then checked himself, wondering if the child had revealed something different—more honest—to Yolanda.

Instead, he said: I'm taking him. Of course he can't make the trip alone.

Then it's all settled, she said.

The sight of Yolanda's broad back, her stubborn avoidance of him, made Lucca want to fire her on the spot, teach her a lesson. This was a familiar dangerous rage, and he closed his eyes for a moment, struggling to master it.

I was in Pueblo Bonito yesterday, he said finally, keeping his voice level. Have you seen our new school? We'll need teachers, a principal, and uniforms soon.

Uniforms, Yolanda repeated, finally turning to meet his gaze.

Do you have recommendations? Lucca asked, knowing her sister-in-law was a seamstress.

I know a man who would make a good principal, Luis said. He's a very senior teacher, has a lot of experience.

Good, Lucca said. We need qualified people, and we can afford to pay them fairly. The actress's generosity has inspired others.

We must use their gifts well, Luis said, talking once more to his shoes.

When Yolanda spoke, her voice was anguished: All this new money. But at what cost?

Since Maria's departure, Lucca had consoled himself with the thought that the Garcias had made their decision. Whether by enticement or coercion, the means were none of his business. But the speed of Dallas's donation—its astonishing sum!—was unsettling.

Now Yolanda's expression was imploring, begging Lucca not with recrimination but for an answer. *What have we done?* And somehow this was worse than blame, the implication that his actions had made his staff complicit in a crime.

Lucca backed out, holding onto the sides of the doorway. He was not the ethics commissioner. His job was to ensure the compound's viability.

I'll be at Head Office for the next few weeks, Lucca said. Thiago is in charge.

Outside, the air was muggy with late-afternoon heat, the sun on its descent. It was the tail end of January, and the temperature would be below freezing in Toronto. Anya had surprised him by suggesting a six-week visit to Head Office, musing that it would be a good trial run for the staff to manage on their own. Now that their fundraising was on an upswing, Anya suddenly seemed anxious to offload her pet project.

We'll map out a timeline while you're here, she'd said. Let's make it ambitious but realistic. This side of Anya was new to him—upbeat and affirmative, brimming with optimism. Start thinking about your next move, she'd joked. We're going to make ourselves redundant.

These days, conversations with Head Office were collegial, even pleasant. What Lucca heard under every lighthearted quip was an apology. And it piqued him. What good was their contrition? It couldn't be traded for his staff's esteem. He could only hope that his absence would dull their resentment and pacify the monster in his chest. This brute was not his own. It belonged to his father, a hereditary weakness Lucca fastidiously kept in check. Yet here was the patriarch, reaching out from the afterlife, pulling his strings.

Lucca left the building feeling jittery and high-strung. But when his feet turned in the direction of the clinic, he felt his body calming. It was a club foot day, and the atmosphere was busy. He'd reinstated the program as soon as Dallas's donation arrived. One call to the health ministry, an afternoon of paperwork, and they'd been assigned an orthopedic officer. Thiago had been dispatched to spread the word, and soon they were inundated and had to expand to a second day. Infants with sickled feet. Toddlers who crawled. Children perambulating in impossible configurations: toes pointing backward or insteps spun so far that they walked on the tops of their feet. Some hobbled or lurched, but more often, their contortions were proficient, their gait hardly notable.

Lucca had assigned Beatriz to act as administrator. When he arrived, she was explaining the procedure to a couple whose child waited on the bench, whispering secrets to her doll.

The foot is cramped like this, Beatriz said, fisting her hand. At your daughter's age, it's easy to correct. Every week the specialist stretches the muscles and applies a cast. Slowly, slowly. Little by little. She straightened the bones of a plastic skeleton and said, Over time the foot relaxes into the correct position.

She *can* walk, the mother said.

But not quickly, the father argued. And it hurts her.

If you do nothing, her feet will become more bent and painful, Beatriz said.

At this warning, the girl began humming and clutched her doll closer. Fishing in his pocket, Lucca found a penny. Catching the child's attention, he revealed an empty hand, then slipped it behind her ear to produce the coin. She grinned, delighted.

Beatriz pointed to a boy who, cast-free, was leaving the clinic with a brace, toes parallel as train tracks, and said, In time that could be your daughter.

The father tugged on his handlebar moustache. We don't have much money.

Everything here is free, Beatriz said.

The mother scoffed. Nothing in this world is free.

This is, señora, Lucca said, cutting in. As director here, I can assure you. And your daughter's feet will be perfect, as if there was never a problem.

The woman was a head shorter, but when she clapped her eyes on him, looking him up and down, Lucca felt small. She said something to her husband, speaking in a dialect he didn't understand, though he caught the word *outsider* and was stung with embarrassment.

It's a cure, her husband urged in Spanish.

Fine, the mother said finally. But if this goes badly—

Impossible, Beatriz said and gave her a number.

When she turned in search of the next patient, her whole face aglow with satisfaction, Lucca caught her eye. *I love this job*, her expression thrilled. *We're changing lives*. He felt her pleasure second-hand, and for a moment they were confederates, delighted by joint success. But almost immediately Beatriz seemed to recall who he was and scowled. Swivelling away, she barked, Who's next?

Lucca slinked off to the treatment area, which was cordoned behind a wheeled curtain. They'd set up a folding table with a foam pad and a cloth spread over top. Here a wailing boy was being restrained by his mother while the orthopedic officer worked on his foot, thumb on the instep, moulding the plaster with quick, gentle strokes.

The medic was a young man with square glasses and a neat off-centre part. He wore an apron and bent to his task, winding strips around the patient's leg, chalky plaster dripping wetly off his rubber gloves.

There is absolutely no force, he assured the wincing mother. We can do this for you too.

And Lucca noticed her stance: left foot straight, right one turned. Her little twisted foot.

A voice asked, Does it give you much pain?

Lucca turned to see Juan at his side, stethoscope folded in the pocket of his white coat.

At least my son won't suffer, she said. I cried for days when he was born.

Lucca was reminded of his words to Inez—*your daughter need not suffer*. He'd assiduously been avoiding all news of Maria but assumed she was having this same treatment in California.

The orthopedic officer urged the mother to consider treatment. You're only twenty-six, he said. You don't have to live like this.

Juan pulled Luca aside. We need a physiotherapist, he said. The small ones are fine, but if we start treating older patients, they'll require more aftercare.

A few months ago, Juan would have said *it would be nice to have* . . . if he'd ventured to ask for anything at all. Now it was *we need*, *the clinic needs*, *what the patients really need*—

I'll get you a physiotherapist, Lucca said.

Morale is strong, Juan said, as they made a circuit of the clinic.

All around, staff bustled with renewed vigour. Even the calibre of volunteers had improved. The current lot included an emergency nurse and a doctor who specialized in tropical medicine. The latter was fluent in Spanish, and from over the din, Lucca could just make out her accented voice, speaking to a patient. Standing here, it was possible to believe he'd done the right thing.

Beatriz joined them, stretching her arms and turning her head from side to side. She made an elongated sound halfway between a sigh and a groan.

Long day? Juan asked.

Good day, she replied.

You're leaving for Toronto tonight? Juan asked Lucca.

They'll be pleased to hear about our progress, Lucca said. You have a physiotherapist in mind?

Juan gave a curt nod. I know two or three, but we'll see who's best.

We have money for everything it seems, Beatriz said. And yet there are things which cannot be bought.

Lucca's father used to say, You can bribe a man to do anything but respect you.

His funeral would be standing room only, packed with employees past and present who, despite their grievances, were loyal to the last. Because for all his faults, Maurício da Silva kept his people employed.

You like your new job? Lucca asked Beatriz, his voice steely.

Beatriz's eyes widened, flickering with uncertainty.

You like this clinic? You like what we do here? he asked, and she squeaked, taking a tiny step back, then another. He went on: You like your salary? Your husband's salary?

He was possessed of an eerie calm, a resolve that required no second thought or pity. He was on the verge of firing her when a voice cut in.

Boss.

The word was an exorcism, snapping Lucca back to himself. He saw his own shock mirrored in Beatriz's expression and then, just as quickly, her revulsion. What had he done?

Boss, Thiago repeated urgently.

His surroundings came into focus, the clinic's hubbub, his second-in-command suddenly materialized at his elbow, worry knitting his brow. He was too flustered to make amends, and there was no time because Thiago, in a low voice, was saying, Señor Garcia is here, and when Lucca startled, he added: Take care. The man is drunk.

Outside, Lucca heard the commotion and hurried toward the compound's entrance where the tall gates stood open and Jorge, vociferous, ranted at the guard. When he reached into his pocket—for a weapon?—Lucca broke into a run. But reaching the guard's hut, he saw it was only a magazine gripped in Jorge's fist. Close-up he could hear it was fury, not drink, that garbled the man's speech until it frothed incoherently.

Spotting Lucca, Jorge pushed the magazine into his face—the Spanish edition of one of those celebrity rags. Lucca had seen this issue, though he hadn't bothered reading it. Dallas and Maria were on the cover.

Why is this woman claiming my child is hers? Jorge demanded. She's calling Maria by some other name, but I know my daughter.

Lucca winced, walloped by a memory: Dallas in the exact spot Jorge now stood, Maria strapped to her.

The guard reached for the baton at his hip, but Lucca gave a slight shake of his head. Jorge was a couple of inches shorter. One foot behind his ankle, a forceful push, and Lucca could trip him backward. But it wouldn't come to that. Jorge wasn't here for a wrestling match.

I don't know what agreement you came to, Lucca said. But if you want something else, you must contact her lawyers.

He heard the staccato of Maria's cries, the tremble in her vocal cords, and the desperate gasping breaths that punctuated each screaming jag.

Who are the lawyers? Jorge asked, flapping the magazine, the wet of his breath spraying Lucca's face. There are no lawyers. There is only you and that one there, a pair of snakes who came and filled my wife's ears with your lies. You stole our Maria. Give her back. I demand you give her back.

It had been a wail of protest, not desolation, Lucca realized, Maria shrieking in vain to be understood and have her own way, her complaints mounting in pitch and frequency as they went unheeded.

Be calm, Lucca said. Be still. Let me understand. After I spoke to you, did anyone else come? They would have brought papers, agreements, something for you to sign.

Idiot, Jorge said. Who comes to see us in the mountains?

The ugly truth he'd been eliding dropped into Lucca's stomach like a rock. Yolanda's words in his ear: *At what cost?* He'd let it happen, forced Thiago to open the gates and made the whole compound watch. He'd allowed Dallas to *take* a baby, helped her kidnap the Garcias' beloved child.

How could you do this? Jorge shouted, gesturing to include Thiago and the guard in his indictment.

Don't blame them, Lucca said, pleading. They've done nothing.

Have you no children? Have you no heart? Jorge hit the air with the rolled-up magazine, a futile vent for his rage. Why? Why did you do this to us?

Because I am a coward, Lucca did not say. Because it was the path of least resistance.

Let Jorge hit and punch and kick him; Lucca would endure the punishment gladly. He would flay himself alive, anything to escape his body, the prison of culpability. Instead, Jorge howled, a cry of helpless agony. His anger was spent, carried away in the hot breeze.

Lucca's voice caught in his throat. He croaked out a sob before swallowing it down. I-I am going now to-to meet with my bosses, he stuttered, fumbling for platitudes. They will see what can be done.

You promised to bring Maria back, Jorge said, quietly now. He held his hands out, a gesture of supplication.

I— Lucca broke off, at a loss for what to say. What use was an apology? It would not magic the girl back. He rubbed a hand over his mouth, staring at the space between the open gates through which he'd allowed Maria to be taken, her bawling turning to despair, the sound wounded and pitiful.

Maria is my daughter, Jorge told the ground. My only daughter.

Real Hero

Claire

The afternoon of the open house, everyone was keyed up, giddy about their fancy new digs and the still-novel feeling of being flush. They had ended the old year on a high note, and a month into the new one, the donations and sponsorships were still streaming in.

It was five, and the team was rearranging furniture, setting out name tags, arranging flowers, and tidying away the flotsam and jetsam of the move.

Everything unsightly into the copy room, Anya called, hefting a stack of flattened cardboard boxes under her.

Better stash me in there too, Crispin joked, making Anya laugh.

Oh, but you've cleaned up so nice, she said. What do the rest of you think? Should we let Cinderella stay for the ball?

Claire was on a stepladder, pinning media clips to a corkboard. Emmanuelle's profile on Crispin was at the centre. It had headlined the weekend section just before the holidays, a splashy three-page feature with full-colour photos. Everyone said it was great publicity, but Claire had been attuned to Emmanuelle's sneering subtext.

The feature began with Crispin's childhood in rural Saskatchewan. Back then, he'd been Robert Gurski, and she charted his transformation from quiet oddball to global star. A musician-slash-humanitarian, Crispin cut a messianic figure, Emmanuelle wrote. Claire had scowled at the word *messianic* and its sarcastic innuendo, but Crispin had brushed it off. The article was too laudatory, too much of the word count dedicated to Children of the World, for him to be a spoilsport. Still, Claire suspected the overall tenor was Art Whylie's doing, his judicious red ink editing away the hit piece Emmanuelle had really wanted to publish.

Claire, I've moved your easels into the corner, Anya said.

These were for displaying the new promotional art. For the last couple of months, Claire and the ad agency had been going full tilt on the #realhero campaign—scheduling photo shoots, writing scripts, and filming ads. No one could believe how quickly they'd pulled it off, but Dallas had been eager, rightly pointing out that they had to capitalize on the spotlight before it faded.

I told you things move fast in Hollywood, Crispin had said.

The visuals were spectacular. Dallas and two of her fellow Sentinels in superhero garb that matched Children of the World's branding and colours. Next week, they'd be projected on electronic billboards in a dozen North American cities. Claire had put in a rush order for a couple of blow-ups to give their guests a sneak peek.

A notification alerted her that the art was en route from the printer, and she took the dolly down to the lobby. Fifteen minutes later, she was impatiently glancing at the time when, through the plate-glass windows, she saw a man approach. He had curly dark hair and a tan, hands hidden in the deep pockets of an open wool coat, a leather messenger bag slung crossbody. He strode in with a rakish, rumpled air of entitlement that made Claire guess he belonged to one of the tech start-ups in the building, whose founders Crispin had invited to the open house.

I'm looking for Children of the World, he said.

You're a little early, she replied, offering her most appealing smile.

I think I'm late, he said, his wide expressive mouth turning up into a smirk as he said the word *late*. Hello Claire, he said, holding her gaze and extending a hand.

The mysterious Lucca, she said. We meet at last.

Resentment had made her incurious, and if she'd pictured Lucca at all, it was always as one of those midlife men who'd aged poorly—paunchy and balding with a pompous goatee or broken capillaries reddening a large nose.

Am I mysterious? he asked, his grip warm.

I was starting to think you were a figment of our imaginations. A mass delusion.

Maybe I am, he teased, squeezing, then releasing, her hand. Maybe this conversation is happening in your head.

Here's the courier, she said when a van pulled up outside. Finally.

But will he see me? Lucca asked.

The poster boards were five feet tall and wrapped in brown paper. The delivery guy rolled them in on a handcart. I need your signature, he said.

Let me make sure they're correct.

Claire ripped off the covering on the first one to reveal Dallas, expression resolute, hands on hips, cape fluttering. Children of the World's name and logo were printed underneath, along with the campaign's tagline: *Become a #realhero*.

That's her alright, Lucca said.

Okay, boss? the courier asked, holding out the digital terminal to Claire.

Yes. Thanks, she said, scrawling her finger over the screen.

The courier turned to leave, and Lucca bumped her arm, whispering, He didn't notice me.

His breath was warm and tickled her ear, sparking a shiver in her belly that rippled down. Her body's disloyalty was vexing, and she was perplexed by Lucca's lighthearted bantering. Was he flirting or making fun of her?

Together, they loaded the poster boards onto the dolly and summoned the elevator. The lift that arrived was narrow. In the close quarters, she could smell his soap—sharp and invigorating with the chlorophyll scent of pine and rough bark—and guessed it had recently been lathered on.

Little cramped in here, he said, as they began to rise.

Self-conscious, she turned away and found herself staring directly at Dallas in her superhero getup. It suddenly struck her as frivolous—all the capes and spandex.

Lucca patted the top of Dallas's head and said: Just the three of us. Very cozy.

It was a relief to arrive upstairs and have Crispin carry Lucca off, leaving Claire to deal with her two-dimensional superheroes.

A couple of hours later, the party was in full swing. Claire circulated, paying special attention to the media guests: bloggers and micro-influencers who were active in the non-profit space and volunteers with strong TikTok followings. She was surprised at how effortlessly Anya worked the room, as charismatic in this crowd as Crispin, and impressed by their tandem manoeuvres, a subtle gesture by one spurring the other to immediate action.

We're sending them to India next, Anya boasted to a man with a white moustache. The office joker, breezing by, muttered to Claire, Her former boss from when she was at CONCERN. And Claire overheard Anya add: They're taking a film crew and making a documentary. We're calling the campaign #realhero.

Clever, the man said. Your idea?

Anya hummed and sipped her drink, but Claire was too distracted to begrudge her. Even as she was swapping small talk with donors and board members, she was paying attention to Lucca, straining to hear him. He was talking about his former life in disaster zones, and their guests were lapping it up, everyone a little star-struck by this international do-gooder with his dishevelled glamour.

Lucca was reminiscing about his time in the DRC as Claire edged her way into the circle of listeners. He'd been based in an eastern town called Bukavu. It was right on the border, Rwanda to its east, on the edge of a lake that was perpetually in danger of erupting. Vast quantities of carbon dioxide and methane dissolved under the surface that could blow at any moment, trigger a tsunami, and obliterate the two million people nearby. The way he described it made Claire feel like she was there, wading in herself and feeling the water's warmth and false stillness.

This was back in '05, at the start of my career, he said.

The NGO he'd been with ran an orphanage. They'd convinced a pharmaceutical company to donate a huge cache of medical supplies, but it had taken Lucca months to wrangle the shipment across the border. In the meantime, he'd made himself useful, rolling up his sleeves and pitching in where he could. Hanging laundry on the line, hauling water. He was a great favourite with the kids who were taken with his novelty. They called him muzungu, the Swahili word for Caucasian.

Not that I'm white, he said offhandedly, in a way that made Claire tilt her head to one side and clock his features more closely. Did he mean because he was from Brazil?

Lucca said the orphanage mainly rehabilitated child soldiers, but they housed little girls too. Some had lost both parents in the war; others had been denounced as witches and cast out by their families.

Witches? Jim Whalen from Robertsons asked. You're joking.

A mother dies. A father remarries. The stepmother wants nothing to do with the first wife's children, Lucca said. Or both parents die and now a relative is in charge. Another mouth to feed when they haven't got enough for their own. The girls were told they caused the bad luck.

Jim appeared appalled, but Lucca shook his head. It's not our place to judge. These people, they've seen things we can't imagine.

Claire pictured Lake Kivu, burping a noxious concoction of gasses. Yes, she thought. She couldn't empathize, not really, but she could understand. Claire and Lucca were around the same age, mid-forties or thereabouts, she guessed, and yet he seemed so much wiser, like he'd already lived several lives. More than once, she caught him watching her. He didn't avert his gaze, just smiled like it was a secret they were in on together. She had to remind herself this was the same man who had been ignoring her emails for over a year, that he was stubborn and intractable and if he'd had his way, they wouldn't be in this #blessed position at all.

Scrupulously, she slipped away to join a group of her colleagues at the far end of the office, only to find them gossiping about the newcomer.

Are we sure this guy's Lucca? Claire joked. I was expecting more cantankerous curmudgeon than life of the party.

You know who he is right? the events manager asked.

Yeah. He's the country director with the email allergy, Claire said, trying and failing to resurrect her resentment.

The events manager claimed Lucca's father had started Latin America's largest media conglomerate. The family were billionaires, the eldest brother the twenty-sixth richest person in the world.

No way, the intern said.

Yes, way. His dad just died. The obit's everywhere.

Then what's Lucca doing here and not at the funeral? Claire asked. Da Silva was a common enough name, and he certainly didn't seem to be grieving.

You're telling me a billionaire wears an off-the-rack suit? the finance director said, shooting a glance at Lucca, who was shovelling cheese puffs like he hadn't eaten in days.

Off someone else's rack, more like, the office joker, said. He looks like he raided his older brother's closet or something.

Crispin had shepherded Lucca to a nearby group, executives from an illustrious B Corp, one of those companies that promised to donate a tablet for every one purchased. Their CEO had just returned from the World Economic Forum, and Crispin was gunning for him to join the board. Earlier, Anya had joked that what Crispin *really* wanted was an invite to Davos.

Now, Claire eavesdropped on their conversation about Ebola. Lucca had been in West Africa during the most recent outbreak. No, he hadn't been worried. Not particularly. When your time was up, it was up.

Meanwhile, the events manager was narrating Lucca's supposed history. Born in Rio but raised all over. Switzerland. England. Boarding schools mostly. Degrees from Cambridge and Columbia. His mother was Italian, a former model for Versace. They howled at that, said now she really was pulling their legs. Claire joined in on the laughter, two seconds late. Lucca glanced toward them, his face a question, his eyes on hers alone. She coughed and ducked her head to cover her confusion.

Talk turned to the Oscars. No one could believe Dallas had been snubbed.

I know, Claire said. It's absurd.

Dallas had been brilliant, utterly luminous, in her starring role, and Claire had taken a best actress nomination as a given. The list, when it was announced, was an unpleasant surprise. Four nods for the film—best script, director, editing, *supporting* actress—but nothing for Dallas.

You carried that movie, Claire had messaged. *You were robbed!* She'd continued in this vein for some length, outraged for her friend and, it must be admitted, disappointed on Children of the World's behalf. She'd shot the text off without much thought and been met with silence. Immediately, Claire second-guessed herself, rereading her words and cringing. Why had she gone off like that? Did Dallas think Claire was criticizing the other cast and crew? Why had Claire assumed the actress would want to cry on her shoulder? She should have been more circumspect or professional or said nothing at all. Instead, she'd crossed the line and put Dallas in the bind of having to respond.

The reply when it finally arrived—*Four noms! The little film that could!*—felt like a rebuke. She regretted her pettiness, that she'd even suspected Dallas's impatience over the #realhero ads were fuelled by anxiety for her Oscar campaign.

How's Dallas taking it? the finance director asked.

Oh. She's a professional. Actors and rejections. It's all part of the job.

She hasn't posted about the baby in a while, the intern said, pocketing their phone.

Claire had noticed the absence, too, with surprise. The most recent photo—sleeping cherub in a beam of sunlight, thumb in mouth—was from two weeks earlier. Since then, there had been only selfies and promotional stills. It was a relief, in a way. Dallas's mothering sometimes made her feel worse about her own.

The events manager said she didn't think children should be on social media anyway. It was a question of consent, something minors couldn't rightly give. She wondered if Dallas was having second thoughts about the overexposure.

She probably has creepy stalkers, Claire said. She wished they would talk about something else. Since her faux pas (was it a faux pas?), Dallas hadn't texted. She longed to return to their former rhythm of mutual commiseration and support.

Look who's here, the finance director said, poking Claire in the arm.

It was Emmanuelle Clemmons, sneaking in, one hand still on the door, glancing around, her entire manner furtive. She had some nerve showing up uninvited, probably fresh off taping another episode of that show.

The Bullhorn was a crowdfunded podcast that billed itself as an independent alternative to the mainstream news but was actually just low-budget talk radio. The blowhard host seemed to be buddies with Emmanuelle. Listening, Claire had been rattled. Not that Emmanuelle was digging into their affairs—that much she'd suspected—but by what she'd found. At first it was only the deprioritized projects. I knew we should have kept those off the website, Claire had said to Crispin, almost relishing the *I told you so*, the confidence she had to speak her mind now.

Anyway, the joke was on Emmanuelle because they were already restarting the work in those countries, a fact Claire blandly tweeted, twenty minutes after the episode dropped.

Emmanuelle, undaunted, had kept going on the show, and Claire wondered at her intel. Some of the issues she raised were things even Anya hadn't known about. Before my time, she'd said. Crispin had brushed it all off, admitting yes, mistakes were made, but they'd learned and grown. It bothered Claire, his laissez-faire attitude, though she tried to suppress her concerns. After all, things were going well now. Still, she couldn't quite shake Emmanuelle's judgmental tone on these interviews, which felt aimed specifically at her.

Claire glided over with a glass of champagne.

So glad you could make it, she said. Here in your official capacity as stringer for *The Bullhorn*?

It was a joke, but Emmanuelle, reaching to accept the drink, seemed to falter. Then she met Claire's gaze, raised an eyebrow, and sing-songed *May-beee*. There was an uncomfortable split second before they both laughed.

For the next thirty minutes, Claire kept Emmanuelle in her periphery, certain that she was here on a fishing expedition.

You're frowning, a low voice murmured, and she was startled to find Lucca at her side. He wagged a finger and said: Bad for morale. Scowling at a party.

I'm very busy and important, she said, straightening her shoulders and holding her head high, adopting his mocking tone. And I'm thinking profound thoughts.

From across the room, Crispin beckoned.

I'm being summoned, Lucca said, and as they parted, she felt his hand, fleeting, on the small of her back.

Claire told herself the alcohol was making her paranoid as well as horny, and she needed to take five. Not wanting to run into anyone she knew, she used the ladies' room on the floor above. Emerging from the stall, she was surprised to find Anya at the sink.

Lucca is quite the bard. Anya spoke in a dusky tenor, with a distinctive rolling creak. She'd once told Claire it was a tone she'd purposely adopted at the start of her career, when she thought pitching her voice lower would be professionally advantageous.

You must have heard stories like that all the time when you worked at Medics Abroad, Claire said, soaping her hands.

Anya twisted open her mascara. Oh, sure. The docs liked to brag. These overseas humanitarian types are all the same. You know how they get on over there, she added, pinning Claire's eyes in the mirror. The war correspondents too. Party hard and fuck like rabbits. STD soup.

Once she was alone, Claire leaned her hot forehead against the cool wall and told herself to get a grip.

A FaceTime call rang. Her ex-husband's name appeared on the screen.

Mama, Theo blubbered, a balloon of snot popping out one nostril. Mama, I hungry.

Charlotte, over his shoulder, was in a temper. Theo kicked me. He *kicked* me.

It's your daddy's week to make dinner, she said, leaving the washroom and heading for the stairwell.

Simon always did this, turned his phone over to the children and wandered away, using her as a virtual babysitter.

Want mama, Theo cried. Want mama. Want mama.

Muscling into the frame, Charlotte got in on the action. My tummy hurts, she whined.

These histrionics never happened on her weeks, and a petty part of her was triumphant. (And he thought they were going to be happy in India!)

I'm sorry about your tummy, Chicken, Claire said, climbing the stairs. Did you tell your daddy?

There was a tussle, and Claire saw fleeting glimpses of the ceiling, Theo's nose, Charlotte's ear.

Kids, I'm hanging up, she said, and that brought the screen right side up, both children in view.

Mama, they cried. Mama, Mama.

She had reached the third floor. Good night, she said. I love you.

Pushing the heavy door out of the stairwell, she stopped short. At the far end of the hallway, Crispin, Anya, and Lucca were huddled by the fire exit. Anya had her pointer finger right up in Lucca's face, and she was whisper-shouting. Crispin seemed uncharacteristically nervous, his body language fidgety, eyes wide. Lucca was the only one who appeared unruffled.

What's going on? Claire asked.

We have a situation, Crispin started to say but was interrupted by Anya exclaiming, The father claims there was no adoption!

For a split second, Claire thought of her kids and whipped around in confusion, expecting to see her ex.

No paperwork. No lawyers. Anya was still ranting. Nothing. Then she turned on Lucca and demanded, Tell her.

I've already—

Tell her what you just told us.

Claire had a premonition and fought the absurd urge to clap her hands over her ears as Lucca described an unbelievable scene. A man accosting him on his way to the airport, raving about a stolen child. A steady thump began in her left ear.

Jorge says they never agreed to the adoption, Lucca said.

No one even asked, Anya added, flinging a hand at Claire as if this was somehow her doing.

Claire's hackles rose. That's a serious allegation. Is there proof? she asked and was chagrined to hear how high her voice had risen.

Are we sure the man is the father? Crispin asked.

He's not an imposter, Lucca said. Don't forget, I met the Garcias when you sent me to force their hands.

Claire, startled, turned sharply to Anya. Was this true? She'd been sure Anya was against the adoption.

I did no such thing, Anya said. You—

Crispin cut in: Lucca, you spent a week with Dallas. What was she like? How did she strike you?

She's like every other celebrity. He glared at Crispin as he said this, adding: They're sincere. They believe they mean well. But they have no idea.

And you let her walk out with the child, Anya said.

It's not my job to stop actors from kidnapping children, Lucca said.

Don't . . . That's an ugly—

Isn't that what you're—

Keep your voices down, Claire shushed, twisting to double-check they were still alone.

No one's saying . . . Crispin cleared his throat and started again, voice lowered. There's no evidence Dallas did anything wrong.

She should have taken Moisés, Lucca said. Then there'd be no trouble.

Who? Claire asked. She worked her jaw, trying to dislodge the beat in her ear.

Anya slammed her palm on the wall. *You* let this happen. *You* allowed a child to leave our care.

Lucca flinched. He rubbed his wrist, and Claire saw fear flicker across his features. She blinked, and it was gone.

That's uncalled for, Crispin said sharply.

I told you it was too fast, Anya said.

You saw the child's feet. There was no time to waste, Crispin said. Still, it couldn't have been an easy decision. Maybe they're having regrets.

Jorge and Inez Garcia, Lucca said.

Right. Them.

Or the father's gone rogue, Claire said. The mother wasn't there?

Lucca shook his head.

It's all very well for Dad to change his mind, but Mom's the one doing all the child care, she said, ire rising on behalf of the unknown mother.

That's not what he's claiming though, Anya said, looking to Lucca for confirmation. There was no parental consent. No adopt—

Quiet! Claire said when she noticed the office door opening.

She was hyperaware of Emmanuelle, circling like a hawk less than fifty feet away. But it was only the intern, peering out. They were about to enter the hallway, but Claire made a shooing motion.

This is crazy, Claire said after the intern disappeared. You're acting as if Dallas . . . as if she . . . I can't even say it. It's absurd.

You should have stopped her, Anya repeated, rounding on Lucca, voice calm but still furious. Instead, you make a mess of things and land the problem on us.

I warned you about celebrities, Lucca said.

You're both getting worked up over nothing, Crispin insisted.

Birth parents get cold feet. It happens. Eventually it'll fade. Especially once they see how well Persimmon's doing.

Stealing a baby? Claire asked. A high-needs baby? Does that even sound logical? I mean it's not . . . Dallas would *never*. Spiriting a child across the border, without adoption papers . . .

Lucca shrugged. In Santa Rosa? It happens. You can bribe someone to act as the mother, get a false birth certificate.

He spoke like it was nothing. *Had* Dallas stolen a child? *Kidnapped* someone's baby? Claire pressed the back of her hand against her mouth.

Claire's right, Crispin said. Dallas could have adopted a healthy baby anywhere, anytime. She had nothing to gain from breaking the law.

Nothing to gain. Claire caught that phrase. Held it tight.

Never underestimate the folly of celebrities, Anya said.

It was just like Anya to dismiss a young woman's intelligence. Claire was glad when Crispin said: Dallas is savvier than you think. Look at her career choices, her online persona. She's strategic about her reputation. And if you insist on being cynical, okay, yes, even with this adoption.

The child has certainly been superb for her image, Anya said.

None of you know Dallas like I do, Claire said affronted. She *loves* that little girl.

Of course she does, Crispin said. Two things can be true at once. And bottom line, Persimmon is better off.

There's a whole team depending on Dallas's career. They wouldn't be so cavalier about risking their livelihoods, Claire insisted, as much to herself as to the others.

Anya appealed to Lucca: If what the father is saying is . . . if there's any basis for—

Lucca held his hands up like stop signs and took a step back.

Anya moaned and covered her face. How could you be so irresponsible? she muttered to herself.

Don't put this on me! Lucca shot back.

Crispin intervened, asking Lucca, What sort of people are they, the parents?

Lucca paused, and in the silence Claire listened to the thump-thump in her left ear.

Inez wants what's best for Maria, Lucca finally said. Jorge . . . The man is a scoundrel. But in this, he is sincere.

What can we do for them? Crispin asked. A monthly stipend. Would that help? Seeing Claire recoil, he added: Don't judge. In their circumstances, any of us would do the same.

I don't think the optics of that are— Anya began to say.

No, Crispin agreed. You're right.

This is a disaster, Anya said. Dallas needs to show us proof.

It was a private adoption between Dallas and the family. It's none of our business, Crispin said sternly.

Anya turned to Claire, eyes narrowed, and said, Ask her.

Claire's mouth was a desert. What?

You and Dallas are bosom buddies.

I—

If the adoption is all above board, you'll be doing her a favour.

Hey Dallas. Just wanted to check on something . . .

Dallas can do something for the family, Crispin said. It would be appropriate coming from her.

Lucca made a frustrated neigh. She should have done it already, from the first.

The talk of money made Claire uncomfortable. Her foot began jiggling, and she forced it to stand still.

This is more about Dallas than us, Anya said, then snorted. Her expression was untethered, two red splotches high on her cheekbones. Oh, I can just see the headlines now.

That's my point exactly, Claire said. Dallas would never risk bad press. It would be career suicide.

She'll appreciate the heads-up, Crispin agreed. Better coming from you than finding an angry man at her door one day.

An angry man. My colleague says he's the biological father. Wanted to give you a heads-up! Would she send the message by email and copy Dallas's manager? Or was it the kind of bad news that was better coming from a friend, over text? Claire felt lightheaded. It had been over a week since their last text exchange (*The little film that could!*).

Lucca dug a knuckle into his left eye and glanced away, back toward the big wooden door of their office. The din from inside was rising. Music and buoyant voices slipping through the gap underneath and ballooning to the ceiling, bobbing toward them.

Dallas, is this adoption legit?

We should get back to our guests, Crispin said. As they left, he turned to Lucca and added, I'm sorry you had to deal with that unpleasantness.

Claire lingered. She didn't want to write to Dallas. She opened her mouth, ready to beg Anya to take care of it, when Anya asked, Have you been to Santa Rosa?

Claire shook her head. She didn't add that before coming to Children of the World, she'd barely known the country existed.

Anya described a car ride she'd taken through the streets of Santa Rosa's capital, many years earlier, before she worked at Children of the World. The potholed roads, the slums with their circling buzzards. The litter. Even the cows appeared malnourished.

In the air-conditioned vehicle, the driver played a local band, marimba, upbeat drums and a double bass. When they stopped at a red light, children surged forward, thumping on the sides of the vehicle, holding up books of postcards that dropped open like accordions. The driver rolled down his tinted window to yell a few sharp words in Spanish, and everyone scattered except for a woman with a skinny baby, tied to her front with rags, cupped hands out. Her face was ashen, her teeth oversized as if hunger had shrunk her head.

In this land of plenty, where the soil and climate colluded to produce a tropical cornucopia, guava, papaya, varieties of bananas Anya had never before tasted, it seemed especially cruel that anyone should starve.

For the rest of the trip, I couldn't stop thinking about that woman, Anya said. There was almost nothing separating us. Just a car window. It seemed so . . .

Thin? Claire said.

Arbitrary, Anya said. In a parallel universe, she's in the van and I'm on the street.

I used to watch those World Vision commercials, Claire said. The ones with Alex Trebek?

She was back in the wood-panelled den of her childhood home, toes sinking into the brown shag carpet, the click of her mother's knitting needles in the background, and Alex explaining that for just the cost of a cup of coffee a day . . .

Those infomercials had made her sob and pry the rubber suction off the underside of her ceramic pig, thumping the coins and folded bills onto her bed. Tender heart, her mother used to call her, but Claire knew her donations were bribes to Fate. She saw the stunted dark children, ribs protruding, their orange furze, and thought of how easily she might have been born in their place.

I worked on that campaign, Anya said. I stuffed and stamped direct mail. Thousands of letters.

Wow, Claire said, struck by the coincidence and the breadth of Anya's experience.

I'd been in non-profit almost thirty years by the time I started here, Anya said. But Santa Rosa has always been different. I didn't think of it as helping strangers. It was more like saving some other version of myself.

Bribing Fate, Claire thought. And now?

Anya shook her shoulders, dislodging an invisible monkey. There's the idea of the thing and then there's the thing itself. What we're doing—international aid—it's a marathon. Sometimes you sprain an ankle.

A burst of music and jovial voices made them turn in unison toward the office doors.

And the . . . what Lucca said? Claire asked.

The woman in Santa Rosa, the one with the baby. Anya made a rolling motion with her fist. She was gesturing for me to open the window. Claire imagined it, the tinted glass sliding down, the baby being passed from one mother to another, the light changing and the car accelerating forward.

Anya rubbed a hand over her face, as if trying to wipe it clean—eyes, nose, mouth, all of it gone. Claire recognized the gesture. It was the one Anya made when she was coming to a conclusion. In a second she would make a declaration. Claire felt utterly sober. Then Anya turned and strode toward the office.

Let me know what Dallas says.

Good Faith

Emmanuelle

Her mother's train got in first, and Emmanuelle took charge of the wheeled suitcase while they waited on the chilly platform for Aunt Martha.

Of course Martha had to come, Emmanuelle said. She can't let you have *one* weekend.

She's done so much for us, Mom said, repeating the familiar refrain.

She's done so much for her own damn self, Emmanuelle said, shoving her free hand into her pocket. She'd forgotten her gloves but wouldn't relinquish her grip on the suitcase.

I would have lost the house, Mom said, stamping her feet against the cold. I would have lost everything.

Martha Winslow was no one's auntie. For the first half of Emmanuelle's life, she'd been the church secretary who slipped her toffees and asked about school. She might have been equally solicitous to every child, but for Emmanuelle, the eldest in a family of eight, grown-up attention was a luxury.

But after her father died, attention became a burden. There were casseroles and braised oxtail, salt cod and pork scraps, Martha Winslow barging in at all hours to deliver groceries and harangue them about homework, taking the Reverend's seat at the head of the table and demanding to be called *Auntie*.

Hunched in a pew on Sundays, doing her best to attain invisibility, Emmanuelle had cringed at the whispers. *That poor woman. Those poor babies. How fortunate they are to have Martha. God is good.*

When she got admitted to journalism school and a modest scholarship, Aunt Martha had said, *I prayed every day for this blessing*. She took credit for everything Emmanuelle and her siblings accomplished, as if their successes were bounties she'd purchased rather than hard-won victories they'd earned. Emmanuelle resented how proprietary Martha Winslow was about her family, how she never corrected strangers who assumed she was their mother's sister.

Nothing was free in this world, Emmanuelle learned, charity least of all. Philanthropy was an expression of power, the receivers indentured to their gratitude.

That woman thinks the sun shines out of her—

Be kind, Emmanuelle, Mom said. Martha doesn't have anyone else.

Maybe there's a reason for that.

The corner of Mom's lip tugged up, and for moment it seemed like she might agree, take one of her rare sardonic jabs, but then she shook her head and muttered, Walk the high road, Emmanuelle.

The speaker overhead crackled on, announcing the incoming train was delayed, and they moved inside the station. The waiting area was puddled with melting snow. Passengers in bulky coats sat amidst their luggage, mesmerized by their phones.

Mom asked after Ben. He was a point of contention, the fact that they were *living in sin*.

Do it for your future children, if you won't do it for yourselves, Mom said, as they found seats by the signs for the bathroom. You *are* planning to have children?

Yes, of course, but you know it's the twenty-first century, right? Everyone's divorced or common law or in a blended family. Or poly.

Piqued by her mother's insistence on being a Martha apologist, Emmanuelle took especial pleasure in describing the domestic arrangements of a particular trio who lived on their street.

Well, Mom said and sniffed. We didn't have these sorts of situations in my day.

Emmanuelle felt a little bad then because her mother took other people's decisions as a personal affront, a critique of her own life choices. They fell silent, letting the hubbub of the waiting room wash around and settle between them. The boarding call for the express train to Windsor. The wheeze of the automatic doors and the blast of cold whenever they opened. A child whining for an iPad.

Emmanuelle's thoughts boomeranged to earlier in the week when she'd crashed the party at Children of the World's new office. After a hearty welcome from Crispin, she'd been left to her own devices, self-consciously orbiting conversations while his employees, in a protective huddle, glared. One young staffer had peeled off from the pack, and for the rest of the evening she'd felt their eyes on her, tracking her movements. They had the faultless attire and obsequious air of an intern, and she guessed they were acting on Claire's orders, poised to intervene if Emmanuelle tried anything brazen. The party was a self-congratulatory affair, fizzy with free-flowing bubbly as online influencers took selfies with cardboard cut-outs of Dallas and her co-stars in superhero garb. Emmanuelle was the only journalist in attendance, but these *content creators* probably counted as media. Depressing thought. She'd been on alert for the visiting country director and had stuck close when she found him, listening as he spun yarns of his exploits. When she'd asked about Santa Rosa, Lucca da Silva had been curiously reticent.

In the train station, a man across the aisle stood, and Emmanuelle and her mother shifted as he squeezed past, a copy of that day's *Herald* tucked under his arm. Mom patted Emmanuelle's knee in a gesture of truce.

I read your article on that charity, she said. Has the paper rehired you?

It was a one-off, Emmanuelle said and was about to add that Art had slashed and burned all the best parts, but her mother was already praising the piece, saying she'd never heard of Children of the World before and had been inspired to visit their website and make a donation. Wasn't it heartwarming what Dallas Hayden was doing for that poor disabled orphan? The rest of them in Hollywood could learn a lesson from her.

Absolutely, Emmanuelle agreed, fake clapping. Brava to her. The performance of a lifetime, far more believable than anything she's done onscreen. Shame it didn't win her that Oscar.

Emmanuelle! Her mother reeled back, yanking her hand away, and Emmanuelle was instantly regretful. It always took a day or two to recalibrate, dial down her sarcasm, and settle into the role of dutiful daughter.

Mom gathered her coat around herself and said: You were never like this before. The city has made you hard.

I'm sorry. I'm sorry. I just feel for the girl's family.

Mom frowned. I thought she was an orphan.

She has two parents and a bunch of siblings, and that's not the half of it, she said.

After an excruciating hour, Emmanuelle had escaped the open house. At the ground floor, when the elevator opened with a ping, she'd been startled to find the intern blocking her path. Early twenties, Emmanuelle guessed. Short with light brown skin and dark hair, styled in a shaggy mullet. They had a fidgety guilty air, gaze flicking in a furtive way that Emmanuelle recognized at once.

Off the record? she'd asked, leading them out the building and into an alley.

Once the intern started talking, all their grievances rushed out: how Children of the World had been on the verge of bankruptcy, how the intern's employment was precarious, and all the organization's marketing materials were full of shit, how no one else acknowledged the tragedy of spiriting a child to another country for a treatment she could have at home. Emmanuelle knew the intern's type, had *been* their type, the only one in the room who saw the naked emperor.

Two million dollars, the intern had said. That's the going rate for a child.

Those parents gave their baby up because they thought it was the only way to correct her feet, Emmanuelle told her mother now. And from the way Dallas goes on, you'd think there were no treatment options in Santa Rosa, but Children of the World runs a free clinic, right in their compound.

Mom listened, grimacing. I wish I'd known all this before I made that donation.

You did that in good faith, Emmanuelle said. Don't feel bad.

What a sin. It's a shame the family wasn't part of our congregation. Something might have been done for the little one.

Your congregation?

Mom said her church had a long-term ministry in Santa Rosa's capital, headed up by a dynamic young pastor and his wife. So many families had been brought to Christ that they had expanded to a small western town, where they'd built a second chapel the year before.

Do you remember Micah Williams from youth group? she asked.

A little, Emmanuelle said.

Micah had always been a self-righteous know-it-all. It didn't surprise her that he'd grown up to become a full-time missionary, saving the heathens from themselves.

I didn't realize the church was doing missions work, she said. When did that start?

Her mother shrugged with a faux nonchalance. Well, I didn't like to talk about it. I knew *you* wouldn't approve.

Emmanuelle waited, refusing to join her mother's guilt trip. Finally, Mom relented, telling Emmanuelle about the missionaries they had sent into the world, how the venture had begun a decade earlier, helmed by Martha.

The Great Commission, Emmanuelle said, caught between pathos and provocation. Her father's big dream.

Dreams are well and good, but it's a serious undertaking, Mom said.

Are you involved with any of that? Emmanuelle asked, wondering at the improbability of finding a source in Santa Rosa through her own mother. Could you connect me with Micah?

Me? No, no. This is all Martha's doing. Mom's eyes twinkled and the corners of her lips twitched up. I'm sure she'd be happy to put you in touch with him.

Emmanuelle smothered a groan. This was the last thing she needed: to be further indebted to Martha, now half a lifetime later.

Talk to Micah, and maybe then you'll understand. Child, you have no idea how much his congregation has thrived.

If charity was a crock, then the religious ones were the worst of the lot, dangling health care or food as a carrot and demanding faith as payment. Emmanuelle couldn't say this out loud though. Already, she was treading on sensitive ground.

But when Mom spoke again her tone was soft with pity: How could we bring people worldly goods and deny them salvation? She pressed her hands to Emmanuelle's cheeks and searched her face. The Lord has blessed you with a good man, a healthy body and mind. Maybe that makes it easy to take His love for granted. But I see how angry you are.

Emmanuelle squirmed, uncomfortable in the familiar intensity of her mother's gaze.

Mom. Okay. Stop. You know I don't believe in any of this anymore. Let's agree to disagree.

Her mother sat back, shaking her head so her beaded earrings quivered. You have no idea how fortunate you are. When your father died, do you know what scared me the most? The thought that I might lose you kids too.

I didn't know that.

Your father and I were never great ones for planning ahead. That's why there was no life insurance or rainy-day fund. Whenever the doorbell rang—especially after the collections calls began—I was certain it was the child-welfare people.

To Emmanuelle, the idea that she and her siblings could have been taken from their mother—who never raised her voice, let alone a hand, to them—was absurd.

The bank was threatening to foreclose on the house. What do you think happens to a parent with eight young ones in a shelter? What do those nice social workers think when they see so many children and a Black mother on welfare?

Emmanuelle was chastened to realize that she knew very well what happened and somehow had assumed her family was exempt. On account of what? Religion, diction, tidy dressing?

Martha told me the church elders took up a collection, but I know she paid that mortgage for months. She got me on my feet. Found me a job. You might bear that in mind when she gets here and see if you can't keep that forked tongue in your mouth where it belongs.

Yes, ma'am.

Mom grabbed her in a fierce hug, holding her so tight her grip almost hurt, but it was a pleasant sort of pain. Well now, she said into Emmanuelle's hair. It's nice to remember I still got it.

I'm sorry, Emmanuelle said. I'm an idiot and an ingrate.

Her mother put her lips close to Emmanuelle's ear, and for a second she expected a kiss on the cheek. Instead, Mom whispered: A small church service. Immediate family only. I won't even insist on a veil.

They were doubled over, laughing, when Martha's train finally arrived.

When Emmanuelle called Micah Williams, she expected tedious small talk and veiled rebukes about her loss of faith. Instead, he said, Do you know about Maria Garcia?

The kid Dallas Hayden adopted? She felt a shiver of trepidation and excitement.

You need to speak to the girl's father, Micah said.

The audio and video quality were both subpar, the internet so patchy they got disconnected three times before they began. But it was important to Emmanuelle that she see Jorge Garcia's face, so they persevered.

He had a complexion weathered by the sun, deep brackets running from under his eyes all the way down to his chin. Thick jet hair and a sparse beard and moustache, shot through with threads of grey. He might have been thirty or fifty. If they were speaking under different circumstances, Emmanuelle could easily imagine him as jovial, the kind of man who burst into frequent riotous laughter.

Today, he was grave, body language impatient. He sat tall and leaned toward the screen, Micah at his right, edged out of the frame.

The Garcias were not in his congregation, Micah explained. They lived in the foothills of the mountains, a three-hour car ride away from his church, longer if, like Jorge and Inez, you didn't have a vehicle and were at the mercy of public transport or hitching rides. Jorge had a cousin in Micah's congregation, a teacher who put him up when work brought him to the capital. She was the one who had introduced the two men, after Jorge had exhausted all his options.

Start at the beginning, Emmanuelle said. Please tell me everything.

The catastrophe took place in October, Jorge said. He'd been working in the city, so he had this part of the story second-hand from his wife. If he'd been present, none of this would have happened. It was Inez and her mother who'd been home, unguarded, with the two youngest children when a stranger arrived, feigning sympathy. He'd heard there was a sick baby in the house, was this true?

Gossipy meddlers, Jorge grumbled of his neighbours. Talking about everyone else's business and paying no attention to their own.

Jorge would later learn the man's name was Thiago and that he worked for an unknown charity.

Emmanuelle had taken Spanish all through high school and university, but Jorge spoke in an unfamiliar dialect with an accent that was garbled to her foreign ear. Several times Micah had to ask him to repeat himself, to slow down. When he relayed Jorge's words in English, Emmanuelle wondered about the fidelity of his rendition and what was getting lost, but Jorge's demeanour required no translation. It spoke of his fury and mettle.

Jorge hadn't realized Maria was ill. The family didn't have phones, and when he was away, he and Inez communicated sporadically, through travelling relations or friends.

And what was the child meant to be sick with? he asked. A pain in the ears? All children had pains. Head pain. Ear pain. Leg pain. Everything was always paining and then it wasn't. Likely the malady would have cleared up on its own.

But Thiago, he was canny. He volleyed Inez with pointed questions. Where is your husband? When will he come home? How old is your child? Is she often sick? Does her fever burn?

My wife is a good woman, Jorge said. But simple. Too trusting. Who is this man to us? He isn't even a shaman. He's just some toady. And yet when he tells her yes, the child's illness is grave, she is on the verge of death, Inez believes it.

After the stranger left, Inez stayed up all night, doing what she did best: expecting the worst, holding Maria close, convinced each breath would be her last.

They've lost two children already, Micah added in what Emmanuelle understood was an aside rather than a translation.

The next day, the thief Thiago returned with a woman Inez mistook for a doctor. Jorge shook his head in disbelief, and Micah unconsciously mimicked him as he translated. You see how easy it is to fool my wife. A strange man tells her Maria needs medicine, special treatments, she must be taken from her home, and what does Inez do?

Relieved at the prospect of salvation, Inez had acted on instinct. It was only afterward, her arms empty and the sounds of her crying baby a memory, that the enormity of her actions set in. By the time Jorge returned from the construction site in the city, Inez was frantic, sobbing that Maria had been disappeared.

The corner of the bedroom Emmanuelle used as a makeshift office was papered in her nieces' artwork. They were safely ensconced in their classrooms, making more crafts. If the school arbitrarily decided to hold them hostage, her sister would take a bat to the doors, march in, and swing at anyone who stood in her way and Emmanuelle would gladly join her. But her sister knew where the school was, had a car, and the might of the law on her side. She pictured the scene in Santa Rosa, another mother, her child vanished. A mother without transport or a phone or so much as a hand-drawn map to follow.

There was a clinic at the bottom of the mountain, staffed by temporary foreign workers. Jorge hitched a ride on the back of an avocado truck. But no one there had heard of Maria. His sons fanned out. Friends, family, neighbours—they all joined the search. Inez was convinced their daughter was dead, murdered.

Despite the poor connection, it was easy to follow what Jorge was saying. There was a coherence to his narrative, an orderly telling that belied oft repetition, the beats of the story falling neatly one after the next, the asides that had likely once been spontaneous (*If I had been home, we wouldn't even be having this conversation*) now fused into the tale.

How must it feel to be forced to repeat these indignities, to suffer each painful memory again and again? How many people had Jorge appealed to for help? Emmanuelle wondered. She, a freelance journalist, without even a paper of record, was only the latest.

A few days later, Thiago returned, Jorge said. But without Maria. Instead, he brought another stranger, a man who introduced himself as the boss of the charity that had snatched their child. This was Lucca da Silva. Jorge had his name correct if not quite his title. It was only then they learned the woman whom Inez had mistaken for a doctor was an actress.

This is who my wife gave our baby to: a professional pretender.

The actress, they were told, wanted to take Maria to the U.S. It was presented as an opportunity. Maria would go to school. Visit special doctors.

Jorge was clear on this: they had *not* given permission. He had demanded Maria's return.

The family waited, hearing nothing, and debated what to do. This time they knew where Maria was being kept and the boss's name. Jorge wanted to find a way to get there and collect the baby himself, but Inez disagreed. They'd been told Maria was responding well to the medications, that she was nearly cured. The men had confused her with photos and videos of the baby and based on this paltry evidence, soft-hearted Inez had decided the kidnappers were trustworthy, that if they were patient, Maria would be brought back, better than ever.

Jorge made a walking motion with two fingers. Maria had club feet, he said. Inez argued the time apart was worth the sacrifice because she'd be cured.

Even as the weeks stretched into months and Christmas approached, Inez said just wait. It wasn't until the new year, when Jorge was back in the capital for another job and making inquiries about this charity he'd never heard of, that he learned the truth from a magazine.

From start to finish, the whole thing was a ruse, Jorge said. The actress had come to Santa Rosa with a single goal: to take his child. Jorge understood how these rich gringos got on. They pretended to be shooting footage for a documentary and captured images of children. This must be how the actress chose Maria. In Santa Rosa, women went to the market for provisions, but in the U.S., everything was selected online. They must get their children the same way.

Emmanuelle did not interrupt this rant, and Micah, she noticed, didn't say anything to correct him either. Perhaps they were sharing the same thought. In a way Jorge wasn't wrong. What had Dallas flown to Santa Rosa for? These kids need rescuing, Children of the World had told her. And you are the hero who can save them.

Did Lucca da Silva say anything about adoption? Emmanuelle asked.

Adoption? Jorge said. Maria doesn't need any adoption. We are her people. We are her family.

The actress claims she adopted Maria, Emmanuelle said.

Jorge hit a fist against his chest. Maria is my daughter. Mine.

These are serious allegations, Emmanuelle said.

They stole my child, Jorge said in English. Stole. Lo entiendes?

Entiendo, she said. Then added: Yo te creo. I have to get your words on the record.

The salient point for the record: no papers had been signed. No legal documents offered or read.

Micah—in English—added what Jorge was too proud to say: both parents were illiterate. Jorge had recognized his daughter in that magazine, yes. But it was his cousin who read the article aloud. Even if there had been legal paperwork, Jorge and Inez would have needed a translator. And their own lawyer, Emmanuelle thought.

How does it work? she asked Micah. In a legitimate adoption, what's the process?

The birth family signs off, and both parties are interviewed by a judge. At first I thought they had forged papers, Micah said. But adoptions are noted in a public register. Neither Dallas nor Maria are listed.

He told her that foreign adoptions were falling out of favour and on the verge of being banned.

My wife and I have been going through the process for two years.

That must be so hard, Emmanuelle said.

The sticking point is our citizenship. Eventually we'll go home. Dallas being a single mother would have been an issue too.

How had Dallas left the country? Emmanuelle wondered out loud.

Fake passports was Micah's guess.

There must be a paper trail, Emmanuelle said. A passenger manifest. But that still left the question of what had happened at the U.S. border.

Jorge snorted in frustration. What were the pair of them talking about? Wasn't this woman rich and famous? She must have a private plane. A pilot who asked no questions. A landing pad behind her mansion.

Emmanuelle was galled by her naïveté. He was right. Borders were for peasants. The super rich had their own revolving doors, invisible to the rest of the world. Still, Dallas didn't act alone. Maria had been under Crispin's roof. From the photos on their website, Emmanuelle had a fair idea of the size and the scope of their operations. The compound would be gated, under twenty-four-hour guard. Dallas hadn't smuggled the child out under her jacket. Someone had greenlit the abduction.

Do you know this Thiago? she asked Micah. Do you think he'll speak to me?

Micah was doubtful. He'd gone to advocate on Jorge's behalf and found the staff wary and guarded. Thiago had deferred to his absent director, their superiors at headquarters, suggested Micah speak to them.

They're protective of their livelihoods, he said.

Emmanuelle scanned her mental Rolodex. Was there anyone she knew, any contact she had at U.S. immigration, at a law firm? But then she considered the stakes. A famous actor. Navigating the legal systems of two countries, if not three. No lawyer would want to touch this with a ten-foot pole and certainly not pro bono. But if there was enough pressure on Dallas, enough bad publicity, if her fans, if Hollywood demanded it, she'd have to return the child. Wouldn't she?

Jorge, I can get your story to the public, she said.

Maria must come home, Jorge said in Spanish, enunciating the words slowly and clearly so Emmanuelle understood. Ella es mi hija. Mía. Ella es mi sangre, he said.

The connection dropped unexpectedly, and Emmanuelle was left staring at her reflection. The whole world had watched a fairy tale, Dallas cradling the baby to her chest and climbing into the jeep, Children of the World's logo plastered across its doors. But now Emmanuelle could reveal the sordid details that had been sanitized out, how Crispin's charity had tricked a poor, defenceless couple and stolen their child.

Emmanuelle rubbed the soles of her feet together. This was the biggest story of her career. It would *make* her career. She felt it in her extremities, the electric thrill of honest-to-god, above-the-fold front-page news. And it would be under *her* byline. All hers.

Change the World

Claire

Claire agonized over it all weekend, phrasing and rephrasing first an email to Dallas, then a text message, then an email again, drafting a dozen iterations. She googled celebrity adoptions and became briefly obsessed with the story of a pop star who had adopted a little boy from Ethiopia only to have the child's father come out of the woodwork. This was ugly but ancient history, the father at first blisteringly angry, softening his stance in later years, only to get inflamed whenever the singer suffered a breakup or was caught sunbathing nude. These stories were always relegated to tabloids, prurient and lurid, accompanied by unflattering photos where both sides appeared loathsome. The child, a young man now, was an entertainment lawyer, and the birth father was most recently on record stating he was grateful to the singer for giving his boy a charmed life. The son, for his part, kept a low profile, attending his mother's events from time to time and never mentioning his biological father.

It was Sunday when Claire, bolstered by this happy ending, finally sent the text. Then she turned off her phone, shoved it in a drawer, and took herself to the theatre where she spent the ninety-minute running time ruminating on what she'd written. *Hey a weird thing happened . . . Just thought you should know*. She'd tried to phrase it as a heads-up, and only now did it occur to her that Dallas might read it as an accusation. What exactly had she said? She reached into her bag only to remember she'd left the phone at home.

She told herself Dallas would respond right away, probably already had. *Oh yeah. That guy. Dunno what his problem is but I know all about him*. And Claire would say, *Sorry to even bring it up*. And Dallas would reply: *I'm glad you did. It's good to have documentation for the lawyers*. Then they'd joke about it. *As if I'd steal a baby. Lol. Yeah. As if.* This would be the icebreaker they needed to put their friendship back on track.

Instead, the weekend passed and the chat remained dormant. Claire's last unanswered message taunting her. What did it mean? Was Dallas offended? Hurt?

Busted?

She was reduced to studying Dallas's social media accounts like tea leaves. All her posts were work-related, but on Wednesday there was a cryptic message—one of those platitudes of uncertain provenance on a generic background that made the online rounds—about cutting toxic people out. Claire saw the post while she was at the office and wondered, *Is this about me?* She reread her message, all the ones they'd exchanged before that, her screed against the Oscars, feeling faint. What did this mean for their #realhero campaign?

Well? Anya asked that same day. Startled, Claire minimized the window on her screen and swung her chair around to where Anya, looming, demanded, Any word from Dallas?

It's none of our business, Claire snapped, surprising even herself.

Anya shrank back, but only for a second, before drawing herself to full height.

I mean, Claire said. It's fine. She turned to her computer, then mumbled: It's like Lucca said. The father is a scoundrel.

At her back, she heard Anya clear her throat and felt the strength of her stare. Claire's stomach clenched, dreading what she might say next.

Good, Anya said finally. I'm glad to hear that.

Facing the document on her screen, all the sentences blurring, Claire's panic subsided. But what had she just blurted out? She couldn't recall a word. Did Anya think she'd spoken to Dallas, confirmed the adoption was above aboard? *Just thought you should know.* She should have phrased the text differently, ended on a question. No wonder Dallas wasn't replying.

Crispin's office door opened and he emerged, expression morose. They're talking about us on that show again, he said.

The Bullhorn, it seemed, had nothing better to report on, and Emmanuelle had become a regular, joining the host a couple of times a week just to chew the fat.

No one listens to that drivel, Claire said. And you shouldn't either.

The last episode she'd heard had gone completely off the rails. What had begun as a grievance over an innocuous picket fence had turned into an unhinged rant about power, Emmanuelle claiming philanthropy was an act of supremacy, the giver forcing their desires on the unwilling recipients.

No one impartial could possibly take Emmanuelle or *The Bullhorn* seriously after that. So when the host denounced Crispin as *a fame whore with a god complex* and called Children of the World *his desperate attempt to remain relevant after Resurrection*, Claire had arched an eyebrow and whispered, Triggered much?

Crispin turned to Anya, who was at the filing cabinet, and asked: How do they know about the fence? Who's she been speaking to?

Flicking through the hanging folders, Anya said: We dealt with it. There's nothing to report.

Claire was surprised by Crispin's reaction. He'd been cavalier about Emmanuelle's feature, joking that she wasn't a fan, but he'd win her over eventually. Yet here he was asking Claire: Have you seen the Twitter essays? And the fake accounts? These anonymous trolls are—

Probably the same anonymous troll, Claire said.

Crispin's shoulders slumped. The Resurrection subreddit used to be this nice, uplifting corner of the internet, but even that's been poisoned.

Your old band, from the *literal* last century, has a subreddit? Anya said.

It's a community, Crispin said, affronted. A group of like-minded—

Are you skulking around there too? Anya asked Claire.

Me? I didn't know it existed, she lied.

If people turn the CEO into a laughingstock, it tarnishes the organization's reputation. Listen to what they're saying, Crispin said and began reading the screeds out, off his phone.

Anya's landline rang, and she made a saved-by-the-bell joke, before striding to her desk.

We have to get used to a little negativity, Claire said. This is what comes with being high profile. Take it as a marker of success.

She was speaking to Crispin but her gaze was on Anya, whose spine had gone rigid, one hand on the receiver, the other gripping her waist.

You're not worried about this from a public relations perspective? Crispin asked.

Not a bit, she said. The #realhero campaign is very popular, especially online, and that'll more than counteract this bit of mudslinging. Anyway, the donations speak for themselves.

It's that priest again, Anya interrupted from her doorway. That's the third voice mail.

Priest? Claire wondered, but instinct cautioned her not to ask.

I thought you were going to deal with it, Anya said, and for a panicked second, Claire thought she was talking to her, that this was about Dallas and Persimmon again. But no, Anya was glaring at Crispin. The Father—

Crispin said, The best thing we can do is ignore—

You need to call the lawyer, Anya said. Today. Now. Get Lucca on that conversation too.

At the mention of Lucca, the skin on Claire's arms prickled.

I have a dentist appointment, she said, shutting her laptop and packing her bag. I'll be working from home in the afternoon.

Let me think about how best to handle it, Crispin said.

This is becoming an issue, Anya said. She whirled around and raised her voice. Where is Lucca anyway? Does anyone know?

A few people shrugged. Claire, standing to leave, stared at a spot in the middle distance and kept her face blank. She was full of a jittery, swooping energy.

I've got it under control, Crispin told Anya firmly, sotto voce.

—

The streetcar stop was across from one of their billboard ads. Dallas, hands on hips, cape flapping behind her, stood larger than life, the tagline underneath *Become a #realhero*. When Claire reached the transit shelter, she found a group of Gen Zeds pontificating. One of them, a young man with a nose ring and microbangs, announced he'd begun to question the whole premise of philanthropy. The non-profit industrial complex, he said, without irony. Intentions are meaningless, like totally impotent, when the system itself is exclusionary and racist.

The master's tools will never dismantle the master's house, his friend, a white girl with dreadlocks, quoted.

Original, Claire thought scornfully, side-eyeing their thousand-dollar smartphones and sleeves of ink. Just her luck to have chanced on *The Bullhorn*'s entire listenership. These dollar-store social justice warriors with their prechewed stock phrases would slouch around sounding off about *neoliberal this* and *capitalism that* while half of Africa starved to death. At least Children of the World was doing something.

The streetcar arrived. Sliding into a single-seater next to a window, she put in her earbuds and caught up on *The Bullhorn* as they clattered down King Street. Claire had never paid the show much attention, but forced to become a regular listener, she had to grudgingly admit their journalism, when it wasn't about Children of the World, was sound.

Emmanuelle and the host had gotten so chummy, they could riff off each other and improvise. Today they were accusing philanthropists of using charity to distract from their misdeeds.

Have you noticed it's the criminals who are the keenest philanthropists? the host asked. Bernie Madoff. Lance Armstrong. The Sacklers. Even Epstein had a foundation.

Credit to the original gangsters, Emmanuelle said. Vanderbilt. Rockefeller. Carnegie. These robber barons, they give and they give and they give, and somehow, funny thing, it never subtracts from their wealth.

The math doesn't math, the host quipped, and Claire had to agree. No one makes a billion dollars, Crispin often said, they *take* it. But when they began dissecting celebrity psychology, she understood why he'd felt targeted.

They're rich and famous, surrounded by yes-men, the host said.

And blessed with generational wealth, Emmanuelle added. These guys act as if they hit a triple when they're born on third base. Naturally, whatever isn't handed to them, they have the confidence to take. I would, too, if I had no conscience and my every whim was bankrolled by Mommy and Daddy.

They've been successful in one area, music or tech or whatever, often through dumb luck or nepotism, and assume they can do no wrong, the host added.

But conflict, poverty, disease, these are complicated issues, Emmanuelle said. Is there anyone less qualified to solve them than an entertainer?

The host guffawed. The truth is they know jack shit about other people's problems.

Claire clenched her jaw, indignant. Why was Emmanuelle harping on about generational wealth? In many ways, Crispin wasn't that far removed from the kids they were helping.

Children of the World loves to boast about their start-up ethos, Emmanuelle said.

Move fast and break things, the host scoffed. Isn't that what toddlers do on the playground?

They think the Global South *is* their personal playground. Whatever outlandish idea they dream up—an app for malnutrition! Have you ever heard of anything more ludicrous?—gets beta tested overseas. Why not? They're accountable to no one.

Claire scowled. This wasn't journalism. It was ad hominem attack.

No one's asking questions or scrutinizing their international operations, the host said. Instead of real oversight, there's a smokescreen of benevolence.

Exactly, Emmanuelle agreed.

The host's family had a saying: Their kindness is killing.

Only nihilists would complain about altruism, Claire thought, standing and gesturing for a man with a cane to take her seat. She'd had enough of these armchair naysayers, in their hermetically sealed sound booth, cut off from the real world, and those kids at the streetcar stop with more graduate degrees than life experience, thinking they knew everything. Meanwhile, the country director in India was reporting a bumper harvest, enough to freely distribute to villages in the area. And the school in Cambodia, the first one Children of the World had built, consistently graduated students who went on to university.

Emmanuelle and her chum began tearing into their orphanages, and Claire, reminded of Dallas's stonewalling, nervously wondered: What did they know?

They recruit locals to be child finders, Emmanuelle said. They roam the countryside searching for kids to snatch.

What you're describing sounds like child trafficking, the host said, and Claire closed her eyes, leaned her forehead against the cold metal of the pole. She had a woozy feeling, as if the ground underneath her had given out.

Emmanuelle said: If Children of the World was sincere in its mandate, they'd help keep families intact. In the West, there's a perception that if it's not nuclear, it doesn't count. But for most of the world, and even here we see this in Indigenous and immigrant households, families are more inclusive. Cousins are adopted in. Kids are raised by grandparents or older siblings.

It takes a village, the host quipped, and Claire opened her eyes, felt the floor solid under her feet again. Okay, they didn't know.

At Sherbourne, she got off and raced for the bus. Heavy clouds had swallowed the sun.

All over the world, institutional care is being phased out, Emmanuelle said. And for good reason. Children in institutions are at higher risk of neglect, sexual and physical abuse.

Like at residential schools, the host said, and Claire stifled a groan. People like Emmanuelle always did this: invoked the Indigenous issue like it was an ace. Even when it had no bearing on the matter at hand. Closing the app with a thumb swipe, she muted the outro theme and was returned to the half-full bus and her fellow riders, the hum of their voices, a panoply of Arabic and Cantonese.

A formless unease gnawed her insides. She couldn't look at this worry too long lest it coalesce into a specific shape. To distract herself, she texted the daycare to ask about Theo. At the drop-off that morning, he had staged a sit-in protest, forcing Claire to carry him while he wailed.

Waiting for the reply, she held her phone, weighing it in her palm. This phone, the tablet at the office, the laptop in her bag, all their electronics were made with coltan mined by children who should have been getting an education. At least the kids at their children's homes were in school.

Emmanuelle's snide voice in her head: *A school they parachuted volunteers in to build, a school they never finished*. A school they *would* finish, thanks to Dallas's donation, Claire argued back.

She cleared her throat to drown Emmanuelle out. An absurd vision: Theo's daycare full of Santa Rosan volunteers, stacking blocks and singing songs and chattering to the children in Spanish. She gave her head a shuddering shake. How lucky they were in Canada, where they weren't forced to make such compromises.

The bus drove past homeless shelters and halal shops, Victorian red bricks that had once been handsome. Claire disembarked at Allan Gardens, legs on autopilot, navigating left and right. Everywhere there was graffiti, threadbare green spaces dotted with tents. The sky was ominous, crackling with lightning, thunder rumbling close by.

At a grey concrete low-rise, she was buzzed in and climbed four flights. The door at the top of the stairs was cracked, propped open with the tongue of a Yale latch. Inside, Curtis Mayfield sang about a junkie named Freddie. Hanging her coat on a hook, Claire unzipped her boots and swayed her shoulders, carried along by the laid-back bass line and the flute in the foreground.

The apartment was four hundred square feet of open space with a mattress on a box spring against one wall and harvest-gold appliances against the other. At the peninsula counter, Lucca stood writing in a notebook. He wore faded jeans, thinning at the knees, their bottoms cuffed, and a grey sweatshirt that was patched over the elbows. At her arrival, he laid his pen down.

Anya's looking for you.

And you've found me.

He pulled her against him, so close she could see the bitten edges of his frayed collar. She sounded pretty annoyed.

Even as Claire said this, she couldn't think of why, the memory of that scene and everything back at the office smudged by Lucca's proximity, the slow burning grin spreading over his features like a taunt. Her pulse was in her stomach, thumping a heavy repetition: yes, yes, yes. He slipped a hand under her shirt, warm fingers splayed against her back.

Do you have anything this afternoon? he asked.

She wound her arms around his neck and shook her head. I'm all yours.

Now that's what I like to hear, he murmured, tracing her lower lip with his thumb.

She bit with deliberate force and watched his eyes glaze, the pupils so dark they merged with the irises, then flicked her tongue over the tip.

Minx, he said, and all the invisible switches flipped on, her whole body humming and buzzing, tiny hairs standing at attention.

Lucca lifted her leg, fingers grazing the hollow behind her knee. Claire put a hand on the counter to steady herself. She closed her eyes. Her insides unfurled like ribbons. Impatient, she tugged on his sweatshirt.

What's your rush? he mumbled, tongue against her collarbone.

She dropped her forehead against his shoulder and groaned. Lucca.

He was kissing her neck with slow deliberation, raking a hand through her hair and making her scalp tingle.

This obsession with efficiency—

Shut up and take off your clothes, she said.

—it's very capitalistic, he said. You North Americans are always in a hurry. So focused on productivity.

Lifting his collar, he pulled the sweatshirt off. Taut torso, dark nipples, a glimpse of a tattoo on his left pec. Claire was ravenous, her desire all sharp edges. She cupped the back of his head and reeled him in. Their kiss was voracious, full of greed. A collision of pheromones and release. He hitched her up, and she wrapped her legs around his waist. Thunder struck and the lights flickered.

Take me to bed, she said.

Groggy, Claire blinked her eyes open and stared at the unfamiliar popcorn ceiling. It took her a few moments to recall where she was. Lucca was housesitting, and the friend who owned this apartment was an artist, or possibly a drug dealer. The whole place smelled vaguely of hemp and microwaved oats. If smell had a texture, this one would be rough.

There was a big skylight but no windows. A furious rain battered the roof. It felt like she was in the belly of an overheated submarine.

Lucca paced, bare feet on parquet, wearing headphones and muttering to himself in another language. When he saw that she was awake, he crawled into bed, pulled the headphones down to his neck and said, Hello.

What's that? she asked, yawning, and he let her listen. Arabic? she guessed.

I'm trying to improve, he said, setting the headphones aside.

Why Arabic? Don't tell me you're job hunting, she joked as he rolled onto her.

You have to earn people's trust, Lucca replied between kisses. Language is one way.

Lucca spoke several, and Claire asked if he felt different in each one. A little. Yes. Take French, for example. In Paris it was very proper. Comme il faut. Even his gestures became guarded. In the south his thoughts raced. Vite, vite . . . that is how it is with Marseillais. But Lucca liked African French best. In West Africa, speech was clipped, sprinkled with loan words from the local languages. There he was gregarious, even his limbs loosened.

She tried and failed to imagine a chummy version of Lucca. She'd never heard him laugh. He was a chameleon, she realized, the person he became in Rome or Port-au-Prince might be wholly unrecognizable to her, maybe even unattractive. If they'd met in Santa Rosa, if she had flown there, who would she have found?

What about Portuguese? she asked, flipping their positions so she was on top. She wondered what he was like in his mother tongue. That would be the real Lucca.

A scowl flickered. I prefer English.

On the floor was an army-green duffel, sweaters and threadbare jeans spilling out, her own clothes discarded pell-mell. A passport on the dresser. A phone and wallet on a wooden crate next to the mattress. As much as she enjoyed living vicariously through his anecdotes, Lucca's life struck Claire as achingly lonely. The rootlessness, being tethered to no one.

What are you running from? she asked, sitting up, knees on either side, pinning him in place. She felt powerful like this, naked and upright, long hair tangled and loose, while he was half dressed beneath her.

Lucca turned his face away, rubbed his chin into his shoulder. Outside, a delivery van honked twice. She'd spoken spontaneously, hadn't meant to pinch a sore spot, but her curiosity won out and she waited, silent.

We should work, he said.

They sat across from each other at the chrome and vinyl table, twin laptops flipped open between them, and when she got stuck on a synonym for *humanitarian*, she paused to watch Lucca. He wore reading glasses and made grimacing faces at the screen, pigeon-pecking with two fingers.

Her phone lit up with a reply from the daycare, a photo of Theo up to his elbows at the sand table, heads together with another child. But rather than make her glad, it brought back the unsettling vision of the Santa Rosan volunteers, and she felt inexplicably sad. Theo so young and vulnerable, out there in the world without her, all alone. And Simon still wanted to whisk the kids off to India.

She thought of Persimmon's birth family and felt a guilty pang. In the absence of a reply from Dallas, she'd been compulsively rewatching the rescue footage, and now the whole thing was seared in her memory. The birth mother, briefly vocal in the background, describing the baby's illness, her anxiety requiring no translation. *She* wasn't the one who had hassled Lucca. Mothers sacrificed for their kids. Fathers preferred the notion of children to their actual care.

It's only a few weeks, Simon had argued. What's the big deal? The question had burrowed in like an ear worm.

Sometimes it seemed like there was nothing tangible tying her to her children, who strongly resembled their father, having inherited more of his colouring and features. She had only her love, the muscle memory of the nine months they'd each spent fused to her. How long before the statute of limitations on biology expired? In darker moments, she despaired of being made redundant. She recalled Persimmon's birth mother—the expression of gratitude and grief as she kissed her child goodbye—and quickly pushed the memory away.

Something wrong? Lucca asked.

Claire didn't want to talk about her children. She didn't want to be a mother here, like this, naked and dishevelled under one of Lucca's shirts. She told him about *The Bullhorn* and Emmanuelle's ludicrous allegations instead. It was a relief to unload on someone who understood first-hand the difference aid made.

It's like she thinks NGOs are to blame for orphans, not war or natural disasters or whatever, Claire said, heat rising with her voice.

Lucca listened intently—it was one of his best qualities—but when she was done, he said: She's right about orphanages. Ninety, maybe ninety-eight per cent of the children have a parent, even two, or some family.

Claire was taken aback. But then why—

It wasn't just Children of the World, he said, telling her about his experience in Aceh, after the 2004 tsunami, when hundreds of orphanages sprang up. Nearly all the children had families. Some weren't even affected by the flooding.

On the podcast, Emmanuelle had used a phrase she'd never heard before.

Paper orphans, Lucca said, nodding, when Claire asked. It's very common.

And when he saw Claire recoil, he added, You didn't know?

What about the girls in the DRC? she asked, feeling betrayed. The ones who were called witches and kicked out.

He frowned. Because their families were poor. Orphanages are offering room and board, school, medical care, everything parents can't afford.

Emmanuelle had called them *pull factors* and made a sarcastic aside about *market forces in action*. Claire had dismissed this as unfounded cynicism, but Lucca's nonchalance made her feel ignorant, then a moment later, irate.

She crossed her arms defensively. You don't seem to have a problem with it, she said.

These people have very limited options, and they make the best choices they can. Anyway, storybooks have given orphanages a bad name. It's just a boarding school.

She stared at him, eyes narrowed, the paltry facts she knew of his life, her colleagues' speculation, rearranging themselves.

What do you know about boarding school? she asked.

What your reporter said about recruitment is true, Lucca said. That's what happens.

She's not *my* reporter.

It was as if he took pleasure in disillusioning her. She felt all the old long-distance enmity then. Did you go to boarding school?

Would it make a difference if I had?

You're one of those billionaire da Silvas.

I don't know why you think that.

She raised her eyebrows, gestured to the borrowed apartment, with its bicycle mounted to the wall, and said, It's pretty obvious.

And it matters to you, who my family are.

If you agree with Emmanuelle, what are you doing here? What do you get out of it?

Are we fighting?

The question was playful, and for a moment she glowered. But then she thought about Dallas, how just as the actress had slammed the door on their budding friendship, Lucca had turned up, and her anger dissolved.

She rubbed her bare feet against the dust-furred floor. The ceiling fan twirled a clump of hair by her ankle. She'd expected Lucca to set her head straight, return her moral clarity.

You were in Haiti, she said. After the earthquake?

Why are you asking?

With Oxfam, she said. Did you know?

This was something she'd learned about on *The Bullhorn*, on one of the rare episodes that wasn't about Children of the World. At first, Claire had been relieved, until she heard what they'd had to say about Oxfam. Prostitutes hired by staff and brought to a villa that was rented with donor dollars, and the charity's flaccid defence: that in Haiti none of this was illegal. The ugly truth had come to light several years earlier, but for Claire the revelation was new.

You've never just put your head down and done your job? he asked.

So you knew.

Everyone knew.

Is it true they used . . . *minors*?

Oxfam denied those allegations. They were never proven, Lucca said quickly. Then he rubbed his nose and muttered: I wasn't part of it. It was nothing to do with me.

No judgment. That's not how I mean this. But how did you keep going?

We set up a canteen and paid locals to run it. Our warehouse was in pieces, and we went in with helmets, formed a human chain, and salvaged supplies. I managed a camp, hired locals to dig latrines, keep the place clean. You'd understand if you'd been there. Most of my co-workers were good people. And if we all quit, then what?

Why do we have orphanages anyway? Claire asked. Why does anyone? Especially if it would be cheaper to give families money and let them keep their kids at home. Don't you think?

Lucca shook his head. This is Crispin's charity. It's not for me to say how he runs his organization.

She told him about the young people she'd overheard. Burn it all down, that's their solution.

Lucca said he'd been just as ardent once, adding: But there's the ideal, and then there are the facts on the ground. It's no use railing against the system. Better to work with what you have.

And work with who we can, she said, thinking of *collaboration*, that Janus-faced word. She was recalling something Emmanuelle had said. Or it might have been a rant Claire had read online. The choir of dissent intruded on her thoughts more and more these days. Claire had expected Lucca to be principled. Turned out, he was a pragmatist.

Doesn't it bother you? she insisted. She'd taken it for granted that their work was unassailable.

He made his hands into fists, holding up first one, then the other, saying: Here are the things I'm proud of, the positive outcomes we manage to achieve. And here is the wider, convoluted clusterfuck that is bigger than all of us. He knocked his fists together. Those are the realities I've been ramming up against for half my life.

But if we're just cogs in this . . . I dunno, doomsday machine, why don't we do something?

The global economy, that's a huge complex system. He held up peace fingers. You and I are two people. We can't change the world.

Scoop

Emmanuelle

A voice full of gravitas and vinegar introduced herself as Quinn Montgomery.

I hear you have a celebrity bombshell, she said.

Thank you for taking the time, Emmanuelle said.

Quinn was a literary agent who represented a former classmate. Emmanuelle had cashed in a major IOU to make this conversation happen.

I've never worked with an agent, Emmanuelle said, not quite knowing how to begin. So I'm not even sure if this is something you—

Drugs or sex? Quinn asked.

Neither, Emmanuelle said. Less salacious, more substantive.

Is it MeToo?

Emmanuelle was thrown off by the terse interrogation, the suspicion that Quinn was multitasking and might hang up at any moment, and found her own answers becoming unnaturally clipped.

Nothing like that, she said. But a crime. Allegations of a crime.

Her friend had suggested Emmanuelle work with an agent rather than pitching editors directly. Emmanuelle knew there were mercenaries who started bidding wars over sex tapes and topless photos, tawdry scandals she skimmed in the grocery line, but she'd never counted her own reporting in that category. Instinct warned her to be protective of Jorge's tragedy.

Well now, Quinn said. We talking A-list?

Yes. Emmanuelle hesitated, then added, It's about Dallas Hayden.

Alright, Quinn said with an abrupt change of tone. I have ten minutes. Let's hear it.

Emmanuelle, despite her qualms, launched in, growing increasingly emboldened as she unravelled Jorge's story, outraged anew by the injustice. Readers would share her indignation. They would want more.

Tell me you have corroboration, Quinn said.

Absolutely, Emmanuelle said. With multiple sources.

Micah had performed a miracle: secured her an interview with a staffer in Santa Rosa. The woman had agreed to a conversation, just one. She didn't want it taped. Micah translated while Emmanuelle took furious shorthand. No, she wouldn't be named. Not even with initials. I need this job, she said and suggested a pseudonym. Call me Persimmon Pink.

Do you know if anyone spoke to the Garcias about adoption? Emmanuelle asked.

Señor da Silva, the woman said. But he'd been acting on orders from above. There had been a call with Toronto. Sin alternativa, the woman had said. *No choice*.

When Emmanuelle was done speaking, there were a few moments of silence on Quinn's end, only the click-clack of keystrokes as she murmured: Hmmm . . . yes. I see what you mean. Okay, she said abruptly. I have the broad strokes. What is it you think I can do?

I was wondering about the *New York Times*, Emmanuelle said, instantly shy. Or maybe the *L.A. Times* would be more appropriate given the Hollywood angle.

But a bombshell like this was surely only the beginning. After it broke, every outlet would jump on the bandwagon. Emmanuelle would take care with the article, weighing every word and sentence, judging their consequence. The goal was to back Dallas into a corner with a single escape hatch, a way to credibly save face. Emmanuelle pictured Dallas appearing makeup free and casual on one of her social media channels, claiming the separation was always meant to be temporary. She'd only taken Maria to get her the most cutting-edge treatment. And then she'd bring a film crew along for the reunion, her triumphant return to the Garcias' home, bearing their child.

You're sure the father will come forward? He won't get cold feet? Quinn asked.

In her notebook, Emmanuelle had underlined the word *determined*. Dallas, Crispin's charity, they had all counted on Jorge being a pushover, someone without agency who could be ignored.

He'll do whatever it takes to get his daughter back, Emmanuelle said.

Do you have photos of the birth family with the child?

Not with Maria, no, Emmanuelle said. But I can get photos of the parents and maybe the other kids too.

Not ideal, but we'll work with it. An exposé and an exclusive. I can sell it, Quinn said, then started throwing out numbers, startling sums.

Emmanuelle was astonished—enjoyed a private moment of victory against faithless Ben who'd begged her to quit—but only for a second. The clock was ticking. Every hour she wasted chewing the inside of her cheeks was another one the Garcias lost with their child.

What do you need from me? Emmanuelle asked.

I'm going to level with you, Quinn said. This is too sensational for the broadsheets. It's more of a tabloid story. The *Sun* or the *Enquirer*. Maybe *Life & Style*.

But it's true, Emmanuelle said. Her stomach plummeted. I have sources at the airfield, Santa Rosa's judiciary—

If this was your child or mine or what have they got in Santa Rosa, a president? If it was his kid, that would be different.

But—

I'm not saying I won't pitch it to the broadsheets first, but realistically we're talking about an A-list actress and an illiterate nobody from the third world.

Emmanuelle flinched, instantly sorry she hadn't heeded her instincts.

I call it like I see it, Quinn said. But okay, I can probably talk them up a little, given its front-page content and we'll have visuals.

Then she named an even higher dollar figure.

That evening, Ben smashed garlic cloves with the flat edge of a knife while Emmanuelle sat on the counter, drumming the backs of her heels against the cupboard doors, and brought him up to speed. They were a week into March, but since her astonishing discovery, they'd called a fragile moratorium on career-change negotiations.

So now what? he asked. Think Jorge will go for it?

We thank God for you every day, Micah had said recently, on one of the catch-up calls they had without Jorge, when Emmanuelle gave updates on her findings and tried to temper expectations. You are an answer to prayer. Jorge's been visiting the compound, and I've been leaving messages for Crispin St. Onge, and we've gotten nowhere. But you—

I'm just doing my job, Emmanuelle had replied, uncomfortable.

We never know where intercession will come from, Micah had said, but the Lord is working through you. Trust in that.

Jorge will agree to anything, no matter how long a shot, if he thinks it might help, Emmanuelle told Ben. They've lost a child. And I'm taking advantage.

Think of it another way, Ben said. Jorge wants you to tell the world what's happened.

Yeah, but Quinn's talking about a tabloid. No one will believe it.

You could sell it to the *Herald*, Ben said and kept chopping, pointedly focused on the knife.

The landlord was coming by with a realtor on the weekend; this year it seemed he might keep his resolution.

Art would take it, Emmanuelle said. But for a fraction of what a paper like the *National Express* would pay.

It *is* a lot of money, Ben said, and Emmanuelle could see him mentally adding the figures, working out which debts they could settle.

And there might be more opportunities for follow-ups, Emmanuelle said, thinking of how much time the story would buy her, before Ben began agitating about a career change again.

What about the other thing . . . that stuff in Indonesia? he asked.

Emmanuelle tapped her fingers on the underside of the counter. To her surprise, the lead had panned out. Her source had replied, not only agreeing to an interview but sending a detailed email about two volunteers who had preyed on a child, returning every few months to abuse her. A couple of months ago, she'd have taken it to Art and insisted he run the story. But now she knew exactly what he'd say.

It's old news, she parroted to Ben. Crispin fired the country director and banned the volunteers—after closing his eyes and sticking his fingers in his ears for years, mind you. But still, Art will say bygones.

The tone is personal, Art taunted in her head. *You and Crispin go way back or something?*

And maybe Art was right. Children of the World would reframe the allegations as a one-off incident they had swiftly addressed. Crispin's apology would sound sincere while eliding responsibility, stress the fact that these events had happened long ago, making two years sound like ten. Behind the scenes, a board director would call Art's boss and remind him of the definition of *newsworthy*, and what stories did and did not sell papers. And for her trouble, Emmanuelle would end up without a byline and another black mark against her name instead.

Emmanuelle was tired of fighting. The call with Quinn had been so *easy*. And the money . . .

She knocked her heels faster, full of pent-up vigour. It seems wrong to be excited about this . . .

Ben caught her eye and said, Scoop.

Emmanuelle groaned. Twelve years of a stalled-out career and finally a break. Of course it would come with strings.

—

Jorge worked long hours, so by the time they talked it was dusk in Santa Rosa and already dark in Toronto. Jorge was still in his workman's clothes, face glistening, hair plastered to his head, slumped in a chair, eyes drooping with fatigue.

When Emmanuelle relayed her conversation with Quinn, Jorge became animated. She believes me? he said.

Yes, Emmanuelle lied, thinking belief likely didn't factor into the agent's calculations.

It'll be in all the newspapers and on television?

One paper to start, Emmanuelle said. But hopefully others will pick it up. She thought about qualifying *there are no guarantees*, but didn't. Instead, she said: The agent is confident she can get the story published. *The National Express* seems most likely.

No way, Micah exclaimed, before he'd even translated for Jorge. No, no, no.

Jorge glanced back and forth between Emmanuelle and Micah.

It's not ideal, Emmanuelle said, but we have to be realistic.

Micah took his time relaying the message in Spanish, and Emmanuelle could tell he was adding his own editorial.

Their circulation is over three hundred thousand, she said. They sell copies at the checkout of every supermarket and pharmacy in the U.S. This will be a front-page story, she added, though that wasn't confirmed.

Micah reluctantly translated, and Jorge nodded enthusiastically.

That's good, Jorge said. People will see. They will know.

It's a chance to tell your side.

In a tabloid that has no credibility, Micah said.

Emmanuelle was irritated, with Micah, with herself. Didn't he understand it was this or nothing? She said, They run legitimate stories too.

Infidelity scandals and extramarital pregnancies, Micah said, in English and Spanish, then added: No one believes what those papers publish. They will make you look like a liar.

I'll be the one writing the story, Emmanuelle said. I won't allow one word of it to be disrespectful.

She didn't mention that she'd have no control over the headline.

It's up to you and Inez, she told Jorge. I won't do anything unless you agree.

What about the newspaper you write for? Micah asked. The *Herald*.

They have limited reach, she said. The circulation is fifty, maybe sixty thousand and mostly in Canada. If we want to pressure Dallas, you'll need more than that *and* U.S. readers.

The whole world should know, Jorge said.

But will it be credible? Micah said. That's my concern.

I think we can all agree that the goal is to get Maria home. The public won't stand for the truth once they know it.

It's a rag that invents alien visitations, Micah said.

Is this true? Jorge asked.

Emmanuelle avoided Micah, focused on Jorge. This is our best chance.

I pray you're right about this, Emmanuelle, Micah said before they hung up. And Emmanuelle heard the subtext of disappointment.

It was after hours, but she emailed Dallas's publicist anyway and was surprised when the reply ricocheted back: *For the privacy of all involved, especially the child, Ms. Hayden won't comment further.* Emmanuelle scrutinized the words *the child* and felt uneasy.

There was one last source to call for comment: Children of the World. Emmanuelle wondered how much Claire knew. Phone between her palms and pressed to her nose, she thought about Jorge, the way his face had fallen when he'd learned about the *National Express*, and how he'd shaken off his misgivings and said, I'll do anything to get Maria back. Even when Micah tried to talk him out of it, Jorge had refused to budge. She imagined him and Inez at the altar, surrounded by Micah's congregation, the laying on of hands, the minister solemnly improvising a prayer. *Lord we commend the Garcias to your mercy. We pray that you will . . .*

Emmanuelle had never made peace with this part of the job. When the story was personal for the sources, and she had to earn their trust. Scavengers only picked over carrion. Journalists sought out the vulnerable and ate them alive.

Gotcha

Claire

At the cabinet, Claire flipped through the hanging folders and plucked a file at random. Catching Lucca's eye across the office, she spun on her heel and strode down a long, little-used hallway. Hearing his footsteps gave her a delicious thrill of anticipation, and she added an extra swing to her hips. Claire was intoxicated with the person she became around Lucca, every movement seductive and sensual. As his departure neared—only five more days—they'd grown incautious.

Entering the copy room, she glanced back to toss a flirty grin over her shoulder and walked smack into Crispin.

Oh!

Crispin jerked his mug away just in time but sloshed coffee on his hand. Hot! he exclaimed, wincing.

Claire, in a confusion of panic and arousal, hyperaware of Lucca on her heels, said, *What?*

That could have been messy, Crispin chuckled. Good morning, you two.

Morning, Lucca said.

Claire put a hand to her waist, the other on the copier, and bent over the touch screen, momentarily bewildered by its digital shorthand. Morning, she mumbled, jabbing haphazardly.

I was just looking for you, Crispin said to Lucca. We should strategize before the meeting.

Claire placed her prop face down on the scanner as Crispin prattled with unusually nervous energy. She caught the words *Tilden*, *social enterprise*, and *novel revenue stream*. Her pulse had calmed, but the tips of her ears were still on fire. She yawned in a pantomime of Monday languor.

Not that there's any reason for concern, Crispin said. Today is just formalities. Sign on the dotted line, etc. Still, it'll be good to have you there.

Claire tucked the unnecessary photocopy into her folder and called a prim All yours as she left. Even before she reached her desk, there was a text. *Stairwell in 10.* She imagined Lucca surreptitiously thumbing the message, nodding and uh-huh-ing as Crispin droned on, and felt a heady, illicit buzz. She was still beaming to herself, mindlessly clicking, unable to focus, when the landline rang. Lifting the receiver, she said: How are you, Emmanuelle? Did you have a nice weekend?

On the other end, Emmanuelle paused before replying. Yeah, not bad. Yours?

A-plus weekend, Claire said. My kids were with their father.

Lucca was emerging from the hallway with Crispin, who had his head bent and was speaking seriously. Lucca glanced her way, curling a corner of his mouth. She pictured the stairwell, her leg hooked over his shoulder, skirt pushed up. Time warped, and when Claire came to her senses, she realized she was listening to silence. Had Emmanuelle said something? Was she waiting for

Claire's reply? Just as she was wondering if they'd been cut off, Emmanuelle asked about Dallas's daughter. How exactly had she found her?

Claire startled. In a neutral tone, she said, Dallas was part of a medical rescue that brought the baby to our clinic.

I didn't realize Dallas was a trained medic, Emmanuelle said, and before Claire could think of a response, Emmanuelle went off on what she called their *voluntourism model* and Children of the World flying in untrained scabs.

Claire exhaled. Okay. The call wasn't about Persimmon after all. She could parry this attack.

I don't think it's fair to denigrate volunteers, she said. Their visits have a lasting impact, transforming lives and shaping our young people to be better citizens of—

Getting back to Maria, Emmanuelle interrupted, and Claire—mid-sentence—almost blurted *Who?*

Persimmon, Claire said, a firm self-correction she unintentionally voiced.

Persimmon, Emmanuelle repeated. She didn't bother to hide her sarcasm, pronouncing the name in a way that made it clear she was attaching air quotes.

That's not—

And have I got this correct, Emmanuelle asked, Dallas brought the baby to your compound where your staff facilitated the adoption?

Where our doctor treated her ear infection. With Dallas's help. We couldn't do what we do without volunteers.

Claire struggled to ignore the awful tumbling in her stomach, the telltale heart drumming in her left ear. Recently even Dallas's assistant had stopped replying to her emails, the ones she sent about the promotional campaign and future travel plans, the ones that had nothing to do with Persimmon.

Is it common for volunteers to adopt children? Emmanuelle asked.

To my knowledge, this is the first time.

And whose idea was it?

Bringing her laptop to life, Claire keyed in her password. Her fingers trembled, and she flubbed the code twice. From across the room, Lucca, now at his own desk, tipped his head toward the exit and raised his brows at her. She widened her eyes at him. *Save me*. Shrugging, he put his glasses on and returned to his screen.

This was one hundred per cent Dallas, Claire said finally. We can't take credit for any of it.

Here's the thing. The Garcias say their baby was kidnapped.

Claire's knee was a jackhammer. Through the glass walls, she could see Anya in her office, shoes off, rolling a stockinged foot over a tennis ball.

The adoption is a private matter between Dallas Hayden and the baby's birth family. Perhaps her manager or lawyer—

Emmanuelle said there was no evidence of adoption. No lawyers, no paper trail. As far as she could tell the child didn't even have a passport.

Mastheads flashed through Claire's imagination. The *New York Times*. The *Washington Post*. CNN's theme song, the volume on blast. She squeezed her eyes closed, tried and failed to breathe from her diaphragm. Emmanuelle was talking as if she'd been to Santa Rosa. Impossible.

These are serious allegations, she said. Opening her eyes, she was faced with the background on her computer screen: her kids in matching overalls, digging in the sandbox. Seeing her father's unruly eyebrows on Theo, her mother's thin lips on Charlotte, her own dimple replicated on each of their left cheeks, Claire was overcome with sorrow.

Emmanuelle claimed she'd spoken with the baby's father. It was heartbreaking, to be honest, she said.

Claire told herself to get a grip. Lucca had made it clear the father was a reprobate, *and* he'd said the mother was in favour of adoption.

What about the mother? Claire asked and was emboldened by the uncertain pause on the other end of the line. Emmanuelle was childless. She didn't have a clue.

The Garcias don't have a television, Emmanuelle said. The nearest movie theatre is hours away. To them, Dallas Hayden is no one. Why would they let a stranger take their baby?

Millions of people had watched the rescue, Claire reminded herself. They'd all witnessed Persimmon's pitiful cries, her blank look of illness and hunger as she lay in that hammock. They'd heard the birth mother's gratitude, the way she'd kissed her hands and laid them over the baby's face. They'd *heard* her begging Dallas to make the little girl well. Emmanuelle's story was absurd. No way LAX was letting a baby through without—

But no, Emmanuelle claimed she'd spoken to an employee at a private airfield who'd been working the day Dallas flew out. There had been a last-minute addition to the flight roster, a Gulfstream V that had arrived with only the pilot on board and left with two passengers: Dallas and a baby.

Passport control is . . . *irregular* at private airfields, Emmanuelle said.

Claire hated these gotcha moments. Who had tipped her off?

Lucca da Silva, Emmanuelle said, and Claire jolted.

What?

Through the line, it sounded like Emmanuelle was turning pages, flipping through a spiral notebook, the kind that was bound at the top and slid neatly into a breast pocket. What's his role?

It's really Dallas—

No comment, Emmanuelle said. A strange response, don't you think? If it was all above—

Children of the World wasn't involved in the adoption, Claire said.

Children of the World, Emmanuelle said. All this emphasis on overseas missions and transforming volunteers' lives. Whose children exactly are you serving?

Claire was frustrated with Dallas, whose silence had forced her into this position of having no answers, and felt the injustice of being misunderstood. I'm not the bad guy here, she thought. If Emmanuelle only knew what she had sacrificed for this job, how hard she worked. Casting about in search of comfort, her eyes landed on their website, the word *community* in bold font. Our projects are more than the sum of their individual parts, she said. In Indonesia and El Salvador and where have you, we're building community.

Emmanuelle's laugh was a snort, an ungainly sound that seemed to burst out of her without warning. It curdled Claire's emotions. She felt beat down and exhausted as Emmanuelle kept pummelling: People have been living in those places for millennia. What makes you think they haven't already got communities?

That's not what I meant, Claire said, tears brimming.

I think it's exactly what you meant.

Why are you attacking me? Claire cried.

There was a long moment of terrible silence. A couple of colleagues looked up, and Claire hunched, hiding her stricken face.

It's my job to ask questions, Emmanuelle said coolly. There's no reason to take this personally.

Claire was mortified. She'd always been unflappable with journalists. I'm sorry. That was unprofessional, she said. But you're sullying the name of a charity that does a lot of good in the world.

Emmanuelle didn't reply and Claire wondered if the interrogation was over. Is that all you needed? she asked.

I spoke to a source in Santa Rosa who says the order came from above. That Lucca da Silva was sent by Head Office to pressure the family. Can you confirm that?

Who told you that? Claire spoke without thinking and then regretted not phrasing her question better. *Pressure the family*. She watched Lucca leaning over from his desk to speak to the intern. Is that how Lucca had described it? What else had he said? She asked, Is this for *The Bullhorn*?

Emmanuelle was silent. Then finally, her voice quiet, she admitted, It's for the *National Express*.

After the call ended, Claire was incensed. Emmanuelle was no one, just an unemployed reporter desperate for a byline. And when potshots weren't enough, she was regurgitating gossip in a rag that photoshopped cellulite onto actresses' thighs. No wonder Dallas's publicist had given her the brush-off. If Claire had known, she'd have done the same, with a laugh, and avoided the interrogation.

Recalling Emmanuelle's imperious tone, her faux sympathy—*it was heartbreaking, to be honest*—Claire seethed. Emmanuelle was acting like Claire had plotted an abduction, when all she'd done was sign up a volunteer. And Persimmon *was* better off.

Automatically, she checked her texts—still no word—and then Dallas's social media. There was a new Reel from the set of the *Sentinels* movie, Dallas in her costume, transforming into Freya.

Claire scrolled, travelling backward in time, February, January, December. She'd been doing this a lot lately, viewing old footage, proof of Dallas's devotion and Persimmon's progress.

Claire paused, confused. Just yesterday she'd rewatched a video from November, of Persimmon blowing kisses through her lips. Now the baby was gone, scrubbed from Dallas's accounts. Was she spooked? Worried for Persimmon's safety?

She texted Dallas: *Emmanuelle Clemmons called for comment. I'm really sorry about all this. LMK if you want to talk it through*.

Claire chewed on her lip. She regretted how she'd handled herself with Emmanuelle. It was a reporter's role to ask difficult questions and a publicist's job to remain unflappable. She didn't recognize her professional self lately, nervous and perpetually on edge. Claire had always kept her composure, even when being grilled on live television about a client's most heinous actions.

Whose children are you serving? She pushed the question out of her mind and focused on another: who told Emmanuelle about the father's accusations?

Striding to Lucca's desk, she said, Can I speak to you? and didn't wait for his reply before heading into a meeting room. He closed the door and reached for her wrist, but she crossed her arms and told him about the call.

Lucca's expression remained impassive as she recounted the conversation. Can you believe her? she finished.

This obsession with celebrities is very strange, he said.

You might not like it and yeah, maybe it's silly, but actors have huge platforms, she said.

Santa Rosa is in the middle of a ten-year drought, he said. She could have brought attention to that. Instead, she made a melodrama over an ear infection.

You're the one who let Dallas take Persimmon, Claire said.

The jab was reflexive, spurred by impatience, Anya's accusation unconsciously aped. Even as the words left her mouth, Claire had already forgotten them.

Lucca shook his head vehemently and made to exit. She grabbed his arm, forcing him to a standstill. Why was he being so evasive?

She said: I assume this man Emmanuelle interviewed, the birth father, is the same one who came to the compound. How did she find him?

Reporters, how do they find anything? he said, shaking her off. You need to ask her.

I think she's been to Santa Rosa, Claire said. Have the staff—

The business with the child, it's nothing to do with me, Lucca interrupted.

Emmanuelle thinks just because she can't find the adoption papers . . . but did she ever stop to consider that there could be extra confidentiality when it's a high-profile . . .

The private jet wasn't the smoking gun Emmanuelle imagined, Claire realized. Of course Dallas wouldn't fly commercial, where any stranger might snap a photo; she'd been trying to shield Persimmon.

Lucca made a show of checking the time and said, I have a meeting.

She asked about you, Claire said and repeated Emmanuelle's claims about Lucca's visit to the family. His eyes widened, then slid away. For weeks now, Claire had suspected a mole. How else would Emmanuelle know about the deprioritized projects? Was *Lucca* her source? She hugged her elbows, feeling exposed.

It's something that never should have happened, Lucca said.

What do you mean?

Lucca turned his head and Claire followed his gaze, out the window to the slushy sidewalk below, where a man pressed two fingers to his mouth and exhaled smoke. How could he say that? What was a little bad press stacked against the lifelong benefits for Persimmon?

That reporter, Lucca said. Did she tell you who she spoke with in Santa Rosa?

What shouldn't have happened?

He met her eyes. This whole thing. You shouldn't have started it.

Claire blinked, taken aback by his resentment, humiliated that he'd been nurturing the grudge all these weeks. She asked, Is that what you told Emmanuelle?

Well, this is cozy, Anya said, as she and Crispin barged in.

Time to meet Robertsons, Crispin told Lucca.

Noticing their postures, Anya asked, What's going on?

Lucca glowered as Claire explained. Crispin listened, shaking his head no, no, no, as if rejecting the news would make it untrue. She's had it out for us from the start, he said.

Claire was jittery and wished neither of the men were here, that she and Anya were alone because soon Anya was going to ask the obvious question and Claire would have no choice but to admit she'd dropped a big ball.

I told you this issue wouldn't resolve itself, Anya said to Crispin. Did you phone that priest back?

Crispin said he'd spoken with their legal counsel, that there was nothing to worry about, then added, But we're on the verge of signing Robertsons . . .

At the mention of legal counsel, Claire grew uneasy. The realization that behind the scenes, other concerns had been raised. Had Dallas taken a short cut, flown Persimmon to the U.S. before the paperwork was finalized, before *both* parents were in agreement?

Never should have happened. She began to wonder if she'd misunderstood Lucca. The thought left her cold, this possibility far worse than a lover's antipathy.

What does Dallas have to say for herself? Anya asked.

Claire squeezed her hands together. I haven't heard from her since before Lucca . . . since before the open house. She's icing me out.

I see. Anya fixed her with a searing stare. Then she sighed, and her shoulders sagged. I was afraid that might be the case.

She wanted then for Anya to call her irresponsible and a liar, to rail at Claire for not following up. Anything but this look of shame that was a mirror of her own.

She had a memory of Simon, slumped in the doorway of their bedroom, at the end of another marathon fight about professional necessity and personal ethics, asking: *When did you become this way? You used to be kind*.

What kind of damage are we talking? Crispin asked.

It's the *National Express*, not the *New York Times*, Claire said.

Those papers are everywhere, Crispin moaned. It won't matter that it's bunk. It'll tank our fundraising.

No one cares about us, Claire said. It's Dallas who'll catch the flak.

We'll get Robertsons to sign today, before it comes out, Crispin told Anya.

Good thinking, Anya agreed.

Claire could tell the reply was reflexive, Anya's mouth on autopilot while her mind turned over the more pressing issue: was the allegation true?

An inconvenient memory, long suppressed, muscled its way to the surface: Lucca's comment about faked birth certificates, his shrugging insouciance that *these things happen*.

Anya sank into a chair, head in hands, while the clock ticked, and no one moved. Finally, she looked up, sought out Crispin.

Tilden is competitive, Crispin said. I'll tell him the grocery category is exclusive and suggest there's another contender, without naming names, let him think it's Farmer's.

While Crispin strategized, pacing and gesturing, Anya turned to Claire. Her eyes had a rheumy film that Claire had never noticed before.

We did a terrible thing, Anya said.

And Claire realized that at some point in the last five minutes, Lucca had slipped away.

Judas

Lucca

Lucca sped down King Street on his borrowed bicycle, his messenger bag strapped tight across his back. Two SUVs blared their horns at each other while a streetcar squealed on its tracks. Lucca swerved to avoid an oblivious pedestrian and felt the whoosh of a taxi accelerating past, the edge of his coat making fleeting contact with its door. Gripping the handlebars, he pedalled hard, sailing through the intersection and zigzagging past a traffic snarl. He was hurt by how swiftly Claire had turned on him, her insistence that he alone was responsible: *You're the one who let Dallas take Persimmon*. He'd never blamed *her* for the confrontation with Jorge. Worse, he was troubled to discover the reporter had spoken to one of his staff.

Since arriving in Toronto, he'd been only sporadically in touch with Santa Rosa, reasoning that Thiago had things in hand. During their first conversation, about a week into his visit, he'd been dismayed to learn Jorge had returned, not once but twice, both times with a minister.

I had to show them all around, Thiago had said. I had to prove we weren't hiding his child. They'll be back. Señor Garcia won't give up.

I've told the bosses all about that, Lucca said. They're handling it now.

Then Maria will be returned? Thiago asked.

That's for Head Office to decide.

But you're there, Thiago said.

Awkwardly cosseted in an ergonomic desk chair, Lucca had heard barn animals in the background, imagined the earthy smell of manure, and been acutely aware of his own surroundings—the antiseptic sounds of keystrokes and murmured voices, the hum of the heating system.

I have to go, Lucca had said, cutting Thiago off mid-sentence. There's a meeting.

On Gerrard Street, Lucca stuck out his hand and veered left, entering a maze of row houses and back alleys, the asphalt cracked and potholed. It was garbage day, and black bins, wheeled to the curb, yawned open, their tops flipped back. Approaching his building, he coasted, swinging a leg over the saddle and crossing it behind the other.

At the loft he took the stairs two at a time to the roof, where a couple of broken-down lawn chairs faced out and pigeons roosted. After that first call, he'd made a habit of phoning Thiago from home. Up here he had a god's-eye view of the houses, pedestrians, and cyclists below, a pair of raccoons skulking like bandits.

Lucca bounced on the balls of his feet and shook out his wrists. He craved extreme physicality, something transportive. A quick hard jolt to the nervous system. A bungee jump. Skydiving. None of the surrounding buildings were close enough for him to leap to.

He pulled up Thiago's number and paced as he listened to the ringtone, surrounded by a white noise of juddering construction, wailing sirens, and the faint strains of a neighbour practising scales on an out-of-tune piano.

Boss.

Thiago never called him by his name, a quirk Lucca had always written off as innocuous. Today it sounded like sarcasm. After that first call, Thiago didn't mention Jorge again, and Lucca assumed the man had resigned himself to reality. But now he wondered if it was Thiago who'd given up, if he'd lost faith in Lucca and taken the matter into his own hands. Claire said the journalist had been to Santa Rosa. Lucca imagined her arriving at the compound with Jorge, Thiago shaking their hands, saying *Señor da Silva is responsible*.

He listened closely, not to what Thiago was saying so much as the tone of his voice, alert to any hint of remonstrance. But Thiago seemed his usual self, frank and competent. Lucca's check-ins were unscheduled and sporadic, yet Thiago was always ready with an update. Today it was all good news. The new math workbooks had arrived. Farm equipment was being repaired. There were three open cots in the nursery and two bunks in the under-five dormitory. Did Lucca want him to go out on another rescue?

Leave it, Lucca said, flinching at the word *rescue*. Immediately, he regretted his brusqueness. That's fine, he said. It's good to have beds available.

Thiago said nothing, and Lucca reconsidered his suspicions. Thiago was pragmatic. He paid the veterinarian and bought the schoolbooks; he understood how Dallas's intervention had reversed their fortunes. But Thiago was aware of other things, too, far more than Lucca. He must know who had spoken to the reporter, who the Judas was. As Lucca tried to think of a way to ask, Thiago began talking about the clinic.

On these calls, Thiago was strictly business, but in Santa Rosa their shop talk was mixed with casual gossip as they chuckled over a child's harmless prank or the not-so-secret grotto to the Virgin Mary that Beatriz had set up in a far corner of the property. Sometimes Thiago shared personal news like his pleasure at being asked to be his nephew's godfather. But now when Lucca asked about the christening, Thiago acted aloof.

My in-laws made the arrangements, Thiago said. It did not interfere with work.

Lucca was dismayed by his careful answer, verging on obsequious. You can always take a day off, he said and was instantly reminded of how he hadn't let the staff protest with the water defenders. The conversation stalled again, and Lucca had an uncomfortable feeling they were having the same thought.

He tried again, asking after Thiago's wife. But Thiago was curt, said yes, the whole family was well.

And how are the others—Beatriz, Enrique, Moisés?

Moisés is counting the days until your return.

The pianist in the building next door had progressed to sheet music, and Lucca paused, mid-step, recognizing the opening bars of "Für Elise," a melody he hadn't heard in years. How had the journalist found the compound? Someone must have shown her the way. Someone had alerted her to the fact that there was a story here at all.

They need me to stay, Lucca said. A few more weeks at least.

You're not returning? Thiago asked.

It is only a slight delay.

Moisés has his appointment.

The eye specialist in the capital. Lucca had forgotten. He imagined Moisés—the bedsheet tied to his shoulders, flapping behind him as he ran in wide circles around the journalist—saying: *Lucca said the doctor would fix my eyes. He promised to take me.*

I can drive him, Thiago said finally.

The disappointment in his voice made Lucca antsy. He resumed pacing and said, Take Beatriz.

Beatriz was a good mother. She'd be a more reassuring presence than him. He weighed the possibility that she was the reporter's source. But for all her vocal critique, Beatriz was timid. She'd never jeopardize her job.

Thiago reminded him that the realtor was expected soon, too, to discuss the purchase of additional land for the conference centre.

I trust you to handle it, Lucca said. I have every confidence in you. *Hago lo necesario*, he thought, then quickly, before he could lose his nerve, asked, Have there been visitors?

Thiago began talking about the volunteers, which groups had left and who had arrived. Anyone unexpected? Lucca cut in. Thiago was silent for a while—confused or caught? Finally, he said: Señor Garcia has been here several times. I wasn't sure you wanted to know.

He's spoken to a journalist, Lucca said, then paused, waiting.

I see.

There will be an article, Lucca said.

Then Maria will come home, Thiago said, and the relief in his voice was unmistakable.

Lucca was tempted to remind Thiago of his own actions—*you* were the one who convinced Inez to give up her baby, remember?—but then he recalled Anya praising Thiago, declaring him the best. A consummate right-hand man, he anticipated his boss's every desire and carried out even unspoken orders. And the one time Thiago had tried to resist, how had Lucca reacted?

He remembered the man's reluctance at the gates. Thiago guarding the switch, his posture stalwart, the tortured half groan as he wilted at Lucca's command. He could feel the swelter of the day, sweat dripping down his temples, the horn blast from the SUV; see the actress, the stubborn compression of her lips, the uncertain flicker in her eyes, her nervous fidget while Lucca hesitated. She'd thrown a protective arm across the carrier on her front and the bundle inside. Possible to imagine it wasn't Maria. Only a doll or a daypack or nothing at all. *Ábrelo*. The mutters and whispers, dismay crackling in the air, and how afterward, barricaded in his office, he'd still felt the compound's reproach.

Whatever happens, it is out of our hands, Lucca said into the phone.

Beatriz, Thiago, Luis, Yolanda, Josefina, they must all be in on it, Lucca realized. He recalled Dallas's quick clip out, imagined the reporter marching in, his staff crowding around, all of them speaking at once. *The boss likes to pretend he's one of us, but he's a foreigner. Worse, he's a coward. He couldn't even commit the crime himself.*

After the call, Lucca remained on the roof for a long time, collapsed in a lawn chair. In his last posting, he'd been working for a German NGO, rescuing refugees in the Mediterranean. All those sailing lessons he'd endured as a child—his father forcing them on him despite, or because of, his sea sickness—had finally come in handy. Lucca had spent three years in that job, been jailed more than once, in Italy, then again in Greece, for human trafficking.

The last group he'd hauled out of a glorified dinghy had travelled from the Ivory Coast. A fifteen-year-old boy and two men, the only survivors of a voyage that had embarked with more than fifty. It had taken time to coax out the tale. They were catatonic at first, after two days spent all alone on the open sea with Italian choppers circling overhead, monitoring but doing nothing. At least they weren't shooting. Anya wrote him off as a braggart, but no one knew these stories. Donors wanted to hear about the drama and heroics, but actual suffering? That was a buzzkill.

A fire truck sped past with its banshee scream. Lucca remembered Maria's hiccupping cries, the one time he'd held her. He tried to force the memory out by conjuring his friends from the Ivory Coast. They had found common ground in French and played hours of euchre and rummy and a game they had taught him. But now he couldn't recollect their conversations, not a single word or phrase, not even the subjects. Maria's wail was all he heard. He cast about for another memory, something deeper, older, more painful, and resurrected his father. A blistering day when his siblings were getting lessons while he heaved his guts off the side of the boat and his father denounced him as *useless*, *a total waste of space*. He rubbed a thumb over his wrist, felt the thin fragile skin, the tendon and blue vein underneath, tried to evoke the feel of the belt buckle and came up blank. Maria sobbed on.

After the 2004 tsunami, he'd been one of the first aid workers on the scene. In Guinea, he'd volunteered as an Ebola contact tracer. Whenever helmets were in short supply, he was always the first to shuck his own. He'd broken limbs, fractured ribs, had guns pointed at him. In Sri Lanka, he'd raced to a bunker while bombs lit the sky, a child in his arms and another clinging to his back. He could set a career of sacrificial valour against this one great and terrible mistake, a singular act of cowardice. But it was vanity. The scales would never balance.

Lucca slid his wallet out of his back pocket, removing a business card. He'd been carrying it around since the evening of the office party. He studied the font and lettering, felt its crisp edges. Considering.

Focus Group

Claire

Dallas stole my baby screamed the headline under the red masthead. The main image was a paparazzi picture from Christmas of Dallas pushing a stroller and turning her face away from the camera, Persimmon hidden by the sun shade. The inset photo was a mug shot of Jorge Garcia, swarthy and unshaven, doing himself no favours with that scowl.

In the days before the article ran, Claire had been convinced that Dallas had committed a reprehensible crime and she herself was implicated. But in print the accusations were so melodramatic, so patently *absurd*, that they could be nothing but fiction.

Without a good editor to moderate her excesses, Emmanuelle was effusive in her disdain. *The flamboyant rescue operation was broadcast on social media. Cropped and filtered in a gauzy sepia hue, this savvy bit of myth-making was accompanied by a soaring soundtrack—a soft launch for Hayden's directorial career, no doubt, and a philanthropic farce.* Claire could just imagine her cackling over the keyboard, as she punctuated the article with hysterical quotes: *They stole my child. She is my blood.* The mother, name-dropped by the father and Emmanuelle, was conspicuously absent from the piece.

Children of the World was a postscript, an innocuous statement from Claire the only evidence of the disastrous interview. *(Despite their high-profile connection with the actress, the organization shrugs off responsibility. "Children of the World wasn't involved in the adoption," their spokesperson said.)*

Claire was savouring her toast over the sink—solitary breakfasts being a perk of shared custody—and catching up on the latest Tupac sightings when Simon phoned.

My god, Claire. Did you have any idea?

It's not true, she snorted. Obviously.

Are you sure? The writer is legit.

Emmanuelle Clemmons is an unemployed hack; she'd sell her mother for a byline, Claire said.

For once, Simon was stunned into silence. Sipping her coffee, Claire languidly turned a page, relishing his discomfort. She heard the scrape of a chair and imagined him in his empty classroom, students just arriving on the bus.

Well, good, he said finally. I hate to think—

The kids have got the dentist at five, Claire interrupted.

That's today? Can we—

We cannot, she said and hung up.

Flipping back to the cover, she examined Jorge's photo. What would happen if Dallas gave Persimmon back to this man? Anyone could see he didn't have the wherewithal to care for her.

Still, she approached the office tentatively, wary of Crispin's and Anya's reactions. At the agency, tabloid potshots raised few eyebrows, but Children of the World had always occupied the moral high ground and weren't used to finding themselves in the gutter press. Through the glass wall of his office, she saw Crispin bent over the phone looking grave, palms planted on his desk. Anya waved her in.

Jim Whalen's disembodied voice filled the room: Robertsons is trying to move away from negative headlines, not court them.

That's why we feel it would be prudent to hold off on announcing the partnership for a week or two, Crispin said.

He glanced at Anya, expectant. But Anya was rubbing a thumbnail against her lip, lost in thought. Crispin made a come-on motion with his hand. When Anya remained silent, Claire pointed a thumb at herself.

I have our comms manager here, Crispin said.

We're only recommending this delay out of an abundance of caution, Claire said. But we're not concerned. The *National Express* is hardly a paper of record. We've run the article past an ad hoc panel, and the consensus is the allegations lack credibility.

Oh, good, Jim said, audibly relieved. That was my impression, too, but you know how it is . . . Some of the senior team members are nervous.

That's perfectly understandable given your context, Claire said, which is why we gathered some neutral opinions.

Well, you can see it, can't you, Jim said, voice light. Just in this photo, just in his face. That's a grifter, if I saw one.

Anya inhaled sharply, and Crispin quickly spoke: It's not uncommon, in high-profile adoptions, for relatives to come out of the woodwork.

Then he regaled Jim with the story of the pop star and her entertainment lawyer son. But Claire was watching Anya, who remained catatonic. Catching Crispin's eye over Anya's head, Claire raised her brows, but he just shrugged back.

After the call, Crispin dropped the receiver and made an exaggerated exhale. Claire, playing along, sagged dramatically.

Did you really hold a focus group? he asked.

If you count eavesdropping on the streetcar.

Okay, Anya said, slapping her palms on her thighs and standing abruptly. Time for the all-hands.

Exiting Crispin's office, they walked straight into a barrage of questions and chatter. The rest of the staff had arrived and everyone was agog, gathered around physical and online copies of the article.

Claire assures us there's nothing to worry about, Anya announced loudly, shutting the subject down.

Lucca alone was at his computer, jabbing the keys with two fingers, his expression inscrutable when they locked eyes. They hadn't spoken since Monday. Without any discussion, the affair had ended, both of them scrupulously avoiding each other. Claire still half suspected him of telling tales to Emmanuelle.

Apart from a handful of donors whose concerns were swiftly assuaged, there was no further fallout. Claire spent the day playing goalie on their social media accounts and there, too, the conversation remained overwhelmingly positive. Elsewhere online, there were the usual contrarians, a minuscule and hysterical faction who tweeted in hyperbole about Children of the World being child traffickers. But as predicted, it was Dallas who wore the bullseye, her comments cluttering up with demands to see Persimmon. When #whereismaria briefly trended, Claire thought surely now Dallas would respond.

—

On Friday, Claire woke to find Dallas had uploaded a new video in the middle of the night with the caption *An update*. Finally!

Dallas, her face scrubbed of makeup and dominated by a pair of dark-rimmed glasses, spoke to the camera: There's been a lot of questions about Persimmon and some wild speculation and conspiracy theories. Honestly, some of it has been pretty hurtful.

Sing it, Claire whispered, feeling vindicated. Putting on her glasses, she held the phone closer, eager to hear Dallas refute Emmanuelle's outrageous slander point for point.

The truth is this journey hasn't always been easy, Dallas said. What you've seen on here, it's only part of the story. Before I brought Persimmon home, the extent of her needs was never made clear to me.

Dallas appeared on the verge of tears, speaking slowly and taking deep breaths between sentences, her lower lip trembling. Claire tilted her head, confused. The authenticity was refreshing but unnecessary. And what did she mean the *extent of her needs*?

The weekly casts, keeping them dry, and just . . . There's been behavioural issues, communication breakdowns, Dallas added, tucking a strand of hair behind her ear. It's been incredibly tough, she said, choking up. I tried so hard. I tried everything. I loved Persimmon. I *will* always love her.

On hearing the past tense, Claire's stomach plummeted.

Dallas continued: But after many assessments and evaluations, her care team felt she needed a different environment, one that was a better fit for her future. So the decision was made to dissolve the adoption.

Claire hauled herself up to sitting. What was Dallas saying?

We've been working through this process for a while, Dallas said. And it's something Persimmon let us know she wanted, too, through gestures and her baby sign language. My heart is broken, but it's the best path forward for her future.

When? Claire wondered. When had she gone to Santa Rosa? Was Emmanuelle involved? She flung the duvet away, feeling clammy.

My heart is broken, Dallas said again, tears flowing, but rehoming was the best path forward for her.

Claire's sleep-addled brain jerked awake. *Rehome.* Did she mean take the baby back home?

She's an incredible little girl, and I don't regret a single second that we spent together, Dallas said. She paused to wipe the back of her hand across her nose. Then she rallied and added, And you guys, I promise, she's thriving with her new family.

Rehome. No, Dallas hadn't returned the baby; she'd dumped her somewhere else. She couldn't be serious. Claire rewatched the video, clocking every detail of the performance—the vocal fry, the crocodile tears. *A different environment. Best path forward. Don't regret a single second*. What kind of a narcissist spoke like this about discarding a child . . . someone else's child?!

The post had already generated a few hundred likes and a couple dozen comments from the night owls, ranging from bewildered to furious, though several were supportive, wishing Dallas and Persimmon *all the best in this new season of life*.

Claire didn't care that it was five a.m. in California. She found Dallas's number and, for the first time, touched the call button. Right away there was a dissonant tone, then an automated voice dispassionately declaring *the number you have dialled is not in service*. Stunned, she skimmed their text history, saw the blue bubbles, all her own messages, dispatched in good faith. The line must have been disconnected all this time. The realization made her furious.

She had to get to the office. Assess the potential damage. Make a mitigation plan. Dallas might have at least given her a heads-up. If she wasn't so self-absorbed. If she considered anyone other than herself.

The children's room was dark and womb-like. Charlotte lay starfished and face down on her bed, blanket kicked to her feet. Theo stood in his crib, suckling on his soother.

Good morning, Teddy Bear, she whispered. On the change table, he squirmed, whining, Cold, cold. And Claire, quickly pulling on Theo's pants, thought of Persimmon, yet another stranger removing her diaper, exposing her naked bum. It shamed her that this was the first thought she'd given to the baby. Barely a year old and already her life had been turned upside down twice. Where was she now? Claire wondered. Who was nuzzling the soft fragile place at the back of her skull?

In the kitchen, she peeled a banana, trading off bites with Theo and imagining a different home, another mother waking up to one more morning without her baby.

Charlotte padded in, face scrunched. I'm hungry. I want Frosted Flakes.

No sugar in the morning, Claire said. How about toast?

Then on instinct, she enfolded her eldest in a fierce hug, feeling a noxious weight in her belly. Six months and every second an eternity of grief for those parents, wondering if their daughter was well or being harmed, did she remember them? Why hadn't Claire ever considered this? She'd been too busy congratulating herself, that was why.

Okay, Mama, Charlotte said, patting her back, recalling her to her own child. Okay.

Claire loosened her grip. I love you, Chicken, she said, a lump like a fist in her throat.

Charlotte considered, her eyes narrowing in a way that reminded Claire forcibly of Simon. Can I have juice? she asked.

There was an accident on Queen Street that jammed her streetcar in traffic. Claire, impatient, scrolled her phone, ignoring Simon who kept calling. No doubt to gloat.

The outrage had already driven Dallas into hiding. The paparazzi had converged at the gates of her Beverly Hills mansion, not realizing she'd hoofed it to her New York penthouse until an intrepid TMZ cameraman caught her sneaking out the back entrance. Claire watched the shaky recording: Dallas all in black, wearing a baseball cap and big sunglasses, chased three blocks by a man yelling her name, asking where was the baby, did she have anything to say to the child's parents, until she finally disappeared into a town car. There would be silence from her fellow Sentinels, Claire predicted. Not one celebrity would say a word in her defence. Schadenfreude, yes, but Claire was also strategizing.

It was nearly ten when she arrived at work. In the lobby, she was surprised to see Lucca step out of the elevator she'd been waiting to enter.

Hey, she said. You look nice.

His flight to Santa Rosa was scheduled for that evening. For so long, she'd been dreading their parting, but now, up close for the first time in days, she was baffled by her former attraction. His bovine eyes, those floppy earlobes—had she really nibbled them? She recoiled at the memory. It was as if all that lust had belonged to a stranger.

I'll see you later, he said, evading her gaze.

Hang on, she said, catching his sleeve.

Three engineers from the fintech start-up on six trotted past, talking volubly. They waved hello, and she broke into an anxious sweat recalling the open house that they had attended, not even two months earlier, the promotional blow-ups of Dallas in superhero garb, proudly propped on the easel. *Rehome*. As if Persimmon was an inconvenient puppy and not a human being. The enormity of her actions, their devastating consequences, crashed over her once more.

Did you hear? she muttered.

Lucca jammed his hands into his pockets and nodded.

We have to find Pers— her. Claire stammered, aware for the first time of the ludicrousness of the name. We have to find the baby.

Lucca's eyes widened. It's nothing to do—

No listen, she said and filled him in on Dallas's disconnected number. It adds up, you know? The ghosting. That was in January. Scrubbing her socials. Now it all makes sense.

Claire turned circles as she spoke. She was keyed up, a cyclone of regret. Her phone agitated in her pocket, but when she checked, it was only Simon again. She banished him to voice mail.

We have to get her back, she said.

Because these new people aren't celebrities?

Because Santa Rosa is where she belongs. With her parents.

He made a dismissive noise through his teeth and torqued his head away. Don't drag me into this.

Drag? He barrelled forward, and she followed. You're the one who—

I have to go.

Your flight isn't for hours.

I have an appointment.

It was then that she realized why he looked different. Under his coat, he wore a suit. Not the mismatched one he'd thrown on for the open house but a tailored dark grey one with a tie. Even his hair seemed tidier.

She gripped his forearms. We *have* to fix this.

He shook her off. Don't put that on me. Whose idea was it to bring a silly actress to Santa Rosa? Whose idea was it to send her on a medical rescue? Who wanted to hire a photographer?

Who tricked the parents? Who let Dallas leave with a baby?

Keep your voice down, he said, glancing at the passersby.

Her breath was coming in short bursts. She glowered at him, feeling bamboozled. Since when do you care what anyone thinks? she said. If I started this, then you finished it.

Lucca glared, expression hard and chillingly unfamiliar. Startled, Claire took a step back.

How convenient for you to have someone to blame, he said, his voice cruel, every consonant slicing her like a knife.

I'm sorry, Claire said quickly. That was out of line.

Lucca blinked, and his face relaxed back to its familiar contours, the menacing stranger disappearing. What *was* that? Claire wanted to ask, but of course it was another side of his chameleon disposition, the person he became in Brazil or Australia, an alter ego he hadn't meant to reveal.

They were at the front doors, and she was reminded of the first time she spotted him, entering the building, full of quiet confidence, perfectly at ease.

Where's the job? she asked finally.

Italy.

The International Red Cross had a ship in the central Mediterranean, ferrying castaways safely to shore. A few months there and then Lucca would be on to the next place.

What about Santa Rosa? she asked, and when he shrugged, she said, Anywhere can be home.

He glanced past her, and she knew he was thinking about his bicycle locked to the rack outside, how fast he could speed away. Quickly she said: What we're arguing about isn't important. We both agree that the baby should never have left Santa Rosa. Help me. Please.

Nothing I can do will make a difference.

I expected better of you, she said, dismayed.

Lucca scowled, and she braced herself, ready this time, to give back as good as she got. But he shook his head as if clearing it and said, They might be good parents, the new people.

They can't be worse than Dallas, Claire said. But she belongs with her family.

Do you even know their names? he asked, exasperated.

Of course, she said but then faltered, ashamed to realize how painstakingly she'd been holding this knowledge, and the Garcias themselves, at a distance.

The Gar— the Garcias, she said, clearing her throat. The Garcias.

Inez. Jorge. Maria. Those are their names, Lucca said. Flipping up his hood, he leaned a shoulder to the door and walked into the drizzly morning.

Upstairs, the office was deserted, all of Claire's colleagues out at meetings or gossiping in a stairwell. In the boardroom, Crispin flicked through his iPad, holding it out to Anya who was vehemently shaking her head. Walking in, Claire experienced a discomfiting déjà vu of a memory she couldn't pin down.

We can fix this, she declared, dropping into a chair. I'll email Dallas, copy her whole team. Reuniting the baby—reuniting Maria with Jorge and Inez, it's in everyone's best interests.

You don't think it's too late? Crispin asked.

It would have been a private adoption, a quiet arrangement with a non-disclosure agreement, Claire said. It can be undone.

She outlined her plan: Dallas flying Maria back to Santa Rosa. A touching reunion at Children of the World's compound, the baby chubbier, improved by her sojourn in California. Maybe the casts were off. She might even be toddling. Dallas could send a monthly stipend to the Garcias. No. She couldn't be trusted. Better for Children of the World to do it. They wouldn't make a big deal about that part though. It was the kind of detail to hold back for later. Follow-up photos a few months out. *With her family's love and Children of the World's ongoing support, Maria is thriving.*

As she spoke, the elusive memory returned: Claire inventing a strategy on the fly, thoroughly in her element. She'd been seated just like this, in the shabby old boardroom, Crispin at her left and Anya across the table. Except then, she'd been mid-interview, responding to a hypothetical. A country director whose financial fraud had become public knowledge, how would Claire, as the publicist, mitigate that predicament?

Now as then, Crispin leaned forward, listening closely, and she realized, with a sick feeling, that the scenario hadn't been an invention. She had walked into the job interview intimidated by her inexperience and strode out knowing the position was hers, believing the crisis scenario had been the clincher instead of a premonition. Crispin and Anya had taken her measure. She wasn't here to live her principles. They'd hired her because she had none.

What's your take? Crispin asked Anya. I think it could work.

But instead of her usual pushback, Anya was uncharacteristically subdued: Whatever you think is best.

As Claire crafted the email on her phone, Crispin returned to the vitriol on his iPad. Can you believe what they're saying about us?

They were right, Claire thought, hitting send. All the anonymous haters were right. She'd been so arrogantly convinced a foreign adoption was the best thing for Maria. In Lucca's place, she'd have sent Dallas and the baby off with a brass band and livestreamed the kidnapping.

We have to win back public opinion, Crispin said, clutching his hair. We won't survive without it.

Let's focus on getting Maria home, Claire said.

We'll ride it out, he agreed, even as his eyes darted in panic. The news cycle always moves on.

It was disconcerting to hear him parrot her cavalier mantra, the one she'd joined Children of the World to escape. Photos of the Garcias a few months after the reunion? What was she thinking? Of course, they couldn't do that.

Her phone buzzed and she jumped, then scowled when she saw who was calling. But it was an excuse to leave. She couldn't stay here a second longer while Crispin spiralled out over all the wrong things.

There's a seat sale, Simon announced.

I'm in the middle of something here, she said, leaving the boardroom. Can we talk later?

The travel agent says now is the time to act, he insisted. We'll never see these prices again. They were booking the trip through an operator, he said, buying a block of seats so the whole family could take over a section of the plane. Can't you picture it? he said, as if they were pals, expecting her to be thrilled. And she *could* picture it, Simon's parents and two sisters with their husbands and a gaggle of small children, an exotic summer camp that Charlotte and Theo had been anticipating for months. Formative memories they would make without her.

Charlie and Teddy's first plane ride, Simon said, a jolly bounce in his voice. I'm springing for business class.

The ache in her jaw, building all morning, radiated down to her shoulders. She said, I don't know, Simon.

Claire, you've been thinking about it for months, and we leave in a few weeks.

It's just such a long time, she said. Are you sure the kids will even like it?

Geez, Claire. It's a vacation, not a prison camp.

Yeah but—

I know you'd like them to forget this, but I *am* their father and my family *are* their blood relations.

Claire had a terrible vision. Simon in India and his new bride, in all their finery, posing for photos with the children, the four of them looking for all the world like a perfect, unbreakable unit. She'd have infinite patience, never raise her voice, put wholesome meals on the table, be a kinder mother than Claire. She deflated, curling into herself.

I just think you need to ask yourself why India is such a problem for you, Simon said.

It isn't a problem—

The kids *are* Indian, he said. You can't wish that away.

Okay, she said quietly, forcing the words out. Okay.

Whistleblower

Emmanuelle

Emmanuelle waited until she landed in Santa Rosa to announce her book deal. The late April sun broke through a dark bank of clouds as she tweeted her big news, alongside a selfie at the airport, the country's name over her shoulder. She always found these kinds of crowing updates vaguely idiotic, and as the replies and clapping emojis flooded in, she pocketed her phone, uncomfortably aware of how dramatically her audience had grown in the month and a half since Dallas became public enemy number one.

The Whistleblower, they called her. The indefatigable journalist who had—on her own—ferreted the story out. In the days after the rehoming announcement, Emmanuelle had done the network rounds, double-enders with talk shows and news programs on both sides of the border, repeating her appeal every chance she got: Dallas could make this right by reuniting Maria with her family.

People began sharing her other reportage: The industrial accidents. The piece about the tenants' protest that had cost Emmanuelle her column. A much older series on a hydroelectric dam that was poisoning an Indigenous community in Labrador.

Emmanuelle was unsettled by the notoriety. She was reminded of Art's admonishment: a journalist can't be the story and report the story. Yet it was this leverage, of being part of the drama through her exclusive line to the Garcias, that had scored her bylines in the *Washington Post* and *New York Times*. And Quinn had parlayed it all into a publishing deal, selling Emmanuelle's book proposal at auction for an astonishing sum.

Suddenly, Emmanuelle was the one turning down editors and commissions. Readers were flooding her inbox, too, strangers who sent tips about unethical employers, financial malfeasance, cops cruising the nightclub district to prey on inebriated girls. Everyone wanted her to right the world's wrongs.

A year ago, even six months earlier, she'd have chosen a tip, reported it out, and pitched the story with relish. But there wasn't time for competing priorities. Even tragedy had an expiration date, and her publisher was pressuring her to rush the book to market. Quinn had suggested a March publication date, to coincide with Maria's second birthday, and the marketing team's glee on hearing the idea had made Emmanuelle cringe.

Her conscience whispered that she was a sellout, sacrificing journalism on the altar of sensationalism. She *would* track those other stories down, she promised herself. Just as soon as she finished this book.

Exiting the arrivals terminal with her suitcase, she checked her phone to see if Micah had messaged as she stepped off the curb. A town car shot by with a horn blast. Emmanuelle pulled up short and caught her shocked reflection, hand on heart, in the tinted windows. She recalled the TMZ video of Dallas being chased down a New York sidewalk by a cameraman before escaping into a vehicle just like this one.

At first Emmanuelle had been hopeful, every opinion piece, trending hashtag, and late-night comedian's joke bolstering her expectations. But as the silence from the actress's camp stretched into weeks and then a month, she realized Dallas was playing the long game. Inevitably public indignation fizzled, attention and outrage pivoting to newer villains. When had she even sent Maria packing? The girl could be anywhere with anyone, lost to her parents forever.

Emmanuelle! a man yelled and she spotted Micah, leaning half out of his car and waving.

Traffic was impatient and there was no time for greetings as she slammed the door shut, and he switched gears. Navigating out of the throng, Micah's brow knit in concentration. She was grateful for the obligatory silence. Even though their conversations had been cordial, she didn't think he'd forgiven her for the *National Express* article.

Once they were on the highway, the quiet in the car turned awkward. Micah cleared his throat, and nervous about what he might say, she shook the broadsheet she'd found at the airport and said, Interesting news.

In Santa Rosa, Maria's abduction still made the front page. The president—a photogenic politician whom the locals called El Guapo—had demanded the U.S. repatriate their citizen. The country's ambassador to Washington was said to be agitating behind the scenes. Now the justice minister announced their human trafficking unit was launching an investigation and that he'd personally filed a complaint with Interpol.

Maria is all of us, he'd said at the press conference, vowing to bring her home. This is our crusade.

There's a corruption scandal, Micah said. El Guapo needs a distraction.

Emmanuelle laughed sardonically, then stopped abruptly when he didn't join in.

Career is his priority, Micah said, not the Garcias.

If the end result is positive, does it matter? she asked, uncomfortably aware of her immodest tweet about her book deal, wishing she could immediately delete it. When Micah didn't reply, she said, I'm meeting the justice minister on Wednesday.

She had a full week of interviews ahead with elected officials, advocates, lawyers, and other NGOs. In service of the Garcias' cause, she told Micah.

And research for your book, he said.

A strained silence settled over the car, and Emmanuelle stared out the window feeling claustrophobic. The book was *for* Maria, she reminded herself, their best hope of getting her home.

Folks at the church are eager to meet you, Micah said finally. They're planning a potluck.

Oh, she said, caught off guard, knowing the bent of her narrative and hesitant to expose his congregation to her critique or worse: give them a free pass.

Micah honked twice, signalling his intention, and switched lanes. Just keep an open mind. Then you can write whatever you want.

Six weeks earlier, Emmanuelle had been ushered into an office in downtown Manhattan where Quinn Montgomery presided in a Herman Miller chair, the city's towers at her back, greenery just budding on the trees. Emmanuelle pegged the literary agent for late fifties, though her face appeared a good decade younger. She wore a leopard-print jumpsuit, red-soled heels, and rubies at her throat.

What the hell is that—*rehoming*? she demanded, her first words on seeing Emmanuelle. Fucking millennials.

Emmanuelle was too stunned to reply, but it didn't matter because Quinn bulldozed on, flattering and praising her reporting. She name-dropped editors and publishing houses, predicted a bidding war. A two-book deal, maybe even three, foreign rights, translations.

I don't sign one-hit wonders, she said and added this could be Emmanuelle's full-time career. One deep-dive book after another, the subject matter entirely her choice. If Quinn wasn't so intimidating, she'd have said wow seven times in a row and then laughed. Instead, she was cowed into silence.

Quinn spoke at a fast clip, as if someone had set her speed to double. Everything she said gave Emmanuelle a whitewater shooting-the-rapids thrill of excitement and terror.

I don't want to write a book about Dallas Hayden or Children of the World, Emmanuelle said. She heard how hesitant her voice sounded and planted her feet, adding: It's bigger than that. It's about our collective complicity.

I'll admit I didn't see the potential at first, Quinn said, but you were prescient. I like the colonialism angle too. It's fresh. It's unexpected. And with who you are—she indicated with both hands Emmanuelle's length—there's credibility. Not every author has that privilege.

Emmanuelle, self-conscious and irked, focused on a spot over Quinn's shoulder until her periphery blurred.

Quinn had Emmanuelle giving speeches now. How did she

feel about a TED Talk? Emmanuelle imagined herself miked up at a convention centre, the clicker in her hand, smoothly going off script and the rapt audience before her. Quinn's certainty was seductive and intimidating. Emmanuelle understood how easy it would be to do whatever this woman wanted.

The book, Emmanuelle said, trying to wrest control.

Dallas is the bait, Quinn said. But then we switch. She said *we* as if this was a group project. And maybe this was how publishing worked. The journalist's experience and writing skills put to use, the narrative shaped by market forces.

To Quinn, Dallas was a lightweight, inconsequential beyond the introduction. The meat of the thing is the industry, Quinn said. Philanthrocapitalism.

She called it a book with brains, predicted it would be shelved in economics. Or political history. She spoke as if the first editions were already printed and bound, Emmanuelle signing copies at the Barnes & Noble in Union Square, a line out the door. Emmanuelle smirked at the thought of Art Whylie assigning the review.

Quinn leaned forward, mouth and eyes narrowed shrewdly. Why philanthropy? Is there something in your—

I'm curious about a lot of things, Emmanuelle said.

Quinn gestured to the floor-to-ceiling bookcases lining three walls of the office, and for a moment Emmanuelle imagined a hunter's trophy room, the collection of Quinn's prizes. Did she ask all her clients this question?

There's autobiography at the heart of all writing, Quinn said. If it's any good.

It was an assignment, Emmanuelle said.

Quinn shook a finger. But you couldn't let it go.

Emmanuelle remembered the *National Express*'s cover, how

afterward on a videocall with Jorge, she'd downplayed the reputational damage while Micah stared at the ceiling and shook his head. To Quinn, she said, I had a hunch and I followed it.

Quinn sat back and assessed her, as if seeing Emmanuelle for the first time. I get accused of steamrolling, she said. People mistake enthusiasm for pressure. What is it *you* want, Emmanuelle?

I want to find Maria, Emmanuelle thought. Out loud, she said, I want to write a book.

Quinn nodded, still thoughtful, and Emmanuelle revelled in what she'd said, that finally there was someone in her corner with the power to grant more than the occasional byline. She was going to have an investigative career. One that uplifted others and didn't exploit their grief.

The kid, Quinn said, pinching two fingers together. All the facts and figures are well and good, but she's the beating heart. I'd like to see you go to Santa Rosa. Into the bush or wherever.

Santa Rosa? Emmanuelle asked, shifting in her seat.

Interview the family, meet them in person, Quinn said. I see their story as a series of interstitials, the narrative through line. It'll keep the book from being too wonkish, and of course the girl is what readers want.

Of course, Emmanuelle thought, deflated. She didn't have the credibility to sell something intelligent. She'd courted a readership that expected beating hearts and celebrity scandal. If she wanted to make a living, her reputation would always be tied to the salacious.

Where do you think she is? Quinn asked.

I wish I knew, Emmanuelle said, then doubted her answer. What action would be incumbent on her if she did? The thought of engaging with the Garcias, further exploiting them, was untenable.

Quinn came around the desk, taking the seat next to Emmanuelle. Leaning across the armrest, she asked, Think you can find her?

I'm not sure—

Interviews with the birth parents and the new parents to bookend the narrative. Wouldn't that be something?

Children of the World's compound was at the end of a private lane. A heavy mist descended from the mountains, but though it was the rainy season, the land was parched, greenery dull and limp. Expecting to be barred at the gates, Emmanuelle had resigned herself to taking photos of signage from afar and zooming in on buildings. Instead, the guard waved them through.

Back at home, Crispin's charity was putting on a good face, still posting sanguine updates: donated rice seeds distributed in Senegal, an upbeat photo of Indian children lining up for inoculation. But there were hairline cracks in the foundation: deleted comments, corporate sponsors who had quietly removed the charity's logo from their marketing materials. It wasn't anything anyone but an obsessive voyeur like Emmanuelle would notice, but she could guess what it meant for their bottom line.

On the steps of the main building, a man hailed Micah genially. Exchanging a joke, they both laughed, clapping backs as they shook hands. Switching to English, Micah introduced Emmanuelle: This is Thiago.

We have a sister church in the village we just passed, Pueblo Bonito, Micah explained, as she shook Thiago's hand. I'm there once a month. Thiago calls when he needs a minister.

Now she understood how Micah had bagged her the anonymous interview. As Thiago toured them around, she scrutinized the female staff, wondering which of them was her source.

Today, there was no subterfuge. Thiago was loose-limbed and content to answer all her questions on the record. She photographed the clinic and nursery, the last places Maria had stayed before being spirited away.

He showed her their farm, pointing out the local varieties of maize sown alongside beans and squash, their vines wrapping up the corn stalks. A group of children shucked, tossing dusty husks into one pile and throwing cobs into barrows.

They worked in shifts, Thiago explained. And then went to class. Both were forms of education.

She'd been cynical about Children of the World's activities abroad; now that she was here, Emmanuelle could find no fault in the operation. They passed classrooms with students, some with heads bowed over workbooks, others rowdy as a hapless teacher failed to keep order. In the nursery, Thiago saw her note the empty cots and said: If they come, we will house them. But we don't go searching.

From her sleuthing, she knew Lucca da Silva was long gone. The sea change was evident. She clocked faces, noting the paucity of foreign volunteers. If their marketing was to be believed, Santa Rosa had long been the charity's most popular destination. Where was the money coming from?

She asked if they expected a new country director soon, and Thiago replied that the locals were in charge now and this had always been the plan. The compound was doing better than ever, morale at an all-time high. Even the children acted up less.

She couldn't tell how much of this was true and how much was a savvy sound bite, something Claire had invented to paper over the fact that they couldn't afford a replacement. Thiago seemed genuine, and she decided that the man believed what he was saying. But later, after he had left her and Micah to roam free, telling them they could speak to whoever was willing, Emmanuelle found herself interviewing a staff member named Beatriz.

We never hear from Head Office, she said, and Micah translated.

Does that worry you?

Before they were very involved, always calling and asking questions, Beatriz said. But since Señor da Silva left . . .

She paused to glance toward the front gates that were opening to admit a man pushing a wheelbarrow. It took Emmanuelle a confused second to realize there was a crumpled child inside. Together, they watched as the barrow was rolled into the clinic.

The money is still coming. But if something should change, Beatriz said, shaking her head, then I don't know. We'll have to find another way.

Now Emmanuelle understood the warm reception, why they'd shown her around and posed the children for photographs. In her bag, she had a stash of local currency—just-in-case funds—and she gave the whole envelope to Thiago before leaving. This was bad journalistic practice. Paying sources. But it also seemed like the most ethical action.

Is it normal to compensate interviewees? Micah asked as they left the compound.

She was ashamed that he'd noticed; worse, that he might assume it was an ostentatious gesture made for his benefit.

They're doing good work, she said. I just want to support that. Still, Emmanuelle regretted her rash action. Micah must be thinking that of all her sources, it was the Garcias who deserved the money.

It was a ninety-minute drive to the Garcias' home. On the way, Micah reported they were optimistic about getting Maria back.

Donations are still coming into the crowdfunding account, he said. That's keeping their spirits up. They'll need most of it for lawyers and travel and whatnot, once Maria is found, but we used a little to dig a well and build them a sturdier house.

Micah said the youngest son was enrolled in school. They were renting a plot of land and growing crops and had joined a co-op in the village through which they would sell most of the harvest. The enterprise meant steady employment for the three adults and kept Jorge off faraway construction sites. The whole family was eating better. Jorge's back had improved.

Emmanuelle thought of the perversity of fate that had snatched their child in exchange for material comforts.

God works in mysterious ways, Micah said, as if reading her mind.

Emmanuelle and Ben had discussed contributing part of her advance to the crowdfunding account, but after going back and forth on the exact amount, the conversation had petered out, not quite forgotten. As Micah praised the generosity of strangers, she was reminded of her good intentions, worthless without action.

Our congregation is praying on Maria's return, he said. We ask the Lord to work in the hearts of the powerful.

Emmanuelle wondered which was more futile: this congregation and their fervent thoughts and prayers or her own impotent efforts. How naive to believe her words could make a difference to anything other than her career.

Glancing away from the road, Micah caught her eye. We pray

for you, too, Emmanuelle, he added, and she heard the unspoken rebuke. *Lord, please make this sinner repent her wicked ways.*

The Garcias deserve better, she said. Everyone's let them down. Self included.

Trust in the Lord, Micah said. Man may be weak, but He always prevails.

Jorge and his mother-in-law were at the farming plot when they arrived, so it was Inez alone who greeted them. There was a ferocity to her hug, and when she finally pulled away, it was to hold Emmanuelle's hands for a long time, staring into her eyes as Micah translated.

Every inch of the property spoke of industry and purpose. Chickens pecked around a coop. There was a kitchen garden, a compost pile, and a firepit. She saw the new well and the deep metal basin propped atop four wooden legs that formed a rudimentary sink. The clouds were spitting, and everything was covered in a wet film.

Inez was proud of the house, explaining how Jorge had led its construction. It was built with adobe bricks on a stone foundation—earthquake proof, Micah explained, an important upgrade—and had a corrugated tin roof that stretched beyond the front door to form a covered patio.

Inside there was a narrow bed at the back, a long table, a dresser, and hammocks. Shucked corn lay drying across every available surface. Garlands of it hung from the rafters. Emmanuelle greedily noted these details, mentally reframing them into compelling prose that would paint a vivid picture for future readers, even as her discomfort grew.

A basket hung from a nail on the wall, and Inez showed her the things inside: Maria's clean nappies, the few clothes she had worn—hand-me-downs from her brothers—and the doll she'd cherished and which Inez had sewn while pregnant.

Tienes hijos? Inez asked.

No, Emmanuelle replied.

Then you cannot know, Micah translated. I love my sons, but I always prayed for a daughter.

The house had a single window, enclosed not with glass but wooden shutters. Inez led Emmanuelle there, still holding her hand. There was a candle on the sill, a statue of the Virgin Mary draped in a rosary, and, taped to the wall beside, a photo of Maria that had been cut out of a magazine. But it was the familiar picture next to it that gave Emmanuelle an unpleasant jolt of recognition.

Inez began speaking again, but Emmanuelle was so stunned she barely heard the translation. It was one of her new headshots. Micah must have printed it off the literary agency's website.

Here is where she prays, Micah said, for Maria's return and your well-being.

Inez was grateful, called Emmanuelle an angel, and credited her with the new house, the corn all around them, every recent blessing.

No, no, Emmanuelle said. No hice nada. Nada. She turned to Micah hopelessly. Tell her, she said. Tell her none of this is my doing.

From the wall her own face taunted her. The photo had been taken at a studio where Emmanuelle had perched on a stool and pretended to be a serious, thoughtful person. She'd been aiming for an intellectual expression, but here she appeared horribly self-satisfied.

It was a relief to return outside. The drizzle had turned to rain, and it beat a satisfying thrum on the roof, dripping into the barrels that lined the house. They sat in plastic chairs under the covered porch, and Emmanuelle pulled from her bag the bottles of Fanta she'd bought at a roadside stand. Micah prayed aloud in Spanish. Emmanuelle closed her eyes and bowed her head, glad for the respite.

Jorge arrived on his bicycle as they said amen. He wore a wide-brimmed hat and a flimsy poncho made of a thin plastic.

What's next? Jorge demanded, after the greetings were over and he had swiped a Fanta. We need to do more.

Inez said she'd been mulling an idea. There was a lot of money in the crowdfunding account, and it seemed to her that what they needed was to hire someone to find Maria.

A private investigator? Emmanuelle asked.

This was just the sort of cliché Quinn would love. Tracking down the child, intrepid reporter saves the day. The prospect of insinuating herself deeper in this tragedy, when every passing minute carried them further away from a happy ending, made her want to flee.

It'll be expensive, Micah warned. And it might not work.

Maria's book will be worth something, Jorge said to Micah, and it took Emmanuelle a moment to understand what he meant.

Maria will be part of the book—with your permission, she said. But it's not really about her.

She tried to explain the crux of what she was writing but could see Jorge wasn't paying attention, wouldn't even face her. She was mid-sentence when he blurted out: When will it be on sale? The question was addressed to Micah, who glanced at Emmanuelle as he translated.

Even as she replied that the publication date was still a year away, that they were trying to sell Spanish-language rights but there was no guarantee it would be available here, that she would send them a copy of course, still Jorge focused on Micah. Because of the language gap? Because she was a woman? This hadn't been the case when they'd spoken online.

How much? Jorge asked. How much for each copy?

Jorge, Inez said.

Emmanuelle was irritated by his grasping, blatant entitlement. She was the one writing this thing, struggling to reconcile journalistic integrity with mass market appeal, and here he was trying to dictate and demand. She didn't like this man. The realization made her uncomfortable.

Maria should be on the cover, Jorge said. If the investigator fails, someone might recognize her from the book.

Emmanuelle felt chastened. *She* was the grasping entitled one.

It might be helpful to speak to a lawyer, Micah said, especially if Maria is undocumented.

They've disappeared Maria, Jorge said. What use is a lawyer if we can't find her?

The improbability of success, the sheer cliff Jorge and Inez were facing. Emmanuelle wanted to be generous to Jorge then. Does he have to be the underdog before I extend my empathy? she wondered. All her thoughts were repugnant today.

I can find a lawyer and a detective, Emmanuelle said. Let me do that.

Afterward, returning to the capital, she felt very tired and unfathomably sad. She couldn't get the memory of her headshot out of her mind. She hated that she was there next to the Virgin Mary, of all people, and the Garcias' vanished child. Inez had taken so much pleasure in showing it to her, did she think Emmanuelle wanted veneration, expected it?

I'm concerned about the crowdfunding account, Micah confessed.

It seems to have done so much good, Emmanuelle said, surprised.

What happens when the interest fades? The plot they're farming is rented. I worry the Garcias think it's going to be like this forever. Not that they're spendthrifts. You saw them. But . . . I don't know. People have short attention spans.

I've never liked charity, Emmanuelle confessed.

Micah laughed then, a deep belly laugh that was so infectious, Emmanuelle had to join him. For a few moments it felt like home, like Wednesdays after Bible study, her father and siblings and church friends all around, Micah somewhere in the mix too. She'd been away too long and should visit, she thought. Maybe even go to church. No. What was she thinking? That was going too far.

The Garcias don't need charity, Micah said. Hell, Santa Rosa doesn't need charity. They deserve reparations.

It reminded her of what Crispin had said months and months ago.

Radical wealth redistribution, she said. Amen to that.

The closed quarters of the car, the goodwill and dopamine generated by the shared laugh, the memories of those earlier days when her conscience had been naively innocent, and maybe Micah himself, his calm, non-judgmental demeanour, put her in the mood for confession. Odd that she'd remembered him as unlikeable and officious. It was me, she realized. I was the officious one.

It feels like the harder I try to do the right thing, the more I fail, she said. Is it even possible to do good when the system is rigged for so much bad?

The wipers swished, clearing the glass for an instant before rain blurred the view again.

No, he said finally. But we have to try.

What would Jesus do? she joked.

Micah frowned, tightening his grip on the wheel. Overturn the tables, he said.

Good Guys

Claire

The conference room was a fishbowl in the centre of the office, its four walls made of glass. Open binders and files spilled across the long table. Pie charts were projected on the screen that hung from the ceiling. All the chairs had been rolled to the side to make room for Crispin and Anya who were stalking around and wringing their hands over the data. The board of directors had scheduled an emergency meeting that afternoon, and they'd been strategizing for it all morning. From behind her computer, Claire gnawed the loose skin around her thumbnail and watched.

The office joker sidled up to her desk, miming a disco. Operation stayin' alive, stayin' alive, oh, oh, oh, oh, he sang under his breath.

It's not funny, the volunteer coordinator snapped, swivelling around in her chair. All my high-school recruitment drives have been cancelled. Do you have any idea how many freaked-out parents I've had to talk off the ledge? Your precious Jaxon and Nevaeh will be just fine. No one wants to abduct *them*. Sorry, she said, glancing at Claire.

Well, it's true, Claire said, returning to her keyboard to type yet another reprimand to the ad agency. She'd pulled the #realhero campaign, but rogue ads remained. That morning she'd ridden a streetcar with Dallas's face plastered up and down both sides of the vehicle. Someone had vandalized several ads near the back, adding horns and scrawling the word *kidnappers* over Children of the World's logo.

Volunteers are backing out, the coordinator continued. The ones who've paid their fees are forfeiting too.

It was the same story with corporate sponsors, the development manager said, joining them. Even companies locked into contracts didn't want the association. Can you scrub these names from the site? he added, handing Claire a Post-it.

Tilden Robertson, anonymous donor. That's gotta be a first, the joker said. Good thing his cheque already cleared. Then he turned serious, adding that they were also losing monthly supporters, and nothing he said could sway them. I'm talking people who've been with us fifteen, twenty years. Even *they* want out.

Claire was only half paying attention. She was reading about Dallas on a celebrity gossip site. The studio had cut her role from *Sentinels II* and put the sequel of her Freya stand-alone on ice. There were rumours of a recast. Insiders claimed Dallas was panicked and trying to undo her mistake. Truth or wishful thinking? Claire wondered. For weeks she'd been leaving messages for Dallas's manager, Hugh Coren, without receiving a reply. If this blind item was to believed, even her agent was about to cut her loose. Surely now Dallas would understand reunion was her only option.

You're wanted in the situation room, the joker said, and Claire glanced up to see Anya beckoning.

To soften up the board, Claire had been asked to compile an overseas win list. Upbeat profiles of their graduates and before-and-after images of kids who'd arrived at an orphanage malnourished, then plumped up in their care. She'd once relished this task; now it was a hateful farce.

What claim did the board have to these children's successes? Rather than giving parents the means to provide for their families, Children of the World was holding the bare necessities hostage and demanding human sacrifice in exchange. *Hand over your kids, and we'll give them a long shot at a better life.* What a perverse economy they'd created.

In the conference room, colour headshots of the board members with names and job titles underneath were laid across the table. As Claire walked in, Anya was moving three photos above the rest: These are the ones to target.

Two men and one woman: a mining executive, a telecom magnate, and a retired media mogul. According to Anya, they accounted for forty per cent of the organization's revenue.

One more, Crispin said, nudging up a fourth headshot.

It was of a youngish-looking man, overdue for a haircut, in a black T-shirt, no tie or jacket. Claire recalled the open house and a bro in chambray, four buttons undone, calling himself a social entrepreneur and bragging about palling around with Bill Gates at Davos.

He just joined, Anya said. He has no history, no loyalty.

While they debated—Crispin arguing for long-term strategy and Anya insisting the wolf was at the door and there wouldn't be a long-term anything if they didn't focus—Claire idly checked her phone. She was stunned to find an email from Dallas's manager: he'd been in touch with the people who had Maria.

Apologies for the delay, Hugh wrote. I've been trying to convince the Olsens to speak with you.

Convincing Dallas to salvage her own career, more like, Claire thought.

Hugh said he'd level with Claire. It would be advantageous for everyone if they relinquished custody. He trusted that Children of the World, with their experience in Santa Rosa, and *their philanthropic bona fides, as it were*, was in the best position to convince the Olsens that the child belonged with her birth parents.

He called Dallas *my client* and said she didn't want to exert pressure on the situation and wouldn't be getting involved—as if Dallas was a disinterested party and not the architect of this calamity. But for the first time in weeks, Claire glimpsed hope. She imagined herself flying Maria home, retracing Dallas's steps and being on hand for the touching reunion.

The Olsens were willing to talk, Hugh wrote, but Claire must realize they had bonded with Lily.

Who the hell is Lily? Claire said out loud.

Claire, we're going to need you to focus, Crispin said.

Good news, she said and read the email aloud.

Is that what the birth parents want? Crispin asked.

We did this! she yelled. It's *our* fault.

Don't blame yourself, Crispin said. Mistakes were made, yes. Sometimes in this work there are unintended consequences.

I hate this, Claire said, thinking of Maria, how even her name had been snatched from her, only to be changed again and again. It's so bleak.

I can't stop thinking about it either, Crispin said. What a terrible ordeal, especially for someone so young. She doesn't deserve any of this.

I know, Claire said, exhaling through an open mouth, still jittery after having shouted.

Anya was turned away, pointedly busying herself over the file Claire had brought in. But Crispin understood. Hugh had arranged a video conference with the Olsens. Crispin would explain everything to them. He'd make it right.

The public is so judgmental, Crispin said. And the industry is totally unforgiving, especially to young women.

Claire, who'd been swigging from her water bottle, choked mid-swallow. She knocked a fist against her chest, coughing. Forget about Dallas. We need to get Maria back to the Garcias. Hugh says the Olsens can talk to us later today. He worked hard to persuade them, and I don't dare ask for another time. This is our only chance, she added, desperation constricting her voice, making it rise to an embarrassing pitch. The board will understand if you reschedule.

Two parents. Siblings. A quiet middle-class upbringing, away from the Hollywood media circus. Being part of a stable family could be the best thing for her, Crispin said.

Maria *has* a stable family with two parents. And brothers. We *stole* her from them.

Claire, come on, he said, closing his laptop and winding the cord. We've been over this. Put yourself in this child's position. Where would *you* rather be?

I can't believe what I'm hearing. Is this what you think too? Claire demanded, whirling on Anya.

I think we have a board meeting to get to, Anya said, tapping the end of the file folder under the photo of the mining CEO who had a soft spot for Santa Rosa and had been the compound's main benefactor since its inception.

Child trafficking is our brand now, Claire said, taking aim at Crispin's pride. She told them about the defaced ads on the streetcar, then repeated what the trolls were saying online. Wayfair and Pizzagate jokes. And that's just the low-hanging fruit. Don't ask about the truly vile stuff, about adrenochrome and missing kids.

We're the good guys! Crispin exclaimed. Why is everyone against us?

What we have to do is get Maria home, feet corrected, better than we found her, and sell this *interlude* as if it was always for the greater good, Claire said. Trust me. The public will buy it.

If the Olsens agree, Anya said, finally meeting Claire's eyes. They probably already think of her as *their* child.

Except Maria isn't theirs, Claire argued. They took her in, so I have to believe they're good people.

Which is exactly why they'll put her needs first—

And give her back, Claire said, triumphantly, at the same moment Anya finished: and not give her back.

Claire's shoulders slumped, and Anya gazed at her with pity, adding: It's hard to change someone's mind when they think they have the moral high ground.

Think of Santa Rosa, Claire said, rallying. There's no reason Maria can't be one of your success stories. Dallas screwed up. But there's a world in which your project comes out clean.

Anya, on the verge of disagreeing, hesitated and closed her mouth. Claire held her breath. Then Anya broke eye contact, slipped her iPad into her bag, and lifted the strap to her shoulder. I don't see it happening. But there's no reason we can't pursue both options.

I know you'll do your best, Crispin said, holding the door as Anya strode out.

My best. Claire thought of the so-called rescue, the catch in her throat when she'd heard Maria's cries, Dallas insisting they had to take the baby away, and Claire's irritation at the intern for calling it exploitation. She had started this. She'd already done her worst.

I'll handle logistics, but as CEO, you're the one with the credibility, Claire said, chasing them to reception, not caring that her colleagues were watching. Speak to the Olsens with me.

I'm sorry, Claire, but I agree with Anya. The odds they'll agree to give their child back—I don't want to dissuade you from trying, but it would take a miracle.

Now it was Anya propping the door open with her back. We need to be downtown, she said.

Crispin, you can convince them, Claire said. You can convince anyone to do anything.

She remembered how he'd signed her CD, then presented it back in both hands; his earnestness at the job interview, when he'd spoken of the charity's genesis in Cambodia, his aura of virtue and how badly she'd wanted to be bathed in that same glow.

Twenty minutes, she begged. Please.

Claire, you're talking about one child. I've got an organization and the well-being of hundreds of kids to think about.

She stared at the set expression on his face and felt a deep, weary disappointment. It's always the forest with you, isn't it? she said, turning back to the conference room and refusing to reply when he called her name.

Ron and Barbara Olsen were a couple in Utah with four other children, all of them high needs. Ron worked in finance. Barbara was a housewife. After their first daughter was born with Down's, they'd adopted three more through the foster system. One was on the spectrum; two had cerebral palsy. Barbara had a rota of therapists—speech, occupational, physio, behavioural—who made house calls. Their eldest was fourteen. They called themselves *old pros*.

Barbara was a pink-cheeked woman with a helmet of auburn hair, a few years older than Claire. Ron appeared younger by a decade, though that might only be the sleeve of tattoos inked down his left arm. At least they seemed like competent caregivers.

Claire murmured encouragingly as they described their other children, the challenges the family had overcome, afraid to cut in, knowing that eventually she must. Crispin would have found just the right moment.

Not everyone is equipped to love on these children, Ron said. But we are called to this work.

Lily is thriving, Barbara added. Though it was a rocky start.

We'll have her speaking English in no time, Ron said. See if we don't.

Claire wondered what they'd expected from this conversation, if they'd already been asked to return Maria, if they had any inkling at all that she'd been abducted.

Can I ask what you were told about her birth family?

Lily was an orphan, Barbara said. She came to us through foster care.

Here's the thing, Claire said and haltingly explained that there were two parents in Santa Rosa, both very much alive. Too late she realized she should have prepared a speech.

The Olsens had been squeezed together, shoulders touching, but now Barbara pulled back, half her face slipping out of the frame. Ron's posture stiffened.

Wait just a minute, he said. Something's not right here. If what you're saying is true, how did our little girl end up here?

Claire tried to explain the family's circumstances. How they'd thought her hearing was in danger and the decision to send her away was made under duress, without proper explanation. But nerves scrambled her thoughts, muddling the story. Ron kept shaking his head and saying it was impossible, that Claire must have their Lily confused with someone else.

She's the Garcias' only daughter, Claire said. They've been desperately trying to get her back since October.

Is this some kind of joke? Ron asked.

It isn't. I assure you. There are videos of Dallas Hayden taking her from her mother, Claire said, realizing even as she spoke, that the videos had been erased. Still, she persisted, bringing up the flurry of press about the rehoming, the articles Emmanuelle had published in reputable papers—the *Times*, the *Post*, the interviews she'd given to CNN and NPR.

I saw something about this, Barbara said, nodding.

Last month, Claire said, hope soaring. It was all over the news in April.

Barbara's brow creased. I didn't like the look of that man, she said.

Ron said they hadn't taken this responsibility lightly. With each of their adopted children, they had prayed on the decision and felt the Lord's conviction.

God blessed us with Lily, Barbara agreed. She's been entrusted to our care.

Now I don't know what you folks are doing over there in Cuba or wherever, but we are loving on this child, Ron said.

Lily had been with them since January, Barbara added, returning full face to the screen. She'd bonded with her siblings.

Claire said they sounded like wonderful caregivers and the Garcias would be grateful to learn their daughter had flourished in their home.

She has six older brothers in Santa Rosa, Claire said, clearing her throat to cover the tremor in her voice. There are aunts and uncles too. Cousins. This has all been a terrible misunderstanding.

She was perspiring. Ron's expression had been bewildered, but now it hardened with distrust.

The Garcias have been praying for their daughter's return, she improvised.

But this is absurd, Ron said. You do realize that, don't you? My wife and I have never heard of your company. What are y'all called again?

We're a non-profit. Children of—

We don't know you from Adam, but you spin us this yarn and expect us to give our daughter to strangers?

Barbara began to cry. Ron put his arm around her and whispered something in her ear. Good, Claire thought. If Barbara sympathized with the birth parents' plight, they could move on to logistics. I'm a mother too, Claire said, appealing to Barbara. My little girl's name is Charlotte. If someone took her from me, I don't know what I'd do.

Barbara blew her nose, then asked, How much do they want?

There's no question of money, Claire said in desperation. Inez and Jorge only want their child back. This is all our fault, she added, appealing directly to the green dot of the camera. Children of the World took the baby from her parents. We promised to return her, and instead we let Dallas Hayden fly her to the States. We made a terrible mistake, and we're trying to undo it. That's all this is about. Please. The Garcias are innocent here.

Lily is a member of this family, Barbara said, sniffing loudly. We won't abandon her.

Please just consider what I've said, Claire said, clasping her hands hard, as if in prayer. Our organization will take care of everything—

We've heard enough, Ron said and hung up.

At the Air India counter, there were huge cardboard boxes encircled with packing tape. Women in saris squatted in front of open suitcases with bra straps and Quality Street tins and Barbie dolls still in their packaging entrailing out.

The line snaked around the stanchions, luggage and people merging with the queues for other flights. Claire spotted her former in-laws amidst the melee, everyone exuberant and animated, on the precipice of adventure. Simon waved from the back of the pack, and Claire wended her way through the throng. She had one hand on the trolley, loaded with Theo and the suitcases, and clasped Charlotte with the other.

We were beginning to think you'd changed your mind, Simon's eldest sister said.

Sara, Simon said, then dropped his voice and added: Shut. Up.

He'd become extra obliging since Claire had agreed to let the kids go on the trip, and now he repeated the itinerary she already knew, promising to text as soon as they landed. Claire listened, razor blades in her throat.

She wanted to savour every last second with her kids, but they'd already squeezed their way between legs to join their cousins. Charlotte would turn seven in India, and Simon whispered about the surprises they had planned. Claire recalled a line from one of

Emmanuelle's articles, about how the Garcias had marked Maria's first birthday in church, praying for her return.

Simon touched her arm. I really appreciate you agreeing to this trip, he said.

She tagged along as far as security. When it could be put off no longer, she crouched and grasped both her babies in a single bear hug, committing every heartbeat and strand of fine hair to memory, the softness of their cheeks.

I love you so much, Claire whispered, inhaling their combined scent, laundry detergent and warm skin. It was taking everything in her power to keep the tears at bay. So so so so so much. More than anything or anyone in the world. I love you two the most.

Okay, Mommy, Charlotte replied, giving her two perfunctory pats on the back. Theo was already squirming, eager to rejoin his cousins.

Ready? Simon said and held his hands out for the kids to clasp.

Claire watched until they were at the front of the line. Simon turned to wave, but the kids had already forgotten her, were through the metal detector, and then out of sight.

Road to Hell

Emmanuelle

The playground was in a bougie part of town, fenced in and hidden behind a copse of trees. It had a Saturday morning vibe. Moms in leggings with artfully mussed buns plus a handful of Filipina nannies. Bugaboos and UPPAbabies and diaper bags stuffed with organic granola bars and cut fruit, children's voices pitched high and loud.

Emmanuelle in grubby track pants and a stretched-out sweatshirt sat with her arms draped across the back of a bench, watching her nieces scramble up a rock wall. Nearby, two balayage blondes huddled together, shooting her suspicious glances. Any moment now they would beeline over and start in on their questions.

Emmanuelle was exhausted. She'd spent the red-eye from Santa Rosa drafting a chapter, ashamed at how easily the words flowed. Disembarking in Toronto, she'd been surprised by Claire's text—sent late the night before. *Can we talk? In person?* And here she was, in a breezy spring trench and white sneakers, sailing through the gate with two take-away coffees in a cardboard carrier.

Emmanuelle was torn between curiosity and suspicion, still

piqued by their last fraught conversation. *Why are you attacking me?* The accusation was so clichéd, Emmanuelle and Ben had turned it into a joke, repeating the refrain in overwrought, mocking tones. Still, the indictment needled.

In her periphery, she saw the Beckys who'd been monitoring her approach. Emmanuelle dropped her sunglasses over her eyes and sprawled lower on the bench, spreading out to claim more space.

Drip or latte? Claire asked, arriving in front of her.

The Beckys stopped short, glanced at Claire, and veered away. Emmanuelle watched them go, gaze narrowed behind her shades, feeling disappointed, relieved, then annoyed. At them, at Claire, at all these wearisome people.

Up close Claire looked rough: bloodshot eyes, dark circles underneath, and a deep crease between her brows. Emmanuelle had a vision of sticking a key in, turning.

Claire pushed the coffees forward. Take one.

Emmanuelle blew air through her nostrils and chose the drip. She wasn't going to be beholden to Claire for more than five bucks.

Only because I've just gotten off a red-eye, she said and sipped.

I found Maria, Claire said.

Emmanuelle sat up, startled. How on earth—

She's with a family in Utah, Claire said. They're a little creepy, if I'm honest.

Claire complained about Crispin's incompetence, how blithely he'd washed his hands of the whole affair. And Dallas! She sent Maria packing in January. Right after the Oscar nominations came out.

Emmanuelle was immediately on guard. Why was Children of the World's publicist suddenly confiding in her? Did she think they were *friends*?

Claire claimed to know where the family lived, his employer, their church, their kids' school, all of it. There was a coyness to these disclosures, and Claire kept glancing away, as if afraid of whatever truth her face might reveal. She wants me to ask, Emmanuelle realized. She's goading me to beg her for intel.

This is on the record, Claire said, gesturing to Emmanuelle's phone, which was face down on her leg. Feel free to record.

Emmanuelle folded her arms across her chest. When's Maria going home?

I begged them, Claire said. I explained it all, but they wouldn't listen.

Emmanuelle watched her nieces navigate the monkey bars, fury coursing through her. Of course! *Of course* they wouldn't let Maria go.

They don't trust me, Claire said. And why should they, I guess.

Emmanuelle silently ran through the options. Hire a lawyer? Alert the justice minister in Santa Rosa? Micah would call this news an answer to prayer. But if these people didn't want to give Maria up, if they believed in their own righteousness, what hope was there? The case would wind through the legal systems of two countries for years, for decades, until eventually Maria was an adult with no memory of her origins. The unease she'd felt at the Garcias' home returned.

Claire was still talking about the family, describing their other kids: Isn't it weird how they're collecting all these special-needs children? Like they're hoarding them or something.

Emmanuelle whirled on her, incensed. Your feelings aren't mine to manage, she wanted to yell. Instead, she asked, What's Crispin's take?

He says we need to respect their decision. *Their* decision. What about the Garcias' decision? What about their right to their own child?

Indeed. What about that?

Claire held up her hands in concession. I started this. This whole chain of events.

And now the ending is out of your control, Emmanuelle finished.

But you can do something, Claire said.

Go to Utah? Break in and grab Maria?

They're an hour outside Salt Lake City, Claire said quickly. Their names are Ron and Barbara—

Emmanuelle sprang up. Stop. Why are you telling me this?

I have their address, their phone number. I can give it to you.

So I can turn up at their doorstep or hide in the bushes with a long-range telephoto lens?

Emmanuelle tapped a restless foot. That was exactly what Jorge and Inez would want her to do. Meanwhile, Quinn would be thrilled. Fool that she was, she'd allowed Claire to entrap her.

From across the busy park, she picked out her nieces' bickering voices. If one of them was being held hostage in Utah, she would fly down with more than a telephoto lens.

Claire gazed up, expression ardent. You have connections with U.S. media.

Ah, so you want me to dox them. Sic the paparazzi on these people, who haven't technically done anything wrong, by the way. And let me guess. You'd be the anonymous source.

I'll go on the record. On camera. Whatever you need.

Emmanuelle marched to the swings and began pushing her niece, Abby. She felt the gut rot of too much caffeine on an empty stomach. She needed a proper meal. She needed to think in peace.

Don't you want their address? Claire said. I know the Garcias are looking for Maria. Well, I *found* her. We can do this. We can get her back.

We?

Abby, hearing her sarcasm, twisted in her seat to fix Claire with a scornful, silencing glare. When the swing flew back, Emmanuelle kissed her niece's head and was rewarded with a conspirator's grin.

A crow cawed. A toddler squealed down a slide. Nearby, a boy admonished his mother: You're taking away all my tools for success. Emmanuelle continued to push her niece, lulled into the rhythmic back and forth, the squeak of the chains. She would speak to Micah, she decided. As soon as she got home.

Well, I'm going to get her back, Claire said finally. With or without you.

You people always think these things are so easy. You'll just ride in on your white horse and save the day.

I don't think it'll be easy. But that doesn't mean I shouldn't try.

These new people have had Maria for three, four months? I'm sure they've bonded with her. They probably feel a sense of *entitlement*.

Claire flinched. I'm not trying to be a saviour or whatever. I just need to fix this.

Does Maria have papers, or is she undocumented? And how will you get her back to Santa Rosa? Crispin have a private plane?

Claire's face crumpled. Emmanuelle was about to snap at her to knock it off, but Claire took a couple of deep breaths and got a hold of herself. Where did you just come from anyway? she asked.

Research trip, Emmanuelle said.

Your reporting has been really impressive, Claire said. Congrats on the book.

Emmanuelle searched her expression and was surprised to find it wasn't grudging.

I have to say, I didn't expect that reaction from you.

What kind of research?

Emmanuelle didn't reply. She was thinking about what it would mean to break the story, what another bombshell could do for her profile. Quinn would say it was too bad they'd already sold the book. Having this intel would have driven up the price.

Oh, Claire said. And then she added, with all the old antagonism, You've made something of this too.

Grasping the chains, Emmanuelle brought the swing to a halt and told the girls it was time to go. Turning to Claire, she said: Must be nice to have a patsy. I trust your conscience is clear now.

We never meant to hurt anyone, Claire said. Our intentions were good.

They always are on the road to hell, Emmanuelle said.

Beggars and Choosers

Anya

FIVE MONTHS LATER

Outside the building, autumn rain rushed through downspouts and lashed the dark windows, whipped up by powerful gusts that sent litter and debris flying, plastering sodden orange leaves against the glass.

Inside the office, the fluorescents were off and Anya was lit only by the eerie glow of her screen. Gripping a pencil between her teeth, she ignored a past due notice from Nepal and made payroll in Santa Rosa. It was closing in on nine p.m. and she was waiting for Crispin, telling herself that his pitch meeting running long was a good sign.

Everyone else had clocked out hours ago, if they'd showed up at all. Head Office was down three staff, and Anya suspected the rest were job hunting.

Logging out of the bank's website, she returned to her financial projections, experimentally setting India to nil and reallocating their budget to Santa Rosa. If they closed the school in Cambodia—no. Crispin wouldn't allow it. It was their oldest project and the one he'd built himself, living there for a year and writing every cheque from his own account.

Alright. Zero out India and Indonesia, throw in Sri Lanka for good measure. The cursor became a spinning pinwheel, then froze. Anya growled, biting harder into wood.

Crispin was having dinner with a cantankerous septuagenarian, a rags-to-riches billionaire who'd turned reactionary in his dotage, allying himself with the hard-right government in his native Hungary. Earlier, when Claire had expressed her dismay—*This is who we're getting in bed with, really?*—Anya had lectured her on beggars and choosers. A year ago, they'd only been broke. Now they were pariahs.

The billionaire was a notorious tightwad, but Crispin hoped to stoke his childhood nostalgia—subtly reminding him of his family's flight from revolution, their arrival in Canada as refugees—and return with spare change.

The cursor blinked. The graphs reconfigured, and Anya exhaled. Twelve months. Okay. Not ideal, but workable.

From down the hall, the lights flicked to life.

Marco? Crispin called.

Polo, Anya called back. Any luck?

Crispin made a sour face and shook himself like a dog. I need a shower. I need to flay off my skin.

Opening her bottom drawer, Anya dug around among the loafers and orthopedic pumps to liberate a bottle.

That's no way to treat a single malt, Crispin said.

I'm an old broad. Let me have my eccentricities.

You're not about to give me bad news are you? he asked, following her to the kitchen.

Crispin, we're broke. Our reputation is radioactive. It should be shrouded in concrete and stored in an underground bunker, for everyone's safety. The board resigned en masse. Staff are quitting. Nikhil has one foot out the door in Delhi, which is just as well because a resignation will save us having to pay severance. All I have is bad news.

Just don't tell me you're leaving, he said, taking a seat at the peninsula counter. I know you could snap your fingers and get a dozen better offers but please, Anya. We *need* you here.

She let him go on for a while as she rummaged in the cupboards, then said: I'm not quitting. Not when there's work to do.

She'd destroyed a family. More than her colleagues, *she* was to blame. Lucca, after all, had only been following orders. And Crispin, vanity and optimism so lethally inflated, couldn't be counted on to make hard calls. *She* was the grown-up. She could have argued harder and made him see sense. But she'd ignored her better judgment, lured by the false promise of yet another big cheque. She felt a hot flush of shame. More than ever, she needed Santa Rosa to succeed.

They perched on high bar stools, next to the glass wall that looked out to the open-plan workspace as she poured them each a finger. Clinking glasses, they sipped silently for a long while, Anya thinking about her projections. Children of the World was finished. That much was certain. But with twelve months of runway, Santa Rosa could be salvaged, made self-sufficient, then break away. After which, she'd retire, legacy secure. But Crispin didn't need to know that.

This feels like a wake, he said.

Don't be superstitious, she said, but privately she was buoyed by his melancholy. She could convince him if he was dejected.

Adding a splash more to each tumbler, she said, I've been running the numbers.

Me too.

This was a surprise. You have?

It's not like I have anything else to do, he said, adding that the exercise had brought him back to the old days when Children of the World was just him and a dream.

We can get through this, he insisted. But our timing is wrong. That became very clear to me this evening. All this effort to win back donors, it's too soon, too desperate. Claire's right. We should sit tight and fade out of the spotlight. Give the pendulum time to swing back.

What else has she suggested? Anya asked, alarmed by his stubborn assurance.

Claire's been distracted . . . He trailed off, sticking his nose in his drink. She wants me to speak to those people, Crispin said.

The Olsens? What good will that do?

She thinks I can convince them to return the girl, like I'm some kind of hypnotist or I dunno . . . Svengali, Crispin said.

Was Claire really so naive? Anya wondered in exasperation. There were some wrongs so heinous, their damage so totalizing, you could never make them right. Didn't she know that?

In the spring, TMZ had found the Olsens, igniting a wildfire of outrage. Anya laughed dryly and said, If the past five months of public infamy haven't twisted their arms, I'm not sure what you can do.

While Claire waited in vain for a miracle, Anya was going to save the seventy children still in their care.

Anyway, I think Claire would agree with this approach, Crispin said. A lot can happen in a year.

Absolutely, Anya lied.

Meantime, we need to scale back, he said, surprising her again.

We could cut salaries by twenty per cent and move to a four-day workweek, she said carefully, floating an idea he'd rejected the year before. It'll encourage resignations and save us on severance packages.

Crispin sighed and made a reluctant gesture of assent, turning away from the sea of quiet desks, with their potted plants and tchotchkes, and toward the impartial appliances.

Anya was disconcerted by his silence, the straight-ahead stare, the jiggling knee. I know you—*we* have been reluctant to scale back overseas. But sometimes—

You have to lose a limb to save the body, he finished.

Anya almost sighed out loud, so great was her relief. She felt for Crispin then, knowing what the concession cost him.

We can keep downsizing quiet, she assured him. Leave the website, all our marketing, exactly as it is.

He'd been fidgety, tapping a nervous staccato against his glass, but as she spoke, he stilled. Gazing at her curiously, he said, If that's what you think is best.

Buoyed by his unexpected pragmatism, Anya outlined her plan: If we sundown Africa, South Asia, and Indonesia, we can focus our attention on Cambodia and Latin America, running both from here.

Latin America meaning Santa Rosa, Crispin said, his expression hardening.

Guatemala and El Salvador too, she added quickly.

India is still attracting volunteers and donations, he said.

India is too complex to run from afar, she explained patiently. We'd have to keep a country director. That salary comes from our operational funds.

Do you know when I cut the ribbon on India? he asked and as she cast about for an answer, he said: No, of course not. *You* weren't here. It was 2002. Nepal in 2003. Indonesia in 2005. Ghana, Sierra Leone, Senegal, those were all before your time.

As he lectured, Anya's vision narrowed on a fridge magnet of a sloth hanging upside down on a limb. When she'd joined Children of the World, it had been hemorrhaging money, staffed with amateurs and charlatans, not a single non-profit professional on the roster, Crispin so far out of his depth he was relieved to let her take the reins. She'd cleaned house, filled the org chart with smart hires, and swiftly balanced the books. She'd taught Crispin everything he knew about fundraising. Thirteen years she'd been here. He owed her.

Crispin was still talking: The projects in Asia are our best-performing. Our most mature.

Yes, and they'll be on the books forever, Anya said. Santa Rosa is different. The end goal has always been divestment.

Haven't I always supported Santa Rosa? he asked.

I've appreciated that trust, she said. It's why—

Even when the numbers weren't sound, he continued. And let's be honest, they've never been sound. Remind me . . . when was the last time Santa Rosa attracted a volunteer, a donor? India and Indonesia have endowments. I can't tell sponsors we're killing their projects in favour of one that doesn't have a single supporter *and* is fatally tainted.

Anya flinched. She took a deep breath, kept her voice steady, then said: Six months. After that, we part ways and Santa Rosa becomes a permanent success story.

A single limb, he said.

Their autonomy will be a springboard for Children of the World's future. Once we prove the model works, that there's a better, more sustainable way to do philanthropy—

Santa Rosa is a liability. It endangers the whole organization.

The land is productive. If we scaled back the dorms, sent some of the kids home. Or charged patients a nominal fee . . . But we have to keep supporting them. Without us, they won't last a month.

Crispin shook his head. I'm sorry, Anya. It's the end of the line.

The end of the line? Who was *he* to dictate to *her*?

I don't stay without Santa Rosa, she said. Package deal.

He rubbed a thumbnail over his eyebrow. I'm sorry to hear that.

This is more than a job to me. That compound, that project, it's the only reason I'm still . . . the only reason I've *ever* been here.

His posture stiffened. I see.

He was bristling now, but she knew he'd relent. It was better this way: everything out in the open. Her project and his, their fates intertwined. He would have to compromise.

Crispin nodded, thoughtful for a moment. When their eyes met, his glinted with indignation. He held out a hand, voice like velvet. It's been a pleasure working with you, Anya. It's a shame to see you go, but of course I understand.

Temporary Measures

Thiago

THREE MONTHS LATER

Thiago glanced in the rear-view mirror. In the back of the jeep, the Martinez sisters had fallen asleep. Aged twelve and ten, they slouched into each other, mouths agape. They'd been sobbing on and off all day and only relaxed when he'd finally quit the search and announced they were returning to the compound.

Up ahead, the guard's hut was deserted. He'd had to let the watchmen go at the beginning of the year, and now they kept the entrance padlocked at night. During the day the gates stood wide open, and driving through, Thiago was slammed by a memory. Lucca demanding he unlock them, his glare a challenge. *Don't defy me.*

Thiago gripped the steering wheel, batting away the tumult of emotion and regret, the big white button depressing under his thumb, the heavy click of the lock retracting, the squeal of the gates as they opened. He willed himself to focus on the present. But the stillness of the compound, its abandoned, desolate air, the shuttered school and dormitory buildings, and the quiet playground were discouraging. He focused on the farm instead, where straw hats bobbed between lines of crops.

The idea to parcel the land and lease it to locals had come from Luis—temporary measures, the farm manager had said, until you can hire me again—and Thiago was almost pleased with how well it was working. The rents, combined with the savings they'd found, kept the clinic open.

It was nearly lunchtime, and the staff were winding down for the break when Thiago arrived.

Seeing the Martinez sisters trailing him, Beatriz raised her eyebrows. Moisés is in the back, she told the girls, pointing with her clipboard. Go play with him.

No school today? Thiago asked.

Suspended, Beatriz said, lowering her voice. We can't trust him alone.

Thiago grimaced in sympathy.

What happened with the girls? she asked.

The Martinez sisters had been living at the compound nearly their entire lives. Thiago recalled the day they were brought in, emaciated with starvation, their single father not faring much better. He'd checked in on his daughters a few times, but after a couple of years the visits ceased. Eventually, they stopped asking after him. It was a sad situation but not so uncommon.

I couldn't find him, Thiago said.

For several weeks now, Thiago had been ferrying their charges home, leaving every morning with a jeep packed with children and returning alone for lunch and a siesta before reloading the vehicle for a second trip. He and Beatriz had taken the task on together, combing through the notebooks that passed for their records, names and addresses scrawled in pen by a succession of country directors, some meticulous record keepers, others careless, leaving behind entries riddled with spelling errors and transpositions or worse: no details at all to suggest where these children might belong.

They called ahead to alert as many families as they could—a vacation was how they described it, an extended Christmas holiday while they made some changes at the compound—but most times Thiago arrived unannounced, unsure of what to expect. The reunions were happy, grandparents and parents holding their young ones tight, but often bewildering too. The disparity between the compound's charges, freshly bathed in laundered clothes, thumbs hooked into backpacks, with their scrawnier, grubbier siblings, and the home beyond, perhaps only a single room fashioned out of scrap wood and metal, troubled him.

The Martinez sisters were a mystery. At the apartment they had on record as belonging to their father, Thiago had found strangers. Patiently, he'd gone door to door, questioning the neighbours. Some said the man had remarried and moved away. Others thought he'd taken a job in the capital.

But if he was moving, why not inform us? Thiago asked.

Beatriz scowled. He'd have told himself it was easier on the girls not to know they'd been abandoned. Especially if there was a new woman.

He may have died, Thiago said.

Or gone to hospital, Beatriz conceded. What will we do with them?

Thiago removed his cap and massaged the back of his neck. He was drained from the long day and all the ones that had preceded it, the cumulative stress and exhaustion of keeping the clinic alive, brainstorming with the staff to cut costs and generate revenue even as he had to, one by one, let them go.

There's nowhere left, he said.

In addition to the ones like Moisés, who had no relations at all, there were a dozen or so children with untraceable families. He and Beatriz had found most of them temporary placements in orphanages and government homes, but even that had been a struggle and now every place was full.

You'll have to ask Josefina, Beatriz said.

Thiago waited until they convened in the cafeteria. Since losing their colleagues, they took turns cooking and cleaning. Today Yolanda and Juan were frying eggs with vegetables. From the kitchen came the sound of oil spitting in the pan, the pungent aroma of onion and garlic.

At a table in the middle of the empty room, Josefina taught the children a card trick while Beatriz and Thiago watched. The sound of the cards slapping against the table echoed in the cavernous space. The morning's trip had shuttled away the last of their charges, and Thiago felt the absence acutely. What a waste that this large facility should be so empty.

The final call from Lucca had come ten months earlier, the previous March.

Boss, Thiago said.

Thiago.

And from the resigned way Lucca pronounced his name, Thiago knew what he would say.

There's been a change in plan—

When can we expect the new director? Thiago interrupted.

But when Lucca was silent, he regretted his abruptness. This was still his superior, after all.

You'll have to manage on your own, Lucca said.

And Thiago realized he'd misunderstood. It was a promotion. For twelve years, Thiago had been a loyal and diligent employee and here was the reward: the independence Head Office had always promised.

He was relieved, too, that he wouldn't have to see Lucca again. Conspiring with the actress was bad enough, but by committing the crime in full view of the helpless compound, Lucca had forced them all into a terrible complicity. Resentment was an open wound, impossible to hide.

Lucca asked if he'd heard the news. Embarrassed that he'd let his attention wander, Thiago lied, Yes.

It is not what I would have wanted, Lucca said, and Thiago wondered how long the higher-ups had been planning this change. Had they recalled Lucca to Head Office only to sack him?

Lucca said, If I'd thought that she would do this . . .

You know the gringos. They make their decisions without consulting us, without any thought to who they affect, Thiago said, privately including Lucca in the denouncement.

I don't like to think of you and the others in this position, Lucca said. It was not your choice.

You mustn't worry about us.

Thiago, Lucca said. If I could go back . . .

He sounded agonized, his voice tight and strangled in a way Thiago didn't recognize. He frowned, unsure of how to respond. It was impossible to muster much sympathy for Lucca, and he was anxious to end the call and share the good news with the others.

I wish it hadn't happened, Lucca said. But the past cannot be helped.

Later, when Thiago learned what the actress had done, how she'd sent Maria away (sold her, Beatriz had said darkly), the conversation had come into a different, truer focus. Lucca's parting words, the passiveness of their construction, how smoothly he'd elided responsibility, even while groping for absolution. It was the worst sort of duplicity.

In the cafeteria, Moisés struggled to dome the cards between his hands. His glasses slid, and he wriggled his nose to urge them back up.

What do you think of your temporary school? Thiago asked.

They have nothing to teach me, Moisés said. I know everything already.

Are the teachers charmed when you tell them that? Thiago said.

The teachers agree he is clever and has an exceptional memory, Beatriz said and tweaked his ear. But they say he must apply himself.

I'm hungry, the younger Martinez girl complained.

Beatriz told her to ask in the kitchen for a tortilla, and when the children were out of earshot, she said, Moisés was suspended for fighting.

Again? Josefina asked. Just look at that child. All thin skin and brittle bird bones. Boys like him are made for diplomacy, not wrestling.

After Lucca's departure, Moisés had turned sullen and gotten into fisticuffs with the older boys. He was an uncoordinated fighter and would have lost every brawl except he fought like a child who had nothing to lose. And since moving in with Beatriz and Enrique, his behaviour had worsened. Beatriz said he'd taken up with a bad lot and run away more than once.

Fortunately, he's not as sly as he thinks, she said. We always know where to find him. But the sooner we can get him back here, the better. At least none of our ones have big ideas about joining gangs.

That child will come to grief if he doesn't take care, Josefina said. Then, turning to Thiago, she asked about the Martinez sisters.

When Thiago explained the situation, she shook her head vehemently and said, I told you already this is the one thing I cannot do.

We've all taken in children, Beatriz argued.

Josefina, young and single, prized her freedom, her nights out with friends.

I have my mother, she said. She needs a lot of care.

You can't be selfish forever, Beatriz grumbled.

If I wanted to be selfish, I wouldn't have become a nurse, Josefina said, tapping the deck against the table.

It's only for a short time, Thiago said. In a few weeks, we'll bring everyone back.

Josefina cleared her throat and fanned the cards before flipping them face up and gathering them into a pile.

You don't believe it? Beatriz said. If you're not committed, say so.

All of you with your husbands and wives and children imagine that is the only way to live. But not all of us want the same things, Josefina said.

I know that, Thiago said, thinking that if anyone could be happy as a spinster it was Josefina.

My mother is not well, she said again.

They are good girls. You might find they are a help.

I don't know why I must be responsible for someone else's choices, Josefina muttered but in a conciliatory tone.

Conversation turned to the budget shortfall.

We could sell the farm equipment, Beatriz said. And the animals.

We'll have to buy them back later, and it'll be more expensive, Thiago said.

El Guapo comes on Tuesday, Josefina said. That could help.

The president was up for re-election, and by a stroke of luck the compound was in his home department, where he'd once been a popular governor. Thiago had arranged for him to take a tour with his propaganda team.

He's made such a fuss about poor Maria, Josefina said. He'll have to give us something after he's re-elected.

Beatriz touched the crucifix at her throat. When you say things like that, it feels like a curse.

The man is corrupt as sin, but if the end result is good, who cares about his intentions? Josefina said.

Beggars can't carry clubs, Thiago agreed.

Great Acts of Altruism

Claire

THREE MONTHS LATER

The familiar bars of the show's opening theme blared through the laptop speakers, the rising crescendo of a piano and the background beat of a bass. The music was ominous, instantly gripping. Claire increased the volume and gnawed the inside of her cheek.

Reveal was one of those investigative programs that trafficked in melodrama and contrived suspense. This episode was right in their sweet spot: true crime with a celebrity angle. The voice-over, in a bottomless masculine baritone, narrated: A crippled child. A Hollywood actress. A brazen abduction.

Emmanuelle flashed onscreen in three-quarter profile. I knew something was wrong, she said. When Maria disappeared off Dallas's social media, I just knew.

Cut to a Black man, standing by a pew and clasping a Bible, saying: It's been a year and a half. How much longer must the Garcias wait to get their daughter back?

Back to Emmanuelle, head-on now, declaring: Rehoming. Transferring custody. These are euphemisms for child trafficking.

The screen filled with a collage of overlapping headlines. *Stolen child found in Utah. Olsens unrepentant. Interpol alerted. Protests mark second birthday.* Photographs whizzed by. Maria strapped into a toddler swing, casted legs pointing skyward, with Barbara at her back, unaware of the camera. Ron, head down, hurrying from a building. An activist open-mouthed and brandishing a sign: *She's not yours.*

An anonymous tip to TMZ from a burner account. That was all it had taken for the media to swarm in. They hounded Barbara down the cereal aisle, photographing the Cheerios she put in her cart. They chased Ron's car as he pulled out of a parking spot. Tabloid reporters and true crime podcasters turned up at the older children's schools, at church, hassled neighbours, teachers, coaches, friends for comment. No place was sacred, no one off-limits. At first, Claire had watched the circus with a grim satisfaction, certain the Olsens would capitulate.

Dallas and her famous pals were inured to unwanted attention. Ron and Barbara were civilians without the buffer of publicists and bodyguards, or the protection of sprawling mansions in gated communities. But the Olsens had astonished her.

Reveal's reporter stood in a studio, spreading her arms wide as she spoke: For nearly a year, they've maintained their silence, refusing interview requests, never releasing a statement, unmoved by the pressure. But that hasn't dampened people's curiosity.

Now came a montage of low-quality recordings: the school-aged Olsens in classrooms, in the playground, at their baseball games and recitals. Claire had almost managed to forget these videos. Seeing them again, she felt a fretting guilt. After the initial flurry of outrage, when the professionals departed for other scandals, the amateurs swarmed in. Classmates recorded gossipy TikToks. Drones circled the Olsens' home, stalked them down the street. Occasionally some tidbit made the leap to the mainstream press. When their eldest daughter was caught smoking under the bleachers, the story ran as proof of unfit parenting. Not long after, as if in rebuttal, another video surfaced: the family at church, singing a hymn.

Reveal travelled to Promise, Utah (population: 2,782), where an eye-in-the-sky showed the neat geometry of a bedroom community—vehicles zipping along streets, the bright green woods all around—accompanied by the perky twang of a banjo. The camera angle changed, and they were inside a car, panning across American flags and a strip mall with signs for Jim's Barber Shop, Used Car Parts, and Wong's Buffet.

The reporter stood in front of a suburban ranch house. Behind her, the home was still, every blind down.

Here in Utah, she's known as Lily, the reporter said, a two-year-old whom neighbours describe as shy and sweet.

The reporter rang the doorbell. Once. Twice. Then she knocked. Hello? she called, peering uselessly at the curtains and tapping on the glass. Hello?

Claire imagined the Olsens hunkered inside, under siege. When her conscience screamed that she had done this, turned their home into a bunker, she reminded herself that Ron and Barbara were colluding in their own misery.

Let's see if someone else will talk to us, the reporter said, and in the next second she was in what appeared to be the town square, interviewing a woman in a prairie dress, hair tied back with a thin bow.

I just think it's unfair, the woman said. They opened their home and their hearts to that poor disabled girl. Not everyone would do that, you know.

She had a stroller with a blonde toddler strapped inside and two older ones next to her. Tradwife and her Children of the Corn, Claire thought viciously, as the camera pulled back to show the small crowd gathered around.

A gammon-faced man in a red trucker cap said: They've got no right to that child. How would they like it if someone snatched one of their own?

Children aren't property, a white-haired woman put in. For we are all born of God.

Red Cap shook his head. But Rosemarie, the good Lord chose to place this child with her own family, and *that* is where she belongs.

Exactly, Claire said out loud.

A man in running shorts spoke up: Well, I call it a witch hunt. I've known Ron and Barb for years. They're a real nice family. He pointed at the reporter and added, You people need to back off.

You people, Claire parroted, rolling her eyes.

It's hardest on the young ones, white-haired Rosemarie said, and here the group was in agreement, adding how the elementary-aged Olsens were being homeschooled, the older ones bullied. They'd dropped out of Scouts and ballet and swimming, were rarely seen in public, and when they were spotted, it was always speedwalking to their destinations, glancing over their shoulders. Claire began chewing her cheeks again, subdued.

They're practically under house arrest, Running Shorts said. They don't even come to church anymore.

They adopted the kid in good faith, but now they know the truth, Red Cap insisted. If they want their privacy, they should send her back to Cuba.

Mexico, a gum-chewing teenager corrected. Y'all voted for the wall. The Olsens . . . fam, they *voted* for the wall. That's facts. Now they wanna keep this Mexican girl?

She's from Santa Rosa, the reporter said, but no one heard. They'd begun shouting over each other, Rosemarie quoting scripture (*whatever you do for the least of my brothers . . .*), the teenager, hand on hip, impatient foot stuck out, saying, You ask me, it's sus.

Emmanuelle, of course, was central to the episode. Seated in a nondescript warehouse, she opined about the case, shamelessly flogging her book, and succinctly outlining her thesis that this incident was a symptom of a much larger system of injustice in which everyone was complicit. We need to examine our own role in tragedies like these, she said.

Emmanuelle's book had recently come out, an *instant New York Times bestseller*, the subway ad boasted. Spotting it on a cramped train ride, Claire had scowled, vividly recalling the #realhero campaign that had once occupied the same space. She could just imagine the publicist's pitch to *Reveal*, the way this episode with its dramatic re-enactments was one tactic in the publisher's marketing plan. March 18: publication. March 26: celebrity book club endorsement. April 3: eyeball-grabbing television special.

A film crew from *Reveal* had travelled to Santa Rosa to interview the Garcias at their church, where the congregation had gathered to commemorate Maria's second birthday with a special service. Inez showed the reporter some of Maria's things. As she spoke in Spanish, the camera focused on her hands, dry and calloused, with long, capable fingers that Claire could imagine wielding a hammer as effortlessly as they comforted a fevered child. Inez smoothed a threadbare blanket and rubbed the head of a cloth doll, as the English voice-over translated her words: For a long time, I would sleep with her things next to me, but they don't smell like her anymore.

A bitter taste filled Claire's mouth. She sat on her hands to keep herself from closing the laptop.

I would like to see a picture, the female voice-over translated. I would like to hear from my daughter. Is she walking? Is she well? Does she remember her family?

When the news broke that Maria was in Utah, TMZ had run photos of Barbara and Maria at the park. Since then, she'd never been photographed. What did the Garcias' daughter look and sound like now? Claire doubted she'd recognize her.

Their minister stood by the couple, a hand on each of their shoulders, as Jorge faced the camera and said in careful, practised English, This is the fight of our lives.

In May, Claire received an unexpected email. She squinted, perplexed, at the sender's name and his two-line message. Hugh Coren hoped Claire was well. Was someone there available to hop on a Zoom? Crispin was sequestered in the boardroom with the accountant, so Claire joined the video conference on her laptop. When she was allowed into the meeting, she saw a room full of suits.

Hugh launched in without preamble: The Olsens have agreed to relinquish custody.

Claire's jaw dropped. Really?

The family was moving and wanted a new start, he explained. They were in an undisclosed location and would remain there until the situation was resolved. It would be in everyone's interests to keep the transfer low key, he continued. No press. No elected officials; they didn't want this turning into a political rally. No recording devices. A strict embargo on the news. Dallas would make a brief and tasteful announcement after the fact.

They've agreed, Claire said, joy and relief soaring in her chest. The Olsens are going to give Maria back?

My client will act as intermediary, Hugh said. She'll bring the child to the birth mother. The father can be present, but he's not to approach my client or speak to her. There's to be no contact with Ms. Hayden afterward. Not by Children of the World (Claire almost snorted) nor the birth family. They shouldn't expect any financial arrangements.

Hugh was at the head of a conference table, surrounded by his henchmen. Claire sat alone at her desk in the silent office, surrounded by empty workstations, their former occupants long gone. She recognized the conversation for what it was: a hostage negotiation, the captors dictating the terms.

Ms. Hayden would like your organization to make arrangements in Santa Rosa, he said.

Leave it with me, Claire said.

Crispin had taken to bringing his guitar into the office and strumming his old hits. The familiar chord progressions were grating, jangling Claire's focus. He was playing "Prophets," humming at first, then softly singing the lyrics, glancing at her expectantly from time to time.

Claire, glasses on, leaned toward the screen where she had several tabs open, comparing flights, weighing stopovers and journey lengths against prices as Crispin sang, without irony, about greedy corporations. It was undignified, the way he was carrying on, embarrassing for them both.

Hugh had made it sound as if notoriety alone had forced the Olsens' hand and Claire didn't doubt their situation had grown intolerable, but she suspected Dallas had dangled a financial carrot. Bought the Olsens a house, arranged their temporary stay in the *undisclosed location*, written them a cheque for two million. And if they balked, Hugh would have invoked the other children, pressing the pedal on parental guilt. This was no life for a child—the relentless hounding, their every word and action subject to public referendum; those experiences were scarring. And here was Dallas, benevolent angel, offering the gift of anonymity. His manner would have been gentle, calibrated to disarm even as it fuelled their anxiety. All the while, he'd be plotting his client's redemption arc—narrating rom-com audiobooks and documentaries by fledgling filmmakers, subtly tying herself to projects with a social conscience, targeting women aged twenty to fifty-five, keeping her voice in their ears, paying penance until the time was ripe for an onscreen comeback.

Dallas couldn't book so much as an adult diaper commercial. When the actors' union went on strike, rumour had it she'd been asked not to join the picket line. Bringing Maria home was her last chance at career resuscitation, Claire thought grimly. A Hail Mary.

Claire chose a flight as Crispin played the song's final notes. He was silent for a while, as if thinking, while Claire double-checked the details, before confirming the purchase. She was charging the trip to her personal credit card because the corporate one was maxed out, all their accounts overdrawn.

The printer churned to life, spitting out the confirmation. By the time she boarded, the bankruptcy would be official.

I thought we would be change-makers, Crispin said mournfully. Not just through our projects, but on the larger international stage. *We* were supposed to be the ones world leaders came to for guidance.

You mean *you* were going to have world leaders banging down your door, she thought, piqued by his ludicrous ambition.

Sighing extravagantly, he hung his head. Without Children of the World, I'm nothing.

Claire almost yelled at him to hire a therapist and get over himself. Instead, she counted to three, looked him in the eyes, and said: Crispin, listen. Let me give you some professional advice. Take a holiday. Six months. One year. Hire an image consultant, and reinvent yourself. Get on the speaker's circuit. Give talks on the upside of cancellation: public censure was humbling, but it made me a better, more authentic person, yadda, yadda. Do your self-deprecating shtick. Don't shirk responsibility; lean into it. You're a white man. Trust me. People will eat it up.

He blinked at her, gormless, then began strumming. Maybe I'll go back to music, he said, playing the opening bars of "Prophets" again.

Claire stood and walked to the copier. I never liked the ending of that song, she said.

No? Crispin sounded surprised.

Too upbeat. It's artificial.

It felt good to wound him, but only for an instant.

At least we tried, Crispin said, lifting the guitar away by the strap. That counts for something.

Gathering her papers, warm from the printer, she let the silence lengthen. When she didn't reply, Crispin repeated himself, plaintively asking, Doesn't it?

Claire checked into a budget hotel close to the airport. She had a general idea of where the Garcias lived—addresses, it seemed, were theoretical in Santa Rosa—but when she asked about arranging a car and driver for the following day, the receptionist pursed his lips and said he'd call around and try to arrange something for the morning.

Claire dragged her suitcase to her room. It occurred to her the driver would be someone's cousin or brother or uncle—just her and a strange man alone in a vehicle for hours, driving through rural areas, in a foreign country where she didn't speak the language. Her phone buzzed. It was Simon sending a photo of the kids.

Simon was getting remarried the next day. His fiancée, a fellow teacher from his school, was a lot younger. Shaking her hand, Claire hadn't known how to feel—smug? jealous?—about the fact of their resemblance.

I really admire what you do, the fiancée had said. You must sacrifice so much, but I bet it's totally rewarding to know you're saving lives.

Her sincerity had aroused a viciousness in Claire. When she raved about Charlotte and Theo, calling them *just the sweetest* and *totally delightful*, and promised to take good care of them, Claire had barked: I'm their mother. They can call you Haylee.

Claire spent a sleepless night, worries ping-ponging between all the things that could go wrong the next day. What if the receptionist couldn't line up a driver? Or they got lost? The Olsens might balk at the last minute.

In the morning, venturing into the lobby, full of trepidation and nerves, she was surprised to see Emmanuelle leaving the breakfast bar.

What are you doing here? They said no media.

You were the kind of kid who always followed the rules, right? Emmanuelle said.

Who do you think gave the Olsens' name to TMZ? Claire retorted.

If it wasn't for Claire, this reunion wouldn't even be happening. Now Emmanuelle's selfishness, her insatiable greed for a byline, was going to ruin—

Emmanuelle rolled her eyes. You destroyed the lives of total strangers to get what you wanted. Let's not pretend these were great acts of altruism.

Emmanuelle had been heading out of the hotel, and Claire had unconsciously fallen in step. Exiting, they were hit with a thick wall of humidity and pollution. It was eight a.m. and already thirty degrees in the shade, the haze that veiled the sun impotent against its heat.

Who are you here with? Claire asked. The *Times*? The *Post*?

A bright red Kia Rio pulled up. The driver turned out to be a fellow Canadian, and after a moment Claire recognized the Garcias' minister from the *Reveal* episode.

Can we give Claire a ride? Emmanuelle asked, sliding into shotgun. She's with Children of the World.

Surprise, then anger registered in the uplift of the brow, a tightening around the mouth, but in the next instant Christian charity prevailed and Micah turned the other cheek, stuck out a hand, and said, Pleased to meet you.

Traffic was heavy and they crawled through the featureless suburbs, windows shut tight against the smog and diesel, past vast parking lots and concrete buildings, before taking the bypass highway that skirted the city. Emmanuelle and Micah chatted like old friends, and Claire, strapped into the back, was reminded of being the third wheel on family road trips. She let their conversation wash over and around her and morph into white noise, dozing at intervals as the sun climbed higher and the car became an oven.

Her dreams were confused, addled by anxiety. Simon's wedding, her children, Dallas, all merging into one. She woke to voices she didn't recognize—*Naw, naw, but what about this though*—and a bray of laughter. When she blinked her eyes open, she was surprised to realize the broad guffaw belonged to Emmanuelle who was holding her belly and saying, Stop, stop, as Micah, animated, recounted a story about a mutual friend named Martha.

Claire had never seen Emmanuelle like this, unguarded and open, so different from the scowling woman she knew, perpetually on the verge of an outburst.

Traffic had thinned, and Micah and Emmanuelle had their windows open, a refreshing breeze blowing in, bringing with it bird calls and the green notes of chlorophyll. They were passing through farmland, following the curve of a wide river. At home, the kids would be up and running amok with their cousins or donning their new outfits. Theo was ring bearer, Charlotte the flower girl.

Emmanuelle, noticing Claire was awake, spoke over her shoulder, We're almost there. Her tone was buttoned up again. I promise to behave myself, she added with a smirk.

The car was ascending toward the mountains.

Los Altos, Micah said. In precolonial times, this was a sacred place. Generations of rulers built their strongholds at the very top. But we're only going partway.

Micah's tone was altered, too, muted and careful. They drove with talk radio on so the upbeat Spanish voices masked the awkward silence, Claire wishing she was still asleep. She felt queasy and didn't know if it was the switchbacks and altitude or the uneasy prospect of coming face to face with Inez and Jorge. What recriminations would they pile on her? What could she possibly say in response?

They turned onto a narrow dirt road, bumping and jostling, foliage brushing against the car.

It's just around this corner, Micah said, and then he was pulling up the handbrake and Emmanuelle was opening the door. Outside, Claire saw a party. Two dozen people, music blasting out of a boom box, young men and old women singing along. There were balloons in the trees and girls threading flower garlands. A woman fried tortillas on an outdoor grill. A man raised a hatchet over his head, brought it down cleanly on a coconut, splitting the fruit in half.

Claire's stomach sank. A quiet handover, Hugh Coren had specified. Just the Garcias, Dallas, and the child. She appealed to Micah. Family only. We agreed.

This *is* the family, he said, pulling the keys out of the ignition.

Maria has six brothers, Emmanuelle said, swinging both feet out of the car. Plus, Inez's siblings, their spouses and kids, Jorge's cousins from the capital . . .

Immediate family, Claire said and heard the tremble in her voice. She recalled the conference room of lawyers. What if Dallas saw the crowd and balked?

Everyone's excited about Maria's homecoming, Micah said mildly.

This isn't California. The Garcias call the shots, Emmanuelle said and slammed her door.

Dallas was bringing Maria all this way, Claire reassured herself. They were en route right now. She wasn't going to renege. Claire lingered in the car, lifting the hair off the back of her sweaty neck. She'd been bracing for Inez and Jorge but was unprepared for the possibility of accusations and ill will of so many others.

Emmanuelle and Micah were being swallowed into the crowd, hugged and kissed by people chatting in Spanish. Claire reminded herself that everyone was here for Maria; no one was paying attention to her.

The scene was picturesque. Ferns and flowering trees, a heady perfume of florals mixed with cooking food. The Garcias' home was unrecognizable from the shanty she'd seen through the lens of Dallas's phone camera. It wasn't just their house; the property was different too. She caught sight of a donkey, several chickens, children sharing hammocks.

She was glad then, for Maria, who would arrive to this joyful reception. And these were only the blood relatives. There would be neighbours, too, and so many others who cherished her. An odd phrase came to her, something her former mother-in-law used to say whenever she travelled to India: *back to the bosom of my family*. For the first time, Claire got a glimpse of what that meant. A refuge, ample and generous.

There had been a caption on one of Dallas's long-vanished Instagram posts: *Us vs. the world #justthe2ofus*. At the time, Claire had read the declaration as triumphant, but now it struck her as pitiful, the poverty of what she in her arrogance had once thought a great boon.

Claire, Emmanuelle called.

She stood with a couple Claire recognized. Inez wore a red and orange dress and had a garland strung around her neck. She was beaming and squeezing her hands together. Jorge, too, was transformed, clean-shaven, dressed in slacks and a wrinkled but spotless button-up shirt. Claire approached, nervously.

Esta es Claire Talbot, Emmanuelle said. Ella trabaja para Children of the World.

Hola, Claire said, and it came out in a whisper. Lo siento. Then in English: What we did, what I did, was unforgivable. I am so sorry.

Her paltry apology sounded a little better when Micah translated. Jorge made a noise of disgust deep in his throat and said something that Micah didn't repeat. Claire held Inez's eyes, her own filling with tears. She was frustrated with herself. She had no right to cry.

Believe me. If I could turn back time . . .

As Micah translated, the rest of the family drew closer, music and voices silenced. Some were muttering. Others sniffing. An argument seemed to break out, though perhaps everyone was only agreeing loudly.

Inez flicked her chin as if swatting away at an irritation. She shook her head no, no, then began talking fast, her words tripping and falling over each other. Her expression was searching, pupils moving back and forth, and Claire willed herself not to look away. If Inez wanted to hurl invective, Claire would take it.

She's asking if Maria is coming, Micah said. Have you heard from her? Have you seen her? Is Maria alright? How long till she—

Alguien viene! The yell came from up in a tree where a child straddled a high limb. They heard the sound of approaching tires and a car engine, and then a white van pulled up.

Maria está aquí! the boy shouted as he scrambled down, dangling by both hands before dropping to the ground.

But when the doors opened and the occupants jumped out, there was no sign of Dallas or Maria, only a half dozen people unloading tripods and recording gear.

Claire rounded on Emmanuelle. Who told the press?

Emmanuelle snorted. Those aren't journalists.

Right, Claire said, shamed by her mistake.

A stocky man with a helmet of curls was calling out instructions. The ambient is good, but let's get the lights set up anyway, he said. Where's the drone?

When he turned to survey the property, Claire saw the bald spot, a perfect circle the size of saucer, on the back of his head.

He pointed to a sunny patch a few feet from the house and said, We'll do it here. Then he wrinkled his nose and said to no one in particular, Can we tidy this up?

Immediately two assistants sprang into action, moving bicycles and plastic chairs, heedless of the people around them. There were barrels on either side of the porch. They hefted one and began carrying it away, water sloshing out. Some of the family members cried out in protest. Micah and Emmanuelle moved to intervene.

Leave the balloons, the little man in charge said. We want a bit of kitsch.

The Garcias, celebratory moments earlier, backed away, huddling together, muttering among themselves. The boy had retreated into his tree, and now Claire recognized Maria's brother, the one who'd been captured on Dallas's video, the day his sister was taken.

The bossy man—Claire had begun to think of him as the director—turned his attention to the family, eyes efficient and dismissive as he scanned the crowd, only flickering to life when they landed on Claire. Which ones are the parents? he asked her. Let's get Mom and Dad by the front door and everyone else out of the way. He made a box with his hands. We want a tight shot. Explain it to them.

Before Claire could speak, there was a shout from the tree. Alguien viene!

The entourage sprung to attention as two SUVs pulled up. Claire tensed. Emmanuelle inhaled sharply. A bodyguard emerged, did a swift visual sweep, then opened the back door.

Dallas climbed out and halted when she saw the crowd. Half her face was obscured by her oversized sunglasses, but Claire saw the way her mouth became a wary line. She and the director put their heads together, voices low. Claire was struck afresh by the terrible possibility that she would change her mind. She imagined Dallas returning to the car, the vehicles spitting dirt and pebbles as they sped away.

There was a loud whirring as a drone rose. The eyes of the party warily followed its progress. Several people cowered as it flew horizontally, hovering over them.

For fuck's sakes, Emmanuelle muttered, and Claire's anger spiked. Dallas wasn't stealing Maria a second time. Together the Garcias could overpower her. Claire would do it herself, throw

Dallas to the ground, pin her down, knee on her back, while the others flung open the car doors and rescued Maria.

She glanced at the bodyguard, feet apart, hands over his crotch. What would he do? Open fire? Use his baton? Claire flinched.

And then Dallas was nodding with the director, raising her voice and loudly saying: Great. So we're all set? An assistant swooped down on her, wielding blotting paper and a brush. The director turned to Claire. Will you tell them? Just the parents. We only get one take.

Claire marched up to Dallas. Where's Maria?

The makeup artist was applying mascara, and Dallas had her face tilted back, obligingly.

Where is she? Claire said again. She was full of adrenalin and indignant confidence, sweat dripping from her hairline, muscles tensed for a fight. She crowded the makeup artist, forcing her back, getting right up in Dallas's face.

Dallas, one eye made up, the other bare, blinked in surprise.

Ma'am, I'm going to ask you to take a step back, said a deep male voice.

Claire held her ground. I'm Claire Talbot, she said.

It's alright, Kevin, Dallas said. And from the corner of her eye, Claire saw the burly figure stand down.

Jorge and Inez have waited long enough, Claire said.

Right, Dallas said.

Up close, Claire saw the dull hollow under the naked eye, the motionless skin on her forehead. She had an impulse to injure, to say something devastating. But she knew, too, that she was furious at herself, her gullibility, how easily she'd been conned by flattering camera angles and her own self-importance. Can we get this done? she said.

Dallas gestured, and the bodyguard moved to the second SUV and opened the back door. Claire was startled to see Barbara Olsen, lumpy and maternal in a sack dress and orthopedic sandals. For an absurd split second, Claire braced for a showdown, Barbara railing against her for destroying her family. But then Barbara reached into the car and lifted a little girl out with both hands.

Inez gave a strangled cry. All around, other family members were speaking: Ah, ahí está! Es realmente ella? Está aquí. Nuestra Maria!

When she'd leaked their names to TMZ, Claire had made the Olsens high-value targets, put a bounty on their heads. Yet there had never been a second sighting of Maria. The family had protected her, Claire realized. Not just Ron and Barbara, their other children, too, putting themselves in shooting range to keep Maria safe. She recalled Lucca saying, *They might be good parents, the new people*.

Now here she was, a toddler in a blue pinafore dress and red sandals, black hair in two fat pigtails, sure on her feet with sweet chubby legs and a round dimpled face, alert and watchful. Voices bubbled, emphatic.

Ella está aquí.

Como ha crecido!

Es Maria?

No es ella.

Es una gringa!

The child sucked hard on her thumb. Seeing the crowd, she buried her face in Barbara's leg. Barbara crouched to speak to her, a reassuring hand on her back.

Everyone in position, the director called.

Hija, Inez cried and moved forward, but the director threw out a hand to stop her.

Somehow, without a translator, he managed to corral his subjects. Even Jorge acquiesced. The videographers hefted their equipment onto their shoulders. The photographers raised their cameras, spares slung around their necks, resting against bellies and waists, lenses phallic and intimidating.

Barbara hugged Maria and whispered into her ear; without hearing, Claire knew exactly what she was saying. *I love you so much. I'll always love you.* In the next moment, Barbara stood and turned Maria around by the shoulders, and Dallas scooped her up onto her hip. The cameras moved in, flanking Dallas as she walked toward the Garcias. The snap of shutters volleyed like bullets. Maria, in Dallas's arms, was sucking hard on her thumb and staring back at the woman she called Mommy. Claire caught a glimpse of Barbara's stricken expression before she vanished into the car. The driver discreetly closed the door, and Claire felt the other woman's sorrow rise in her throat like vomit. Maria, bewildered, began to struggle, arching her body away from Dallas.

Here we are, Dallas said cheerfully, halting in front of Inez and Jorge as Maria reached toward the SUV and screamed: Mommy. Mommy. Want mommy. Want mommy.

Claire heard the English words, the American accent, and flinched. Above the quartet, the drone hovered.

Dallas switched to Spanish: A su casa. Mira. Madre. Dropping to one knee in front of the Garcias, she set Maria on the ground.

Mommy, Maria bawled, straining to run back even as the SUV carrying Barbara Olsen drove away. No, Mommy. Mommy. No. No. No. No. No.

Estoy acquí, hija, Inez said, picking her up, covering her head with kisses even as her daughter flailed, striking out with feet and fists. Maria, Maria, Inez repeated, a name the child didn't know.

Lárgate! Jorge shouted at Dallas. Lárgate de aquí pinche gringa!

He horked, letting loose a glob of phlegm and spit that landed at her feet. Then he hustled his wife and child into the house, slamming the door. Other family members quickly barred the way and took up the chant: Ay, pinches gringos, lárgate! Lárgate!

Dallas appeared stunned for a moment, staring perplexed at her shoes. Inside the house, Maria shrieked at the top of her lungs. Tears streamed down Claire's face.

Take my car, Micah said, handing the key to Emmanuelle, after Dallas and the film crew had beat a speedy exit.

You're staying?

I'll get a ride back to the city with Jorge's cousin, he said.

Claire waited by the Kia while Emmanuelle said her goodbyes. The mood had sobered, people gathering in smaller groups, heads together but barely speaking. Even the men wiped their eyes. Dallas and her people were long gone, the heavy tire treads of their vehicles the only physical reminder of their fleeting presence. Maria continued to wail, her frantic screams awful in the silence. Claire imagined Inez, holding her daughter tight, trying to comfort this foreign child who'd once been a part of her.

After their trip to India, those interminable six weeks, when Claire had met her children at the airport, she'd been struck by how they'd altered. Taller, hair longer, redolent of cardamom and sandalwood, unfamiliar soaps and detergents. Charlotte had spoken with a different intonation, emphasizing certain syllables and not others, pronouncing the letter *t* with a soft *th* sound. There were new phrases in her repertoire, and Theo, while abroad, had begun potty training.

Emmanuelle was stooping to touch foreheads with one of the elderly aunts. From this angle, it appeared as if the older woman was comforting her, Emmanuelle's back softening and sagging. She pulled away reluctantly before returning to the car, her face thoughtful. But once she'd gunned the engine, her demeanour shifted, switching gears with unnecessary force, jaw clenched. Her rage was incandescent, and Claire made herself small, shifting to the far edge of her seat, pressed against the door. It was selfish, but she wished Micah was with them and she was in the back.

They drove in silence, Emmanuelle navigating down the mountain like she'd done this many times, zipping past villages and roadside stalls, heedless of the speedometer, glowering at the windshield. Claire felt the nauseous rise and fall in her belly. What would happen after Micah left, how would Maria understand? When would her parents and brothers feel like loving family again rather than frightening strangers?

Es Maria? No es ella. Es una gringa.

Is that Maria? No, that's a foreigner.

For the past year, Claire's hopes had been pinned on getting Maria back home, reversing the catastrophic sequence of events she'd set in motion. She hadn't thought past the reunion, telling herself that to do so would be a jinx. But in reality, she'd been evading the truth. The upheaval she'd wrought, the irreparable harm.

Claire groaned involuntarily, unable to stop the strangled noise, covering her mouth too late. Emmanuelle slammed the brakes, and they lurched to a stop, just in time to watch an emaciated cow amble across the road, tail swishing against the flies.

It was the right thing to do, Emmanuelle said, the first words either of them had spoken in over an hour. She eased off the brake, and the car picked up speed.

I'm not sure there is a right thing. Not at this point. Everything was going to be the wrong—

Maria belongs with her family, Emmanuelle snapped.

I know that.

Emmanuelle jerked the wheel and Claire's stomach careened as they swerved off the main road.

Gas, Emmanuelle said and parked in front of an old-fashioned pump.

While she filled up, Claire stretched her legs. The village they were in was dusty, pretty in a faded way. A parched fountain in the centre of the square, the arched entrance to a covered market, a stone church with a stout bell tower. A sign caught her eye, the English words out of place. Emmanuelle, holding the nozzle, followed her gaze.

Is it far? Claire asked.

Ten-minute drive.

You've been there, Claire said.

Once. And it was enough.

While Emmanuelle paid the attendant, Claire stared at the key she'd left in the cup holder and imagined giving in to curiosity and taking off for the compound. It would be a quick detour. But Emmanuelle would be furious when Claire returned. Worse, she'd scoff and call it rubbernecking. And for what? To see the place that had loomed so large in her imagination? Compare its reality against Dallas's cropped and filtered images or Lucca's anecdotes?

Last she heard, Lucca was in Kyrgyzstan, helping with post-earthquake rescue. They'd had a couple back-and-forths and then he'd gone silent. The next day Claire had seen the news. An after-shock had triggered a second quake.

Shaking her head, she spun away from the keys. Anything Claire found could only be disheartening. Leaning against the car, she checked her phone instead. There was an Instagram post from Dallas: a carousel of shots. In the first: Dallas on bent knee, a supplicant at Inez's and Jorge's feet, Maria between them. The camera was at her back, capturing only the toddler's pigtails and the crisscrossed straps of her dress. It was her parents who were the focal points: Jorge's gentle expression, Inez in the act of bending down, arms out, face alight. The next one was of the family trio, Maria in Inez's arms, her face blank—frozen in the split second between crying jags when she'd paused to draw breath—and Jorge leaning in, his arm around his wife.

In the photos, Santa Rosa appeared Edenic. Inez with her flower garland, Jorge clean-shaven, Maria cherubic, placid as a doll. The appealing play of shadow and light. It was a scene from a storybook, flattened and antiseptic, intolerant of nuance.

Vamos, Emmanuelle said, returning.

They had shut their doors when a boy raced over. He was thin with curly hair and a dimple in his chin, comically big glasses slipping down his nose. Eight, Claire guessed. Nine at a stretch. Emmanuelle rolled the window down, and they bantered in Spanish, the boy attempting to convince, Emmanuelle dissuading, both of them keeping up the pretense that this was all a joke. Emmanuelle pressed a few bills into his hand, and Claire eagerly emptied her wallet too.

When the boy turned to Claire, she saw he had a lazy eye.

U.S.A.? he asked.

Canada, she said.

He was pensive for a moment, then brightened and asked: Ottawa? Vancouver? Montreal? Toronto?

Toronto, she said, delighted by his unexpected knowledge.

You take me home?

Cute kid, Claire said after they were back on the main road, Emmanuelle navigating more carefully, no longer speeding.

I don't like giving them money, not when it's going to end up in some kingpin's hands, Emmanuelle said.

Crispin is filing for bankruptcy, Claire said. Has done. By now.

Edging into the opposite lane, Emmanuelle accelerated to pass a cyclist. You have something lined up? she asked finally.

I'm going to Robertsons, Claire said.

Ah.

Comms director.

There was a clarifying honesty to for-profit. It hardly mattered what key messages she drafted, what evasive jargon she put in the CEO's mouth. Everyone understood it was insincere.

I read your book, Claire said, and when she saw the rise of the eyebrow, she added: I thought it was really good. Persuasive. I should have had it two years ago. Then maybe none of this would have happened.

Two years ago, you wouldn't have believed it, Emmanuelle said.

Claire thought of Dallas's photos and everything left out of the frame: the SUV ferrying Barbara Olsen back to the airport, the rest of the Garcia family, Dallas's entourage, Emmanuelle and Micah, even herself.

Yeah, Claire agreed. But maybe after all that's happened, someone else will.

They continued down the mountain and merged onto the highway, alongside tractor trailers and motorcycles, a river of traffic flowing to the capital.

In the opposite lane, a bus flew past, its roof laden with produce and flowers, black clouds farting out the exhaust pipe.

Exuberantly painted in purple and green, it sported an imposing chrome grill and a hood ornament, polished to a shine, of a busty scantily clad woman.

Inside, people napped, heads bouncing off seatbacks as a hot breeze rattled the open windows. At the back, a boisterous crowd blasted reggaeton through a portable speaker. Overhead, among the backpacks and plastic bags, a chicken sat in a woven basket, bright red comb and wattle bobbing in time with the music. The driver—the regulars on this route called him Speedy Gonzales—slammed the brake and veered hard to exit, flinging the standing passengers into each other.

Pueblo Bonito, next stop, he called, nearly clipping a motorcycle.

When he pulled up at the plaza, two men hobbled off, the younger with his arm around the elder's waist, holding him up. There had been an accident at the factory, equipment falling on the older cousin, crushing his foot. Glancing around, at the squat buildings washed in muted pinks and yellows, a boy lolling in the shade, they spotted the sign. Though it was in English, a language neither could read, they understood its meaning and followed the arrow, making their way, in fits and starts, a slow, dragging journey toward the mountains.

After an hour, they were rewarded by the sight of a crowd. A dozen men, women, and children, coughing, injured, emaciated, all of them gathered at a ten-foot-tall chain-link fence, beyond which they could just make out a white-washed building with a distinctive blue and white *H* painted on the closed door. There was a hut by the fence, a place where a guard might be positioned, granting and denying entry. Even without craning, it was obvious the station was deserted.

A couple was arguing loudly. Between them, a little girl sat on the ground, both legs fully casted, stretched out in front.

We never should have started this, her mother said. Didn't I warn you that nothing was free? Didn't I say never trust a gringo's boasts? They come here with full pockets and empty promises, only to slink off in the dead of night like thieves.

They're just closed for lunch, the father insisted, pulling on his handlebar moustache.

The girl rocked a doll in the cradle of her arms as she hummed tunelessly.

A cure, the wife scoffed, her voice affected in an imitation. Her feet will be *perfect*. As if there's *never* been a problem.

Her mother's solution was to do nothing, the man said, appealing to the crowd. Just let the child suffer.

The girl hummed louder. Everyone who'd been avidly watching the drama now became very busy, staring at the sky or at a gecko in a tree, scratching their noses and ears.

The wife crossed her arms and glowered as she said: She could have learned to get along. People *learn* to get along. But now what? Her legs are trapped in these cages.

The cousins conferred. They'd come all this way. There was a private hospital two towns over, but it was expensive. Meanwhile, the elder's toes were black.

Have some patience, an old woman called. They will open after siesta.

Shrugging, the cousins joined the line of people waiting outside the padlocked gate.

Gratitude

First and foremost: my editor, Anita Chong, without whom this novel would not exist. Thank you, Anita, for your curiosity, wisdom, and willingness to start all over.

Stephanie Sinclair has championed my writing for a decade, first as my agent, then as my publisher, and always as my friend.

For their faith and patience, I'm grateful to Kristin Cochrane, Jared Bland, and everyone at McClelland & Stewart and Penguin Random House Canada. Special thanks to Rebecca Rocillo, Crissy Boylan, and Peter Norman.

Martha Webb shields me from a lot of things I cannot face. Bless you, Martha. Thank you, also, to everyone at Cooke-McDermid Literary Management and Transatlantic Agency, especially Rob Firing.

Grants from Canada Council for the Arts, ArtsNL, and the City of St. John's provided important funding during the novel's long gestation.

Key research sources for *Good Guys* include Anand Giridharadas's book *Winners Take All: The Elite Charade of Changing the World*, Canadaland's podcast series *The White Saviors*, and reporting by *The Guardian* and Al Jazeera.

Beatriz Rodriguez Rubio helped put Spanish words into my characters' mouths. (Mistakes are intentional or mine alone.)

She insisted on the exclamation marks, loaned me her name, and did a close read of a late-stage draft. Gracias, Betty!!!!

Good Guys was written in solitude with the support of community. Thank you to the Port Authority: Melissa Barbeau (who pointed out that I was writing about money), Jamie Fitzpatrick, Carrie Ivardi (who let me borrow the expression "STD soup"), Morgan Murray, and the wonderful Susan Sinnott, who we miss very much.

Elisabeth de Mariaffi weighed in on plot and point-of-view, and indulged endless whiny texts. Kelley Totten whisked me out of town for writing retreats. The Slow Writers offered companionship and camaraderie during a lonely pandemic spell. I'm grateful to Melanie Mah and Tom Cho for their invitation and friendship. Daria Boltokova and Beth Schwartz welcomed me into their academic writing circle. It's humbling to know that as you're fiddling with clumsy metaphors, the chemist next to you (Lindsay Cahill) is solving the scourge of nanoplastics.

Thank you to everyone who read my debut novel, attended an event, sent a friendly message, or invited me to a classroom or book club. Invariably, when I was having a hopeless writing day, an acquaintance or stranger would stop me on the street to say they loved *The Boat People*. Dear readers, your kindness means more than I can say.

The librarians at the A.C. Hunter Public Library unearth books from the basement, make me feel at home, and treat my dog like a celebrity. Many thanks to every bookseller, the small independents especially, who keep me in business. Festival organizers are doing the Lord's work.

My father is a great one for a shaggy-dog tale and taught me my first lessons in storytelling and satire. The family aphorism "their kindness is killing" comes from him. Generosity is second nature to my mother. She, along with my Uncle Suranjan and Auntie Rohini, quietly change lives, without strings or fanfare, exactly the way good deeds should be done.

It's great fun living with a mathematician who, without irony, calls his work *art* and describes his research in such fantastical terms as to seem wholly fictional. He also files my taxes. I love you, Tom.